TA LĘ

BOOK I: KNOWLEDGE

YESSOH G.D.

ISBN: 978-1-7775594-1-0

Thank you for buying this book.

For bonus content, info on new releases
and other great reads, sign up for
our newsletters or visit us online at
www.thetaleseries.com

Contents

Whether it's the code dwelling in the nucleus, or the spirit—
they live within me, and for this, I am eternally grateful.

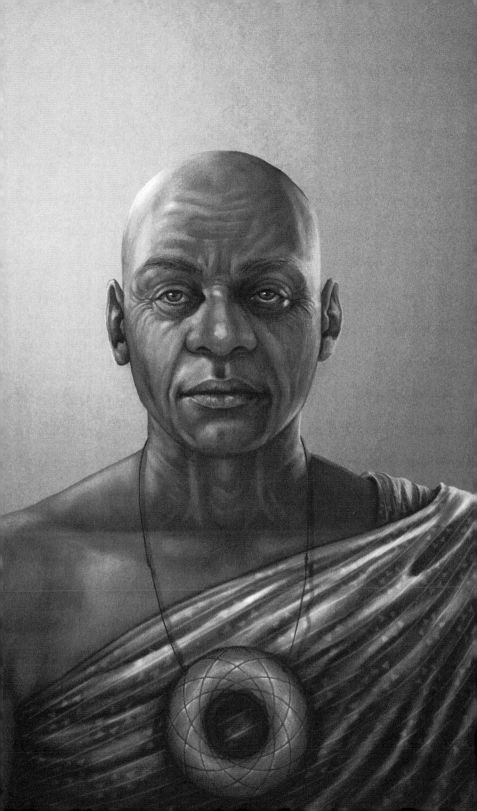

CHAPTER 1

Sector o

Kone is typing on his silent keyboard, his face lit by his bright display. He sits in a spacious room where shelves six feet high stand behind him, filled with books and folders, mainly constitutional compendia and government documents. Many of those books and files are piled on the left corner of his polished wooden desk, open and leaning toward him. None of the books spread on the table relates to governmental affairs, and the closed folders have the "classified" seal stamped red on their khaki covers. Kone has been in the room long enough to leave only two of the many lights on. These two lights on the ceiling are more than sufficient to fill the office, at least where he is, although it is dimmer toward his section. The dark circles under his eyes and the slightly curved posture he has adopted suggest at least two nights without rest. He leans back for a moment on his black leather couch, his right palm barely covering his lips, as if he needs a second to think, and then leans forward to type a question to the person on the other side of the screen. He waits for the flashing cursor until the answer comes: *Yes.* Kone lightly scratches his temple with his left index finger and stares at his screen, waiting for another answer or maybe thinking.

The ringing of his phone startles him. He is expecting a call sooner or later, with the response he just received, but this is too soon, too fast, and at five in the morning, it only confirms the severity of the situation. Kone pulls the phone from the left inner pocket of his unbuttoned dark-gray suit and presses *Answer*. "Yes?"

"An important minister is dead. I am getting calls from everywhere. Do you have any information for me?" asks the man on the line.

"I know a minister is dead. Since the autopsy revealed a heart attack, I thought it was one of them. I am still waiting for confirmation to close the file," answers Kone.

"I contacted each of them. They have nothing to do with this, and it's becoming a concern. You know how this works. In case it's not someone I know, I have to contact you. Your people are the best with unexplained death," says the man on the line.

"Why would one of our own want the death of a white minister?" Kone prompts carefully. "Do you at least know why he has been killed?"

"That's why I believe what they say," responds the man. "There was apparently no reason for him to die, and this raises questions. Since this death isn't their doing, they fear they are losing control. It'll be on the news tomorrow. The experts say it's a heart attack, and this is going to be the official statement, but we both know better, don't we? I have been on the scene … things are beyond what they seem."

Kone allows a brief pause and releases a short breath. "Okay, let me check with my sources and see what I can find, but I doubt it's one of us. I'll get back to you as soon as possible."

"I'll be waiting," says the man before hanging up.

Kone springs from his chair, tightening his loose, striped, dark-blue tie, and exits without closing the door. At the end of the corridor, fifty steps away on his right, is the presidential office. He rushes to the door, which is slightly open and guarded by two agents in black suits, one on each side. The personal guards of the president stay close and will leave him under no circumstances. They hear everything, but nothing will make them breathe a word. Kone passes them, and despite his six-foot stature, he is still three or four inches below them. He quickly pushes the meticulously carved golden door handle and enters a bright, wide room to see President Dablan standing behind his large desk, leaning slightly forward, with both fists on the table, his chin tucked in and face staring down.

"It's not them, Mr. President, and they believe it might be one of us," Kone hurries to say.

"I know, Kone," says the president calmly. "This was my concern."

"But there is no reason to kill a white minister," says Kone, his face brimming with questions.

The president leaves his table and walks around to the long beige couch in the center of the room. His calm, well-balanced pace makes up for his five-foot-nine stature. He sits on the puffy left arm of the couch, with his pinstriped marine-blue suit unbuttoned. The long night has meant his dotted purple tie is left on the presidential table. President Dablan looks at Kone. "We don't know yet. Contact the head of Sector 0 and tell him my people will pay him a visit. Call the head of the S-cell, call a meeting in twenty minutes, and bring me Kobenan now."

"Understood, Mr. President." Kone, whose grip never loosened on the bronze-painted Victorian handle, is leaving when the president calls to him.

"Yes, Mr. President?"

"Make sure this stays under the table until we figure out what it is," says the president, looking intently at his most trusted man.

"Understood, Mr. President," Kone replies and leaves the door half-closed.

*

During Kobenan's two years in the presidency, he has stepped into the presidential office only twice, despite his office door facing Mr. Kone's. The first time was when he was introduced to the presidential house after President Dablan requested he be sent here as an analyst instead of working for the S-cell, as he was chosen to do. The second time was on the verge of a *coup d'état*, when the president needed his brightest and closest team, Mr. Kone and Kobenan, to find the source and figure out a solution within twenty-four hours. There have been many threatening and delicate situations, but Kobenan usually answers directly to Mr. Kone, so he knows before knocking at the presidential door, where he stands towered over by the two agents, that there must be a crucial situation ahead. Or is the summons simply because he still has not completed the files he was assigned three days ago?

Kobenan clears his throat and knocks twice. "Mr. President, you asked for me?"

"Come in, Kobenan," answers President Dablan.

Kobenan widens the door enough to enter and pushes it back to its initial position. President Dablan has not moved since Kone left. Palms joined, his fingers interlocked below his waist, forearms resting on his thighs, he looks in the direction of the door. This is the first time Kobenan has seen the president without a tie. He looks for a second at the president's white shirt, with the collar button undone, and then looks at his face. *Has he been up all night?* The unbuttoned suit and collar button, the tie on the table, and his face—though hardly noticeable, his face shows signs of fatigue.

"Come, sit down. There is something I want to talk to you about," says the president, waving him over.

If Kobenan has been summoned because of the delay on these files, if the president requested him just for that, then he is in serious trouble. Mr. Kone could have made an appearance at any time to ask for those files, which Kobenan has been working very late to solve. But he didn't visit Kobenan's office this week, so Kobenan didn't get a chance to report the status of the files. And now the president has requested him.

"I am sorry for the delay, Mr. President. I have closed the analyses you requested, and the reports are almost done."

The president smiles and sits on the couch, while Kobenan sits on the other one, facing him. A small wooden table with an antique bowl of pied Saintpaulia separates them. Kobenan looks down and makes sure to pull the tips of his shoes away from the white carpet, just enough to avoid any unwanted stain. It's the same reaction he had when he first sat on this couch.

"How old are you?" asks President Dablan.

"I just turned twenty, Mr. President."

"You know you are a pride of this country. Never before have we accepted a person this young to an important presidential job," says the president with a smile.

Kobenan takes a short breath. *This might be a relief. Maybe it's not about the files after all.* But with what feels like a lifetime of training, most years of his childhood, he has wanted to work for the S-cell; he still does, but the president requested he work at the presidential house instead. It's a great honor and sometimes an intense responsibility, yet Kobenan has set his mind on the S-cell since he was fifteen, and he has been forward about it with President Dablan. The president has asked him not to bring up this subject again, so he is careful with his next words. "Thank you very much, Mr. President, but this wasn't what I was aiming for after my formation."

A brief pause tightens between Kobenan and President Dablan as the president stares in Kobenan's eyes. He has to admit, the boy does not shy away from expressing himself.

"How long have you been here?"

"Twenty-two months, Mr. President."

"And how many files have you solved? How many behaviors did you predict?"

"I have solved 1,024 files, sir, and 527 behaviors."

"See? More than any of your predecessors. That's why I wanted you close to me. There is something about you, and now, more than ever, we will need this gift of yours," says President Dablan.

Kobenan is speechless. Should he rejoice at these high honors from the commander-in-chief, or is it a warning about the work standard he has to maintain? Still, he wonders what the president means by *now, more than ever, we will need this gift of yours.*

Someone knocks at the presidential door. "Mr. President, Biafle Herbert, head of the S-cell," says a deep voice behind the door. Kobenan moves his head a little but does not turn. Did he just hear "Biafle Herbert"? A name whose owner he has never seen, yet he feels like he has met him every day since he started working here at the presidential house? A name plastered on the most crucial files, the most crucial cases to the safety of the country he has studied and solved for the government and S-cell these eleven months? This man, whose reports sometimes don't make a single spark of sense, no matter how many times Kobenan reads the lines or flips the pages—yet the words always feel coordinated and leading somewhere—Biafle Herbert, the head of the S-cell, the only agent in this nonexistent organization, working alone on the most complex and crucial investigations, just set foot in the presidential office.

"Come in, Mr. Biafle," calls the president, standing up. Kobenan immediately follows suit and turns to the door. A tall man in a black suit and plain dark-gray tie enters the large room. The suit is far from worn out but definitely not new, still decent enough to meet a president. He is followed by Mr. Kone, who closes the door behind them. Mr. Biafle quickly walks to the president and extends his right arm.

"Mr. President."

"Mr. Biafle," greets President Dablan, shaking his firm hand. He allows everyone to sit and follows suit. The guests take seats on the long beige couch facing the president. Kobenan dares a quick glance, not even with the intention of looking, just to process the two people sitting on his right side. He and Mr. Kone have never both been in the same room with the president, not even when the *coup d'état* threatened. And here he is with his superior, President Dablan's right hand, who holds no official title, and Mr. Biafle, the head of the S-cell.

"Everyone is present. You should know that this meeting never happened," says President Dablan. Kobenan's focus sharpens. "Four hours ago, the minister of primary resources of Brazil died of a heart attack in his mansion. We know it's not a natural death, and the secret societies deny any involvement. They are concerned ... and so am I. I just got information that it could

6

be at the hands of an African, so Mr. Biafle, I want you to head for Sector 0 and investigate. You'll be assisted by Mr. Kobenan, our most brilliant analyst."

Mr. Biafle looks for a second at Kobenan on his left, next to Mr. Kone. "Mr. President, with all due respect, this person is too young for Sector 0. There might be some serious repercussions."

"We have no time to worry about that," snaps the president. "We don't know how long this situation will be under our control. I need the best at this task. He will adapt."

"Understood, Mr. President. We are leaving now," says Mr. Biafle, standing up after the president.

Kobenan stands up with no words, his head racing with questions. He can't interrupt such a high assembly with what he feels are personal concerns. President Dablan gives him a last look, which lasts maybe half a second, but it is enough for Kobenan to catch the president's alarming yet serene expression. He picks up one thing that requires no words: *I am counting on you.* Kobenan follows the tall S-cell agent through the presidential door. He can still hear President Dablan giving important instructions to Mr. Kone as he pulls the lever and leaves the large door in its half-closed state.

*

Kobenan stares vaguely at the moving trees through the closed window of a black SUV. They left the city one and a half hours ago and are now driving along a single-lane road covered with dense trees on both edges and bearing nothing but a few cracks. Silence creates a tense atmosphere in the car. Kobenan in the front passenger seat is still trying to figure out why he is in a government vehicle heading to a remote place, the name of which he first heard only two hours ago. He is an analyst, not a field agent, and never trained to be so. His skinny five-foot-eight frame says plenty; he is not like the well-balanced six-foot-two or -three man on his left. He has no experience whatsoever outside the presidential house, no defensive skills or protocols that he knows of. And from the many quaint, disturbing, and sometimes frightening files from Mr. Biafle that he has solved, he knows he is not ready for this trip.

He wanted to speak of his concerns back at the presidential house. He wanted to tell the president that he will be more of a rock stuck to Mr. Biafle's foot than actually a help to him on this case—a case about which he has not a single clue, no information, nothing to start on. But whatever he would have said might have come out very wrong in this *crucial situation*, as President Dablan described it. So here he is in a heavy SUV with the head of the S-cell. There is a reason Biafle Herbert works alone. It's not rocket science; he does not want any partner, and the president basically ordered him to break his rules and work with an inexperienced, defenseless, and flimsy analyst.

Kobenan has questions but dares not say a word. Better to wait for the right moment, if it presents itself at all. He knows this man is probably not the happiest right now, but he has to follow presidential orders. Everyone has to. So, despite his lack of experience and this blind case, Kobenan will do what he does best and maintain the standard of the expectation President Dablan has placed on his shoulders, not shying away but analyzing and doing what's required to get results.

Sector 0. One of the many questions floating in his head. Why does this name feel new? He's never heard of Sector 0 anywhere in the files he worked on, even during his formation in his youth, before the presidential job. He never heard it anywhere. He would remember if this name was mentioned before or if he'd read it. He would know; he never forgets what he sees or hears. He has a perfect memory of everything crossing his senses, an annoying burden for his mind at times but extremely useful in what he does. That's probably why he is the only member of the fourth analysis department at the presidential house, along with the fact that he can solve highly improbable files. He is certain there are other people somewhere in the presidential house doing analyses and answering directly to Mr. Kone, as he does, but the things he has worked on so far are partially for the S-cell and on some occasions even files other departments were unable to make sense of.

Despite the fact that figuring out problems comes fluidly to him, he sometimes faces cases so confusing, he doesn't even know how he manages to solve them. He doesn't know how he manages to solve half the files he receives. Of course, there is logic, extensive knowledge, and learning he has accumulated through the years, but most of the time, you can't make a dent in the documents with those. He knows he is lucky to still be able to solve these files and wonders when his luck will run out.

"How old are you?" asks Biafle, pulling Kobenan from his deep thoughts. Kobenan looks at him. Biafle glances at him and then back to the road.

"Twenty," responds Kobenan.

Biafle glances back one more time before bringing his eyes back to the road. "Twenty?" He pauses. "The president must be very confident in your skills to send you into this."

This. What is *this*? Is that the case? Sector 0? Kobenan remains silent. A short moment of inattention as he is absorbed in the conversation makes him miss a right veer by Biafle onto a large, newer road still lined by trees at the edges. He looks through the windshield and perceives something at the end of the road about five hundred yards from them. The flat, straight terrain shows from well afar the rectangular shape of a large edifice. Biafle drives until what looks like a tall wall is clearly visible, still around three hundred yards from them. He stops the car in the middle of the road and turns off the engine. "Get out," orders the man, taking out the car keys and pulling his door handle. Kobenan opens his door and descends from the SUV. He walks to the front of the car, looking at the strange edifice.

"Why are we stopping here? We are still far from it," asks Kobenan, lost in the blackish walls and quietness of the surroundings.

"No machine works beyond this point," answers Biafle, turning before the front of the car.

These words snap Kobenan out of his contemplation and back to his partner. Kobenan locks his eyes on the tall man's right hand in the inner pocket of the black suit as his profile gets closer. Biafle pulls out a necklace of intertwined brown cords covered with animal fangs, human teeth, and what looks like dark, crystallized rocks.

"What's this?" Kobenan ventures cautiously, following the hand with the eerie necklace.

"Protection," says the man, shoving the dangling object in Kobenan's face for a very close look. "No matter the situation, do not remove this from your neck. It'll keep them away from your body."

Kobenan looks up to Biafle's charcoal irises. "Who?"

Biafle squints at Kobenan's troubled face. "So, you don't even know what Sector 0 is?" He holds the necklace with both hands and slips it onto Kobenan's head. "I am sure there is a reason the president wants me to work with you on this case. Let's go. I'll brief you on the way," says Biafle, walking away.

Kobenan and Biafle advance toward the large edifice. It is a long, silent two-minute walk before it really dawns on Kobenan. It's not the silence between him and his partner. This place emanates an odd quietness. Forests cover both sides of this large road, dense with what resembles *Ceiba pentandra caribaea*, among other trees. *How come there's no birdsong? Not a single sound?* And the air, this very thin, light air. All of this makes him more on edge than he already was. As they approach what looks like a fortress, he realizes how high this wall is. It easily stretches forty feet, maybe more. Everything about this edifice screams *protection*, yet there is no one around. He feels like his partner and he are the only people in this place, maybe the only souls. He takes a look to his left. Mr. Biafle is rolling some kind of cord around his wrist, pale red in color and shredded into many twines. It might be some kind of protection, like the one Kobenan wears on his neck.

This reminds him that communication is established, at least enough for Kobenan to ask some of the questions troubling his mind. "So ... Sector 0?" he says, looking at Biafle. The man continues twining the red cord on his wrist. He has no need to watch the road, as it runs plain and empty before the edifice. "The biggest and most secure prison for the deadliest sorcerers, djinns, and lost spirits," says Biafle, tying a small knot on the inner left side of his wrist.

It takes a few seconds for the words to sink in as Kobenan stares at the tall man. Then his heart skips a bit. "Sorcerers?" he softly repeats, trying to confirm to himself what he just heard. He looks back at the approaching edifice. This bizarre construction is a prison. He feels his heart pounding. *Sorcerers.* Kobenan has encountered this word a few times in his files, less so with djinns. But his main focus was not on them, mostly a situation surrounding men he had to solve; nothing close to djinns or sorcerers or spirits. He never worked on a file with the word *spirit* in the lines. He did hear of sorcerers and djinns during his youth, but they were merely explored in the books he studied, waved away with hazy details here and there.

He was told that if he were to be received into the S-cell, he would have a year of intensive training. Maybe this was to learn about these sorcerers and djinns. But he's never had the chance to work at the S-cell, and now he is approaching what he was just told is a prison for sorcerers.

"I am surprised you don't know about this place. How long have you been working for the government?" asks Biafle.

"Twenty-two months," answers Kobenan, his eyes stuck to the wall. "Was I supposed to know about it?"

"You are close to the president, and he seems to trust you," says Biafle.

Kobenan wouldn't call that *close.* His office might be steps away from President Dablan's, but he seldom sees him. Maybe close in other ways, with Mr. Kone frequently in the president's office and him working under Mr. Kone's direction. "I know about the S-cell and secret services. I have been analyzing documents for both sectors," says Kobenan.

"And how many mistakes did you make so far?" asks Biafle.

"None," says Kobenan, fixated on the approaching wall. "When was this created?"

"We don't know," responds Biafle. "Legends have it the first guardian of Africa built it. As far as we are concerned, we were guided to it by two powerful sorcerers centuries ago."

Kobenan cannot take his gaze from a large door carved into the wall. The door borrows from this aberrant structure's color, or lack thereof, drawing closer to him with every step he now calls a foolish mettle, maybe because he feels a hint of security with a partner of this caliber at his side. One thing that sticks in his mind in all those many years of hazy details is that no one can really protect you from a sorcerer except yourself, if you are knowledgeable—and Kobenan is not. He tries to fathom the idea of what lurks inside these walls, but nothing comes to mind. Maybe this medley of fear, wonder, and curiosity plays a confusing role. What bothers him most is this large, closed door with an emptiness before it, quite alarming for a secret prison holding the most dangerous sorcerers. "Why are there no guards in front of the gate?"

"There are," says Biafle. Kobenan breaks his stare and looks at his partner. "Where did you get this?" asks Biafle, pointing at Kobenan's forehead.

Is Biafle trying to distract him from this hazardous situation? Lighten the tension? That won't work. Kobenan is an analyst; he learned about these standard procedures of subject change when tension arises to calm the mind. Why does Biafle use these now? It doesn't even look like his style of work. *What do you mean there* are *guards? I don't see any.* Those are the words burning on Kobenan's tongue, but he will play along.

Kobenan points at his forehead, to a small, lightly pushed-in circular mark, barely visible if you don't pay careful attention to his face.

"This?" He says. "I don't know. It's a birthmark, I guess. It's always been there. Never really paid attention."

"And your parents never told you why it's there?" asks Biafle.

Why is he so interested in this barely visible speck? "My parents? I don't think they noticed it. My mother never mentioned it."

"This is a mark of vision. You might be smart, but your ability to read people and files comes from this. Some of the best and smartest people in this country work at the presidency, but only gifted ones work in the close entourage of the president. You should have known that," says Biafle, pulling up his right sleeve and brushing Kobenan's forehead with the shredded red cord, as if cleaning. First sweep, second sweep, and he pulls his arm away from Kobenan's face. Kobenan turns his head toward the gate and freezes.

The chill cascading down his spine is so intense, he barely feels his legs. The blood has rushed to his feet, yet he feels nailed down, unable to move a toe. He loses all strength to budge any muscles. He just stands, with shuddering and increased breathing. His mouth is locked open and eyes wide, ready to pop out, staring at what walks before the edifice. Biafle observes the confused young man, lost in what his shocked mind is fighting to believe or disbelieve. Two humanlike creatures, each as tall as two men combined, stand on the road at each side of the gate. Creatures of disturbing morphology, twisted and crooked, the likes of which he has never seen before, patrol the very top of the wall. Biafle stands with no words, motionless, following the boy's reaction.

Kobenan has lost his vocal cords. The strength needed to scream has vanished. He barely moves and doesn't seem to have control of his shaking body, constricted with fear.

"Please advance. The Great Chief awaits us." The sound of a strong, slightly vibrating voice pierces Kobenan's right ear. The accent and low tone are completely unfamiliar. He jerks to his left, snapping his head in the voice's direction. He loses his balance and sits on the road, dragging himself away. There stands something in the shape of a man, something or someone with a complexion so deep, he barely looks like he has a skin, or has a skin so dark he seems calcified. Stretched eyes, free of eyebrows and red, as though filled with blood, stare down at Kobenan, whose heart might stop at any time. He quickly looks to his left, searching for the only man who can protect him right now, Biafle, but he sees only another dark man with gaze locked on him. It may well be a state of extreme shock or the mind breaking under such stress, but not a single word or sound escapes Kobenan's mouth.

Biafle observes him, staring silently. All three look at the young man. No one has ever behaved this way here, though they do understand this drastic reaction.

"Get up, Kobenan. He is waiting for us," says Biafle calmly.

This is not the moment to flinch. He can't allow himself to confirm what Mr. Biafle might already be thinking: that he is a scared, flimsy analyst. Despite the dread in his eyes and the stiffness of his body, Kobenan collects himself somewhat and stands up, now avoiding eye contact with the creatures by his side. They might be disturbing to look at, but he doubts they will hurt him. This is surely the only thought keeping him in this place right now. And again, he is with the head of the S-cell, even though he has to be extremely careful where he stands and where he is going. He takes a trembling, deep breath, arranges his suit, and stands even closer to Biafle. He is one move away from holding his partner's hand.

They continue their walk, with the humanoid creatures leading. A plain brown piece of fabric dangling between their thighs and stopping by their knees covers their waists. It looks like the only piece of clothing on their thin, peculiar, athletic bodies. They both are around the same height, barely under Mr. Biafle's. These two must be some kind of guards, and he wonders if they have been walking alongside from the moment they stepped out of the car.

The large gate is opening as they approach. The pace of the doors catches Kobenan's eyes. It has a few short drags and uneven movements. This does not seem mechanical. He remembers Biafle mentioning something about machines not working in this area. What, then, is opening these twenty-five-foot doors? Kobenan slows down for a brief moment and quickly catches up with Biafle. The gate is revealing something more confusing than the outside of the edifice, but what disturbs him most is that he's getting closer with each step to these long creatures at each side of the gate. Their erect shape only suffices to bring back the chills in his spine. They easily stand above thirteen feet and don't seem to be bothered by him or his partner approaching. Their gaze points straight ahead, focused on the horizon behind him. Kobenan does not dare turn left or right when he and Biafle cross the tall gate. His head is fixed stiffly forward.

The quaint architecture inside the walls breaks this stiffness; he has to look around. The awe on his face before these strange materials and unwonted constructions is hard to conceal. They are somewhere between archaic and extremely elaborate, if not advanced. He can't wrap his head around a few shapes and forms he notices, which seem impossible to build. He just looks around at this edifice, which feels odd, old, and bears a strong sense of emptiness and calm, the opposite characteristics of a prison. He still makes sure, while half-gawking, to stay as close to Biafle as he can. They are approaching a smaller door of aged wood, which has enough holes from the middle to the top section to clearly see the whole interior of the edifice. When one of the guards escorting them pushes the handle to open the door, Kobenan takes a look at the extensive room. Never before has he seen a place so unnerving, so unique—a quaint, twisted architecture unlike anything he knows.

Large, curved spaces follow contours. Wood and rocks define walls. African masks decorate them; many of them he recognizes from his books. Masks with definition and purpose, things he barely believed when he was reading. Now he sees them. They are real, and from what he has seen so far, their purpose must surely be real too. Kobenan notices two short men walking toward them, forcing him to curb his contemplation. The first thing that draws his attention, apart from their roughly four-foot height, is their hair, braided thin and covering their weirdly broad shoulders. The natural light slipping into the room and hitting the strands gives some of them a strong sheen. Either they have a hard yellow color or there are literally gold hairs on these two men, who look very much alike. One of them has a shorter set of braids than the other, but their faces seem like one shared by two people. The short height, the hair color, the fanned feet—Kobenan has only seen those traits in one of the books with a plain black cover and no title. Books handed to him by his instructor after reminding him that he was sworn to secrecy and could die just by pronouncing a word written in the book. "Are those …?"

"Pygmies? Yes," responds Biafle, looking at the approaching men.

CHAPTER 2

The Soul Eater

They are said to be mythical and hidden from the world. Many of the secret tribes of very short men scattered around the continent are believed to descend from pygmies, but none of them carry these unique traits of golden hair and fanned feet. Kobenan is staring at the strands glistening in the natural light when he starts experiencing shortness of breath. He first squints and wonders where this is coming from; there is plenty of air in this spacious hall. The shortness of breath heightens as these men approach. He loosens his blue tie, but it doesn't seem enough. Reasoning and controlled behavior stop, and he is starting to suffocate. He grabs his neck with his right hand and puts out his tongue, coughing. He falls on all fours, choking and spurting saliva. What is happening? His whole body feels numb, with his blood rushing in his veins. He can feel the liquid coursing through him. His body is shaking, but not with fear this time. Something is happening to him. Why does he feel every inch of his body and guts? He coughs, spurts, sweats. He has stopped thinking. The only instinct now is to find a way to breathe. His lungs burn, as if someone has lit them on fire. His eyes are filled with tears. His mouth keeps dripping saliva on the rugged granite floor.

"Try to regulate your breathing, in and out. Your cells have been disturbed by their energy. It's normal. It's the first time you've met them," says Biafle, looking down at Kobenan. The dark guards bow when the pygmies stop before them.

"Ubuntu," says one of the guards.

"Ubuntu," respond the pygmies.

"Thank you, brothers, we will take it from here," says the pygmy with long braids. The guards bow and leave the edifice, closing the door behind them. The two pygmies approach Kobenan, who is still struggling with his respiration. He seems to be getting some air through his nasal pipes. He tilts his head slightly and looks at them with watery eyes. They are so close to him, he can't help but notice the brown leather on their waists, their large, almost flat nude torsos, and their hair, which now that he is only three feet from them looks more yellowish than gold, with a few white strands.

"First time?" asks the pygmy with short braids.

"He just opened his third eye," responds Biafle.

"This must have been a shock for him," says the one with long braids, staring at Kobenan.

"He is handling it pretty well for someone who just opened the third eye. I have seen people lose their mind," says Biafle, looking at Kobenan gasping on all fours, trying to breathe.

His eyes are burning, and he still can't close his mouth, but his body has calmed down, and he is starting to feel his normal senses. The pain is slowly fading. The pygmy with long braids, the closest to him, kneels down. "You'll be all right. Try to relax; let your cells get accustomed. It won't take long. I am Nianbou, and this is Djengdjeng," he says with a quick glance to the short man on his right. "We are the brothers of Congo, high-level guardians of Sector 0. We are here to escort you to the Great Chief." The pygmy stands up.

"Can you do something about it?" asks Biafle.

"We already concealed a major part of the radiation when we saw him," says Nianbou.

"I'm okay," interrupts Kobenan. "I can breathe normally. We can move on."

He has not been chosen by the president to be a burden. He

slowly stands up and wipes away his tears. The burning has stopped. He still feels his lungs, but he can breathe. No one should be waiting for him.

"The boy's all right. Let's go," says Djengdjeng, the pygmy with short hair.

They lead the way to a staircase on the far right of this grand space, naturally lit, with pouches of darkness in a few areas. "There are people from Congo here?" Kobenan asks.

"South Africa, Nigeria, Cameroon, and the best in each African country using sorcery," says Biafle. "The brothers of Congo are the most powerful pygmies and two of the strongest earth beings we know."

Kobenan and Biafle follow their guides in this strange place, which seems to extend two stories up. Kobenan notices shadowy corridors as they walk toward the wooden stairs. Five, if he has counted correctly. Five corridors spread across this spacious room, each leading in a direction of its own, each blending into the dark areas. They reach the stairs, and he quickly takes a second look when he realizes what he is stepping on: a circular stairway of old wood linking to the next story. One that seems commonplace if you don't look closely, a kind of detail that hardly escapes Kobenan's eyes. This stair adds to the many mysteries of the odd constructions puzzling him in this place. How did they manage to make a spiral out of wood this size? It's practically impossible to build a stairway with a single trunk, and yet this is exactly what it looks like: an insanely large trunk carved to perfection to create a spiral staircase with embedded steps, not separately built ones. Most of all, how did they relocate such a trunk? It certainly doesn't appear to be native to this land, considering the species Kobenan has seen outside.

Better focus and brace himself for the person they are going to meet. If he experienced this acute unpleasantness from these two short men, what is to come from their chief? Biafle and Kobenan walk two steps behind the pygmies, and Kobenan can't help but stare at the golden hairs before him and this place, giving him chills at times. "So ... Biafle, how did you end up with someone so weak?" asks Djengdjeng, the pygmy with short braids. He is clearly talking about Kobenan. And with what has happened so far, it has just confirmed the increasing weight he might become on Mr. Biafle's foot.

"He has been assigned to me by the president," responds Biafle.

"There might be a reason he is the president's choice," says Nianbou, the pygmy with long braids.

"He is a competent analyst," adds Biafle.

"Then protect him with whatever you have. The president assigned him to you. Be careful this time," says Nianbou, turning his head but not looking at Biafle behind him.

Someone already died under Mr. Biafle's protection. So that means Kobenan's safety is not guaranteed at all with a man of this caliber. But what can he do if not stay close to his partner?

"Here we are," says Djengdjeng, turning to the guests before a covered entrance. "The Great Chief awaits."

It's an entrance with no door, only an embroidered curtain covering most of the interior. Kobenan is familiar with this type of fabric. *Kente* it is called, or *Kita*, depending on the region it comes from, a fabric deeply woven into several of the local ethnicities' customs and used on diverse occasions. This particular curtain seems to be old, and the motifs, though recognizable in their pattern, are disparate. Kobenan can see an orange light escaping from torches inside, painting the floor underneath the curtain. Djengdjeng, the pygmy with short braids, makes a gesture for the guests to enter. Kobenan follows his partner, who bends the heavy fabric on the side to step in. The Great Chief stands before them, a man with a frame Kobenan has never seen, judging by his controlled reaction.

The Great Chief easily stands six-foot-five, and it's very unlikely he's ever made any attempts at stretching in this room, since the ceiling is very close to his head. But what makes Kobenan hesitate for a brief second before stepping further into the small room is the unusually large body of the man before them. His shoulders greatly expand and tend to slightly lean down because of his trapezius. His large hands and the well-defined muscles coursing through his arms and shoulders alone speak of a strong man, if you ignore for a moment the name "Great Chief," which Kobenan knows might speak to something else. His head is bare, his face showing short, tangled chin hair with a mixture of gray and dark. He wears white paint covering a great deal of his face and extending to his pronounced chest and almost flat belly. Several necklaces of different sizes and forms rest on his neck.

Biafle, standing with what Kobenan interprets as the utmost respect, bows with his right palm on his chest. "Ubuntu," Biafle says.

Kobenan, who follows every movement of his partner, quickly copies the gesture and the word.

"Ubuntu," responds the Great Chief with a bow, his right arm resting on his ample chest. No choking, no shortness of breath, no burning eyes or chest—Kobenan wonders if his body has already become accustomed to these beings. What he experienced earlier should be worse with the Great Chief. Or is he concealing his energy, as the pygmies did? If that's the case, then he is doing it pretty well, for Kobenan feels nothing.

"How are you, Biafle? Please, have a seat." The Great Chief lightly pulls up his torn pants of African textile, held to his waist by cords, and sits on the floor. The guests follow suit.

"I am well, Great Chief. This is Mr. Kobenan, from the presidential analysis department," says Biafle.

The Great Chief turns his head to Kobenan, sitting with legs crossed in imitation of his partner and the important man before him. "His first time feeling the energy. It's a unique experience. So, do you know why you are here?" The Great Chief turns back to Biafle.

"Great Chief, President Dablan asked us to come and meet you. Apart from that, nothing," Biafle says respectfully.

"Nine hours ago, the guards were patrolling the cells department when prisoner 204 said, 'An important man is about to die.' He doesn't usually talk, and knowing him, he would never have spoken a word if this important man didn't affect him in some way. So, I contacted the president to warn him and ask him to inform me in case an African president, leader, or king dies. So, what happened?" asks the Great Chief.

"A white minister died. Apparently, it's not a natural death, and their secret societies deny any implication."

"Was it on African soil?"

"No," says Biafle.

"Why is it our concern?"

"The circumstances of his death, Great Chief. Everything on the scene ties to sorcery, the African imprint."

"Are you sure these secret societies are telling the truth?" asks the Great Chief.

"We have very little data at this point, but there is no reason for them to lie. They usually kill for a precise reason, when the person doesn't work according to their plan, and the public is usually never aware of their involvement. But when an unplanned situation like this happens, they all have investigators looking for answers, and one of them called us three hours ago," explains Biafle.

"But why would an African kill an important white leader? They don't need this kind of attention," the Great Chief wonders.

"Unless we are missing something," says Biafle.

"Okay, let's go and see the prisoner," says the Great Chief, standing up. Biafle and Kobenan follow.

"We don't want to disturb you, Great Chief. There is no need for you to come. We will handle it."

The Great Chief smiles. "You really think this necklace will help? He is too weak for that, and where we are going is the department holding the most dangerous sorcerers and djinns."

The large man grabs a can, dips his right hand in it, and draws on Kobenan's face with white paint. Kobenan stands still, pressing his lips to avoid letting the liquid seep into his mouth. "You stay near me, son," orders the Great Chief. Kobenan nods, with the white liquid wet on his lips. They leave the room and head downstairs. The Great Chief leads them to one of the seemingly shadowy corridors near the wooden stairway. It gets clearer as they approach. Carved pillars stand before the entrance. The intricate carvings, the signs—these are totems. But Kobenan can't quite make out the carvings. He has surely never read about them before. The corridor holds small holes for the light to illuminate the whole path, revealing aligned masks on its rocky wall. This path of uneasy feeling looks short, as Kobenan can see the next room's yellow light.

"Great Chief, what do you know about this prisoner?" asks Biafle.

"His name is Namien, sorcerer soul eater. Very powerful, very smart. He was a former member of the Tugbe, a group who eat only successful families."

This might well be the first hint in this investigation since Kobenan left the presidential house. Unnerving place or not, Great Chief or not, this is not the time to hold any doubt or concern. "Very powerful ... So, who captured him?" Kobenan steps in. His face paint is almost dried up.

"Nobody. He gave himself up." The guests look at the Great Chief.

"He was tired of eating people ... or he was running from something," says the tall chief, letting in the bright light after pushing a door wide open. They enter a circular room lit with torches hung on the walls. The room is filled with cells and metal bars, the first things Kobenan has seen so far that make this place resemble a prison. Something sets them apart from the standard cell he knows. Many are locked with nothing but meshes from dubious sources or dark strands of hair. Others simply have no doors. He can't help but turn his head when his eyes meet a giant creature in chains walking twenty feet from him, escorted to its cell by an old woman barely holding herself up on a stick of wood. Next to the creature's cell is another one, wide open. Only a black cat sits at the entrance, as if guarding something inside. Kobenan, intrigued, turns his head to look at the cat. He turns to look one more time before they head for a dim staircase of concrete.

The walk takes two full rounds to reach the next floor. There is almost no light. But Kobenan can still see his feet next to the Great Chief's. There, at the floor, where torchlight bleeds a few steps down, three guards looking barely human stand before a small wooden door, around sixteen feet from the Great Chief and his guests. Only their profile makes them close to something recognizable. Their red eyes, their lifeless faces, are a vivid reminder to stay closer to the Great Chief. One of them untangles a mesh of cowrie shells and raw gold nuggets around the door and opens it when they see the chief. They immediately close the door when Biafle, who is last to enter the dim alley, passes the entrance.

Kobenan feels the chill air around him, the quietness, a presence down his neck. He slightly jerks his shoulders and looks behind to see if someone touched him. Only the closed wooden door stands behind. "Don't forget to breathe, son. You will be all right," reminds the Great Chief, advancing on a straight path with cells running on either side. Kobenan's vision is quite clear in this narrow place of little light. He notices in his quiet walk beside the Great Chief that the cells, unlike the circular room downstairs, stand apart from one another. He crosses one where the metal bars are connected with dark hair and small round balls resembling nuts. A woman stooped in the corner slowly lifts her head of long, grimy hair and follows him with her eyes.

Another cell doorway to his right holds no door. A small tin can slowly moving around inside makes him look twice before he double-checks to make sure he is close enough to the Great Chief. The next cell his eyes fall on holds a glass bottle erect in the center. The face in it, flattened against the glass contour, stares at him with a large smile.

"Here we are," says the Great Chief, stopping before a locked cell a few steps further down. "Namien, these people have come to see you."

A man, seemingly naked and sitting on a stool nine feet from the bars, raises his head. His almost vague gaze falls on Biafle.

"Mr. Namien, my name is Biafle Herbert, head of the S-cell, and this is my partner, Kobenan," says Biafle.

The sorcerer smiles.

"Since when does the S-cell accept djinns as head in their organization? Times are changing, aren't they?" says the sorcerer. "Biafle. It's the name they gave you. It's ... different. And you are the new guy." Namien turns to Kobenan. "Your energy is still disturbed by all of this."

As weird as it may seem, Kobenan feels no fear at the sight of the man, maybe because of his human traits. He can relate to something he already knows. But again, the Great Chief said he is one of the most dangerous sorcerers they know of, so Kobenan is more than careful and stays close to the Great Chief, as ordered. He observes the man talking. His posture on the stool exudes confidence and power. His gestures suggest someone experienced.

"You could have brought someone older, Mr. Biafle," says the sorcerer with a semblance of a smile, turning back to Biafle.

"What do you know about the assassination?" asks Biafle, barely acknowledging the words of the sorcerer.

"What makes you think I know something? I am as in the dark as you are," responds the sorcerer. "But I want to know more."

"Why?" insists Biafle.

"I have my reasons, and you don't need to know them ... but I can help you," says Namien, looking coy.

"I am listening," says Biafle in a serious tone.

"No ... I want out," says the sorcerer.

"We are wasting our time." Biafle turns to the Great Chief.

Kobenan can't read the sorcerer. His body language is too well controlled. He is far different from the few men Kobenan has had to read during some of his cases. He divulges no information in what he says. His microexpressions are as plain as a white board. Everything whispers that he knows nothing more than what he speaks, but Kobenan feels different. It's the same feeling that floods him when he reads a file and knows something is wrong, even though every word, photo, and proof in the file says otherwise. Namien is hiding something. Kobenan knows. This feeling has never betrayed him, not yet.

"You want to know more because someone you care for might be affected by this assassination. It's the beginning of something that might reach this person," says Kobenan, staring at the naked man.

Namien shifts his gaze to Kobenan. His light face hardens, a confirmation for Kobenan. The sorcerer's countenance changing means only one thing: whoever it is, they are very important to him. The sorcerer gazes silently at him.

"Who?" asks Biafle.

"Someone very close to him," responds Kobenan. "This person might be the reason he gave himself up."

The Great Chief looks at Kobenan, thinking, *This boy knows nothing about the sorcerer. How does he come up with suggestions so tangible?*

"What did you do? You made a deal … for their protection. Is that why you are here?" asks Kobenan. "Otherwise, why would you want out now? Because this deal might be compromised."

The gaze of the sorcerer does not waver. Every part of his body, including his eyes, has stopped moving. The Great Chief quickly detects this, and he moves closer to Kobenan.

Biafle stares at Namien. The words somewhat make sense. "He wants to make sure the deal still holds. He has no interest in running, but he wants to be sure the person he is protecting is still safe. The Great Chief would never have allowed him to leave, so he made sure the information came to us so we could help him clear his concern," says Biafle.

The sorcerer does not budge, his gaze nailed to Kobenan.

"This might be someone in his family, a brother or his child," adds Kobenan. The thick metal bars bend open in a blink. Kobenan's reflexes can only flicker his eyes. The Great Chief quickly grabs the bars and forces them back to their initial state.

"Calm down, Namien. There is no need for this here. If you know how to find answers, just tell us. You don't need to be out for that," says the Great Chief.

"You'll never find the place of these people without me," affirms Namien, his gaze still dead set on Kobenan.

The men are all thinking the same thing. If that is really the case, if Namien wants to ensure the safety of someone, then it's a very weak link for a sorcerer of this caliber, which is highly improbable. There might be another reason, but the only way to confirm this is to go with it.

"It's the only lead we have so far." Biafle turns to the chief. "Is it possible to leave him in our custody, Great Chief?"

"The situation is critical. I don't have a choice here. The boy is right; if he made a deal, there is no need for him to run. My bat will follow you," says the Great Chief.

Biafle digs his left arm into his inner pocket and pulls out two bracelets of braided dried palm leaves. Stained white fibers cover them in an intertwined fashion. The many broken fibers sticking out attest to the worn-out state of the bracelets. Kobenan can't quite make out the material of these white fibers. They definitely look like nothing he knows. "Put these on," orders Biafle.

"I don't need spirit bracelets," prompts Namien, looking at Biafle from the corner of his eyes, his head still fixed in Kobenan's direction.

"Safety," retorts Biafle, tossing them to him.

Spirit bracelets. This name rings a bell from one of the files Kobenan read. They are designed to bind the spirit of the wearer to his body. One of the many tangled sentences he couldn't make any sense of. Kobenan looks at the sorcerer as he puts on the bracelets and stands up with his gaze locked on Kobenan. He stands close to six feet tall.

Kobenan is still reeling at what just happened. Everything went so fast; he is still questioning what he really saw. Did these large metal bars just bend open by themselves before his eyes? Did the large man by his side just push them back in place through sheer strength? A heavy hand on his chest pulls him back to awareness. The Great Chief is pushing Kobenan behind him as the sorcerer is exiting the cell.

"Okay, let's go," says the Great Chief. "There is no time to waste. My people will escort you out of the prison."

A djinn. One of the first words of the sorcerer when he was addressing Biafle. Kobenan knew that there is a djinn in the S-cell. It's plastered on most of the files he solved, and based on what he put together in these two years of work, this djinn has been working for the S-cell for more than fifty years, but only twelve years ago did he become an important lead. And this coincides with the time Mr. Biafle became the head of the S-cell. So the sorcerer was talking about him, about Biafle. *He is a djinn.* Kobenan takes a brief look at his partner walking to the black SUV, escorted by the two dark guards, with the prisoner. His knowledge of djinns is more than vague, but from whatever recollection he has from his books, they are far from having human morphology, and Biafle is everything a man should be. If all of this pans out correctly, it means Namien was in that cage for a long time, if he didn't know Biafle was the head of the S-cell—at least twelve years.

Kobenan has very clear fragments of equivocal details about djinns that he stumbled upon through the years. They are mostly irrelevant for analysis or in decision-making, but they will do for now until he learns more. Djinns are sparsely dispersed throughout several zones of the continent. They vary greatly in shape and form. Their location is unclear, but many reports have mentioned various forms dwelling in the far, sometimes isolated regions of the country. The great majority of them, it is written, are invisible to the human eye. One of the conjectures is the mind failing in interpretation, but nothing is set in stone, for the S-cell documents Kobenan has stumbled upon lack data. The many redacted pages did not help either; he simply was not authorized for more information than he needed on the subject. The lines about djinns he has read in the books and the many cases he has solved don't portray them as friendly, nor are they classified as a foe, but they certainly are dangerous.

Biafle opens the trunk of the car and pulls a cardboard box toward himself. He grabs a light-blue shirt patterned with fading red flowers and black pants and presents them to Namien. The sorcerer glances silently at the clothes, then looks at Biafle. "You do realize I am invisible to the naked eye, correct?"

"I know," Biafle responds calmly, his hand extended toward the sorcerer, "but you are too visible to us right now."

Namien grabs the pants and slips them on. They are slightly shorter than his legs. He grabs the shirt and wears it without buttoning. The cardboard box is full of clothes. Biafle must encounter many of these naked men in his line of work, Kobenan thinks. Biafle opens the left back-seat door and signals that the sorcerer should enter the vehicle. "Let's go," says the head of the S-cell, getting in the driver's seat.

*

It's a prominent neighborhood. That's the first thing Kobenan notices after two hours' drive back to the city, when the car enters a vast area of big, widely spaced houses, each unique. The sun is strong in the sky, and only a few pedestrians traverse the quiet neighborhood. Namien asks Biafle to park in a spot close to one of the houses. Biafle kills the engine, removes his jacket, and opens his door. "Leave your jacket here. We don't want to draw attention," he says, leaving the car, followed by Namien. Kobenan follows the instruction and joins his partner in front of the SUV.

"The protection the Great Chief drew on you worked well," says Namien, turning to Kobenan. "I couldn't detect the third eye. That's why you have been so quick to read me, but I am warning you, if you say something ... anything ... they will detect you, and believe me, they will hunt you down and make sure you disappear. You sit. You don't speak. You listen. Hopefully they will make a mistake and say something helpful."

"Okay," says Kobenan, in a voice that barely escapes his mouth, after a brief silence.

"Who are *they*?" asks Biafle.

"Enkonhi," responds Namien.

They exchange a sharp gaze, and Biafle looks at Kobenan. Though Kobenan has never worked for the S-cell, his formation as a candidate for the organization brought him across many names he was never meant to think about a second time if he was not selected. Enkonhi was one of these names. *Enko-n-ni,* he remembers the orthoepy, a vocal sound from an old tribal language of the southeast, which closely translates to "became demons." It refers to sorcerers and sometimes couples who have killed and eaten all their siblings, children, and grandchildren throughout the ages. They are extremely rare and sometimes incredibly powerful. "These two are well known for having delicate information. They are close to the source," says Namien. "They are by no means friendly, so be on your guard and have an escape plan ready."

They walk by two houses before reaching the one where Namien stops. Green bushes and flowers four feet tall surround the two-story house. It's a beautiful abode for those who can't see, one heavily fortified for those who can. Kobenan spots in his brief observation many small fetishes lying about on the grass. He and Biafle stand before the entry of the house, as their guide does. It takes a few minutes before they see a hand appearing from the window, waving them over and disappearing into the house. The door gently opens halfway. "Let's go," says Namien.

Kobenan, following the steps of his partner, is walking toward the door when Biafle stops him and makes a subtle move with his head to the left. The window is the door.

The sorcerer goes in first, followed by Biafle and Kobenan. They enter a modest interior, which seems to be the living room. Kobenan takes a look around as he slips his second leg into the room.

"Welcome. Please come in," says a woman with a smile. She's in her mid-fifties, in a yellow T-shirt, with a fairly new sheet of African textile—bogolan patterns, judging by the print—wrapped around her waist and dropping to her heels. She goes to the extent of shaking the guests' hands and shows them to another room in the center of the house. There stands a smiling man in short green pants and a white T-shirt. He extends his arm to shake their hands and invites them to sit. Biafle is the only one who stays standing up next to Kobenan after moving his chair to the side, maybe for security purposes, Kobenan thinks.

"Oh, a djinn of the forest!" exclaims the man, looking at Biafle. "It is a long time since I have seen one. Your kind has become very rare nowadays. Which forest are you from?"

"East, Manguela," answers Biafle.

"Oh, Manguela. I've heard there are very few of you left there. Pfff, what a pity," says the man.

"What do you expect, with this deforestation happening everywhere?" says the woman, looking at her man. "Oh, sorry, where are my manners? Can I offer you something to drink?"

"You know we won't take it, so can we get back to the purpose of our visit?" prompts Namien.

"Sure, please," responds the woman, maintaining her smile.

"I believe you know what is happening right now. Do you know who did it?" asks Namien.

"Of course we do." The man smiles. "Every sorcerer is talking about it. Rumors have it Mother Nature is cleaning."

"Mother Nature!" exclaims Namien. "You mean the guardians of Nature killed a man? That's not possible."

"Why is this not possible?" says the man, his smile fading. "It happened before, and you know it, even if it was a long time ago. It's happening again. Mother Nature is targeting everyone who is a threat to her, and these people are right in the midst of it."

Who is he talking about? Kobenan wonders. *Might it be people like the minister who died? Or is he generalizing to a broader group?* His focus should be on their every word right now, not overthinking.

"They don't care." The woman takes over. "As long as what they want is within their reach, they use it extensively. Their baffling ignorance is flaring everywhere. So maybe the guardians are setting things right." She shrugs.

"Well, they believe their technology will save them when the time comes," says the man. "They don't know it's a big part of what is coming."

Kobenan looks at Biafle on his right and then back to the couple.

"Technology isn't the problem," Biafle steps in. "Their understanding of it is."

"Whatever," says the woman dismissively. "It's their technology, their way of thinking."

"What did the white minister do?" asks Namien.

"He was thinking of processes for electricity that would have wiped out entire forests if realized and was planning to launch a proposal about it," says the man.

Namien looks at Biafle and gets back to the couple. "Are you sure the guardians did this? It's very rare for them to interact with creatures of nature."

"Well, are you sure they consider themselves creatures of nature?" asks the man.

"I was thinking ..." Namien begins.

"What?" interrupts the woman. "That someone who broke the rules did it, and your child isn't safe? That your deal is off?"

Namien's brown irises snap at the woman. Biafle, standing one chair away from the sorcerer, moves his eyes toward him. *Kobenan was right; he does have a child.*

"We know that too," says the woman with a smile. "You are a very selfish man, Namien. After eating the souls that others offered you, you don't want to offer your parts? You really think the deal you made will protect your child? You are mistaken."

Rage without warning propels Namien toward the smiling woman. His spirit bursts out of his body, screaming loudly in her calm face, but cannot detach from his wrist. Kobenan jolts right from his chair but remains on his seat, his heart skipping, shocked. The bracelets on the sorcerer's wrists stretch as the spirit struggles to leave the body. When the loud and brutal roar stops, the spirit glares with all the stretch it can get into the eyes of the serene woman. "You really thought we didn't know? We are looking for him, and we will find him. You know how important and gifted he is; that's surely the reasoning behind your desperate presence here. Someone may have acquired your child, if an assassination such as this occurred."

The sorcerer can't touch them. His spirit returns to his body, and he to his seat and takes a deep breath. "I think we're done here," he says in a low tone.

Kobenan tries to maintain his calm.

"Spirit bracelets ... You've become sloppy, Namien, if you thought we wouldn't know you were in prison for his protection," says the man with a shake of his head. "You can't save him. He is already dead, and so are you."

"Don't try anything we could both regret," says Biafle calmly. "I can free him anytime, and I am a djinn of the forest."

"Nooo, we aren't stupid," says the woman, laughing. "We know what djinns can do."

"Normally, we would have let you roam lost in this house until you died, but we didn't plan to come across a djinn of the forest. You know how to leave this house. Next time we see you, it won't be in such a pleasant manner," says the man.

"Follow me," says Biafle, crossing by the hosts. Kobenan does not need another word from his partner; he is already up and following closely. Namien is next, standing up and giving a last look to the Enkonhi before heading for the stairs on the trail of the agents. Biafle leads them to the next floor, where four doors align before them. He gestures carefully before the first door, moving his left palm around, with an expression as if he is trying to feel something. The others remain close behind him. Kobenan takes a quick look downstairs, only to see the chairs empty. He takes one more step closer to Biafle.

Biafle shifts to the two doors on their left after hovering his palm around. When they reach the fourth one, he stops after his hand has made a pass and slightly touches the wood. He starts gradually punching the top left of the door at precise spots. The grayish brass lever steadily turns by itself, and the door slowly opens. They enter a room full of folklore masks and African pots. Kobenan looks around. A bed lies before them, surrounded by quaint statues of wood. "Don't touch anything," warns Biafle, moving in a specific pattern around the pots. Kobenan and Namien follow every step of the djinn to the bathroom. A window next to the sink is the way out.

"Kobenan, do you have something for me?" asks Biafle when they reach the black SUV after a silent walk.

"They lied," responds Kobenan. "The guardians of nature didn't kill this minister. They know the person who did it, and whatever is being prepared has a serious connection with Namien's child."

"Of course they lied," confirms Namien. "They agreed to meet us to find out what we might know. Now they have confirmation that we have nothing. This talk was a diversion. The guardians of nature agreed not to touch any human being after what happened last time. Someone powerful enough to have influence in Brazil did it… These blood-seekers are looking for my son. "

"Your daughter," says Kobenan.

Namien looks at Kobenan. "What?"

"Your daughter," repeats Kobenan. "Back in their place, you tried to attack them when they said they were going to find him. But you went back to your seat and took a deep breath. You were relieved they didn't know it was a girl. And yes, you know they are going to get her; this just bought you more time."

Kobenan's feet leave the ground, and he slowly starts gliding upward with a stiff neck, his eyes turning red. "Put him down, Namien," warns Biafle, clenching his fist, transforming it to sharp, intertwined roots. "There is no need to kill him. If he is right, we'd better find a way to stop them."

Kobenan is choking. The sorcerer remains silent, staring at Kobenan.

"Don't force my hand, Namien. Put him down," comes a second warning from Biafle. Kobenan falls with a rushed and long inhale. He holds his throat and tries to find some air, spurting sharp coughs.

The sorcerer looks down at him for a moment and then opens the car's back door. "Bring me to my cell," he says, entering the vehicle.

Kobenan is regaining his breath. "He wants ... to ... es ... cape ... but ... he ... can't. He's bound ... by your ... spirit bracelets."

"Is your neck all right?" asks Biafle, looking around for any eyes that might have witnessed what just happened. No one seems to be close enough to trust their sight. He takes another look at Namien through the window, his sharp root reforming into a hand.

"I can ... breathe," responds Kobenan, still on all fours.

"Then get in the car," prompts Biafle, opening the door to the driver's seat. Three houses away, perched in a mango tree, is a bat, watching over everything.

The drive seems longer than Kobenan previously experienced, maybe because of the nerve-racking atmosphere in the car. He can see the dark guards from afar, standing, waiting for the SUV to stop where it should. When Biafle turns off the engine, they approach and stand by the back door. Biafle descends, followed by Kobenan. The djinn opens the back door. Namien, in the middle of the seat, does not budge, seemingly torn between descending and staying. "Namien," calls Biafle.

The sorcerer turns his head without looking. It takes a few seconds before he slides to the door and gets out. One of the guards attaches a thin, torn piece of cloth to his heel—the same strip they removed before he left the prison. The guards walk by the prisoner's sides, followed by Biafle and Kobenan. The Great Chief's grand stature grabs Kobenan's attention when they cross the main gate. He awaits them, standing in the large room of quaint hallways. He is the one waiting for them this time, maybe because of Namien.

"His energy is disturbed," says the Great Chief, looking at the dark guards escorting Namien into one of the dim hallways.

"His child is in danger," says Biafle, looking at the sorcerer walking away. "You were right, Great Chief, this is bigger than we thought. We don't have all the pieces, but it might be the beginning of something we won't be able to control if we don't find answers. The death of the minister looks like the start of a chain, and whoever is behind this knows what he is doing. "

"Yes, it's a problem if no one was able to detect a sorcery like this until after the fact … and I presume the child of Namien is connected to all of this."

"We don't know yet," responds Biafle. "Namien killed many of his family's children. It might just be a payback, and he doesn't want it."

"I understand," says the Great Chief. "This is common among soul eaters; they eat their family's children, but they don't want their children to undergo the same fate, so they make a deal to protect them. But this scenario has never happened before. Why would a sorcerer like Namien make a deal to give himself up to protect his child, and who made him take this deal?"

"We don't know yet. But I am sure he'll attempt to break free," says Biafle.

The Great Chief smiles. "You know that's not possible. This isn't a common prison. The doors alone are a weakness for the prisoners. He can't approach them. And we are among the best sorcerers, djinns, and spirits from Africa who guard this place. Don't worry, he knows he can't get out unless we allow him. That's why he is disturbed."

It will probably be wrong, downright disrespectful, but Kobenan has to speak. Whatever he heard out there felt nothing like payback. This is something different. Maybe worse than what Mr. Biafle and the Great Chief think. And this child might be the answer. He somehow has to find a way to convey it. "We have to let him go, Great Chief," Kobenan says suddenly. "He might be an important lead in this situation."

They both look at Kobenan in a brief silence.

"My apologies, Great Chief. We will be on our way. We have to brief the president," says Biafle.

"We don't free sorcerers," says the Great Chief, his gaze still on Kobenan. "It's the first rule of this prison."

"But there might be an exception, Great Chief," prompts Kobenan. "His daughter is connected to all of this. He might be of great help."

"Sorcerer soul eaters don't help," says the Great Chief. "They think only of themselves, their interests, and they have no problem killing for that. You of all people should know that by now; you can barely speak. He wanted to know if his child was still under protection."

"We will be on our way, Great Chief," Biafle says respectfully. "Thank you very much for everything."

The Great Chief looks at Biafle and nods.

"But ..." Kobenan begins.

"That's enough," interrupts the Great Chief in a calm tone.

Biafle bows, and Kobenan follows. He knows it's not at all wise to insist at this point. They leave the prison, with the dark guards stopping before the main gate.

Biafle leads quickly and silently. Kobenan struggles to catch up, mainly trying to convince his partner of the mistake he thinks they are making. He who usually works alone in his small office and mostly trusts his instincts to get results has to convince someone else this time about something he knows is true. His feelings have never failed him, and this one is too strong to just ignore it and listen to the Great Chief. This girl is connected to all of this.

"Mr. Biafle, we are leaving a precious lead here. We need him to find answers," pants Kobenan, one step behind Biafle. The head of the S-cell walks straight, looking straight ahead. "Believe me, his daughter is connected to all of this, and she is very important, not only to him. Why would he give himself to a sorcerer prison? You heard what the Great Chief said—no sorcerer can escape this prison. Why would one of the deadliest sorcerers give his life to protect his daughter unless she has something special? He could have made some other deal, so why the most secure sorcerer prison? The Great Chief said this has never happened before. Mr. Biafle, do you hear what I am saying?"

Kobenan follows his partner to the driver's door. When they reach the car, Biafle turns and brutally grabs Kobenan's collar with one hand, pulls him, and pins him to the door with a loud bang.

The slam on the SUV is sharp. Kobenan's hands cling to Mr. Biafle's solid grasp on his collar. The stretch on the back of his neck is rigid, almost painful. His heart is pounding at an increasing rate, and his eyes, wide with shock and fright, look into Biafle's pupils, which show a serious intent to hurt. He was merely talking about the severity of the situation, and now he is pressed against the door with his feet barely touching the ground.

"I'll explain to you in detail what happened to my former partner," Biafle begins. "He was brilliant, stronger than me, extremely resourceful but reckless. He made one mistake during a mission, one, and two weeks before he died, he was not the same anymore. He couldn't eat or drink. He was vomiting dark blood, and the stench of his skin could only remind you of something putrid. His innards were rotten. His soul was still in his body, but he was already dead; his body was deteriorating. The entire cell never thought someone of his caliber could be struck down by a sorcerer, but he is dead. Do you hear me? Dead.

"You are very weak. You don't know much about the sorcerer world, yet you act like you do. If you are stupid … good for you … but don't be reckless under my watch, not while the president assigned you to me, or I swear I'll kill you before a sorcerer lays his hand on you. Is that clear?"

"Clear," says Kobenan.

Biafle releases Kobenan's collar, which is now rumpled to an unrecognizable state. Kobenan finds balance again when the back of his feet touch the road. Biafle pushes him to the side and opens the driver's door. "Okay. Now get in the car, we have a briefing to do," he orders.

Kobenan takes two steps toward the hood of the vehicle. He has to make a whole turn to reach the passenger's door, but he suddenly stops. Maybe his tongue will kill him today. If this harsh pinning to the door was just a warning, Mr. Biafle's way to make a point, then Kobenan's next words might be the end of him. But he can't swallow them. He doesn't want to die, but he can't stay silent.

"The president assigned me to you because I'm the best at what I do." He turns to Biafle. The tall man, who was about to enter the vehicle, pauses. "And I'm sure you've noticed that,"

Kobenan continues. "I know I'm not strong. But I also know that if we don't get this guy out of prison, what will happen will be disastrous. His daughter is the key to all of this. You might think I am reckless, and maybe I am, but I have to act this way to understand the situation or the reaction of the suspect and foresee his next move.

"The president assigned me to you because I can quickly figure out what happened and what will follow, and you will be there to protect me in case of problems. So we can sit and figure out how to get Namien out of prison now or waste time on a briefing while they are closing in on his daughter."

A brusque silence falls between the two agents. Kobenan clenches his teeth and prepares himself to receive whatever is coming his way, his heart pounding as he refuses—or maybe is hesitant out of uncertainty for his immediate future—to break eye contact with his partner. The strength he just experienced pressing on his neck with only one arm means this man can break his neck with a flick of his fingers, and right now, he doesn't look too happy. This piercing regard, this statuelike pause, presages nothing good at all.

"So, if I understand well, you don't want to brief the president." Biafle finally breaks the silence.

Kobenan takes a deep breath of relief. "Unless Sector 0 belongs solely to Côte d'Esperance, I highly doubt only President Dablan could release Namien. And from what you described about this prison and the people guarding it, it must be international, hence many approvals could be required. I don't think the other presidents will agree to free a sorcerer, especially Namien, and we don't have time. I want to brief the president, but this will make him an accomplice to what we are about to do, and we don't want that, do we?"

Biafle looks at Kobenan for a brief moment before he continues his slide into the seat. "Get in the car."

Kobenan hastens around the front of the car to the passenger's seat and enters the vehicle. Biafle, who had the engine started, turns and leaves the prison.

Biafle's former partner, this man, it could only be agent Malik Lotoumbe, the former head of the S-cell, the agent who is said to have bent and changed many rules inside the agency. His name appeared at times in Mr. Biafle's reports, but never as a partner or even a former partner. It was always agent Malik Lotoumbe's thoughts or theories or conclusions, when Biafle wanted to invoke his name on a specific subject they had faced or similar to the case he was writing on.

Agent Malik Lotoumbe was probably the one who pushed for Biafle to be the next head of the S-cell by changing the rules. *That's why Namien said when he saw him that times are changing.* Maybe making a djinn head of an important governmental agency like the S-cell would never have been possible if not for agent Malik Lotoumbe. His death or details relating to it never appeared in any research book Kobenan read when he was learning about this man. Cursed by a sorcerer; maybe that's the reason it was simply written that he retired.

CHAPTER 3

The Choice

A loud bell rings all across the building, a joyful sound for many. It's time to leave after a heavy eight hours of study, so it doesn't take long for chattering noises to follow. The gate of the four-story building opens for a flock of young men and women to leave for their respective homes. A substantial flock but still far less prominent than the average school. Cars are parked on the pavement before the privileged establishment. Taxis pile up as potential clients stand in numbers at this hour of the day. Drivers and a few parents await, some in their luxurious cars, others standing by their car doors, mainly to signal their position in the row of vehicles. While many of the drivers open the back door for their masters, a few children jump in the passenger seat after a kiss on their parent's cheek.

Many students are still chattering before the school's main gate, which is seven feet high, and those whose stomachs were emptied during the long hours of writing lessons buy food at the nearest stores around the school. Joel is leaving the building, his face relaxed from laughing. His friend Roland is still in the midst of a barely contained laugh.

"You should have seen his face when he got his mark—price-less," says Roland, arranging the backpack with one strap on his right shoulder, leaving the other strap dangling.

"I saw it," responds Joel with a giggle, digging into his khaki pants pocket. "I think next time he will think twice before challenging us."

He pulls out his phone and switches it on. He follows the rules and does not want to lose it, as it is mandatory to have your phone off during class, unless you want it ending up in the principal's drawer for the rest of the year. Roland looks toward the row of cars and yellow taxis on his left. "I think your driver is here," he says, waving at the driver. The man waves back with a smile.

"I am not going with him," says Joel, making a sign to the driver. The man, who seems used to the gesture, nods and heads off.

"I don't understand. Why are you wasting this opportunity?" asks Roland with a disappointed expression. "That's just dumb. I am telling you, if I had what you have, I wouldn't be walking home."

Joel looks at his friend. Poor choice of words for someone who has a whole flat to himself. "Seriously? Let's just go home."

"Just sayin'," Roland continues. "I mean, look at these threads, man. You're killin' your shoes."

"I'll buy another pair," says Joel with his focus turned away on the pavement before him, troubled by the crowd between him and what he stares at.

"What are you looking at?" Roland follows Joel's eyes further down the pavement in front of the school's main gate. "Please don't. You two are from different planets."

"What do you mean?" Joel asks passively, barely listening to his friend.

"She is too cute for you, man," says Roland.

"So ... I am ugly," says Joel.

"Like I need to tell you that." Roland pats Joel's shoulder. "Don't scare the poor girl. I am your friend, and I care deeply about you. Listen to me."

Despite his mocking humor, Roland is probably right. This girl, Miranda Tedry, is the most beautiful girl in the class. Her five-foot-nine-inch height makes her stand out from the other girls. Her lean figure with generous curves is the talk of many boys in the school. She is what you would call high-class, but she always looks and acts grounded, hanging out most of the time with her girlfriends. There she is in a crowd of chatty students before the school gate, talking to one of her friends, not too far from the exquisitely shiny gray sedan with her driver waiting. Everyone knows who her father is, some important colonel who seldom visits the school. Hence, few mess with his daughter.

Miranda is the dream of many boys, but not Joel. He just knows her as his kind, beautiful classmate, and they only exchange a shy "Hi" when their paths cross. Something else has caught his attention. Something standing right next to her and moving when she does. He has seen this kind of creature before, but never in school. The scrawny creature, with his prominent ribcage and a face Joel could barely describe, stands around six feet tall on her right. It is fixated on the girl and occasionally looks around. When it looks on the other side of the road, Joel follows, until he descries another creature gazing at him, one of a height more frightening than the first one. Joel quickly breaks eye contact and turns to his friend. "Let's go," he says.

Roland, who is staring at his friend enchanted by the beauty of their classmate, shakes his head. "Damn, where does this come from?" He chuckles, turning to the edge of the pavement. "You had an epiphany or something?"

Joel is ahead as they cross the road, keeping his head straight. He dares not flinch to check if the creature is still looking at him. Why are the creatures he usually sees on streets and junctions following someone? And she is completely oblivious to their presence, as is everyone else around. The thought of these things near her troubles him. He has seen too much suffering when they show up for it to be just a coincidence. He walks on, oddly quiet and distant.

"You heard about the inspection tomorrow? Pretty random, ain't it?"

"Han?" Joel snaps from his thoughts. "Yeah, I heard it's because of the coming exams."

Roland smiles. "You'll see how Professor Nobli will behave tomorrow."

These last words fall on deaf ears as Joel is pulled back into his disquietude. It takes an hour and a half when he and Roland decide to walk home, which is every day for Joel. It takes almost two hours for Roland to reach his apartment. But there is always nattering, on subjects from girls to weird teachers to learning more about the history of other continents instead of their own. This has always baffled Roland, and he couldn't care less about this class.

Joel is silent today. He looks around at times and appears distracted when they cross a road. He has learned over the years to forget about the accidents he can predict when these creatures are around. But this is different. They never get this close to a person. Their action, as far as he knows, is mostly directed toward groups of people. Something is not right. It seems like the number of creatures he routinely sees at the crossroads he uses to reach home has doubled, maybe tripled. Ten more steps and they will be at the signal where he and his friend part ways.

"You okay, bro?" asks Roland.

"I'm good. Just tired."

"You sure? Someone's falling hard for Miranda," teases Roland.

Joel smiles. "You're crazy. See you tomorrow."

"See you," responds Roland. "Just wash your face with water tomorrow. It'll go away."

Joel chuckles with a light shake of his head. They take opposite directions after a fist bump.

Joel, who is now in his neighborhood, walks slowly. He can hear the yelling at the gate, probably because of him again. The rear metal gate, rarely locked before ten at night, stops below his chin and makes a thin, squeaky noise when he opens it. He heads for the second metal door in the garage, which opens tightly onto a wooden door. He usually avoids the main entrance. Fewer eyes on him if nobody is paying attention, not like today. The yelling is pronounced at the wooden door, mainly his father's voice. He used to wait behind this door, his hand on the knob, until the voices calmed down. Now he just enters and goes straight to his room. He turns the knob and opens the door to the dining room. His mother stands at the table, seemingly exhausted by the dispute. His father, whose energy is fueled by anger, raises his voice again when he sees Joel. "What's wrong with you, son? Why won't you ever take a car? Tell me why!"

"Let the boy be," says Joel's mother. "If he doesn't want it, he doesn't want it. You can't force this. Baby, go to your room, please."

"I don't understand why he can't be like normal teenagers," says his father, pausing with his hand on the table, frustration etched on his face. "Why can't you be normal? You even avoid buses. I specifically told you, if you don't want to use cars, at least take the bus. You're always home late because of that. Look at the time. Or is there something you are doing out there that we don't know?"

"Baby, please go change, and then you can have dinner." His mother turns to him. Joel, who had removed his bag at the door, lets it hang in his left hand and walks to the stairs. He can still hear them when he closes his bedroom door.

"He's a good boy, Philipe. You should know that. He has good marks, and his walking home has never been an issue. He doesn't want to take the car or the bus. What's the big deal? Scolding him like this isn't good."

"Oh, so you want something to *happen* before you make a decision, is that it?" demands Joel's father.

Joel lays his bag on the blue carpet before the door and sits on his bed. He looks down and exhales. He should be used to this by now, but it doesn't seem to get old, at least the tension at home when there is a dispute. It is true that most of the students go with a parent or drivers. None take the bus, and the only ones who walk are very close to the school. For some, vicinity is no reason to discard their vehicle. Even Roland complains at times. He doesn't mind walking, as long as he is not alone, but Joel knows that Roland walks because he does. Joel hears his mother's voice calling him at the door. He responds, leveling his stare. She enters, closes the door, and approaches him at the bed.

"You must be tired of all of this," she says, sitting next to him.

"That's all right," Joel almost whispers.

"I'm sorry you had to hear all that. You know your dad loves you. He's just concerned for your safety. You're a grown man now, but you'll always be his child—our child. That's why he's acting like this. He doesn't want anything to happen to you. You're our first, and you have to set an example. Your little sister is looking up to you." She lays a palm on the back of his head. "I'm sure you have your reasons. Just be careful, okay? I love you so much."

"Okay, Mom," responds Joel.

She smiles and stands up. "You're going to have dinner with us, right?" Joel nods. "We'll be waiting for you downstairs." She gives him a long kiss on the cheek and leaves the room.

Safety. His parents have never really understood him, and he doesn't expect this to change. There is nothing he can do to make them understand. He quickly stopped showing them what he was seeing when he realized he was the only one who could see. When he was twelve, the therapist said that though this was late for a child his age, it might just be a phase. He hated medication and so stopped talking about what he was seeing. There was no point at all. Now he is seventeen, and he has to manage a different issue altogether: safety, as his parents frame it. But it doesn't matter, anyway; this year is his last. He will be gone soon to another city to continue his studies, as he already discussed with his parents. That is, if his application is accepted—it has to be. He is tired of hearing yelling almost every day. At least over there nobody will be complaining, and he will visit his family every other weekend. Roland has also applied, so hopefully they will be together. He will miss his parents, but not as much as his beautiful little sister.

"Poutchou, you there? You didn't give me kisses when you came," says a little voice from behind the closed door. Speaking of his sister, there she is. The only one who never knocks twice before entering his room. Sometimes she barely knocks at all. *Poutchou*, as she calls him, is always followed by the door handle turning before Joel has the chance to say "Come in." She has turned eight now and is more stubborn about the knocking. You'd think she would grow up with a better understanding of her big brother's privacy, but she just gets cuter and sillier. Princess enters in her yellow dress and smiles at him.

"Hey, little monster." He opens his arms, and she approaches. He gives her so many kisses that she starts laughing. This is the only moment in his days that makes him forget about everything else.

"Give me a few minutes," says Joel. "I'll shower and come downstairs. We will eat together, okay?"

"Okay, Poutchou," she replies, her smile widening.

Princess jumps off the bed and leaves the room. As she is about to close the door, she grimaces with a silly face. "Oh my goodness, you're ugly," says Joel, covering his face. She laughs and shuts the door. Joel stands up and walks to the laundry basket near his closet. He empties his pants of the pennies he uses for snacks on the road and removes his clothes, avoiding eye contact with a short, tan-colored being who has always been in his room for as long as he can remember.

At first, he experienced dread and nightmares every time he had to sleep in this room when he was younger. After failed attempts to sleep elsewhere, which always resulted in him being brought back to his room by his parents, he started waiting for them to go to sleep and then came down in the living room to sleep on the couch. But that only lasted for a very short period, as they quickly realized he wasn't in his room most nights. Years have passed, and fear has become avoidance. Joel just pretends this being is not in his room, and everything works fine. He has never done anything to harm Joel, so Joel goes on with his daily life without bothering with him.

The being sometimes stands near the closet at the wall's corner or sits with legs crossed on Joel's study table. Today he stands near the laundry basket, gazing at Joel. Joel cannot call his fixations hostile; *threatening* might be the appropriate word, or *extremely intimidating*, as though he waits for Joel to make one wrong move, to acknowledge he sees him, before something happens, something he could deeply regret. So, Joel never gives him this satisfaction.

On the rare moments when Joel happens to face or have him in his field of view for a few seconds, he can feel the tan man's intense stare. A stare with eyes that don't appear to blink. He hardly reaches four feet and has been in the same clothes since the first time Joel cried in the room. A brown cloth covers most of his body, leaving legs and feet bare. He wears a belt of straw and cowrie shells and a strange necklace of cowrie shells and shiny, small black rocks. Two of the things that almost always catch Joel off guard before he starts ignoring the short man are his bloodshot eyes and his insanely flat and large nose. Of course, he is used to it, but something always makes him hesitate before entering the room when he sees the man. So, he has made a habit of entering the room head down so he can prepare himself to ignore him.

Joel leaves his underwear on and goes to the bathroom. When he opens the door after his bath, tightening his white towel around his waist, the short being with bloodshot eyes and dark pupils stands before the bathroom, staring up at him. There's half a second of a barely visible jolt, but Joel just walks past him to his closet. The being follows him. Joel dresses and exits the bedroom, which this short being never seems to leave.

Everyone is already at the table waiting for him. A savory smell has claimed the dining room. Fried chicken and mashed potatoes, his favorite. "Come, baby, sit," says his mother.

"Yes, come, baby. Sit," repeats his sister.

"Stop that, Princess," Joel's mother says passively.

Joel smiles and pulls his chair out.

"I believe there is an inspection tomorrow," says Joel's father.

"Yes," responds Joel. The school must have called all the parents, as they always do before inspection each year. It's a fancy way to say, "We take care of your grown-up children, and they will be coming home early, since there won't be much study this day."

"So you will be home early, right?" asks his father.

"I will, Dad," answers Joel, turning his plate.

"Do you want me to come and pick you up?"

"It's okay, I'll manage. I will be home early. Don't worry."

"Okay, then." Joel's father turns his plate. "You reassure me. Let's have the delicious dinner your mom cooked for us."

Dinner is silent, punctuated by clanking silverware. When they finish eating, Joel helps his mother and sister clear the table and wash the dishes. His father goes back to his study to resume work on his miniature buildings. He has been working on his project for months now, a contract on the construction of a new building downtown. Joel knows this because his father told them months ago he would be home most of the time, but very busy, so they won't see him much until he is done with his models. He always tells them when he is about to start a long project.

"Are you okay, baby?" asks Joel's mother, who has noticed her son's pensiveness.

Joel looks at her. "I'm okay."

"You sure? You seem far away. What's wrong?"

"I'm okay," Joel repeats.

"You can tell me anything, you know that, right?" says his mother, rubbing the foamy plate in her hand.

Joel smiles gently at her, rinsing the plate he receives and handing it over to his sister, who wipes it with a cloth and arranges it next to the row of plates. The dishwasher is encased a few inches below the countertop, next to the sink and in perfect condition, but they almost never use it. Joel used to wonder why, but it became apparent with the years. His parents want their children to acquaint themselves with cleaning on their own. His father does the dishes at times, but always alone, and when he does, he has cooked for the family. When there is no more rinsing to do, Joel gives his mother and sister a kiss and walks up to his room. He crawls into bed and covers himself from head to toe. The thin, almost see-through cover allows for an unsolicited peek at the short man sitting with legs crossed on the table. He turns on the other side, giving his back to the being, and closes his eyes.

"Don't get involved in this."

The words force Joel to quickly open his eyes wide.

Joel remains in his bent position, his left palm below his head. This is the first time the short man has ever spoken. Joel does not budge and closes his eyes. Though this one is starkly different in form and size, it would be foolish and reckless to contrast him with those beings he spots on the road. What does he seek? Joel doesn't know. He doesn't want to know, for he doesn't want to find out what this being might do to him. Things are manageable as they are right now. But Joel knows this short man is far from stupid; he has seen Joel crying countless times in this room. Nonetheless, it is safer, and it has worked so far, to fake ignorance of this being in his room, as with the many unsettling ones he has met on the road through the years. Nothing good can come from this if they know he can see them, that he may well be the sole witness to these unexplained accidents. It takes a few hours for Joel to fall asleep.

*

The third alarm ring compels Joel out of bed after a late sleep. He showers, kisses his mother and sister, and leaves for school. As always, he walks. Class started seven minutes ago, and the school gate is closed, but Franck, the doorman, is a good buddy of his, so he opens the door for him after a little begging. Joel is rushing up the stairs when the words, "Before six …" float down from the upper floor. He slows down and hearkens.

"What about her great-grandfather?" asks the second voice.

"He doesn't know we are aware. Before six. I will take care of the rest," responds the first voice.

"Someone's here," says the second voice.

Joel, who has stopped on the stairs, resumes his ascent. A man in a gray suit and flat black tie stands alone two steps down before the next floor. Joel crosses by him and salutes him, avoiding looking in the direction of the tall creature facing the man. He can almost feel their gaze down his neck as he enters his classroom. Joel braces himself for the censure of Mister Nobli, the physics professor, who does not mince words with late students. When he knocks, the professor, writing on the long blackboard, looks his way. A head gesture suffices for Joel to rush for his seat next to Roland and empty his backpack on the table with his notebook.

"What was it this time, Mr. Kouadio, tying your laces?" says the teacher, continuing to write on the blackboard. The class gives a short laugh, with some throwing a glance at Joel.

Joel smiles as he pulls his physics book from his backpack and opens it to the lesson of the day. He gives a fist bump to Roland, who doesn't seem to care much about the formulae on the board. It's a half-day. He must be eager for the school bell. Joel looks at him in his boredom and shakes his head. A second gander past Roland falls in Miranda's direction, one row of tables before the entrance. The smile is quickly wiped from his face. He almost forgot for a second what he saw yesterday. The rush to his seat made him overlook the creature standing next to Miranda, the same one. There is another standing by the entrance. He quickly shifts his gaze to the blackboard; he can't rouse any suspicion. The last thing he wants is to show any sign that he can see them. Two, he thinks. Two creatures standing in his classroom. He only recognizes one from the day before. Or does he? They tend to resemble each other, apart from a few that stand out, with their shape and size.

His sight is shortly forced back to the entrance, as is everyone else's, for that matter, when a man in a gray suit enters the class. Joel's focus instantly turns to the two creatures following the man. One of them lowers its head to pass the doorway. Joel takes a light, trembling, deep breath and restricts his eyes to the man in the suit, the one he met on the stairs. Rules and custom demand students stand up when someone other than themselves enters the classroom. "Sit," says the man, heading for the back of the classroom, where he drags over a chair and ensconces himself. This man is the inspector, the one evaluating the professors' performances.

What is happening? What do they want with her? Why her? Joel follows Professor Nobli with deafened ears, fazed by what he sees. What should he do? What *can* he do? There is nobody he can tell about this. No authority in their right mind will believe him. They'll surely think he has some sort of mental disorder, hold him until his parents are called to pick him up, and Miranda will be dead by then. Warning her, whatever form it may take, will trigger an early reaction, advance their agenda, and they will both be dead before the end of the day. And unless he wants to come across as deranged, there is no reason to warn Miranda. What should he do? There must be something he can do to help her, something. One of the creatures appears before Joel, the one who lowered its head when it entered the classroom. Joel is smart enough to conceal his short jolt of surprise and dread with an ear scratch, as though something pinched him. The creature slowly bends, bringing its face next to Joel's, and looks him in the eyes. Joel does not budge his head from looking toward the professor.

He feels the heavy breathing on his face as sweat drips down his armpits. He shall not betray any expression. He tries to remain as calm as he can, his trembling breathing under careful control. He keeps a serene countenance directed toward the blackboard, praying his heartbeat is not as loud as he hears it. The creature is fixed on his face, looking for one mistake to take him down. When it sees a sweat drop on Joel's temple, it raises its fist.

Joel maintains his stiff posture, seeming attentive, his heart drumming in his chest. If he moves, he is dead. If he doesn't, he is dead. "Weird. He is not picking on anyone today," whispers Roland. Joel fakes a chuckle.

"Something funny, Mr. Kouadio?" asks Professor Nobli. "Care to share it with us?"

"No, nothing, sir. It was a cough," responds Joel.

"A cough?" says the professor, looking at him. "I heard a chuckle."

"No, sir. Sometimes it sounds like a chuckle," responds Joel. It's his only chance to confirm his ignorance to the creature.

"Sometimes your cough sounds like a chuckle," says the professor.

"Yes, sir ... sometimes," says Joel, lowering his voice as he completes his sentence.

The class snickers as Professor Nobli stares at Joel. His glasses resting on the tip of his nose, his head slightly tilted down, with his darting eyes pointed at Joel and physics book open in his right hand, the professor stands silent a solid five seconds before opening his mouth. "Mr. Kouadio, don't cough again, or I'll have to kick you out of my class. If what I'm teaching isn't important to you, it might be to others."

"I'm sorry, sir," says Joel, grabbing a green pen on Roland's notebook. His friend who started the whole thing follows the class in a laugh.

Joel remains immobile, the large fist hanging over his head. He feels the breathing of the creature drawing closer to his face. Maybe it knows. Whatever Joel just did didn't work. *It knows.* The thought pulsates in Joel's head. He feels like his heart will give up soon. The creature raises its fist, when it suddenly looks in the direction of the inspector. Joel is stark in his seat, his eyes on the board or the professor as indistinct thoughts bounce in his head. The one or two seconds of waiting for the fist to strike down feels like time is hanging. The creature straightens up and leaves the table. Joel is shaking, confused for a brief moment, and then breathes. He nearly met his death.

"What's wrong with you?" Roland asks with vague intrigue.

Joel turns to his friend "What do you mean?"

"Look at your shirt."

Joel didn't realize how much he was sweating. Luckily, only his armpits and his face show significant perspiration. Roland is not the only one who noticed it, but the embarrassing moment that just happened with the professor explains plenty. Roland digs in his bag and hands Joel a tissue to clean up his face. "I'm good. It's just ... it's hot in here," says Joel, wiping his face.

"Dude …" says Roland, pointing with his thumb at the air conditioning.

He knows now. He is convinced. She will be dead before the end of the day, before 6:00 p.m., if the inspector was speaking about her in the stairway. The inspector seeks anyone who might be a threat to this operation. They didn't make him out, or he would be dead by now. Joel is extremely careful and does not take his eyes off the board. He even takes notes doubtfully related to the professor's words. The inspector stays for another class following Professor Nobli's and leaves after a brief conversation with the professor of history. Only the creature standing next to Miranda remains in the class when the inspector leaves. Its skeletal shape; stretched, rugged skin; and bloody dead eyes intensify the already deep unsettlement and confusion in Joel's mind. The creature moves to the entrance and takes the same position as the one who was there before it.

The loud bell reminds Joel of what will happen to this girl if he stands idly by. He has to figure something out, and quick. *Think, Joel, think,* he keeps repeating to himself. Every second now is a step toward her death. Joel suddenly looks at her, talking with her girlfriends. Maybe he can. He doesn't know these creatures, but he knows enough. He has witnessed more than enough "accidents" to know what they mostly use: vehicles. The car. It clicks in his head. Her driver is surely waiting for her. He doesn't know what really happens during these accidents. It is always so sudden and fast. But speed is one factor. If only he can find a way to make her walk home. She must live far if she has a driver, or maybe because she is the daughter of a colonel. In any case, he has to find a way to convince her to walk. If this creature at the entrance doesn't know he is aware, he has a chance to guide her away from danger. But what can he possibly tell her to make her understand she is in great peril? Nothing without driving her away, appearing a fool, and accelerating everything, with the creature warned. But he has to. Roland catches Joel's attention, follows it, and sighs.

"You didn't wash your face, did you?"

"What?" asks Joel, turning to him.

"I told you to wash your face with water to make this deeeep love go away. She's like, from Venus, and you're like, I don't know, from Anobilekro," says Roland.

"That's a village."

"Exactly," says Roland with a smirk.

Joel smiles and pats Roland's shoulder when he gets up, as if to say, *I am going to try it anyway.*

Roland looks at him leaving and shrugs. "I've got a lot more tissues, don't worry."

Class is getting quieter, with students walking out of the classroom. Miranda stands at her table, chatting with three of her girlfriends, occasionally tucking a notebook or a pen into her handbag. Linda, one of Miranda's friends who sits behind her, is the first to notice Joel approaching. She quickly touches Miranda, who looks at her and then looks in his direction. Denise and Nadia follow Miranda. Joel would have veered for the door three times now if his mind were not in a different state. He salutes them with a smile and turns to Miranda.

"Can I talk to you for a moment?"

The girls look at Miranda with an expression only they can understand and leave for their respective bags. The creature at the entrance glares at Joel and edges closer to the girl, staring at Joel. No one should disturb its mission.

Joel breaks the silence. "Exams are coming up, and if I tell you I know something about physics, I am lying, big-time."

Miranda merely squints. Joel might not have the best grades in physics, but he is far from bad. "What makes you think I'll help you?"

Joel pauses as he looks into her brown eyes. He didn't anticipate this reaction. She always seems so smiley and nice to everyone, he thought her next words would probably fall under, "Which chapter don't you understand?" not this one she just threw at him.

"It would be a waste of being so beautiful and not nice, don't you think?" The words escape his mouth before he can evaluate them.

Miranda smiles. Despite the pressure surrounding him, with this creature's beaming eyes on him, this smile, now that he sees it so close, forces his heart to smile back. She really is beautiful.

"And what will I get in exchange?" Miranda asks.

"Everything. Whatever you need. Cars, planes, cruises, just ask," says a more relaxed Joel.

Miranda breaks into a laugh and looks at him. "I didn't know you were that open. You seem so shy."

"I'm not," Joel says gently. "But seriously, I saw your grades in math. I think I can help you with that. Deal?"

Miranda pauses with an awkward silence and gives him one of the most beautiful smiles he has ever seen. Joel waits with the most strenuous anxiety disguised as confidence. He hopes he made the right approach.

"Deal," Miranda responds.

"What do you think I get to know your place today so we can start tomorrow?"

"Hmmm ... works for me," she says with a playful expression.

"Okay. Give me a minute. I'll tell my friend here that he can start crawling home, because I'm not following him today."

Miranda giggles and nods. "Okay."

The creature's sharp gaze has not budged from Joel. It eyes Joel as he gets back to his seat, ignoring it. Roland followed the whole scene and has an amused expression on his face when Joel turns to him.

"See, I'm from Venus too," says Joel.

"Nah, you're not," says Roland. "Go. Just don't screw this up."

Joel packs his bag, and as he arranges his notebook and book in the sections, he notices his pens, red and blue. There is a brief pause before he grabs the blue one and tucks it in his pocket. He doesn't really know why, but having something to defend oneself with is better than nothing at all. It's the only close-to-sharp object he carries in his bag. He leaves Roland with a fist bump and joins Miranda, who is waiting for him. The creature is right next to her, gazing at Joel when he reaches to hold the door for her. He grabs the lever as his head slams into the door. Joel falls on his back, holding his nose.

The pain is deep, very deep, as Joel groans under his cupped palms. The situation should be alarming, but Miranda can't help but laugh before she gets close to him. Roland slowly puts his hands on his face.

"Are you okay?" asks Miranda, trying to contain her laughter.

"I'm okay," responds Joel, getting up. He ignores the creature and looks at Miranda.

"What happen … oh, you're bleeding," she says, hurrying to her handbag for a tissue. "Here."

"I must have lost my balance," says Joel, holding the tissue under his nose. It's a lie. He felt a hand pushing his head against the door. There is no need to guess whose that was. From what happened, maybe the creature wanted to stop Joel without alarming the girl to the point that she chooses to stay for him. This push was not a heavy one, but Joel could feel the strength on the back of his head. If this creature wanted to kill him with a slam of the door, it would have.

"Maybe you should see a doctor. We can do this tomorrow," says Miranda in a more serious tone.

"Oh, don't tell me I won't see your fortress because of that. See? I'm fine." Joel shows his wiped nose to Miranda and quickly puts the tissue back to it. "Don't make me curse this door for the rest of my life," he says with a smile underneath his hand.

"Okay. Let's go, then," says Miranda. "I'll get the door, don't worry."

Joel chuckles. "All right … walking?"

"I have my driver waiting downstairs." Miranda turns to him.

"How long will I get to know my new friend if I'm in a car?" asks Joel.

The voice coming underneath the tissue with the closed nostrils forces a smile onto Miranda's lips. "Okay, we'll walk."

Joel makes sure to hold tight to the railing in his descent. Better to avoid any unpleasant surprise. The face of Miranda's driver is at first a confused one, but he quickly gives an agreeable nod before he starts the car. Miranda has probably never walked home, but who is he to say no to the daughter of a colonel? He leaves without a word.

They walk along the road, talking and laughing, her more than her companion. Joel's bleeding has stopped, and he walks carefully and very aware of the position of Miranda beside him. He shifts sides often when he sees a potential danger for the girl. He can feel the creature growing more and more suspicious as it walks sometimes close to Joel to check his face. But Joel doesn't break eye contact with the road or his friend. The creature leaves Miranda's side and approaches Joel, breathing right down his neck. When they arrive at a bridge, Joel stops.

"You okay?" asks Miranda, turning to Joel, her vague inattention ending with the sudden halt of her companion. Maybe she is thinking the blow to Joel's head is taking effect now.

"Yeah," responds Joel after a brief pause. "Is there any other way to your house?"

Miranda smiles, her short moment of concern dissolved by Joel's words. "No, there isn't. What, are you afraid of bridges? Be a man, Joel," she says mockingly.

Those are hardly words young men want to hear from a beautiful girl. Joel is no different. "Of course I am ... with everything in place," he adds.

"Everything in place ... you're an interesting guy."

"I'll take that as a compliment," Joel says, looking at her over his shoulder.

Of course, he would have taken any other direction if there was a chance he could avoid the bridge. Apart from the fact that it is high above ground, many accidents he has witnessed happened on bridges. And there is no real position he could be in that will guarantee Miranda's safety. Both sides of the sidewalk open to a dangerous situation. On his left is a highway, where cars might be moving at an average of forty miles per hour. The small protection dividing the road from the sidewalk won't be of any obstacle to the creature if it tries anything. On the other side stands the railing, with nothing but wind and air beyond. The cars he perceives passing underneath the bridge are tiny. Joel can only protect Miranda from one side, and this gives more opportunity for this creature behind him to hasten any action it is to take. Joel shifts to the rail, where she could easily be thrown onto the road below. For the road on his left, he will have to keep both eyes on the cars passing by.

"Why do you move around so much?" asks Miranda.

Joel glances at her and looks back at the road on his left. "I like doing that," he says.

"Oh, I thought you were being protective," she says, almost patronizingly.

"I am."

"No. Otherwise you would be on this side, where cars are passing." She points to her left. "Well, there is not much to protect me from anyway."

She is right. Three minutes on the bridge, and only two cars have passed by on the opposite side of the road. It doesn't seem like a well-used bridge, or is it because of the time? People are still at work at this hour of the day. That means there aren't many eyes to force the creature to hesitate. So he has to stay alert.

Joel smiles. "Hmm, you might be right."

"I am right."

"Still far?"

"Maybe thirty minutes." Miranda glances at him "So … tell me about your family."

"What about me?" says Joel, dodging the question.

Miranda looks determined. "You aren't getting away with that. We have plenty of time for you. I want to know more about your family."

Joel, who has his eyes peeled on the empty road, looks at Miranda. If this can make her overlook how tense he is, why not. "Okay. I'm the first of two kids. I have a sister who I love very much, a wonderful mom, and a strict dad."

Miranda smiles. "We all have a strict dad. It's for our own good."

"My dad is something else," replies Joel.

"Yeah. My dad is an army colonel." She gives Joel a look as if to say, *Your dad can't be worse than mine.*

"Okay, you win. So, what about you?" asks Joel.

"I am an only child. Lost my mother when I was ten ... hmm, that's pretty much everything."

"I'm sorry about your mom."

"It's okay. It was a long time ago. Oh, and I have a wonderful great-grandpa, who visits me all the time. So, I'm not always home alone. Sometimes it almost feels like he is checking on me or something."

Joel looks at Miranda for a brief moment and then gets back to the road. How come a girl so beautiful feels so lonely? She is popular at school, with everyone running around to be her friend or boyfriend. Yet now that she has said a few words about herself, it feels as though she really needs a friend. Someone who is there for her. Someone with whom she can open up, and maybe he could too. The thought of a real friendship crosses his mind. Joel smiles. "Your grandpa loves you very much."

"I know. He is a great pappy."

The creature's suspicion is clearing. This young man behaves like he is protecting the girl. It steps closer, breathing down Joel's neck.

Joel blinks to his right and quickly looks back to the road. He made a mistake, a big mistake: he blinked right. Did the creature notice? Did he? He doesn't feel any more breathing on his neck, as if the creature has moved back. What is Joel going to do? He can't turn to confirm what the creature is doing. If it doesn't know Joel knows about it, turning will surely confirm all its doubts. He can't stay in this limbo. It's too dangerous. He doesn't know where exactly the creature is, what it is about to do. There, Joel can see the end of the bridge.

Almost there. He brings his eyes back to the roadway, his mind saturated with trepidation. A vehicle is coming, a truck. Joel notices it when he attempts to locate the creature with a semblance of attention on the road behind him. He can't feel the creature. He doesn't know where it is, where it is going to attack from. Joel pinches his heart, gulps his saliva, and slowly grabs Miranda's right hand. Miranda looks at his hand and smiles. She doesn't object, but she can see Joel's anxiety. Maybe his trying takes a lot out of him, and she won't be the one to make it more awkward than it already is. The breathing comes back on Joel's neck. But this is different, a rapid breathing, furious, the breathing of something ready to kill. Joel can't talk. The vehicle is approaching. He steadies Miranda's hand in his. The creature is furious. The breathing brushes Joel's neck and vanishes. It is there. It is going to do something. Joel's heart pounds in his chest, his hand moving tightly around Miranda's.

Miranda looks at her hand and looks at Joel. The squeezing continues. "You're hurting me, Joel," she says. Joel can't hear anything; his eyes dart to the road, expecting the truck to drive by any time now. There is no sound around him, only the thought of what this creature is going to do.

"Joel," Miranda calls, looking at him.

Joel doesn't respond, staring forward.

"Hey! What's wrong with you?" she snaps, ripping her hand from his. "I said, you're hurting me."

Joel feels the yank from his hand and comes back to his senses, looking at Miranda.

"I-I'm sorry. I didn't know I was hurting you."

"What's with you?" she says, rubbing her right hand. "You know, I think this whole thing was a mistake. I'll go home alone. Maybe another ti—"

Miranda is brutally pushed onto the road, with the truck only a second away. She is about to fall when Joel desperately manages to grab her hand and pull her back. They both fall onto the sidewalk, and the truck doesn't stop.

"Are you okay, Miranda?" asks Joel, getting up.

"What just happened?" asks the girl, disoriented and looking around.

"I'm sorry, Miranda," says Joel, reaching for her.

"Don't get any closer … please." She stops him, still in shock.

"I'm sorry," repeats Joel, trying to find out if the girl is all right.

"You almost killed me. Please, let me go home," she says, turning her back on Joel, looking for some tangible support to process her troubled thoughts.

"Wait …" says Joel, stretching to reach her, when he is brutally hit on the base of his neck. He falls on his knees, lost, unaware of what is happening to him. Miranda quickly turns to him.

"Joel? Joel, what's wrong? *Joel!*"

She is rushing to him when she sees him suddenly pulled away. She screams with her shaking hands on her mouth, staring, eyes wide, at Joel being dragged down the road.

The shock turns to paralysis and dread. What is happening? The dizzy young man is struggling to free himself from something wrestling with his collar as it pulls him. Miranda stands on the sidewalk, trembling, staring at Joel lying in the middle of the road holding invisible hands that are choking him. She breaks out of her stiffness and runs to him. "Joel!" she screams. She is suddenly bashed away. She hits the edge of the sidewalk and remains immobile.

When his neck is freed from a hand for a brief moment, the creature glancing at the girl as she lies on the edge of the road, a thought flashes into Joel's head. Maybe a reflex or survival instinct, but he remembers the pen in his pocket. He quickly grabs it and stabs the flank of the creature. The creature, which still had its head turned toward the girl, snaps back at Joel with dead eyes and a shriek bound to freeze the warmest blood. Joel doesn't stop, despite the horrifying sound. By some miracle, he's made a hole in its body. He keeps stabbing and stabbing until the creature, disturbed, trying to choke and simultaneously stop Joel from deepening its wound, jumps away from Joel to recover for a second. It glances at the broken pen in its flank. The next look, directed at a weak and dizzy Joel, radiates rage. It is about to finish the job when a car smashes it away and stops to check on a young man struggling and this inert girl on the roadside. The driver felt like he hit something hard, and he glances behind him when he rushes out of the car, but his concern is with this boy lying on the road. The creature, bleeding from everywhere, appears momentarily in a state of despair and then vanishes, moving slowly away on all fours.

A few cars, including those on the other side of the highway, have stopped to see what is happening, and many are converging. Two of the drivers help a weak Joel get back onto the sidewalk. Miranda lies with a couple standing next to her, a phone to the woman's ear.

*

It's calm, quiet. There's only the hum and beep of a machine. A nurse has been checking on Miranda for a few minutes now, and she is leaving. Joel looks at Miranda, in her light-green hospital gown, lying on the bed, bound by a cord on her left arm connected to the beeping machine. A plastic tube runs along her nose to other equipment. She seems stable. It's now past seven, and Joel still doesn't know what to do at this point. He has not even been able to clearly explain what happened. He can't leave her alone. His mother will be worried. He doesn't even want to think about his father. He told them he would be home early, and here he is in the ICU. The doctor didn't say much about Miranda's condition. Of course, Joel is not family, and they probably think he is the cause of what happened to her. At least the doctor told him not to worry, so he takes that as a good sign, and he has been kind enough to let Joel stay next to her.

A lever clanks across the room. Joel, sitting in a chair at the corner, levels his head at the door on his left. A man with a sheet of ribbons plastered on the left side of his chest, standing just above six feet tall and clothed in what Joel can only interpret as a military outfit, approaches. From the look of it, it's an outfit worn by high-ranking officers. The man stares at Joel and walks over to Miranda. He stands by the bed, watching her, ignoring any other presence in the room, and then sits in a chair next to her bed. He exhales, grabs her hand, and kisses the back of it. "I'm sorry I wasn't there, baby."

Doctor David Amangou, the one who took care of Miranda and told Joel not to worry, enters the room. He looks at the man in uniform holding Miranda's hand on his forehead with his eyes closed. The doctor approaches Joel. "Can you wait outside, please?"

"Okay," says Joel, getting up from his chair and heading for the door. He leaves the room and stands by the window. He is too anxious to sit on the couch by the adjacent room. Is this man Miranda's father? He must be. That's the first time Joel has seen him, and not in the best of circumstances. It was seven hours before he showed up. He must have been very far away to come only now, knowing his only daughter had a serious accident. Joel should really think of what he will say when the colonel asks him what happened to his daughter.

*

"What happened?" asks the man in uniform.

"We don't really know, Colonel Tedry," answers the doctor. "She received a violent shock to her head for reasons I can't really explain. It's just a concussion, no permanent damage. She's only unconscious. She was with this young man when the ambulance picked them up. He has trouble explaining what exactly happened. My guess is he was playing the interesting guy when this accident occurred."

The colonel turns to the window for a clear sight at Joel, who meets his gaze for a moment before looking down. "She never walks home. How come she decided to walk home today?"

"Friends," says the doctor. "Maybe this young man influenced her. The most important thing right now is that she's safe. She'll be okay. She just needs rest."

"Thank you, Doctor, for everything," says Colonel Tedry. He gets up and walks out of the room.

"I'm really sorry, Mr. Tedry," rushes Joel when the man closes the door, glaring at him.

"I'm going to throw you in a cell for so long, you will never consider going after a colonel's daughter again," says the man, looking straight into Joel's apologetic eyes.

"I'm really sorry, sir. I never meant for any of this to happen," says Joel.

"I don't care," says the man in a controlled, menacing tone. "You made my daughter walk home. Do you have any idea of the danger you exposed her to? You'll spend half your life in prison. There you'll have plenty of time to be sorry."

"Don't," says a voice, approaching.

The colonel directs his gaze behind Joel to an individual in a blue suit walking toward them. Joel's eyes widen, and without any conscious control, he steps backward. The only thought filling his head right now as blood rushes to his feet is to get out of this place, leave, and run as far as he can.

"Don't be afraid, son. It's okay," says the old man.

Joel stares at him, trying to manage his quivering body. The strong and tall posture does not give him the air of someone worn out by time. Only his facial traits and well-groomed white beard suggest otherwise. Joel's primal need to run is not because of the old man; no, a large creature, well above six foot five, tailing them, is what keeps his body from settling. Another individual a little shorter than the old man, wearing bracelets of cowrie shells on his wrists and what looks like a skirt of wheat straw around his waist, walks by the old man's side. If no one else in the hospital has their gaze plastered on him, it only means one thing: Joel is the only one who can see him and this dark-skinned creature. A creature with the silhouette of a man, a visage resembling a man, and eyes so red and so small they seem filled with blood.

"Grandpa!" the colonel calls, as though surprised at the visit. "Who told you she is in the hospital?" Either he is used to these two beings following the old man or he is completely unaware of their presence. Joel looks at the colonel. The colonel doesn't see them. He would have at least glanced in their direction if he did.

"She is my great-granddaughter," the old man states casually.

"This boy is the one who put her in here." The colonel points at Joel.

"Let him be."

"*What?*"

"Let the boy be. Go home, son. It's late." The old man turns to Joel.

Joel cannot take his gaze off the towering creature positioned before Miranda's door, as if standing guard. Is he going crazy? No, this can't be. He has seen many creatures imperceptible to others, but never something like this. Who is Miranda? Who is this old man?

"What's he looking at?" Colonel Tedry is staring at Joel, gawking up at the door.

"Do you hear me, son?" the old man calls once more, pulling Joel from his daze. "Leave this place. Go home."

Joel looks at the old man in confusion.

"Is this boy normal? Get out of here," orders Colonel Tedry.

Joel walks to the couch where he left his bag, grabs it, and heads for the lift.

"The doctor says she is okay."

"I know." The old man eyes Miranda through the window.

"How did you know she was here? I am the only person they contacted."

"We will talk about it later. She needs you by her side," responds the old man.

"I'll get back to her," says the colonel, clearly irked by the preposterous decision to let the boy who put his daughter in this situation go free. He has to listen and comply. Aside from being a very influential man in the government, he is his grandfather, and respect comes first when it comes to family lineage. Better leave him to his odd, almost senile practice of standing alone for no reason whatsoever and talking to himself. Colonel Tedry opens the door and closes it behind him. He sits by his daughter's bed and holds her hand.

"They know," says the old man, fixated on his great-granddaughter.

"They knew long ago. They needed to take action now," says the man in the skirt of straw, his gaze in the same direction.

"Reducing half my power, why now?" asks the old man.

"She holds half of your knowledge as well. Maybe they want to know what you know," answers the man in the skirt of straw.

"Strategic information. There is no war," says the old man.

"Then there is one coming. They want you out of the game. You represent a serious threat," replies the man in the skirt of straw.

"They almost got my great-granddaughter. If not for this boy … After what he's done, they'll all be looking for him."

"We can't interfere with that. It's a family matter. He'll be in danger only if a member of his family exposes him," says the man in the skirt of straw.

The old man looks at his companion. "You know what will happen."

"Don't put yourself in a situation that will slow us down. We have to find out who did this and what's being prepared."

The old man exhales deeply. "War is coming."

*

Joel cannot clear his mind of what he saw in the hospital and what happened to him on the road with Miranda. He feels like many faces, many bodies and hands squeezing his neck are invading his brain. He is in disarray and walks with the calm of someone who doesn't know where he is going, someone wandering the night. He does possess a general knowledge of the area. They brought Miranda to the closest hospital to the accident, the one not too far from his school. So, the road, apart from a few new turns, is the same. A road he can close his eyes on and still find his way home. He has to clear his mind, snap out of it. This is not the first time he has seen creatures, accidents, and people dying. Why does he feel so strange? As if it's the first time he has seen something like this. That's the feeling this creature, this tall, dark man with bloody eyes instilled in him. His hands are still shaking just at the thought of it. Even almost dying this afternoon doesn't appear as strange as this. He is alive, Joel remembers. He really almost died this afternoon.

It all went so fast, so abruptly. But he can still sense the constriction on his throat. The excruciating squeeze that shut off every ounce of air. Joel looks at his right hand, the one he used to stab the creature. There are still a few crusts of blood on the back. He didn't clean his hands well at the hospital. They were so shaky under the running tap, and his alertness was doubtful at best. The doctor thought it was Miranda's blood and was alarmed at first, until he saw the concussion and came to ask Joel questions Joel couldn't begin to answer. Miranda is safe, and he is not dead, not in jail either. So, that's the most important thing. Now he has to find an excuse for his parents, if he can't get to his room without being spotted. He is too late. It's almost nine, and he has never come home so late. He can't even imagine the state of his father at this point. He has to find an excuse, a good one, or this night will be rough. Laughter catches Joel's attention at the gate of his house.

Joel recognizes his mother's laugh, his father's. They rarely laugh that loud. Joel opens the gate and reaches the second door. They really are laughing. At least they are not fighting because of him today. Maybe he is not in trouble after all. He opens the wooden door after the metal one.

"Is that you, Joel? Come, we are in the living room," calls his mother, who must have heard the clicking sound of the door closing.

Princess, in her cute sky-blue gown, is leaving the kitchen with a happy face, a smile she almost always wears when she doesn't have nightmares. She holds a plate carrying a bottle of water and a glass.

"Hey, Poutchou! Grandma is here. Come," says the little girl, heading for the living room.

Joel drops his bag from his shoulder and follows his sister into the living room. His grandmother is here. It has been so long since her last visit, two or three years, he thinks. And the last time she stayed for about a week. A nice week, if he recalls, for him and his sister, especially Princess. She was the one who spent the most time with their grandmother. Her visit is timely. No shouting from his father today, or at least it will be delayed until Joel escapes to bed. Princess enters the living room and turns right to her parents and her grandmother. "Here's my little girl," says an old woman's voice.

Joel follows Princess's little steps into the living room and freezes when he turns to them. Blood flushes from his head. His thoughts vanish in an instant. *NO* is the first word that shapes. *Please*, follows in his head, and then blank again. He doesn't know what to do. He has no reaction. Terror, despair, the thought of bolting out of this place, the thought of screaming to warn his parents, the thought of grabbing his little sister and protecting her with his body flood him all at once. He stands like a log staring agape at his mother laughing, his father smiling, his little sister pouring water into his grandmother's glass. In all things happening before him, this deafening sound in his ears, he can only feel his heart pounding against his chest.

"What a cutie, my granddaughter," says the old woman with a smile.

"Thank you, Grandma," says Princess, finishing pouring the water.

"Joel, come say hi to your grandmother," says his mother. "Don't just stand there."

Joel approaches when he hears that. He doesn't know what to do, what to say without provoking any reaction toward his family. Maybe doing what he does best will buy them time: ignorance. Act as if he doesn't know, he doesn't see.

"Ohhh, it's okay. Let my grandson be. He is a sharp little man. Aren't you, Joel?" says the old woman, grabbing Joel's hand. "Here, sit near me, my son. I missed you both so much. So what were you looking at?"

"Nothing," responds Joel.

"Are you always this late from school?" she asks.

"He's like that. He doesn't like to take transport," says his mother, smiling.

"Is that so?" says his grandmother, looking back at him. "It will be very difficult for you to move around in this day and age, my son."

"Yes, he promised me he'd be home early today, but apparently not," says Joel's father, frowning at him.

"Ohh, that's all right. They're teenagers. It's the age. I'm sure he will grow out of it. So, Joel, what did you do after class?" asks Joel's grandmother.

"Nothing. I just walked home," responds Joel.

"Is that so?"

"Yes. May I go to my room to bathe? I am a bit tired," presses Joel.

"Of course, baby," responds his mother. "We will be downstairs for dinner."

"Don't take too long, my son. We have so many things to share," adds Joel's grandmother.

Joel stands up, avoiding eye contact with the two creatures looming behind the couch the old woman sits on. He exits the room, losing sight of his school bag on the floor, and rushes to the stairs with a forlorn glance up at his room door. He rushes, disturbed, desperate. He can't fathom the idea of what is coming. He doesn't want to, blocking it out as the thought forces itself into his mind. Blocking it as tears flow onto his cheeks. He struggles to maintain one thought at this moment. The thought that impelled him to exit the living room. The thought that at this very instant makes him race up the stairs. He opens the door out of breath and looks at the short man sitting with legs crossed on the study table.

"What are they doing here?" he quavers, with a voice on the brink of collapse.

The short man looks up in silence at Joel's face, smeared with panic and tears, the handle of the door tight in his shaking grip. Joel proceeds to close the door and hastens to the short man, looking at him straight in the eyes. "What ... are they doing here?"

"I told you not to get involved. Apparently, you didn't listen. They are here for your family," answers the short man.

These words—the thought he was struggling to chase out of his mind, the thought he was desperately trying to run away from—have caught up to him.

"No ... no no no no, please no. Not my family, please ... Princess," says Joel, in tears, rushing to the door.

"What are you doing?" asks the short man.

"I have to warn them," says a panicked Joel.

The short man budges once, as if hesitating, questioning the action he should take. "There's nothing you can do," he finally says. "From the moment she walked into your house, it was already done."

The words fall on deaf ears. Joel ignores the short man on the table and opens the door. He perceives one of the creatures exiting the living room. Joel hurries back in the room and locks the door.

"He's coming here!" he exclaims, wide eyes turned to the short man.

"They spotted me," says the short man, hopping from the table. He removes his necklace and presses it into Joel's hand. "Here, wear this. It will protect you. Listen to me. Your parents are already gone."

"No, no," interrupts Joel.

"Listen!" says the short man. "They are gone ... but your sister, she is too valuable. They won't touch her. You are a threat, and they will kill you as soon as they lay their hands on you. You want to save your sister, save yourself. Take the window, get on the ground. Use your father's machine, and go as far as you can from this place. I'll try to hold them off." The short man walks to the study table, grabs two of the legs, and breaks them with one pull.

The muddled young man puts on the talisman with his uncontrolled hands, a talisman of cowrie shells; old wood; small, pale green feathers; and black, shiny small rocks. He rushes to the window and tries to unlock it with all the calm he can muster. The creature from downstairs crashes into the room, breaking the door to the nearby closet. The short man who dodged the brutal opening of the door in his face breaks the table's legs on the creature's temples with a violent smash. There's a split second of shock before the creature bashes the short man into the same closet. Joel, dazed, tries to maintain his calm and open the window as fast as he can, his hands shaking so severely he can barely control them. He sees the creature dashing toward him, and the most primal of reflexes kicks in. He crouches and covers his head, with his eyes ready to close, when he sees the creature receding as if something has pulled it away. The short man, who has a grip on its ankle, brings it toward him and smashes its head with both fists.

A savage and brutal fight begins, dragging them around the room, breaking everything in their way. The bathroom window, Joel remembers. He left it open this morning. Joel slips on all fours before getting up and running to the bathroom. The creature shrieks as it sees Joel moving away. When it turns, the short man does not stop with his violent blows to its neck and jaw. The creature manages to pull itself away from the short man with a harsh elbow in his flat nose and rushes to the bathroom. It sees Joel in the window, ready to jump. It throws a sharp roar and dashes to the young man. It quickly loses its balance as the short man snatches its ankle from the ground again with a straight pull. He grabs its head with one hand and shatters the bathroom sink with its face, muting the creature for a moment. Then he shatters the toilet seat with it. The creature screams in pain and rage, pulling the short man onto his back and throwing him against the tiled wall.

Joel has only a moment of hesitation, looking at the mango tree branch, too far from his reach with even a jump. And this window does not allow much room for stretching. But he has no choice. He leaps as far as he can and fights to catch the branch. He holds fast, struggling to keep his balance, as only his left arm has a good grip. His right arm manages to find its way to the branch, and he then tries to lift his left foot up. The branch snaps, locked in his firm grip. He watches the other section receding as he falls.

CHAPTER 4

The Plan

Biafle and Kobenan are miles down the road, with silence reigning in the car. Briefing the president is protocol, but they don't have much, apart from what Kobenan found so far, and if he is right, then time is of crucial essence. Losing more than two hours to brief the president and await instructions might not be a smart move. Not briefing the president on the current situation is a serious code offense. But this has never been Biafle's concern. Breaking into Sector 0 is a whole different situation, and he has the life of this boy to protect. But Kobenan has been correct in his analysis so far, and Biafle can't ignore this fact, even though following protocol is the right and sound course of action. Biafle slows down and parks in rocky red sand extending about twenty-five feet past the road before falling steeply to a cliff. Wilderness and landscape expand underneath. Kobenan looks at Biafle, surprised, awaiting some kind of explanation for this unexpected stop.

"Even if we get in without raising any suspicion, the chances of getting him out are too slim," says Biafle, looking down as if thinking out loud. "You are the one who will suffer the most when they figure out what is happening." He turns to Kobenan. "You do realize we will never leave this prison if we get caught."

"We have no choice," responds Kobenan. "Unless you know someone else who has leads. We go in, you distract the Great Chief while I free Namien, and we find a way to escape."

The words of a true ignoramus. But maybe that's why it could be an idea.

"You really don't know this prison, do you?" asks Biafle. "There's nothing happening away from their vigilance. The moment Namien gets out of his cell, the main guards will feel it. You will be dead before you reach the first door. And there's no way I'm letting you near Namien. He'll kill you before you have the chance to speak."

"So, we make it official," says Kobenan. "Requested by the president ... We still have the advantage of time. We haven't been gone for long. The only person who should stay in the dark is the Great Chief. There's no other way. You're the only one who can distract him. He will want to verify the clearance from the president. And you said it yourself, as soon as Namien is out of his cell, the Great Chief will know. You can do something and buy us some time. You have to trust me with Namien. My principal concern is the main gate ... How are we going to open it?"

Biafle looks at Kobenan as if assessing him. The young man who could barely talk this morning is proposing to walk alone into a sorcerers' prison. He is either suicidal or he is adapting very quickly to this whole situation. In all cases, his proposition is plausible.

"The main gate isn't an issue for any prisoner, as for me," Biafle answers. "The thing to worry about is the barrier before the main gate. It weakens the sorcerer to near death, and this means we will have to drag Namien to the car, and the way I see it, if there is a fight, as there will be, I'll be alone."

"If we manage to exit the prison, what about those giant guards in front of the gate?" asks Kobenan. "I don't see any way we can escape from them."

"The Dokouni?" answers Biafle. "They watch for something else, not the prisoners. If I can manage to block the communication between the Great Chief and the guards, it should buy us some time for the escape before things get out of hand. But again, I don't know whom the Dokouni directly take orders from. It's a gamble we'll have to take. They should always be looking straight ahead. If they look at us, it's already over. It'll mean they have received orders, and yes, there's nowhere we can escape from them if we're not dead in the seconds following their gaze."

The Dokouni. Kobenan doesn't remember any word close to this. Another name added to his lexicon of confusion. That's the name of the giant creatures, which didn't even bother to look at him and his partner when they first crossed the gate to enter Sector 0. So, they are meant to always look straight ahead, watching for something else. What? Now is not the time for this question. If they don't bother about prisoners escaping unless they are given orders, then that improves the odds.

"So, what do we do?" asks Kobenan.

"We act smart and use our weakness to our advantage," responds Biafle.

"Our weakness?" asks Kobenan, intrigued.

"You. You're so weak, it will be difficult for them to notice you, unless they figure out who you really are."

Is this an insult? Is Mr. Biafle trying to be funny? Kobenan doesn't see a trace of a smile on his face. Kobenan knows he is weak, and he doesn't see how this is going to help in any way.

"Thank you for being so keen about my weakness," says Kobenan.

"Focus," says Biafle. "Your energy is sparse and therefore difficult to detect. Two kinds of people use that: the strongest and the weakest. The strongest because they know how to control every inch of their body, and the weakest because they have very low energy. And since you'll be in the prison and walking free, it can give the impression of being very strong. It'll give you a free pass in some areas. We'll use that. The prison doesn't have surveillance cameras. They don't need them. I'll leave you at the entrance of the hallway leading to Namien's cell, and you find your way to him while I distract the Great Chief. You should breathe slowly … very slowly, until you free Namien. One mistake, and we're done for."

"Understood," says Kobenan.

"Listen carefully," begins the head of the S-cell in an even more serious tone. "This prison has some of the deadliest guards in all of Africa, known for their sorcery and strength. You've already met the pygmy brothers, but there are those stronger than them. No matter what happens, do not freeze or run away out of fear. Ground your feet, and try to stay in control. As soon as we get Namien, your main objective will be to reach the car as fast as possible and start the engine. We won't be able to last in a fight.

"It's very likely that they will strengthen the field before the prison when the alert is triggered. It'll be tough, but you'll have to make it to the car, or we're all dead. Remember, once we start this, there is no turning back. We'll be outlaws until we finish the mission." Biafle opens the door and puts his left leg on the rocky sand, ready to get out. "I have to make a call. Stay in the car."

Kobenan's gaze follows Biafle through the windshield as the head of the S-cell walks around on the red sand, waiting for an answer from the other side of the line. The windows are closed, so sound from the outside is barely audible. But Kobenan can tell when Biafle opens his mouth that someone answered his call. There's a brief exchange before the head of the S-cell hangs up and gets back in the SUV. Biafle lays his left hand on the wheel and exhales quickly.

Despite the strangeness of this man, it doesn't take a genius to see that he is uneasy about this choice. Kobenan can see why. In addition to the fact that the risk of his dying shoots straight up because Biafle will not have his eyes on him, this whole undertaking jeopardizes Biafle's position and all the respect he has acquired through the years at the S-cell. And this is not even speaking about the repercussions of what might be considered high treason. Apart from dying, Kobenan has no problem. He is just taking orders from a higher rank, so everything falls on Mr. Biafle's shoulders. But if they want answers, they have to free Namien. On this they both agree.

"We should never have brought him back to the prison. It

would have been much easier," says Kobenan. "I'm sure he would have followed us."

"We wouldn't have gone far," says Biafle. "It was the first time they let a convict out of the prison. Who knows what they had set up in case Namien tried to escape? Remember, Namien went through many hands before he was passed on to us at the prison hall. His dying minutes after he had somehow managed an escape wouldn't be useful, would it? Probably ours too if we had a helping hand in his escape." Biafle momentarily closes his eyes and scratches his forehead. "And you forgot the Great Chief's bat. No one can hide from it."

The Great Chief's bat. Kobenan didn't even know the bat was around at all. Thinking back at the prison, the Great Chief did say that his bat would follow them when they were taking Biafle to the sorcerer couple. So Biafle kept track of the bat all along, Kobenan thinks. The bat must not have been present when Biafle clenched Kobenan's collar. Otherwise, Biafle would never have allowed Kobenan to talk at all.

Kobenan gives Biafle a sudden look, as though the words of his partner have caught up to him. "How do we know that if they actually did something to Namien to prevent his escape, it's not still in effect?"

"We don't. At least they're not expecting what we're about to do. The Great Chief doesn't expect it. Our odds of dying are not worse. Take this." Biafle pulls a washed-out yellow ring from his inner pocket. "It'll sustain the pain and damages of your body, but be careful, it has its limit, so keep an eye on the color. The darker it becomes, the more critical your health. I hope you remember your lessons about fetishes. All the security is made of those in this prison. Do you know what Klebla is?"

Kobenan does remember this word: a state of deep meditation performed only by the highest ranks of sorcery. It allows the performer to divert his energy toward something of focus to strengthen it or give it properties. It is said in the books that some fetishes are created this way, while others require transferring souls. Kobenan nods.

"The guardians in Sector 0 use Klebla to strengthen the seals of the cells," says Biafle. "We move now. They can't budge when they start the incantations. This will buy us time."

The wait is around forty minutes before Biafle starts the engine again. Despite a plastic watch fastened to his wrist, he has relied on the position of the sun to decide the time to leave. Apparently, the sun might be more accurate when it comes to this Klebla. Biafle makes a turn and drives away.

*

There is no welcome party this time when they enter the grand room inside Sector 0. As Biafle anticipated, the pygmy brothers, too, must be strengthening their seals. Biafle turns to the guards.

"You may leave us here. We know our way to the Great Chief. Thank you very much."

The dark guards bow and recede to the door, closing it behind them. Kobenan has only a brief moment of contemplation of this soundless and empty room before Biafle taps him on the back to remind him that it's time. Kobenan follows Biafle, heading for the quaint wooden stairs.

"This place is so calm, as if there were nobody here. But even I can feel something," whispers Kobenan, looking around as he tails his partner.

"Anybody here will feel this pressure," says Biafle. "It's in all of us. That's why we can sometimes feel a presence around us. It's strong in some people and weak in others, but everyone possesses it, and most fear it. They don't understand. Don't forget to breathe slowly. This is what will differentiate you from the weak. We move together until I reach the stair, then you go for the hallway on your right.

"Remember, no one in this prison is normal, no one—adults, children, animals, so be on your guard. They won't stop or question you because you walk free, and this means you have a pass. But make a single mistake, and they'll spot you. Stay away from the children. They can easily detect weak people.

"I'll reduce the communication between the Great Chief and the prison, but as soon as Namien is out, you'll have to move fast. Good luck."

There's a smooth separation between the partners as Biafle steps on the stairs and Kobenan turns to the somber hallway a few feet to his right. He follows the instructions of his partner and keeps his breathing steady and slow when he enters the lightly curved passage. Holes in the right wall allow thin rays of sun to illuminate a few areas. Twenty feet into this strangely lit place, Kobenan stops. He turns to look behind him. He can still see the spacious room, but this path looks somewhat different. That's the same hallway the Great Chief, Biafle, and he used to reach Namien's cell. At least the same entrance. But why does it feel so different from before? Kobenan can't turn back to verify the entrance, although he is pretty sure it was the only entrance next to the wooden stair. There is no chance he would be able to leave this hallway, with what he has noticed on the left wall.

Biafle was right; *they* are everywhere. Kobenan stares at them. He knows them. Basic but deadly security fetishes he can counter if he doesn't fail the instructions. Maybe not the first wooden mask plastered against the wall at the entrance. The one that might blind him if he tries to walk back into the spacious room before he reaches the other side of this hallway. In fact, all of these fetishes plastered on the wall or laid on the ground have a specific purpose. Their shape, style of sculpture, and colors define precisely what they are and what they do. Fortunately for Kobenan, he has met most of them in his books. The only thing he can rely on now is the lines in these books. The fetishes seem to have been arranged in such a way that they are connected to one another, so he should be able to bypass some of them if he is extremely meticulous and careful. One mistake will mean him closing the door to the living. He sincerely hopes he has read enough about fetishes, or this will be a drastically quick operation.

Kobenan moves cautiously, planning every step he takes. He stops at a few points, crouches, and draws signs visible only on the tip of his index finger as he strokes the ground. Or he takes some strange stances and makes odd gestures before he advances. This hallway, which now runs straight, seems to stretch deep. Kobenan feels it extending as he walks. Nothing is moving. Nothing has changed. Even this light at the end seems to be at the exact same distance as it was when he first saw it. He is calm, patient. Yes, one reason is the instructions of his partner, but also because one fetish he recognized at the entrance monitors his pace and movements. So, any rash action could cause his heart to stop. He is not exactly sure of the patterns on the left cheek of this mask, if it's the fetish that he thinks it is. But he'd better not take any chances. So Kobenan keeps walking steadily, looking around and anticipating which fetishes he should stop to deactivate.

Kobenan's walk is long and steady, and the orange light at the end of the tunnel doesn't seem to be getting any closer. There must be one fetish in this hallway that won't allow him to leave. Did he miss it? He doesn't think so. He would have been dead or lying inert on the ground with only his eyes left to blink if that was the case. He is still walking, which means he has his whole motor functions. He can still clearly think and analyze, so nothing has reached his head yet. And he can clearly see. *Unless...* Kobenan thinks. Unless he only thinks he is sane, when he actually is not anymore. Maybe he was affected long ago. But nothing seems to suggest that. "Let's keep walking," he says to himself.

This fetish around sixty feet from him, standing in the middle of the pavement, seems different from any of the ones he has crossed before. He stops at a safe distance and squints. He can't see enough detail to decide, but this is not a fetish. All markers point to a totem. Kobenan can't risk getting any closer. Totems' effects are far more direct and broader than fetishes. Not only can distance be a trigger, but also the wrong movement. The carved pillar of wood stands before him, with the small yellow light farther away. A glimpse of light from a hole in the right wall feathers the totem. It does allow Kobenan to notice a few patterns carved on the right side if he squints hard enough. But that's not sufficient to decide what kind of totem this log of black wood is. Identification is key. Failing at this step will make him circle this hallway for the rest of his life—if he doesn't get a stroke before that.

It is extremely hazardous, but Kobenan has to, so he takes one more step toward the totem to get a better view of the carving on the log. The right side painted with light seems to be okay for Kobenan, but the left side is concealed in shadow, and he can't risk another step closer. Nonetheless, he does remember seeing four totems like this one with similar markings on the right. The carvings on the left trouble him. He can't quite make out the writing, and this means any gesture he attempts right now might be his last. There is only one gesture he remembers from his book. And the gestures for the four totems are very distinct from one another. The closest he can see, matching this pillar to what he has read, will be putting his leg to the right. It should be the simplest one. Now, shouting with all his strength also matches this totem, but he has limited information on the left-hand carvings. And shouting may raise an alarm and end this mission before he has even started. Memory is his best ally now, and it does not suffice, for his sight is limited.

He cautiously looks around, moving only his eyes. There is no fetish nearby, only this totem. This makes him wonder. It might be the only thing controlling this section of the hallway. He looks at the hole on his right, the one that lets the light brush near his hand. He slowly moves his fingers underneath the beam of sunlight. There is no temperature, no breeze. Kobenan closely looks at the dust in the beam and notices no movement. Where is he? Nothing is moving. He uses his index finger to nudge a few particles, which move under his interaction but stop immediately after. They should continue their course, as the laws of physics demand, but their stop is sudden and constant. Something clicks in Kobenan's mind. He has to verify it. He slowly turns his hand and forces his eyes down to look at his watch. He smiles. How did he miss this? He was so caught up trying to stay alive that even the lack of ticking in this dead, silent hallway didn't affect his ears once.

Wherever he is, time has laid down its pen. He is confident now. This step shall be the one. Kobenan tries to wrap his head around this idea, and if he is right then everything has stopped in this section. Nothing should travel away from this hallway. He takes a deep breath and screams with all his strength at the pillar, which gradually vanishes before his eyes. He coughs for a moment, catches his breath, and instantly hears the continuous ticking. He looks at the dust motes in the beam of light. They are slowly gliding about. Kobenan continues through the alley. The yellow light seems to be getting bigger. The door becomes clear as he approaches; an ajar door lets light escape from the next room. Kobenan is not out of the hallway yet. This totem might not be the last one, so he keeps his pace calm and looks around to make sure he doesn't miss any other fetishes.

The door gives way to a wide, illuminated room. Kobenan carefully enters the area. He recognizes this place—the wide, circular room surrounded by cells. This is the place where he saw an old woman escorting what he can only describe as a monster. There the black cat sits in front of the empty cell. The cat he kept turning to look at when he first came here with the Great Chief and Biafle has not budged an inch. Kobenan is heading in the right direction. *Calm and slow breathing,* he reminds himself before taking his next step toward the stairs, which should be where he will find Namien. Something shadows his vision and passes inches from his nose. Kobenan's heart jumps before his body halts. He slowly turns to see what this was. Long legs. Something with disturbingly prominent legs walking toward an entrance. It is slow, queerly disproportionate, with its flaccid hands dangling past what Kobenan can only refer to as knees. A head deprived of a neck. Its silhouette of around seven feet bends to vanish through an entrance where the yellow light can only extend a few feet past the frame.

Calm and steady, Kobenan reminds himself one more time. When he takes a deep breath, another one walks past him. Kobenan keeps his calm. Something around his size. A man, a woman, he can't quite differentiate. He or she wears a pile of necklaces made of bones, cowrie shells, and gold. It slowly looks over its shoulder but doesn't stop. Kobenan starts noticing them all around the circular room, one after another. Strange individuals of varied size and shape wearing nothing, clothes of odd fabric, and necklaces of rocks, pearls, and metal of quaint origin. Kobenan notices dogs with subtle behavior he can't quite place. Their pace, their eyeing toward each other and toward him, could push him to lose his composure if he doesn't keep his head.

A man approaches a little girl in a white gown, makes the same gesture Kobenan has come to know since entering this prison, and hands her a document of a light-brown color. The little girl with short, braided hair, about eleven years old, standing barefoot, grabs the document and peruses it. Kobenan, whose attention has been caged in this circular room, looks at her. She appears to have a high status: the man laid his right hand on his chest and bowed before handing her the document. Though it must be a standard greeting here, for a man of this size and age to await approval from someone this tiny shows something. The little girl in her white gown, fading to dirt brown near her calves, is looking through the document when she suddenly levels her stare at Kobenan.

Kobenan snaps from his contemplation. He can't get caught now. The stairs, he has to reach the stairs. Kobenan starts walking at a calm pace toward what he remembers to be the path to the next floor. He makes sure to breathe slowly. The little girl follows him with her gaze. She hands the document to the man by her side, with her eyes locked on the young man. Kobenan stops. Is this the place? It should be. That's the same direction the Great Chief went last time. But there are no stairs here, only an entrance to a dim alley. He doesn't have the luxury to search around for them, not with this little girl in the vicinity. And if this circular room is anything close to the hallway of fetishes he just passed, then this dim alley should be the direction.

Kobenan enters the alley. A short and narrow path gives way to another room with only one exit. There, the stairs, he recognizes them. But something else quickly captures his attention. Two sculptures of black wood stand on each side of the stairs. Their shape, their size, this specific sculpture. He knows them, he learned about them, and the first thought that flashes through his mind is deviation, to return from whence he came, which is nowhere safer.

The fetishes of truth. Powerful spirits trapped in tribal statues of wood. Whoever dares speak a lie in their presence shall be paralyzed for this life and the next. And if his recollection is correct, as soon as you see them, they see you. There is no turning back. There is nothing he can do but advance. Kobenan wants to keep his calm, but the sweat from his forehead keeps dripping on his face. He cannot stop it. His objective is to free one of the deadliest sorcerers for reasons that are not even confirmed. What can he possibly say to these fetishes to let him turn back? No, he can't turn back. There is no way he can leave the prison at this point. Death or eternal paralysis awaits him at either end of this. He can't step back, and if he steps forward, he has to speak. What is he going to say? What can he say?

If he can't leave, better move forward. Standing in place will not help, either. Time could be running out for Biafle. He doesn't even really know how long he has been in this prison. Kobenan takes a deep breath and steps forward.

"What is your name?" echoes a loud masculine voice.

"My name is Kobenan Jean Marc," answers Kobenan, walking toward them.

"Why do you come to us?" echoes a loud feminine voice.

Kobenan stops before the statues of wood. *Just speak what's in your mind*, he says to himself.

"I come to borrow one of your prisoners, the sorcerer soul eater Namien. He is an important lead in our investigation."

"And who are you to request a high-ranking prisoner?" the loud masculine voice rings out.

Kobenan takes a deep breath. "I am the main analyst at the presidency of this country, Côte d'Esperance, and I only stand before you because this is a crucial situation."

"Do you have an authorization?" echoes the loud feminine voice.

There's a short moment of silence. Kobenan gulps a big glob of saliva and starts breathing unevenly. He can't speak a lie, only truth.

"No. No, I do not have any authorization, but you know I speak the truth when I say this prisoner is a key to avoid a dire situation this country might endure."

Silence seizes the room. Kobenan remains speechless. He has to maintain his calm. How could he? Knowing he could drop on the ground any second now and not be able to move a muscle. Just waiting for a guard to find him and throw him in a cell for life, or worse, one of these eerie creatures sees him and starts feeding on him, leaving him to watch his flesh be torn apart until his eyes are next. Kobenan tries to control his breathing and shaking. He stands erect, waiting for any response at all. But these statues have gone silent, and what could be his next move in this situation? Run? Where?

"You may come in," intones the loud feminine voice.

Kobenan exhales. "Thank you very much." He passes the fetishes and takes the stairs. The sole reason he entertains for a second this dubious conundrum after all that just happened is because of his feeble knowledge about these fetishes of truth. Their sculpture, as written, is real. But the conversation occurring between the spotted person and the fetishes is said to happen in the victim's head. Yet he fails to distinguish at which moment he stepped out of that illusion and to the stairs, if it was an illusion. When Kobenan looks over his shoulder for a last check, the statues are still present.

It's the same dim path. It confirms the direction, but he'd better prepare for what's next. Two times now, he has reached areas that were not there during his first visit with the Great Chief and Biafle. This is beyond what he can rationalize. The only thing he can do is brace himself and hope that whatever is ahead has been mentioned somewhere in one of his books. He never thought in a million years that they would be so handy or even save his life. He didn't take the books seriously, mainly because they didn't make any sense at the time. He only read them because it was a requirement of his instructor. A lot of the writing still confuses him when he thinks of it, but he is quickly starting to piece things together with what he has witnessed so far. So, what could be next? What lies at the end of these stairs? Will he be able to bypass it this time?

The torchlight bleeds onto the steps. A good sign—he remembers this. Kobenan reaches the end of the stairs and turns right. The small wooden door is sixteen feet before him. Yes, that's the same distance. The three guards, barely looking human, are in the same place. Their red eyes and distorted faces strike Kobenan. He has to stay close to someone. No, he is alone this time. He has to advance alone. Kobenan steadies his breathing, clenches his fists for courage, releases them, and approaches the three guards.

"I come to see Sorcerer Namien," he says in a voice feigning confidence.

"Do you have a pass?" asks the guard on the right, the one who seems in charge.

Kobenan doesn't have a pass, and he would assume it must be granted by the Great Chief. But he was just allowed to take the stairs, his only coin of exchange. "I have the authorization of the fetishes of truth."

"Then you may come in," says the guard in the middle.

Kobenan turns to him. The one on the right is not in charge. Or maybe none of them is.

"You enter at your own risk," warns the guard on the left. "We have orders to stay in front of the door, whatever the situation."

Kobenan turns to the creature on the left and nods. The creature in the middle detaches the mesh along the door. The guard on the left barely opens it enough for Kobenan to slide in.

The same cold, dark feeling creeps over him. This time, he will have to rely on himself, and that means managing to reach Namien's cell without being snatched away by one of the other prisoners. He has a strong feeling that these metal bars aren't really a protection for him. Hell, some cells don't even have any. The only thing he can do right now is conceal his fear. In any case, he can't defend himself if he is attacked, so it's better not to entice them. Slow and steady breathing. Head straight. Kobenan walks the path with an even pace, remembering to look forward until he reaches Namien's cell. It will be hard to miss it. It's the last cell on his left.

Each cell Kobenan passes provokes the curiosity of the occupants. They stare at him as he traverses the paved path. They know this is not a place for a weakling like him. Some burst out laughing so hard, it echoes around. Others throw a disturbing giggle, which emanates as a shriek, piercing ears and chilling bones. Kobenan keeps his calm as he walks, rolling his ring around his thumb with stress. He reaches the cell, and only at this moment can he allow himself to turn and verify whether he is at the exact place he wants to be. He might be too close, so he takes two steps back, looking into the cell.

The sorcerer is sitting on a stool in the same position as Kobenan saw him the first time, legs open, elbows resting on his thighs. The only difference is his clothes. He kept the clothes Biafle gave him. The laughter around has calmed down, but the shriek, the piercing giggle, continues in a few cells. Kobenan looks at the sorcerer. He sweeps up whatever courage he has left and opens his mouth, first with no sound as Kobenan hesitates on which word should come first.

"Still meditating?" The voice almost loses its strength when it escapes Kobenan's lips.

The next thing Kobenan hears is a chuckle. He stares at the sorcerer.

"I know you're reckless. But I never thought you were so stupid as to present yourself alone in front of me."

The doors break open with a violent shock, swooshing before Kobenan's face as his reflexes pull his head back. When his startled mind tries to grasp the situation, he feels a harsh palm on his throat, only to hear the shock of his head against the opposite wall. Kobenan has no time to realize what is happening to him. The only thing he can see is the deadly eyes of his aggressor so close to him.

"You dare come here and speak to me," whispers the sorcerer. "I'll crush you bone by bone and throw you to one of those flesh-eating creatures."

Kobenan is pinned against the wall, his legs floating above ground, his tongue out. The sorcerer throws him to the end of the path. Kobenan smashes into the wall and falls on his shoulder. He slowly tilts up his head, only to see Namien walking, unhurried, toward him. Quietness has fallen on the cells around.

"What a shame," Namien says calmly. "You seem to be a brilliant analyst. I wonder if they'll find another one like you."

The sorcerer looks down at Kobenan. "This is what we do. We kill successful people. And you're a successful analyst. It gives us power, and it slows the country down. We get more control over everything. There is no such thing as a shortcut, and the repercussions of eating soul and flesh are very severe, but this is Africa.

"I gave it up for my daughter. She's the one who made me change. She will be dead in a few days. I won't eat you ... but I'll kill you ... very slowly."

The addled young man slowly pushes himself off the floor and sits with a struggle, using the wall as a support. The pain seems bearable, but his nose and mouth drip blood on his suit. He spits to the side and slowly looks up at the sorcerer.

"You can kill me now ... do whatever you want and go back to your cell ... or you can let me help you."

Kobenan sees himself lifting off the ground, his arms and legs helpless, his throat clogged, forcing him to cough and seek a way to breathe. He stares into the eyes of the sorcerer as his vision gets blurrier.

"You can't help me. Nobody can," says Namien.

"I can," Kobenan forces out. "Why ...do ... you think ... am ... here ... alone?"

Namien's eyes and face slightly relax. Kobenan's throat unclogs, and he starts coughing and breathing heavily on the sorcerer's face. Namien doesn't blink. Kobenan, with his fixed limbs open in the air, catches his breath and levels his head at the sorcerer.

"Biafle is distracting the Great Chief as we speak. We can still save your daughter … but we need your help. I'm the only chance you have right now."

Namien stares at Kobenan, calculating. Why come here alone? How could this boy get him out of this cursed and treacherous prison?

"Listen to the boy." A voice emanates from the cell next to Namien's. "You know what's being prepared, and they will reach her if you do nothing. Be sure of that. It has already started."

Kobenan falls onto the floor and slowly gets on all fours. He feels numbness in his extremities, but it seems to be fading.

"What do we do?" asks Namien.

"We have to reach the main hall," says Kobenan, standing up.

"I'm following you," says Namien.

Kobenan barely feels pain, but his partner warned him to keep an eye on the color, so he checks his ring. The golden color seems to have grown paler, as though worn out by time or recurrent use. It's quite difficult to assess the damage; the color before this one was not that vibrant either. Maybe he is all right. Now that he has Namien, the next step is the hall.

Kobenan takes the lead and walks to the only entrance of this terrifying hole. They stop before the closed door, and he gives Namien an uncertain look before knocking. There was no planning how he would pass these three guards with the sorcerer. But the first coin worked, so it's the only thing he can use right now.

"I have to borrow the sorcerer Namien."

"Do you have an authorization?" asks one of the guards.

"I have a pass from the fetishes of truth," answers Kobenan.

"Only a pass from the Great Chief can allow us to let him out," answers another guard.

Kobenan looks at Namien. That's as far as he can get. Biafle never talked about these guards. Maybe he was expecting

Namien to step up in this situation. But whatever the sorcerer does will inevitably raise an alarm, and they are very far from the hall—too far. Namien clenches his fist. Kobenan looks at it and steps back. A part of him wants to ask the sorcerer to stop, but he doesn't see any other solution, and the expression on Namien's face right now is far from being soothed by any word.

They both know it's a desperate move at this point, but Namien is willing to do anything to get out. Better this than going back to his cell. The sorcerer is raising his fist when a voice rings out.

"Let them pass. I authorize it."

Namien immediately drops his fist. Maybe this dim lighting is playing a role, but Kobenan sees a glimpse of fear in the sorcerer's eyes, even restraint and respect for the little voice that just spoke.

"As you wish, Third Great Chief," says one of the guards, pulling away the meshes enrolled around the door.

Light washes onto Kobenan and Namien as the door slightly opens for them to pass. Kobenan looks at the little girl approaching, the same girl who spotted him earlier. Her walk, the way she carries herself, shows the poise of a grown-up. The guards have their hands on their chests, with their heads down, awaiting her. She lays her hand on her chest in response and looks at Namien for a moment, then looks at Kobenan.

"Bring him back," she says.

"I will," says Kobenan.

The little girl steps aside and gently moves her hand to show the direction to the stairs. There is no thinking twice here. Kobenan walks to the stairs, followed by Namien. He stops at the steps and gives a last look at the little girl staring at them.

"Thank you," says Kobenan.

"Don't thank me," says the little girl. "The fetishes of truth let you in for a reason. I believe you know what you're doing. I hope you're prepared for what's coming to you."

Whether Kobenan is prepared or not, he just illegally freed one of the deadliest sorcerers from the most secure sorcerer prison. There is no getting away from this without terrible repercussions for his life and his partner's. But is this what the little girl is talking about? He is not sure. He nods and leaves by way of the stairs.

The stairway leads directly to the circular room; no fetishes of truth, no small room or dim narrow alley. Kobenan is not surprised, but his concern heightens for any unexpected change like this on their way back to the hall, the large room where he and his partner were first greeted by the pygmy brothers. He slightly turns to his left, the ajar door leading to the hallway of fetishes. He starts walking toward it, drawing a few gazes in their direction. Kobenan avoids eye contact, but he knows these stares follow him. No one has moved so far, and Kobenan prays it remains this way until he reaches the door.

Nobody seems to be following them, just the staring. Biafle was right. Kobenan walks free, and that means he has a pass. But Namien follows Kobenan, and Namien is of interest to these eyes in the circular room. If he is walking in this area with this boy, he must have been allowed to. Kobenan doesn't want to test the limit of this theory. His pace is calm and steady, but he tends to accelerate at times. They have to quit the spotlight before anyone asks questions. Kobenan exits through the door with only one thought in mind: leave this circular room. Only when he passes the door with Namien and brings it to its initial ajar state does he remember the traps in this hallway. He freezes and looks straight ahead.

"What?" asks Namien.

"This hallway," responds Kobenan.

"Whatever you experienced was your first and last time," says the sorcerer.

Kobenan looks at Namien. "What about you?"

"I wear a holder; it won't affect me."

Kobenan looks at the torn piece of cloth wrapped around the sorcerer's ankle. The band they removed before he left the main gate and reattached before he entered the prison when they were back from the sorcerer couple.

"What is it?" asks Kobenan.

"It doesn't allow me to leave the prison," says the sorcerer, staring ahead. "You said you and Biafle planned this." He looks at Kobenan. "Did you think about the barrier before the gate? If they remove this from my ankle and I'm not escorted by the prison guards, I won't be getting anywhere."

"Biafle mentioned this. I'm not sure what he planned, but when we reach the hallway, he takes the lead," says Kobenan.

The hallway appears shorter than before, about the same length Kobenan first traversed with Biafle and the Great Chief. He can see the large room. Namien walks by his side, looking ahead.

"Something's wrong," he says.

"What?" asks Kobenan, looking at him.

"It's too calm," says Namien. "The Great Chief has eyes and ears on everything in this prison."

"Biafle told me he'd distract him to give me time to extract you."

"As strong and smart as Biafle is, it's impossible for him alone to keep the Great Chief in the dark for so long," says the sorcerer. "Either someone much more powerful is helping him, or we're heading into a trap."

"Do you think it's that little girl?" asks Kobenan.

"I don't know," responds Namien.

"Who is she?"

The sorcerer glances at Kobenan, as though surprised for a second about the question. "Eyra," he answers. "The third in command in this prison. The Third Great Chief. Stay alert. When they remove this fetish from my ankle, no matter how strong this person is, the Great Chief will know. The fetish is directly connected to him. When they are removing it, get behind slowly and hold on to me at my signal."

"Okay. But what if it's a trap?" asks Kobenan.

"If it's a trap, we're dead."

Kobenan perceives the dark guards walking toward them on his way out of the hallway. He doesn't know how, but his guess is they probably felt the sorcerer. He made it to the hall. All he can do is wait for his partner. He and Namien walk in the grand space toward the guards. Better say something when they meet, to avoid any suspicion. He hopes Biafle knows he is here, otherwise it will be a long wait, and who knows what can happen. The guards reach Kobenan and Namien. Their eerie eyes on Kobenan, ignoring the sorcerer by his side, need no words. But Kobenan is almost certain they await an explanation for the presence of the sorcerer here.

"I borrowed him for national matters," says Kobenan. "Authorization of the Great Chief. I'll bring him back before sunset."

One of the guards turns toward the exit door and waves once. Kobenan looks outside through the few windows near the door and watches the heavy main gate slowly opening. The second guard kneels beside Namien. Kobenan brings his eyes back to the sorcerer. He has to stay alert. Namien warned him. Kobenan slowly steps behind the sorcerer while the guard is detaching the cloth from Namien's ankle.

Kobenan follows the dark hands loosening up the knot and untwining the strip. The guard is pulling the cloth away when a violent explosion shakes one of the upper floors. Kobenan jerks his shoulders and snaps up. Someone is blown off the third floor and is in free fall. He witnesses with his mouth still open thick roots growing urgently before the Great Chief's entrance room and wall. The loud impact of Biafle's fall snatches Kobenan's attention to the ground. Biafle quickly gets up from the debris of polished granites, slightly dazed, and staggers before he quickly finds his balance on his way toward Kobenan.

"AAAAAAAAHA," roars the Great Chief. "You dare try to deceive me, Biafle? You made a huge mistake."

The split second of the intense burst forces the guards' attention up before they realize what's happening. The one still kneeling on the ground, the strip in his hands, rushes to touch the sorcerer's ankle as Namien shouts Kobenan's name. Kobenan lunges to clutch the sorcerer's right thigh. The sorcerer unleashes a brutal force field, casting it over everything in the vicinity, including Biafle. He manages to deepen his fingers, turned brown, in a corner of a granite tile. The shock is uneven, harsh, and short. Kobenan manages to hold strong to the sorcerer's thigh with his eyes shut.

They hear loud impacts on the third floor, crude, constant impacts. The Great Chief is breaking free from the barrier of roots. Biafle hurries up. "Let's go, let's go," he says, hustling toward the exit door. Namien and Kobenan follow.

Biafle bashes open the hall's exit door, with Namien and Kobenan on his tail. They are running toward the main gate, which is now closing.

"The barrier! What about the barrier?" yells Kobenan.

"Namien, get behind me," says Biafle.

Biafle passes the invisible barrier, followed by the sorcerer. Namien falls inert on Biafle's back. The agent quickly crouches to get a hold of the sorcerer on his shoulder and continues toward the prison's main entrance. Guards are converging on the gate. Biafle throws his left hand into his inner pocket and pulls out a few seeds and small balls of sand. He puts one of the seeds in his mouth, waters it, and tosses it in front of the gate. The seed grows before Kobenan's wide eyes into a curved tree, deepening its roots in the ground and blocking the closing gate. Biafle licks one of the sand balls and hurls it at the tree trunk. The ball explodes in a compressed wind, dispersing every guard before them. The agent tosses another ball, and it explodes in a thick smoke of dust on impact.

"Grab my hand," shouts Biafle.

Kobenan hastens to Biafle's left hand before they dive into the smoke. He sees nothing but gray dust all around; even the large, heavy gate has vanished in this thick smoke. When Kobenan can see again, they are outside the prison. Biafle releases Kobenan's hand and points to his left with his arm before running forward. Kobenan knows what this means: get as far as possible from him and reach the car. Kobenan turns to his left only. His eyes fall on one of the giants standing before the main gate with his gaze ahead, unchanged. Kobenan can't advance a few steps without a look in their direction. "If they look at us, we're already dead." Those were the words of his partner when they were planning this prison break. He has to stay focused, but he can't help but turn to verify they are still looking straight.

"HAAAA!" Kobenan squeals when one of the giants suddenly looks at him. He loses any function in his legs and falls on the ground, unable to make any move, waiting for the inevitable. One second. Two seconds. Nothing happens. The giant stares at Kobenan with no movement. "Get up, get up," Kobenan keeps encouraging himself to move his frozen body. "Get up," he says, rushing up and dashing away. The giant didn't attack. He saw him but didn't move. That's not luck. The car, he has to reach the car.

*

The field is already starting to pull. Gravity is increasing, and the air is getting thicker. Biafle runs in wide steps, with Namien bent on his shoulder. Biafle looks over his shoulder. Something is coming at great speed toward him. He turns, leaving the sorcerer's body to fall, and blocks the hit with his left arm turned to roots. The smash propels him feet away before he drags onto the road.

"Bad call, Biafle ... bad call," says Nianbou, the pygmy with the long braid.

Biafle stands up, the roots on his left arm spreading to his torso, stretching the fabric of his suit. "I had to do this."

"You leave us no choice," says Djengdjeng, charging toward the djinn of the forest with his brother by his side.

Biafle has never fought the pygmy brothers before, but he doesn't need his extensive knowledge to know that he is at a serious disadvantage with these two guardians, especially here. He grounds himself and blocks the violent blow aimed at his face with his crossed arms of roots. The second blow slams his forward leg off the ground, leaving him unbalanced. The djinn is bashed away from Namien's body with the intense shock on his arms. He rushes up and dashes to the pygmy brothers with his stark fist of roots. He can't let them anywhere near Namien.

Both brothers attack in complete coordination. The points of impact are harsh on either side. Biafle is blocking the heavy strikes from many angles. They step as one, move as one, their attack well-coordinated or synchronized, as if they speak with no words. The field is getting heavier, weakening Biafle, but more so Kobenan, who is breathing heavily and walking with elephant feet. Gravity is growing unbearable.

Kobenan doesn't stop and doesn't give up. He falls on all fours, gets up, and continues to walk. The lack of air and strenuous effort keep him winded, his vision growing blurrier as he advances. He keeps walking. He has to reach the car, which he can barely see now.

Biafle is overwhelmed. The attacks from all fronts with the strong field slow him down. He manages to block most of the heavy blows, but he is stressing the resilience of his body. The brothers' attacks have lost speed—Biafle can see the difference from when this fight started—but not nearly as much as his. Moving has become an effort now, while they can still be swift. One of the pygmies sweeps Biafle off the ground. The second one, in the air, falls on his chest with his whole weight. The impact pins the djinn of the forest to the road with a burst of soil, and the fight ends.

Djengdjeng walks to Namien and grabs his ankle. Nianbou, the pygmy with the long braid, still on Biafle's chest, raises his fist to end the djinn, when a sound from above forces them to leap away from the loud explosion. The pygmy brothers remain on guard, waiting for whoever has landed to stand up so they can see who they are up against.

"As always ... you're late," says Biafle from his back.

"I'm sorry. It's not the village next door. And you owe me a better phone. This one is no good," says the heavy shape, standing up. His right fist of rocks and thin roots retracts from the impact it created on the ground.

"You think you can handle them?" asks Biafle.

"Leave it to me," responds the heavy shape.

Rocks, thin roots, and leaves grow down to his feet, stretching to tear the white tank top and the moss-green shorts. A djinn of the mountains. The pygmy brothers recognize this rocky shape, a large silhouette standing six-foot-four.

Kobenan has flattened on the road. He is crawling with one arm. He can't see much, but the blurred dark spot of the car is very close to him. He must be close to the edge. The gravity is extreme. He is slowly pushing forward with his hand wearing the ring. Breathing has become so strenuous, he can't feel much of his lower body, but he can still move. He can do it.

The djinn of the mountain walks toward Biafle and grabs him. "Desks don't suit you, my friend. You're getting weak."

"So I've noticed," says Biafle.

The pygmy brothers keep distant. Caution is the wisest move. They know djinns of the mountains, their incredible strength and tenacity. But they can't let him walk away.

"Don't worry. I'll keep them off your back until you're out of range," says the djinn of the mountains. "But you owe me a better phone. These humans are good at creating addictive things."

"Indeed they are," says Biafle. "I'll buy you a new one. But don't rely too much on it. This is one of the reasons why all this trouble exists today."

"Are you comparing me to a human?" says the djinn of the mountains. "I'll throw you first. Namien will come next."

"All right."

The djinn of the mountains hurls Biafle before he feels the strikes of the pygmy brothers on his neck. They awaited the moment when all his attention was directed elsewhere to try to take him down. Biafle, who saw the attack before they hit the djinn, has to forget about it and think of his landing. The djinn of the mountains has hurled him high enough for him to land as close as possible to the black SUV, but gravity seems to be pulling him down way too fast. Biafle slams to the ground at the edge with no rebound and sees his feet still in the strong field.

He pulls himself away, gets up, and notices someone flattened on the road not far from the SUV's back tires. Kobenan has his right hand stuck out of the field and his body flat with his mouth open, drooling, his eyes looking at his partner. Biafle shakes his head and walks toward Kobenan. He grabs his hand and pulls him off the field.

"Thank you," says Kobenan, regaining his strength.

"Start the car," says Biafle, getting in position for Namien.

The head of the S-cell awaits, but no one shows out of the field. They can't leave without Namien. There is no point; they are already on the blacklist. The pygmy brothers played smart. They awaited the right moment to strike. The djinn of the mountains is strong, but they should never have taken their eyes off these two guardians. The car is on, and Biafle still waits. Thirty seconds have passed now. He can barely see what is happening out there. This strong field has created some kind of haze around the prison. A body is coming at great speed toward him. Biafle sticks his hands out, only for the body to fall on top of him. He stands up and grabs Namien. He rushes to the car, opens the back door, and swings the sorcerer inside. He gets in the passenger seat and looks at Kobenan. "Drive." Kobenan hits the gas.

*

The fight is fierce. Whatever the djinn of the mountains touches explodes. Three African dogs spring out of the prison and go after the car. The bat follows. The djinn, under heat from the pygmies, manages to smash one of the dogs, which rolls on the ground. It is no more. The two other dogs continue the chase. This instant of inattention allows Djengdjeng to jump on the djinn's feet and sweep him off the ground. When he budges to try to get up, every high-ranking guardian stands around him, and more are coming. Men of quaint form, djinns, spirits, cats. They all stare down at him. There is no more fight. The djinn of the mountains smiles, slowly gets up, and stands tall. One of the guards attaches a strip of cloth to his ankle.

"Give him a cell," orders the Great Chief.

"They had help from within the prison," says Nianbou, the pygmy with long braids. "But I heard the fetishes of truth let the boy pass."

"False information was constantly being fed to me since those two entered the prison," says the Great Chief. "Biafle couldn't do that. Eyra did. Only she has enough power and precision to reduce the communication."

"The Third Great Chief, for what purpose?" asks Djengdjeng, the pygmy with a short braid.

"I'm sure she has her reasons," says the Great Chief. "She is wise. I'll talk with her. Get everything in place and double the protection. I have a conference with the presidents and leaders concerning this incident."

CHAPTER 5

Talk with the Secretary

Namien lies in the back seat, seemingly moribund, his motionless body on the brink of rolling and shoving itself between the seats with the abrupt movements of the car. Biafle turns to check on him and prevents the fall with a quick hold on the left flank of the sorcerer. He opens the glove compartment with his free hand and digs out a small glass bottle of pale-orange liquid. He moves to the back of the car and helps the sorcerer sit up. Namien can barely maintain this stance with assistance. Biafle opens Namien's mouth and forces the liquid down his throat.

"Drink this," he says. "It'll restore some of your energy."

The pupils of the sorcerer mildly contract. His right hand flat on the seat, palm facing up, barely twitches a small finger. His head, leaning to the left on a neck devoid of strength, tends to unbalance his body before Biafle pushes him back up. The sorcerer makes a languid blink. He is slowly moving his fingers. Though vaguely, he can now secure himself in the seat. Biafle leaves him and gets back into the passenger's seat.

"They're getting close," Namien says slowly.

"Yes, I felt them," confirms Biafle.

"Who? Who's getting close?" asks the troubled young man who, for a brief moment, had a glimpse of relief with the distance between him and this unsettling edifice.

"The prison dogs," responds Biafle.

"What do you mean they're getting close? We're in a car!" exclaims Kobenan.

"I told you that nothing in this prison is normal. These creatures are among the strongest and fastest dogs Mother Nature can offer, and they won't give up until they retrieve Namien."

"No, I got that. I'm saying *we're* in a car," says Kobenan.

"We have to find a way to lose them, and fast," says Namien. "I feel only two."

Kobenan, who has yet to envision an SUV being chased by dogs, sneaks a look in the mirror. They *are* dogs. They look like dogs, brown in color, and they are gaining on them. Kobenan quickly glances at the speedometer: eighty-five miles per hour, almost eighty-six. He doesn't understand. He looks back in the mirror, and the dogs are getting closer still.

"This is insane!" yaps Kobenan, almost losing control of his hands.

"Focus," prompts Biafle. "The road."

"Are you sure your speedometer works?" squeals Kobenan.

"It's a government car," says Biafle. "Just drive."

They are supposed to be solid, fast vehicles, but Kobenan doesn't feel this at all right now with these dogs on their tail. It is as if all efforts to put some distance between them are pointless. Kobenan glances one more time in the mirror and no longer sees the dogs.

"Where are they?" He turns to Biafle and then brings his eyes back to the road.

A crude shock on their left side shakes the car, forcing the tires into a brief skid. Kobenan, who has a firm grip on the wheel, manages to keep the car on the road.

"Daaaaaaaaaamn!"

He takes a quick look in the mirror and notices one of the dogs running closer to the back door.

"*Dogs*, you said!" screams Kobenan.

Another shock from the other side disturbs their straight course. Kobenan struggles to get back on track.

"If we don't do something, they'll flip the car, and that'll be it for us," says the sorcerer, lifting a lazy hand.

Biafle brings the sorcerer's arm back down to the seat. "Don't. Your body has suffered enough. You'll add some serious damage to it. Let it recover. We have no choice but to use this now."

Biafle pulls from his left inner pocket two miniature statues shaped from black wood. He clenches them for a few seconds and throws them by the window. They enlarge as they bounce and spin on the road. Dogs of wood with red eyes speed up when fully formed and catch up to the dogs of the prison. They lunge at the brown dogs' sturdy back legs and unbalance them. They all fall on the road, rolling for a while before attacking each other. A ferocious dogfight begins.

"You know those fetishes won't last long. And there's no one better than them to trail us. They'll find us," says Namien.

"I know, and we can do nothing about that," says Biafle. "But we *can* delay them. Kobenan, keep the wheels straight. No mechanical thing works on the bridge we're about to use."

Biafle slips his right hand through the window and lays it on the door, his ring in contact with the metal sheet.

"What bridge? What are you talking about?"

"Just keep the wheels straight," says Biafle. "We have to get rid of this bat."

Kobenan squints and brings his eyes closer to the windshield, as he feels at first they might be playing a trick on him. The straight road does seem to elongate. The rows of trees bolting by on his left are pulling and distorting as they pass. Colors he can identify and many he can't create a warped feeling before his eyes. The sound of the engine dies, forcing Kobenan's attention to the vehicle. All lights shut off, with everything around the sliding vehicle growing darker, only to allow a few hints of rich brilliance flashing through. Numbness envelops Kobenan's ears and drums with the sudden absence of sound. He feels a swoop of low gravity as he slightly lifts from his seat before he feels it again under him and once more sees the road flashing before his eyes. Reflex pushes his leg to slam the brake pedal in the middle of the road. He sits there, blankly staring at nothing. His stiff hands are clawed on the steering wheel, his body frozen to the bone.

"Why did you stop?" asks Biafle.

The silence of Kobenan quickly alarms the head of the S-cell. He shakes him and pulls him from the driver's seat. There is no time to waste. This short gain will only last if they stay in motion.

"Kobenan," Biafle calls one more time, to no response.

"You've given the boy too much to take in," says the sorcerer, pulling on his now fully functional limbs. "I'm surprised he hasn't lost it yet."

*

Kobenan is in the driver's seat, calm, silent, gazing ahead with dead eyes. Something is not right. Why does he have this strong feeling of déjà vu? This windshield, this road, this car, this instant, or was it the instant before? Is he losing his mind? From all he has read, déjà vu after a shock can manifest when the mind starts losing sense of its surroundings, of time, confusing what is and what is not. He might be losing his mind. He has to stay on the ground, keep it together. He is thinking. He might still be sane if his brain is thinking. Or is it too much thinking right now? Is he lost in his thoughts? Is he sane or not? "Stay grounded," Kobenan says to himself. "Stay grounded."

"Ho!" He feels a loud, rather harmless slap on the back of his head and promptly turns to look at Biafle. "Where are you? Keep it together. The mission's not done."

"What was that?" Kobenan asks after a brief silence of blank staring.

"What we traversed? The sorcerers' space. The one they use to travel. We bought ourselves some time," says Biafle.

Kobenan slowly turns back to watching the moving road.

"Don't think about it, or your mind will try to process it," says Biafle, glancing at Kobenan. "It's not ready yet. Give it time."

He should not think about what just happened. He can still hear Biafle. And the sorcerer is still in the car. Kobenan takes a look behind. He still has his normal senses. He is still sane. "Don't think about what happened," Kobenan repeats to himself.

"Kobenan," calls Biafle.

"Han?" responds Kobenan with his gaze on the road. "I'm here."

"All right."

"I didn't know djinns of the forest have the power to switch space," says Namien.

"We don't. This is a gift from my former partner," says Biafle. "So where are we going?"

"The Black," responds the sorcerer.

"The Black?" asks Kobenan. The name bounces in his head more than once as he clearly recalls this location.

"The most renowned black market. A place where you can find almost anything you seek," says Namien.

"Why there?" asks Biafle.

"To meet the secretary of the Wiseman," says Namien. "The man we have to see to get answers."

"The secretary of the Wiseman is located in the Black?" asks Biafle.

"A young Dioula who goes by the name of Blackys," says Namien. "He sells high-end phones, but this is just a front. Only a few high-level sorcerers know of his connection with the Wiseman. If you don't meet him, you will never meet the Wiseman."

"Kobenan, are you listening?" asks Biafle.

Kobenan turns to his partner and then looks back to the road. "I am."

"The Wiseman is a powerful sorcerer who has the ability to switch bodies at will," says Namien. "We'll have to follow each word of the secretary, or we'll never meet him."

"Namien, if we're going to help you find your daughter before they do, we have to know everything you know. What happened, what's coming, and how you ended up in this prison. Kobenan will figure something out from that," says Biafle.

*

107

The Black is the new destination, a market Kobenan often visited during his childhood. There is only one place on the African continent called the Black. Kobenan was very excited to learn this when he was nine, visiting for the first time with his mom. The place is in Abidje City—the commercial town of Ebile, to be more specific. It is a very famous, or should he say infamous, zone in Côte d'Esperance. Only in this peculiar market could he and his mom afford articles for his school and their life. It wasn't a place for a child, she always said, but they had to if they were going to survive, before he was picked up by the government. Kobenan remains silent, staring at the road, but more importantly listening to the sorcerer behind him. He has to stay focused. Biafle is right; the mission is not over yet.

"When I left the confederation, I knew they would come after me," says Namien. "But I wasn't concerned, because my wife and I were among the strongest."

"Why did you leave?" asks Biafle.

"Eating souls and flesh gives power, which lasts a short time and then demands you eat more to get more. We all knew we weren't doing any good to this country by killing the most successful people, either to assuage our thirst or in accepting bribes from a few to eliminate their competition … until we reached one of the family who was meant to change everything for the better. We knew this would have a direct impact on us and everyone else in the country. Not like the previous ones we ate. My wife and I refused to participate.

"The confederation was convinced we refused to kill him because he was our blood. He was part of our family. We then left the confederation and didn't associate with these practices afterward. We thought it better to choose the long path and learn with nature in our search for strength. Many of their attempts to kill us failed, until my wife started to weaken because of her baby. We thought at first it was them, so we fled to a distant village where we could find protection.

"When she delivered the baby, she couldn't support the energy drained from her body. I knew when looking into the eyes of the baby that my days were also numbered."

"Why?" asks Biafle.

"She had the sparkling eyes of a person cursed with the pupils of time. Cursed with the body as a vessel of an immense energy that can only be used by very powerful sorcerers. A person whose appearance in the world comes every two hundred years when it's a boy—"

"And every thousand years when it's a girl," says Biafle.

Kobenan turns to Biafle. "Why a thousand years for girls?"

"Because girls aren't meant to be griots," says Biafle. "But when Mother Nature chooses a girl, it means the energy trapped in her body will change the world if it comes to be released. Female griots are uncontrollable and powerful. But most of all, they appear when the world is about to enter a period of despair."

This might not be the same name, *griot*, as Kobenan recalls. The one he knows, also called *jali*, is from an old tribe of the African desert, a name meant to tell tales and predict the future of kings, sing of their lineage, and praise their exploits. Namien said a person cursed with the pupils of time, so he could be talking about the same griot Kobenan knows of. But nowhere did he read about this kind of immense energy. What griot are they talking about? There is so much he doesn't know. Better to listen.

"We were the only ones who knew it was a girl," Namien continues. "But the other sorcerers felt this immense energy and started to look everywhere. I had no choice but to rely on someone much more powerful."

"The Wiseman," says Kobenan.

"He is a former member of the wise circle," says Namien. "The people behind the biggest decisions of life. When I met him, he said he was waiting for me. He left the wise circle ten years back because he knew I'd approach him for something bigger than himself. And I had the choice: either he kills the child, because of the great danger she represents, or he protects her, but I have to pay for my crimes and surrender to the sorcerer prison.

"It has been thirteen years since the Wiseman hid my daughter. She is becoming more and more unstable because of the energy she bears. I don't know where she is, but I do know that if we can't feel her, it means she has mastered how to control the emission, and this is killing her. If a sorcerer powerful enough to unlock the power inside reaches her, it will be the end of the life we know. Everyone. Those beyond the sea won't even know what's hitting them."

"Then we have to make sure this doesn't happen," says Biafle.

"If the Wiseman left his group ten years before your child was born to protect her, I don't think he'll be happy to see you. I don't think he'll want to see you at all," says Kobenan.

"He's a wise man. I'm sure he's aware of what's happening," says Biafle.

"One more reason he won't see Namien," says Kobenan. "They both want to protect the girl for different reasons, and the Wiseman will make sure Namien never reaches her, because he'll think we might be followed, or if not, when we take the child, we'll be found by the people looking for her. I'm sure Blackys has been warned about him."

A row of tables at the very edge of the side road filled with sundry merchandise of various sources indicates their arrival. The market is now within walking range. Biafle finds a spot to park and turns to Namien.

"The kid might be right. You stay in the car. We'll talk to him."

"Okay," agrees the sorcerer. "But be careful. If he has any suspicion, he'll flee, and you won't find him again."

Kobenan gives a skeptical look to his partner, but he quickly grasps the situation. It is true that right now Namien has no reason to escape. If Kobenan is right, Namien's best chance to see the Wiseman is to stick with them and follow Biafle's instructions. Someone willing to give his life for his daughter won't try to jeopardize the best chance to find her.

"We have to find him first," says Kobenan.

"He sells phones. We know where to go," says Biafle, leaving the car.

"He's made a reputation. Ask for him," adds Namien.

"I want you to wear the spirit bracelet, but you're too weak right now, and we need you alive. Is there anything I should know before we leave?" asks Biafle.

"*The boss* is the word," answers Namien.

Biafle is walking away with his partner when Namien calls him. He looks at the sorcerer without completely turning.

"Whatever you do, don't let him touch any walls."

Biafle and Kobenan enter the Black, a rich, vibrant place of diverse voices and scents. The odd and unique way people have of shouting and vouching for their goods to attract the pedestrian evokes memories for the young man. Nothing has really changed since he last visited this place when he was a kid. Thin lines separate one merchant from the next. Happy and energetic people share exchanges and products. Young people run everywhere and approach with confidence potential clients with their one product in hand. It's difficult to move forward, since many use the same path. Space is scarce. Walking sideways is sometimes the only solution.

Only one word fits this wonderful and intriguing place: *loud*, to cover the many silent and important transactions behind walls, where one can trade anything.

Biafle and Kobenan are finding their way into the market. As chaotic as it may seem, things are extremely organized for the accustomed and those who know what they seek. It doesn't take long for the agents to find the phone sector. New and second-hand phones from diverse and sometimes doubtful origins are sold to the one who knows the universal language. Someone is approaching.

"*Vieux père*, the last of the lasts. Powerful, cheap, only for you. Give me a price."

Vieux père. A name spoken only to someone older than oneself as a sign of respect, or in this case, to charm the client. Kobenan does remember that this name is largely used in places like the Black and mainly poor areas of the city.

"We're looking for someone," says Biafle.

"Who?" asks the confident young dealer, following the agent with energy and hustle, as if he has no time to waste.

"Blackys," responds Biafle.

"*Vieux père*, it's the same thing he's gonna sell you, believe me, and he's very expensive. I'm the best deal for you. It's the best phone on the market right now."

"We want to talk to him," says Biafle, his fleeting gaze on the people passing by and the many tables in a row offering wide ranges of phones and accessories.

"Talk to me, *vieux père*. I have other products for you if you want," says the young dealer, tucking the phone in one pouch and pulling a gold watch from the other. "Look at this, gold, *vieux père*. it has no battery, full mechanic. Look at the back, only glass, and water-resistant. Whatever product you want, I'll get it for you."

Biafle stops and turns to the young dealer, no more than sixteen years old, in black jeans and with no top. "No. We want to talk … to him."

"Oh, okay, talk to him," says the young dealer.

"Do you know where we can find him?" asks Kobenan.

The young dealer turns to Kobenan. "He moves around a lot, but you can ask that guy over there. They're close."

"Thank you," says Biafle.

"No problem, *vieux père*. If you want something, you know who to approach. I'm very cheap." The young dealer walks away.

"Yes, thank you."

Biafle and Kobenan approach a man sitting on a table, his feet hovering the ground. Phones are aligned in a grid by his side.

"Look and choose, brother. I'll give you a good price."

"We're looking for Blackys," says Biafle.

"Blackys? I don't know; he was there a few minutes ago. Hey, Issa, have you seen Blackys?" The man turns to another dealer on his left.

"Who wants to see him?" asks the second dealer.

The man on the table points to the one on his left. Biafle and Kobenan walk to the second dealer, merely three steps from the previous table.

"Do you know where we can find him?" asks Biafle.

"Who wants to see him?" repeats the man, looking at them.

"Tell him we want to see the boss," says Biafle.

"Hey, Mamadou, call Blackys. People want to see him." The second dealer turns to a third on the other side of the small, dusty road.

The wait is brief. A skinny man barely toping five foot five in torn blue jeans and white tank top approaches. It seems he just made a pleasant deal, judging by his bright smile. He is clearly enjoying the counting of his money, Kobenan can see.

"Who wants to see the boss?" asks Blackys, his eyes fixed on the fresh bills.

Biafle is about to answer when Blackys suddenly raises his head. He looks at the two agents and dashes in the direction he came from, leaving the money behind. This abrupt reaction is only a surprise for a split second before Biafle and Kobenan launch into pursuit. They can't afford to lose him.

Blackys is a child of the Black. His movements around the crowd, under and over tables, speak of his agility and ease in this place. Every path in this whole market lies at his fingertips. He jumps here, slides there, takes shortcuts and subtle turns. He seems to be heading for a specific area.

"Blackys, we just want to talk," shouts Biafle, with Kobenan right on his tail. This place is too crammed, and they are slowing down between making their way around tables and avoiding people following the scene. Kobenan perceives what may look like an exit; the same exit used by Blackys. A wall stands at a running distance from them when they enter an area devoid of people.

"The wall!" yells Kobenan. "He wants to touch the wall."

"I know," says the head of the S-cell, grabbing something from his pocket.

Blackys, now about six feet from the unfinished wall flashing with graffiti of charcoal, is extending his arm to touch it when he is sharply propelled away. He falls on the hard, sandy road. He hastens to stand up, ready to throw himself at the wall, but Biafle already has a hold of him, forcing the young dealer into an uncomfortable, inescapable position. Biafle lets a short, twisted rope fall on the ground and looks at Kobenan.

"Restrain him." He then turns to the young dealer, still struggling to break free despite his inability to move an inch of his body. "We don't want to hurt you, Blackys. We just want to talk."

"I don't want to talk to you or anyone linked to this guy. I have orders."

"Namien, I told you to stay in the car," says Biafle, holding the young dealer tight for Kobenan to fasten the knot on his wrist. He relinquishes Blackys and helps him sit on the ground.

"He was about to get away," says Namien.

"He wasn't," replies Biafle.

"I couldn't give him a chance to escape."

"What do you want?" interjects Blackys.

"What every sorcerer wants when they approach you," responds Biafle.

"It's not possible. You will never meet him," says Blackys.

"We have to talk to him," says Kobenan. "It's a matter of national security. I'm sure you know what national security means."

"I don't care if it's continental security," prompts Blackys. "I have orders to disappear as soon as I feel Namien's energy."

"We're wasting time, Biafle. He'll never get us an appointment willingly."

The young dealer lifts from the ground and starts levitating, his tongue out, choking as if his windpipe is pinched. It seems he can only breathe with arduous effort.

"And you're slowing us down," says Biafle. "Put him on the ground."

Kobenan, a step away from his partner, is closely observing the young dealer. These subtle twitches of his fingers should not occur, at least not that quickly when someone is trying to find air. His eyes moving up to his brain is never a good sign.

"He's dying, Namien, release him!" calls Kobenan.

Blackys briskly looks at the sorcerer with a different expression. Air seems to be no more a concern of his body. The shaking of his hand has stopped.

"Namien, put my boy down ... now," says a new voice with Blackys's lips.

The sorcerer instantly lets the boy fall to the ground. Kobenan stands starkly staring at the young dealer.

"I have to talk to you, Wiseman, otherwise I wouldn't have gone this far."

"There is nothing to talk about," speaks the voice. "Take your friends and leave before this conversation turns into something disagreeable."

"We can't, sir," says Biafle, looking at Blackys. "The only reason we're here is because what you know might be crucial for the safety of this country. The girl might be in danger."

"And what makes you think she will be safe in a different place?" asks the Wiseman. "I can't let the love of a father interfere with this. She'll be extremely dangerous in the wrong hands."

"That's why we're here, Wiseman," says Biafle. "We believe someone very powerful is pulling the strings. If we don't act fast, he'll achieve whatever he's planning. Namien's child is in the center of what's happening right now."

"He doesn't know," Kobenan says softly.

"And what is happening?" asks the Wiseman.

Biafle looks at Namien. The Wiseman is not aware of the situation. How is this possible, when the Enkonhi couple knows so much about this assassination and everything else brewing around it?

"Please, sir, let us talk to you in private," says Kobenan. "Here isn't safe for such a delicate matter."

Stillness swipes the area for few seconds before Blackys comes to his senses, or almost, as he still seems lost, looking at the ground.

"He granted you access ... You may go."

"Where?" asks Namien.

"His third location," says Blackys.

"His third location?" asks Biafle, turning to Namien.

"The entry of Benoumin," says Namien.

That's at least fifty miles from Abidje, the city they are in now, Kobenan thinks. Biafle doesn't waste time. He leaves Blackys on the ground and asks Kobenan to untie him. Kobenan does so and reaches the car with the S-cell agent and the sorcerer waiting for him.

"You took your time," says Biafle.

"I tied him too hard," responds Kobenan, entering the car.

*

It's an hour of silent voyaging to the village of Benoumin. Biafle slows the SUV and takes a right for the woods on Namien's instructions. He stops the car before the trees a few feet from the road and gets out. Kobenan and Namien follow. The sorcerer points to what may look like a house deeper in the woods. It's barely visible through gaps between trunks. Biafle and Kobenan follow the sorcerer to a stop about thirty feet from the house, when he raises his hand and stands still. They don't move for a few seconds, looking occasionally at each other. Despite his sharpened awareness, Kobenan can't help but drift away for a brief moment in his surroundings before the sound of a door opening brings him back to the ground. They can now go inside, it seems, as Namien is walking toward the house.

It's a calm place of repose, Kobenan can feel. He looks around at the large carpet of green grass encircling the house of wood standing in the very center. Trees have only grown beyond the circle of grass, leaving the house a grand space. The wind is gently rocking the tall branches and the small blades of grass around them. This subtle dance of the trees feels harmonious and at ease. The birds' chants seem to appease the vast, roaming energy sifting around. Their iridescent green plumage, if he sees right under the soft blue sky cradled with sunrays, pertains to the Sturnidae. They are certainly glossy starlings.

"What would have happened if we didn't stand still?" asks Kobenan.

"You would have thought you saw a house," says Biafle.

"It becomes invisible?" asks Kobenan.

"It shifts space," says Namien.

"No wonder it's impossible to see the Wiseman if he doesn't want you to," says Biafle.

Kobenan remembers this word: *space*. A word his partner asked him not to think about because his mind was not ready. Whatever it is, it's clearly beyond his understanding. But he is all right. He has managed to forget about it and get rid of the shock he received after they traversed it. At least he thinks he has.

"What's space?" asks Kobenan, looking at Biafle.

The head of the S-cell glances at him and looks back at the house. "You might have a better understanding if I say *dimension*, but it's not, and I can't really explain that to you. You'll have to find out by yourself when the time comes."

Not really what Kobenan was expecting for an explanation, but again, nothing has been normal or close to comprehension since he left the presidential house this morning. He will have to accept what has been given to him: some sort of dimension but not quite.

Namien stops in front of the house and asks Biafle and Kobenan to remove their shoes. The agents comply and await his next instruction.

"Please come in," they hear from inside the house.

The agents follow Namien into a fairly dim house. The light seeping through the windows highlights the contours of masks and statues of various tribes erected on the floor. Biafle and Namien remain cautious, as they doubt their real purpose. Kobenan contemplates the flat, almost empty house of wood.

A man stands in the center of the room, dressed in what might look like a white embroidered *agbada*, an attire composed of pants and a large robe, usually worn by nobility or elders. His doesn't seem to have sleeves underneath or pants, just the large robe covering his body from neck to heels. His short gray beard

117

is more prominent in this dim light than his face. Kobenan is unaware of the wise men's influence and knowledge in this world, but most of all, he is ignorant of how old and powerful they are. Namien and Biafle, on the other hand, have some knowledge of the wise circle and the power they wield. They are very careful and aware of each of their movements in the room, showing the utmost respect for the man standing before them.

"Please be seated," says the Wiseman when the guests reach him.

The three men sit on stools in front of the Wiseman, who grabs a stool and follows them. His fixed regard after sitting demands the utmost attention of his guests.

CHAPTER 6

The Djekoulé Stone

Fear is Joel's worst injury from the tree fall. The branch that snapped must not have been that far from the ground, or else he has no time to think about pain. Joel shoots up and sprints for the garage, with his racing mind unable to grasp the situation he put himself into. He jerks down under the violent sounds emanating from his bedroom but keeps moving. His senses heightened, his hands shaking, his heart beating to the terrifying noises around him, he struggles to open the unlocked vehicle door.

Loud crashes of destruction sound from the bedroom, and they are as close to Joel as he can hear when the short man and the creature are propelled from the window onto the ground, smashing each other in the most brutal and chaotic way. Yet they seem to follow a certain pattern of sharp reflexes and intense strikes, a merciless fight demanding fists, palms, knees, feet, and anything within the vicinity falling into their hands. The loud noises have woken up the neighborhood. Everyone is outside, wondering what is happening in the Kouadios' house. They see nothing but metal doors bending, walls and pillars exploding, glass bursting. No one dares to approach the house, but the authorities have been called.

Joel rushes into his father's pickup truck. He fastens his seatbelt, grabs the key from under the sun visor, and controls his shaking hands to start the engine. The back door shatters inside the garage, forcing Joel to jump from his seat. The stiffness of his body and the dread in his eyes when he perceives the second creature glaring at him from behind the car is more than enough to make him lose control. The creature charges, but before it can get out of range, despair or adrenaline urges Joel to hit reverse and pin the creature to the wall with the truck. Joel keeps the vehicle in reverse until they break into the kitchen. He feels the four-by-four tires rolling over the creature until he hits the fridge and loosens his foot on the pedal. Joel shifts gears with his jittery grip and leaves the kitchen at full speed. He hears a crash of metal and quickly brings his confounded, overwhelmed gaze to the mirror. It's not dead. The creature is furious and hooked to the back.

The sleek, midnight-blue pickup truck smashes what remains of the portal without a flinch of deceleration and dives into a loud skid on its steep turn. The short man, bleeding from his many wounds, is bashing his inert opponent sprawled under him when he perceives the vehicle passing by. He grabs the side of the car and with a swift hop gets onto the cargo bed. The fight left him in severe shape, with a crushed throat and one barely functioning eye. The loose back bumper detaches under the creature's weight, which had most of its solid grip on it to hold onto the car. It drags on the road for a brief moment and stops. Its rage seems out of control, with a harsh punch on the road before it launches into pursuit.

The creature uses everything to propel itself closer to the car. When panels or signals fall out of range, its leg movements are unmatched. Joel throws a look in the mirror and sharply turns to verify through the rear windshield. He turns back to check the speedometer. He can't seem to accept what he reads. The needle is bumping at seventy-eight miles per hour. He looks back in the mirror and perceives that the creature is getting closer. Joel hits the gas as strongly as his foot allows and tries to put some distance between himself and this monster, but speed seems to be of no help; it is getting closer.

The short man sits on the cargo bed, his right hand holding to the side edge. He has trouble keeping his eye open. He knows it's a matter of time before he loses consciousness. He has lost too much blood.

The creature leaps and breaks off one of the advertising panels on the road. It falls back, speeds up to the left back tire, and with uncanny strength throws the panel at it. The sharp explosion of condensed air bounces the car forward, causing instability, and before Joel can react, the vehicle is spinning, breaking, smashing. It rolls and veers off the road into a steep slant.

His mouth is red with blood, his hands resting on the roof, his body hanging in his seatbelt. Joel is numb inside the flipped car, his eyes loosely flickering out of extreme shock and concussion. He has not lost consciousness but cannot move. He tries to lift his hand an inch before the limb falls dead on the roof. He hears a scraping sound and then harsh metal breaking as the door is pulled away with no effort. Joel feels strong hands clasping his chest and khaki shirt, but the resistance of the seatbelt is what hurts the most under this strong pull. The second yank drags him right out of the car after the sound of a breaking seatbelt. He can feel the grass under his neck. He can hear the tires still spinning. His blurred sight can clearly identify a leg lifting above his face, the bottom of a foot hanging right on top of him, ready to stomp his skull.

The creature looks at Joel like the vermin that he is, or with the satisfaction of finally fulfilling its task. Its face will be the last face Joel will see. The leg drops toward Joel's head, but something disrupts the creature, unbalancing it. Its large foot does not reach Joel's face as the short man leaps onto its back, holding its arms as the one foot maintains stability on the grass. He locks the creature's movements in a struggle, which pushes them to fall into the weeds. The creature is violently jerking around and fighting to break free from this strong grip.

The short man manages to hold a red rock from his amulet with one hand and the neck of the creature with the other. The elbow strikes, head knocks, grabs, and scratches of the creature are of little effect.

"We'll leave this world together. Joel, seek the Djekoulé stone," says the short man in a ragged voice before his eyes stop moving and his strong grip loosens. The creature starts squirming and moaning in extreme pain, clutching and scratching its chest as if the atrocious pain originates from there. It grasps the weeds, the dirt, and squeezes, as life leaves its body. The writhing slowly fades into minor twitching. Death follows seconds later.

Joel is lying on his back, suffering from his wounds, looking at the dark sky. The faraway sound of sirens alarms him. What will they do if they find him here? Arrest him? Protect him? They can't protect him, not after what he has seen. Better not to stay here. Joel slowly holds his ribs and struggles to stand up. He can barely get up, but he has enough strength to put one leg before the other. Joel drags himself away from the car into the bushes, with no direction in mind. Stay as far from the police as possible is the main goal—the only goal. He sees next to nothing, with the dark and the thin drip of blood from his forehead. He just needs to remain in motion. Every inch of his body aches, and he can feel the weight of his chest as he breathes, but he has to keep pushing forward.

After a long strain, numbness sets in. His vision gets blurrier. The dizziness grows acute, and his body is unable to follow his will. Joel can walk no more. He has to push further—he has to. He can still hear the distant sirens by his dad's car. Joel falls on the soil, left cheek–first, mouth open, and slowly closes his eyes.

*

The bright sun burning the side of his face forces Joel to slowly open his eyes. A subtle movement reminds him of the acute pain in his armpit. He can feel the other injuries, but they seem bearable as he steadily stands up. He should get out of here and find his way to the road. Where is he? There is no siren. Joel looks around at the bushes surrounding him. There, between the holes of branches and leaves, he can see something. Something resembling a road. Joel knows which direction to take.

When he reaches the edge of the road, he instantly recognizes the area: Ebile, the commercial town. Did he walk this far the night before? He can't remember. He used to walk this way when he had free time to reach home. It's thirty minutes longer than his usual path, but it was worth the time if he could spare himself the sight of accidents. But the worries of his parents wouldn't allow it every time, only when he was done very early at school. If he walks about ten minutes from here, he should find himself under the Mekou Bridge. Joel remembers someone selling phone services under that bridge.

The Mekou Bridge's shadow is a perfect spot for the very few who prefer to catch customers on their way to work. Some stop by to check the front pages or buy one or two newspapers. Phone services like cheap calls of a few minutes to phone card recharges are a profitable business in Ebile. Joel approaches a man on a used plastic chair lost in the paper he is reading. Beside him stands a table of various tabloids.

The vendor levels his eyes at Joel after he notices a shadow on his paper. The dry blood on Joel's forehead causes him to pause.

"What did they take … your phone?"

The confusion of the question is momentary. This is Ebile, the town of the black market, which happens to be very close to the Mekou Bridge. This man must be thinking Joel got mugged.

"Everything," responds Joel.

"You must have been walking in a very dangerous area," says the man.

"Do you sell phone services?"

"Yes," answers the man, handing over one of the phones on the table, a rather old one with a small square display and keys unveiling only fractions of letters from the excessive use.

Joel takes a few steps away from the vendor, where he can make his voice difficult to eavesdrop on with the cars passing by. The phone is ringing. Joel waits impatiently for someone to pick up, when his eyes lock on one of the newspapers on the table. A chill traverses his body at the very first words.

YOUNG MURDERER ON THE LOOSE IN CITY screams the bold and large heading on the cover of the paper, with his face plastered next to it. The ringing sound turns dull when he notices the same subject on most of the newspapers on the table. Thoughts of walking away while it's still possible invade his mind, but Joel keeps calm. He slowly tucks his head into his chest and shows his back to the vendor, who is checking on him with his piercing gaze.

The ringing continues with no response. Anxiety rises as the man keeps his eyes on Joel. Maybe it's just a standard precaution, because this is Ebile and he doesn't trust a stranger with his phone. Or he has doubts about Joel's face. All Joel can do is wait and pray for someone to pick up. This number is the only one he can turn to at this moment.

"*Allô?*"

"Roland," responds Joel with a short sigh of relief.

"Joel! Thank God you're alive," exclaims Roland. "I was worried sick about you. Where are you?"

"I didn't kill them, Roland. I didn't kill my parents," says Joel.

"Bro, come on, just tell me where I can find you."

"Ebile. I'm under the Mekou Bridge right now."

"The Mekou Bridge," repeats Roland. "That's not far from Mami Tchetche. It's better you head there and wait for me."

"Mami Tchetche, there are too many people there," says Joel.

"Better. That's the last place people will go looking for you. Just don't look at them. Your face is everywhere. Find a corner and stay put."

"I have to go. The newspaper guy is staring at me."

"Okay, okay, but be careful. I'll be there in like twenty minutes."

Joel searches in his pocket for pennies after giving back the phone, the pennies he always keeps in his school uniform for candies. The man stops him with a raised palm. Joel pauses and looks at the vendor, still unclear whether he should start walking away. He can't run. Not with this pain in his armpit. But he will be long gone before the police arrive, even if this man calls them now. He won't leave his goods to follow Joel.

"It's okay. It's on me," says the vendor. "You should see a doctor for that injury on your head."

"I will. Thank you very much," responds Joel.

Joel leaves. He advances cautiously, avoiding eye contact with the few crossing his path. Those turning to him on occasion give him a long stare before they continue on their path. Joel quickly realizes that the dried blood on his forehead is the center of attention and wipes it off with his saliva. His destination should be about a mile from here, but it's becoming harder to walk with the unbearable pain in his armpit. There, he can see it from afar, the popular establishment.

The restaurant owned by Mami Tchetche is praised among the locals. She is well known for her *attiéké, poisson grillé*. It must be midday, with this large flock of customers. Now that he is close, Joel doubts the safety of this plan. A restaurant so well known, at this time of the day, might not be the smartest place to hide. People will easily recognize him. He has no choice, though; it's the only place where he can meet with Roland.

The fresh scent of grilled fish and cassava greets Joel at the open doors. A wide, flat area of chairs and tables is filled with people savoring or ordering for more. Joel keeps his head low and looks for an empty place in the corner. It must have been twenty minutes or more since Joel started walking to this place. Roland should already be there but is nowhere to be seen. He should be able to blend in with his khaki outfit. There is a large number of students in the restaurant.

His wandering eyes checking for any sign of Roland make him stumble into someone looking at him. The man eating his meal throws occasional glances at Joel, until they become more and more frequent. Joel dares not raise his eyes to look at him. The man elbows another man by his side to look at Joel. Joel lifts his hand to scratch his forehead and covers his face. When he raises his eyes again, both men are looking at him. He is found out. The few people talking around the table push others to turn in his direction. Even if he wants to leave now, he won't be able to outrun them. Where is Roland? Joel looks around one more time, but there's no sign of his friend.

People seem to know who he is. Otherwise, why look at him

this way? He cleaned the blood from his forehead. Is it his khaki shirt? It can't be; the dirt is not that obvious. He can't be the only one who comes here with a dirty shirt, not with all the construction in the area. More eyes are converging on him. What should he do? Joel can feel blood dripping down his armpit. Maybe he should leave. Someone gets up from the table across the room and starts walking toward him. Joel is sweating. He should walk out of the restaurant now. They might start chasing him. They will if he moves. The man is close enough to identify him. Many are looking at him. A hand touches Joel's shoulder.

"I knew you'd be here. I told you to wait for me at the store. You're something else, aren't you? Let's go."

Joel doesn't think twice about the nonsense of his friend. He stands up with a smile, which requires as much strength as he needs to walk out of the restaurant, and they quickly reach the taxi before the doubtful customer has a chance to react to the scene.

Roland almost has to carry his friend to the underground parking lift of his building, with the help of Issa, the only taxi driver he has been calling since he was fifteen years old. Issa leaves them at the lift doors, gets his fare with a thank you from Roland, and returns to his taxi.

It doesn't take long for Joel to pass out on the lift's tiled flooring on their way up to the fourth floor. It's a struggle for Roland to pull him out alone while constantly looking around for anyone who might be walking the hallway. Luckily, his apartment is not far from the lift, and he quickly gets the key in the door before anyone walks in on him. Roland lays Joel on his bed and removes his shirt, which has turned red under the armpit. He notices the large wound stretching to his shoulder and panics. He has absolutely no clue what to do. He sits on a chair next to the bed and looks at his unconscious friend. He grabs his phone and is about to dial when the bell rings.

Roland jumps out of the chair and rushes to the door.

"At last."

"I had to wait for my friend to cover for me," says the woman, entering and removing her jacket.

"I told you, he's in really bad shape," says Roland.

"You also told me to come alone," says the woman. "How am I supposed to leave the hospital unnoticed? Where is he?"

"In the bedroom," responds Roland. "He fainted when we arrived."

"What happened?" asks the woman following Roland.

"An accident."

She approaches Joel at once to check on him. "I can take care of his wounds, and I don't see any signs of internal bleeding, but I'm not sure … Roland, he has to go to the hospital."

"He can't," says Roland.

"Why?" she asks, turning to Joel. "Wait … is that …?"

"Babe, listen to me—we can't bring him to the hospital. They'll send him to jail."

"Of course they will send him to jail … after he's feeling better."

"All right, take him," says Roland, throwing his hands in the air. "Don't even bother to visit the hospital."

"Is that sarcasm, Roland? You're doing this right now?"

"I'm sorry … I'm sorry, baby … I'm freaking out, okay? And you're the only one I can trust."

"He's a criminal. Haven't you seen the news? He killed his parents."

"Baby, look at him. Does he look like a criminal?"

"Because it's written on their forehead, right?"

"He's my best friend. He didn't kill anyone. Trust me. Besides, you swore an oath, right? Why are you asking all these questions? Make use of your oath. Invoke it or something."

"You lied to me."

"Oh my God." Roland holds his forehead. "The man's dying, and you're talking about my lying to you."

"He's not dying. He's just unconscious. Just pray there is no internal bleeding. What's this thing on his neck?" asks the woman.

"An amulet. Don't touch that, okay?"

The woman sighs. "Help me turn him. I'll clean the wounds and treat them."

She reaches for her bag, grabs a notepad, and starts writing. "Get me these medicines. Don't take more than two in one pharmacy." She tears the paper from the notepad and gives it to Roland.

"Okay. Listen, babe …"

"Don't *babe* me right now. Just go get the medicines."

The tone is enough for Roland to shut it and leave the apartment. She has the exact same look when she is mad at him, and now is not the time to smooth-talk her out of it.

Roland hastens to the drugstores where he knows someone and brings the medicines as she requested. He remains silent and attentive to the process and helps her when she requires it. She said Joel is not dying, so that's a relief. But Roland is still on edge, with his best friend unconscious.

After two long hours, with no other signs but stable breathing, Joel finally opens his eyes, and Roland is the first person he sees by his side, sitting on a desk chair, looking at him.

"Man, you scared me," says Roland.

Joel looks at his bandaged wounds. "Who did this?"

"My girlfriend," responds Roland with a smirk of pride.

"Your girlfriend? Isn't she in law school?"

"Shut up," urges Roland in a low voice. He quickly peeks at the door and gets back to Joel. "Do you want her to bring you back to your previous state? She is my third girlfriend, okay?"

"Okay," responds Joel.

"I'm sorry, bro … for your parents."

"My sister!" Joel remembers. "She's still alive."

"Whoooa. Where do you think you're going?" asks Roland, holding Joel down on the bed.

"I have to find her," says Joel.

"Not in this condition. I'll help you, but you need rest."

Joel lies back in the bed and takes a deep breath.

"They found only two bodies at your place and assumed you must have murdered them. And you kidnapped your sister. It's all over the news, bro. What happened?" asks Roland.

"You'll think I'm crazy."

"Try me."

Joel exhales deeply and takes a moment before he turns to his friend. "I see things. Things I'm not supposed to see."

"What things?"

"Creatures … things … I don't know what they are or where they come from. But they've always been in my life. Yesterday they came to my house with my grandmother, and after that …" Joel stares into the void with watery eyes. "It went so fast. My father … my mother … Princess … If not for this short man, I would have been dead too."

"A djinn."

Joel looks back at Roland. "You know them?"

"Not really, but when my parents were killed, I was given an amulet so that the sorcerers from my family won't be able to detect me. The person who gave this to me talked about them."

Roland reveals his own amulet of intertwined thin black cords and small pearls. Now that Joel sees it for what it is, it does look unique. He has always assumed it was one of Roland's accessories. That and the many bracelets of small pearls he keeps changing every day.

"I thought …"

"What … accident? That's the official version," says Roland.

"I'm sorry."

"It was a long time ago … you know bad things will happen in your life. You have to hold on to the good things and never let go. And right now, I'm your only good thing." Roland smirks and then gives Joel a straight face again. "I'm here for you. Your sister is still alive somewhere, and we'll find her."

"Thank you, bro. I don't know where I'd be if not for you."

"Jail … with cockroaches and everything."

A smile escapes Joel's tired face, but it quickly fades when he looks down, as if something came to mind.

"What is it?" asks Roland.

"Djekoulé stone." Joel looks at Roland. "He told me to seek the Djekoulé stone."

"The djinn?"

"Yes. I'm pretty sure I heard his voice after the accident."

"What's that?" asks Roland.

"I don't know, but I have to find out," says Joel.

"A stone … at least we have something to start from. I know where to go."

"Where?"

"To his protector," says the woman, entering the room to pack her bag. "That's what you call him, right?"

"*Guardian* … my guardian … pffff. Joel, Raissa, my girlfriend … Raissa, Joel."

She's svelte and beautiful, Joel can see, exactly Roland's type. She is probably three or four years older than him, but that's never been a problem for his friend.

"Thank you for taking care of me," says Joel.

"It's a miracle you're still alive," says Raissa, grabbing her bag. "I saw the car in the news. How the hell did you survive that accident?"

"I don't know."

"Well, he's here and kicking, right?" says Roland with a smile.

"You need rest," says Raissa. "Roland, he needs rest. Don't make him leave the apartment to see your illusion-seller. His wounds are still fresh."

"I'll be careful," says Joel.

"It's not about being careful. It's about letting your wounds heal."

"Okay, sweetie. He'll stay here. I'll make sure he doesn't move," says Roland.

"I'm going in for my shift. I'll be back tomorrow to check on him."

"Two minutes. I'll see her out." Roland catches up with Raissa on her way to the door.

When he comes back, he lets himself down in the chair and makes a spin. "So, tomorrow. Have a good rest."

"But you told your girlfriend we were staying."

"Have you ever heard of the saying, 'No brings war'? Trust me, she would still have been here if I didn't agree with her. So, tomorrow."

*

Morning is painful but far less severe than the day before. At least Joel can walk without feeling the whole weight of his upper body in his chest. And moving his left arm is not as much of an ordeal anymore. A dark green T-shirt and old blue jeans are his pick from Roland's closet after a long and troubled bath. They quickly get breakfast, and Joel takes his painkillers, as requested by Raissa. Roland packs some of the food in a plastic container and leaves the apartment with his friend. Issa the taxi driver has arrived and is parked underground, waiting for his clients.

"You look better."

"I feel better, Issa. Thank you very much for yesterday," says Joel.

Issa nods and turns to Roland. "So where we go?"

"Tumi Road," says Roland.

"Tumi Road it is."

Only when they are free from highways can Joel sit up. His face is still in the newspapers, according to Issa, and Joel can't take the chance of being recognized on the road. It is true that they have known Issa for a long time, especially Roland. But despite his relaxed face, he is risking too much driving them around. He might be right when he says, "I don't know you, and I don't read newspapers," the perfect alibi if they get caught by the police.

Roland, on the other hand, is a completely different case. Those at school who know Joel know Roland as the one who's always with him, and vice versa. Joel can't think of what his friend will say to protect himself if they get caught. He is helping a criminal, he is an accomplice, and Joel knows that the penalty must be severe for this. But here Roland is, even more relaxed than Issa, or he just doesn't seem to care about this whole situation he put himself in. Is Joel the only one who realizes the consequences of just being around him? But again, Roland has never been one to really worry about anything. He has always had a way of getting around problems. Maybe it's the freedom he got at such an early age that made him who he is.

He seems to act without any supervision or fear that someone will reprimand him. His older brother, who is always between countries, seldom checks on him; at least that's how it would seem from the countless times Joel has been in his apartment. And there is really no reason for the school or social services to worry. He has good grades, and you'd never know just by looking at his always joyful or calm face that he is without guardians.

"Long time I used this road," says Issa.

"I know. I have been so busy," says Roland.

"First time you bring Joel with you."

"Yeah ... he's my brother," says Roland.

"You're my friend, I'll give you good price," says Issa.

"Why you do that to me all the time? Han, Issa? Nooo, you know how much I'm going to give you. I know what your 'good price' means."

"Everything expensive now. Gas, food. It's not me."

"I'm your best client. Don't do that," says Roland.

"Okay, okay. Only because of our friendship."

"Ahh, now we're talking," says Roland with a smile.

How they can talk with so much ease in a situation like this, Joel can't comprehend, but this silly, friendly banter between Issa and Roland puts a smile on his face for a brief moment.

"Who's this guy we're going to see?" asks Joel.

"His name is Bredou," answers Roland. "He spent ten years in the forest with djinns and animals, learning the secrets of healing and power of the forest. He's the one who helped me stay alive."

"Stay alive?" says Joel.

"He came to me and explained what I was going through," continues Roland. "He said he felt like my guardian and gave me the amulet. Since then, I stopped falling sick and having nightmares. That's why I recognized yours. I don't know what your amulet does, but you're feeling way better than when I picked you up yesterday. I doubt that's only Raissa's work. I'm sure Bredou will give you something to start from."

"How much does he take for his services?" asks Joel.

"Nothing. He says money is the source of many diseases of this world."

"Nothing? I thought it was his business," says Joel.

"I thought so too," says Roland. "He says it's his purpose and that those who take money know why they do. He accepts food if you bring it to him, but if you don't, he'll help you anyway."

"You've known him for a long time?"

"Since I had my first painful nightmare when I was thirteen," responds Roland.

Issa has been a taxi driver long enough to know where police control is prominent and makes sure to avoid it. They are not leaving the city of Abidje, so they won't have to pass the main road control. Issa parks the taxi halfway off the road after a forty-minute drive. Roland and Joel leave the vehicle for the tall coconut trees on the roadside. Joel follows his friend on the many turns with nothing to see ahead but more trees and soil. It's a ten-minute walk of finding their way in the coconut field before they reach an open area with a tent by one of the trees.

The tent of braided coconut leaves with a split requires bending to enter. The fresh, deep-brown soil bares some of the leaves piled in the center of the area. Joel's eyes wander in his surroundings. It's a very quiet area in the middle of nowhere. He'll probably lose his way if he has to walk back alone to the road. Someone leaving the tent with a woman brings Joel's attention back to the entrance. The man hooks one side of the split entrance to the bottom corner of the tent. Roland taps Joel's shoulder. The half-open entrance is the sign that he can go next.

"When you get in, sit and put the food in the bowl on his right," says Roland. "Speak only when he asks questions. Don't say less, don't say more. Only what he asks."

"Okay," says Joel.

He enters the tent with a last look at his friend, who gives him two thumbs up. A first glance around requires Joel to keep his calm. A small wooden statue stands in the corner. It has a face that commands a second look. Many bowls of carved wood and coconut shells are spread on the sandy ground, bearing colored powder, grains, and liquids of dubious purpose. A strong scent hits Joel when he approaches them. It pervades the whole tent. He can't identify it, but he knows it is coming from these bowls. He sits beside them in front of a middle-aged man with closed eyes.

The man sits with legs crossed, head down, as if he is meditating. His flabby, naked torso shows paint of white and yellow, which seems to extend to his back. Amulets and bracelets of many sizes and shapes repose thick on his neck and wrists. The sound of colliding pearls and cowrie shells is inevitable at the slightest budge. Something resembling a fly-whisk lies by his side. It has a carefully crafted grip of wood. Whatever it is, flies are not the target. Joel has not seen a single one around since he and Roland arrived at the tent. He crosses his legs to follow the man's posture and puts the food in the carved wooden bowl as instructed.

"Joel," says Bredou.

"Yes," responds Joel.

The man levels up his head and looks straight in Joel's eyes. "You can see them."

"Yes."

Joel noticed them the moment he stepped into the tent: two dark men with faces as unique as the one who gave him the amulet. They sit on each side of Bredou, legs crossed, necks straight, eyes closed. They are probably what Roland calls djinns. Bredou throws three cowrie shells on a short, flat stool before him and looks at them.

"You missed death."

"Yes," confirms Joel.

"Show me your protection," asks Bredou.

Joel pulls his amulet out of his shirt and holds it out to show the man. One of the djinn opens his bloody eyes and stares at it. Joel looks at the djinn on his left but can't bring himself to hold this terrifying gaze. He quickly looks back at Bredou.

"A djinn's amulet. I can't see what awaits you. This amulet won't let me. What do you seek?" asks the man.

"The Djekoulé stone," says Joel.

Both djinns turn to gaze at Joel.

"The forbidden stone. Nobody knows where it is," says Bredou. "I'm sorry, I can't help you."

Joel's face falls in desperation. Where else can he go? This is the only lead, the only chance he has. "Please ... please," he implores.

"This stone has been lost in legends for centuries," says Bredou. "Everything about it has been destroyed. And even if I knew where it was, you'd be dead before reaching the place. The djinn gave you this amulet for a reason. You should hide."

"He gave it in haste," says Joel.

"Djinns don't know haste, and they never give their own to humans. Whatever is chasing you might be of the highest rank. Hide."

"He's the one who told me to seek this stone," says Joel.

The man peers into Joel's eyes in silence. The surprise on his face is subtle but noticeable. He shakes his head slightly. "I can't help you. I'm sorry."

"They took everything from me. I have to find my little sister ... please," says Joel, on the brink of tears.

"I don't know the location of this stone. I can't help you."

Joel stands up, ready to bend for the exit, when the man calls to him. He searches in a small bag of old leather and pulls out a polished black stone.

"Go to Adou Godi, my village. Show them this rock and ask for guidance. Maybe you'll find something there."

"Where is it?" asks Joel.

"Dosoville."

"Thank you. Thank you so much."

"Your life is on the line now," says Bredou. "I don't know why this djinn said what he said, but never let anyone see your amulet. The ones who know you have this will kill you without hesitation to get it. And whatever happens, don't remove it from your neck."

"I won't," says Joel. "Thank you. Thank you."

Joel leaves the tent to join his friend by a tree.

"What did he say?" asks Roland.

"Dosoville."

Only when Joel speaks with Roland does his attention veer from this rock. Even then, his eyes have trouble looking elsewhere. He examines front, back, side, and brings it closer, as if he might uncover something before they reach Roland's apartment. But it's just a rock. Eerie, true, but still a rock. Maybe it's its unique form and texture that incites so much curiosity. Nothing extraordinary with every inch he has been observing, but he knows this is not common. Joel probably never studied this rock in geology classes. If he did, he surely doesn't remember. He was not the most enthusiastic student in those classes anyway. But Roland has no clue either, and he had better grades.

The rock resembles granite, with smooth, rounded corners, one side tapering more than the other. One thing bothering Joel is the way it shines under light. Is it a rock at all? Joel scratches his forehead. Maybe he should have paid more attention in class, now that he thinks about it. The shaman said Dosoville. When he reaches Adou Godi, the shaman's village, there is no telling if anyone will help. If he knew what kind of rock this is, its name, at least there would be a chance to find the area it came from, and maybe even find this Djekoulé stone.

Roland looks at Joel, lost in thought, staring cluelessly at the stone. "It doesn't speak. You know that, right?"

"His face changed when I said Djekoulé stone," says Joel. "Bredou?"

"Yes. He said I will die before I reach the place."

"That's promising," says Roland.

"What do you think it is?"

"The Djekoulé stone? Don't know … a stone."

Joel looks at Roland. "Yeah, I really haven't thought about that."

"What d'you want me to say?" Roland shrugs. "I have no idea what that is. Don't worry, we'll find out."

"What do you mean, 'we'll find …'" Joel pauses. "No, no, Roland, you have already done too much for me."

"I'm not letting you go alone."

"Did you hear what I just said? What Bredou told me? I can't let you risk your life because of me."

A glance at the entrance of his building forces Roland to take a second look at the window.

"What is it?" asks Joel.

Joel is turning to follow his friend's gaze when Roland pushes his head down on the back seat.

"Get down!" hisses Roland, hiding from the window. "Issa, don't stop. Go on, go on."

Roland slightly raises his head only to show his eyes to the rear windshield. Joel follows and perceives two men in black suits entering the building.

"Who are they?"

"Government agents, or maybe S-cell," answers Roland, getting back in the seat.

"Who?"

"An organization that chases sorcerers."

"What are they doing at your place?"

"What do you think?" asks Roland.

Joel takes his seat. "They think I'm a sorcerer?"

"I'm not sure who they are, but with what you told me, it's probable. I heard they rarely take prisoners. We have to leave the city, now."

"Someone at school must have tipped them off." Joel looks at Roland.

"I doubt they visited the school. Bredou told me that only a few know they exist, and if you see them, it's just a matter of time …"

"Shit. The phone call I made to you."

"No, one of my friends made my SIM untraceable." Roland sighs. "Maybe they have something to trace it."

"But why now? I called you yesterday," says Joel.

"Raissa." Roland raises his head, staring at nothing.

"Your girlfriend?"

"She was the only one besides Issa who knew where you were."

"You think it's her?" asks Joel.

"No ... no, she wouldn't do that. I don't know, man. It doesn't matter right now. We have to leave. I guess extra money's not an option anymore. Issa, Neri Station." Roland leans forward to the driver. "Travel buses are our best bet."

"Will be double fare, Roland," says Issa.

"It's all right," says Roland, leaning back in his seat.

Roland is right, Joel thinks. Neri Station is twenty minutes from his apartment, and Issa will have to take some detours to avoid police, but if they manage to leave the city while it's still possible, at least there is a chance to find this stone.

Roland remains quiet during the whole drive to Neri Station. This is the first time he has been so worked up about something. These two men, this S-cell, must be an entirely different problem from the police. And now they know where Roland lives because of Joel. He put his friend in a dangerous situation the moment he called for help. Roland is already an accomplice, and Joel doesn't even want to think about what will happen to him if he stays in the city. Despite the fact that he doesn't want his friend to risk his life, they have to leave the city together. That's the best course of action right now.

"I'm sorry, bro."

Roland looks at Joel. "What for?"

"Dragging you into all of this," says Joel.

"Don't say that, come on. You'd do the same for me. Don't worry, we'll find Princess."

Neri is a large station, but between fast walking and occasional jogging, it isn't long before Joel and Roland cover all the bus stops. Nowhere can they find the one for Dosoville. Asking around quickly clears the confusion. They will have to take the bus to Dogboville, then the one to Assina, before they reach Dosoville. There is no direct road to the city. They passed the Dogboville stop a few minutes ago, just a couple of stops back.

Neri is packed with people disembarking or buying tickets for another city. Vendors wander, presenting their goods to potential customers on the buses in transit to another city. Joel and Roland stay close to one another. One could easily lose sight of the other in this high traffic.

It's Joel's first time setting foot in a bus station. He, who steered clear of any kind of public transportation because of what he knows and what he has seen, is compelled to take one today. There is no picking which kind of transport suits their situation. It's either bus or go to jail, or maybe worse.

Roland leaves Joel in a spot near a sweets merchant and goes to the cashier for the tickets. Better to avoid any risk of exposure to the cameras.

"It's a long road," says Roland, handing Joel his ticket.

"How long?"

"Three hours to the first stop, Dogboville. Get on. I'll get some snacks."

Joel nods and heads for the bus, only a few steps from the sweets merchant. He presents the ticket to the conductor at the door and is allowed to step in. Half of the ticket has been torn by the conductor. He is instructed to keep the other half for further checking. Some of the seats in the back rows have yet to be claimed, and the ones not far from the left window seem hidden away from most eyes. He will just have to leave the seat by the sliding glass to Roland to avoid being seen from outside.

Only five minutes, and the bus is almost full. The droning engine suggests departure very soon. Joel has had to apologize twice now for holding up a free seat, but there, by the window, he can see Roland with a white plastic bag on his way to the bus.

"Excuse me," calls a passenger standing by the side, another one about to request the free seat. "Can you move?"

"Oh, my brother is on his way," says Joel, turning to the passenger. "He just went out for foo—"

"Hey!" yells a voice outside, catching the attention of many around. "Stop!"

Joel follows some curious passengers gathered by the window to see two police officers chasing someone running with a plastic bag. It doesn't take him long to realize that Roland has caught their attention by running to draw them away from the bus. Joel hadn't even noticed the policeman posted at the door, talking with the conductor. They are looking for a young man, for him, or they wouldn't care about someone his age running from the station.

"Officer, I don't want to be behind schedule," says the frustrated driver, looking at his watch. "I have seventy-five miles to cover."

"He's right, officer," says the conductor.

The police officer raises his hand for the men to pause while he responds in his walkie-talkie. He taps the metal sheet of the bus twice and waves to authorize the departure before he follows the direction of the previous officers. A woman who would probably have missed her trip if not for this unexpected delay enters the bus. The only free seat she finds after looking around is the one near Joel. Before she can say a word, Joel shifts his legs outward to let her sit by the window. The bus is heading out of the station.

CHAPTER 7

A Road for Normal Men

Hours have passed since he abandoned his friend at the station. His neck relaxed on the headrest, he stares blindly at the back of the seat before him, silent, distant. Did Roland manage to get away? Did they catch him? Is that why they allowed the departure of the bus? These questions strain Joel. He might never see his friend again. He can't think of any safe way back to Abidje right now. And even if he manages to return, what are his chances of making contact with Roland again? Roland is resourceful. Joel gives a long sigh. Maybe he didn't get caught. Maybe he is okay. But the police officer let the bus go. Why?

"Son," calls a voice near Joel.

The hand of the woman on his forearm brings him back to the bus. He looks at her, by the window seat on his left, and then turns to his right.

"Where are you?" says the conductor, erect by his right in the narrow aisle. It seems he has been standing near Joel for a while now. "Your ticket."

"Sorry." Joel hurries in his pocket and hands the second half of the ticket to the conductor.

The man tears off the slip of paper, hands it back, and advances to the next row of two behind Joel.

"Is something bothering you? You seem lost in your thoughts," asks the woman.

"I'm a bit tired," says Joel with a hint of a smile. "I didn't have the chance to sleep well yesterday."

"Well, we still have hours ahead of us," says the woman.

"That's true," Joel agrees with a nod. "Thank you."

The woman squints at him. "Do I know you from somewhere?"

"No. No, I don't think so," says Joel, looking back at the seat before him.

"It's weird. I feel like I know you."

"It happens," says Joel, tilting his head just enough for the conversation. "Maybe you're confusing me with …" He sharply straightens and turns to the window.

The woman glances outside and then looks back at Joel. "What is it?"

"Excuse me," says Joel, pushing to the window.

"What is it? What are you doing?" asks the woman, compelled to lean deep in her seat and allow Joel to gaze at the empty road.

"Please get back to your seat," calls the conductor by the bus door.

Joel looks at him, then at the many passengers whose attention he caught with his scene. He slowly gets back into his seat.

"Are you all right?" asks the woman, stumped.

Joel understands exactly what she means by her tone and countenance. *What's wrong with you?* would be the straightforward, impolite question.

He knows what's coming, what he has always witnessed from afar. Joel is unable to stay still, unable to bring his mind to one thought. Everything is rushing in his head as he looks around. The man two rows before him next to the narrow aisle is passing a bottle of water to his wife. The one right across from Joel's seat is reading a gray book of many pages. The woman behind is feeding her baby, smiling at him, rubbing his nose. They are all alarmingly unaware, too calm. Of course, they can't see what lies on the road; they can't see these creatures standing very sparsely at what one could guess is an equal distance, following the bus passing by with their gaze. Joel knows what's to come if he stays in his seat. But what can he do? The bus. He has to stop the bus before it's too late.

The woman looks at Joel, annoyed by his incessant move-ments. "What's with you, son? Why are you so …"

"Sto-o-o-p!" Joel shoots up, startling many of the passengers. "Please, stop!"

A few wake up at his sudden bark. The whole bus turns to the young man.

"Please take your seat," the conductor says calmly.

"I can't … I can't hold it anymore. I have to go."

Smiles and laughter ripple through the passengers. The bus driver shakes his head and gives a smile to the conductor.

"We can't," says the conductor, trying to keep professional with a straight face. "We have a schedule to meet."

"Please, sir, since this morning I haven't been able to sit cor-rectly. I'm sure I'm disturbing this poor woman with whatever she's smelling here. I can't hold it anymore."

"I'm sorry, boy," says the conductor. "We're already late. We can't stop. Just try to hold it a little longer to the next station."

Joel looks at the window and leaves his seat.

"Boy, please get back to your seat," warns the conductor.

"What's he doing?" asks the driver, with his eyes glued to the road.

Joel hurries to the driver and grabs his seat. "Sir, I'm sure you don't want me to do it in the bus. I'm sorry, but at this stage, trust me, I'll do it anywhere … *any* … where."

The conductor holds back his laughter. "Just give him five minutes."

A few minutes of delay is not exactly a thrill for the driver, but he has to park. "Do it fast," he says, watching Joel head out.

Joel gets down and walks in front of the bus.

"What the … is he crazy?" yells the driver, rushing out of the vehicle. "Hey, what are you doing? The forest isn't comfortable enough for you? You want to do it in front of my bus?"

"I'm sorry, sir, but I can't let you go farther," says Joel, sitting before the bus.

"*What?* What are you talking about?" asks the astounded driver, looking down at Joel.

"If you go down this road, they'll kill everyone."

"Who? What's wrong with you? Are you out of your mind? How can you say things like that?"

"Hey, what's wrong?" asks the conductor, joining them.

"This boy's crazy," says the driver, turning to his second in command.

"Sir, please, you have to listen to me. There is death on this road."

"I have taken this road for twenty-five years, and I've never had an accident, and you, crazy fuck, want to ruin my day?" the driver shouts. "Get in the bus, or I'll leave you here."

The delay and voices attract the curious passengers outside, only to see Joel sitting before the bus.

"I can't let you go." Joel looks up at the driver.

"What's with this boy?" asks one of the passengers.

"He doesn't want us to leave. He says there'll be an accident if we try to," responds another passenger.

Murmuring spreads through the passengers standing by Joel's side and those still coming out of the bus, wondering what's happening.

"See what you're doing? You're making people worry about their trip. I can assure you, people. No such thing will happen." The driver turns to the group standing outside the bus.

"Throw him somewhere, and let's go," says a passenger. "We're wasting time. If he doesn't want to come, leave him here."

"You'll leave a teenager on these roads?" asks a woman trying to calm her crying baby.

"He's wasting our time and telling lies. There are other buses using these roads," says another passenger.

"Boy, move. Don't make us decide," says the conductor, pulling Joel from the front of the bus. Joel struggles.

Arguments quickly break out among the passengers and the driver. Leaving a teenager on these roads will be irresponsible, but then again, what can one do if the subject himself does not want to leave?

The woman who was sitting next to Joel approaches and looks him in the eyes. "I remember you. People think you're dead after your accident. You're the kid who killed his parents two days ago."

The buzzing of a fly can be heard at this very moment as everyone stares at Joel. Some eyes grow wide, and jaws drop in recognition.

His mind goes blank for an instant before he dashes in the opposite direction with whatever speed his feet can muster. He runs as fast as he can, as steadily as his body allows. He can't afford to get caught now, not without finding his sister first. Joel glimpses back to check if anyone might be close to him, but no one is chasing. They have not moved, watching as he distances himself from them. Joel runs until he can breathe no more. When he stops and holds his knees to catch his breath, he looks in the bus's direction. It's gone.

The aching of his feet and chest compels him to sit at the edge of the road to calm himself and take in some air. The brutal start he took to get away is having a heavy effect now. He is dizzy for a few seconds, with pain coursing through his body, but it is at this moment, this instant, that everything floods him. Unable to think, completely lost in the middle of nowhere, sitting alone with only the delicate wind and leaves' harmony for support, Joel dissolves in tears. He cries because he cannot bear the thought of everything he has lost in just two days—his father, his mother, Princess, his best friend.

He is now just a fugitive, constantly on the run for his life. He cannot understand how this has come to be. What has he done to fall into this nightmare he prays to wake up from? Joel won't stop crying. He can't. The weight is unbearable, and he feels like his head will explode.

Here he is in the middle of nowhere, with no food, no drink, and only the infinite road and the forest to rely on. His hands clasped to his head, he gazes at the wet soil under him with his drowned eyes. His tears won't stop dripping. His short sleeve is soaked from wiping his face, and the only thing he can do is look down at the soil.

No. No, he has to keep it together. He has to. Otherwise, he has no chance to make it out of this. He cannot use the road. He doesn't know the forest. "Think, Joel. Think." Joel makes a rash turn to look at the road, when he hears a faint noise. He looks around, but nothing suspect presents itself. This is not a safe place for him to stay, not with what he has seen on the road. He stands up, wipes his face one more time with his shirt, and walks into the forest.

The next station is Joel's best bet. He will just have to follow the direction of the bus. For how long? He doesn't know, but using the paved way would be signing his death warrant. He will take a few steps into the forest and walk parallel to the road. At least this way he will be safe from unwanted eyes.

Joel quickly turns to check once again. This noise was prominent, somewhere behind him. Joel sees nothing but the trees he just passed. He changes pace. Whatever they are, these noises are not random. He hears crackling leaves and stops to look back. He hears branches breaking. Joel dives into an aimless run. He knows something is out there, something he can't see, and he won't wait until it is close enough to catch him. He races between trunks, hops over roots, and keeps in a straight line if the trees allow him. The cracking sounds are now constant; he can feel them behind him. Joel turns for a quick glance when he perceives them.

They are agile, swift, jumping from branch to branch with ease. Joel has never seen these creatures before. He perceives only two in the trees, but sounds on the soil speak for more. It takes less than a second to register this glimpse, but they seem humanoid, with long legs, or maybe it is their arms, and their outlines are seemingly hunched over. Joel tries to speed up between trunks, but he can hear them gaining ground. A swoosh bursts the bark of a tree before him. Joel ducks out of reflex but doesn't stop his path. More bark explodes inches from his head as he blitzes through the forest. There are no thoughts in his mind. There is nothing but running for his life.

More bark is destroyed behind him. He cannot engage a straight line; he will be a dead target. The random placement of the trees is the only reason he is not agonizing on the dirt. There's another burst by his face as he ducks past a curved tree. One of the rocks hisses past Joel's left earlobe and disturbs his course. Joel stumbles on a root and splashes face-first into the soil. He promptly stands up, but panic gets the best of his balance. Joel falls on all fours, trying to steady himself before he can get up.

One of the creatures drops onto the soil and advances with wide steps toward him. Joel is lurching away, begging for his life. The creature snatches a rock off the ground and raises it high at its target. Joel brings his arms to his head before there's a brutal smashing sound. His sharp scream is never unleashed.

Joel is frozen. He stares, mouth agape, at his attacker flattened on a tree trunk on his right. It takes him a few seconds to realize that he is still alive. He slowly turns his dazed eyes to a man standing before him.

The man blocks the daylight before him. Joel is tense, ready for an escape. But this man just saved his life, and even if he wanted to, how can he possibly get away from someone like this? The man looks down at Joel.

"Thank you, sir. Thank you. Thank you." Joel rushes up, trying to quickly prove that he is no threat at all before he becomes the next target.

"What are you doing here?" asks the man.

It wasn't just because Joel was butt-deep in the soil. This man is tall, maybe six foot five, wearing only a brown cloth from his waist and two bracelets attached to his heels.

"Sir, I was being chased by these creat—" A projectile rips into Joel's right chest before he can point at anything. He hits the ground, eyes half-closed, mouth open.

The tall man looks down at Joel and turns to the five creatures.

"Give us the child," says one of them.

The tall man eyes the three creatures on the ground and then looks up at the other two in the branches. "Take a good look around you. You are far past your territory. Leave … now."

The two creatures in the branches drop to join the three walking toward the tall man. Two men appear from the trees' shadow behind the tall man and walk slowly to his side. They are as tall and large as he. They wear the same dun cloth around their waist. One is chewing a stick of wood and the other herbs.

The creatures stop their advance and stare at the three men standing, waiting for them. One of the creatures taps the one beside him, and they all fall back. The man with the stick of wood, the biggest of them, looks at Joel with no expression. "He's dying," he says, walking back to the shadow he came from.

The tall man crouches beside Joel and stops the bleeding with a quaint movement of his hands. He grabs some of the chewed herbs from his companion, the youngest of them, and applies it to Joel's wound.

"He needs to see Old Paapa. This won't hold for long. His chest bones are badly damaged."

"We have no authorization to bring him into the village," says the man with the chewed herbs.

"You need authorization to save someone?"

"What if he's a mole?"

"He isn't," says the tall man, showing the amulet on Joel's neck.

*

Joel's eyes slowly flicker open. The sluggish movement of his head allows for a distorted view of his surroundings. He fails to identify objects with this blurred vision, but something, someone just moved by his side.

"Look who's awake," says a voice. "Don't move. I'll bring you some water."

"Where …" Joel slowly gulps down saliva. "Where am I?"

"Don't worry, you're safe here."

"Where is … Mo-o-om! Da-a-ad! Princess. Where is my sister?" cries Joel in a frail voice.

"Calm down," says the short being, leaning toward Joel. "They aren't here. Don't move too much, or you'll open your wounds."

149

Joel slowly reaches for the blanket on his stomach. "I have … save … my … little …"

"Hey, don't … Paapa!" calls the short being, turning to the entrance of the hut. "Old Paapa!"

"What is it?" An old man enters. "Hey, don't move. You haven't fully recovered."

"My … little… sister… I … have … to …"

"Calm down, my son. You need rest."

The old man gently strokes Joel's forehead twice and then presses his palm on it. Joel falls into a deep sleep.

"What happened?"

"He started calling for his parents. Is he in shock?" asks the short being.

"Probably. But he wasn't supposed to wake up now." The old man looks at Joel. "His bones have almost recovered. Watch out for him."

"Okay, Paapa."

CHAPTER 8

Listen

A voice echoes in his head. Someone is talking from afar. He can hear it, but he cannot quite understand. The voice is too far away. Is this a man talking? Yes, it is. What is he saying? All is dark, and this faint voice is Joel's only focus now. He can really hear it. It is not in his head. It is somewhere around him. Joel opens his eyes. The voice goes on, still indiscernible, but it wasn't a dream. The roof of straw over his head is his first visual contact.

There are tightly assembled piles of straw, with a center standing higher than the rest. He follows the tapering curve of wood binding the piles together and finds a wall of dried red mud, neatly smoothed. Joel can see a round wall. He is in a hut. He can feel the straw fibers of the bed on his back, strong enough to hold him, soft enough to feel comfortable. A table the height of the bed stands to his left, a round table of wood holding calabashes of leaves and powder and a bowl of liquid, probably water, judging from the clarity. Where is he? By his feet is an entrance, the source of the voice. He can see an orange light dancing.

Joel budges, but the atrocious pain shooting through the right side of his chest warns him to stop. The pain is so deep, he has to grit his teeth for a few seconds before it dies down. Moving might not be the best option. Joel can afford to open his eyes only when he feels a slow swarming on his muscles and nerves. The blood flow, the heat, and crunching—he has never experienced something like this. Joel slowly lays his head back on the cushion of cloth and straw at the first sign of relief.

Someone shows his head at the door and enters the hut. Joel looks at the entrance, and the surprise is momentary at the sight of the short man. His flat face, large lips, and nose seem peculiar, but it is his skin of dark brown with light patches that demands attention. The sleeveless piece of plain cloth on his torso extends to his knees. A few motifs, though seemingly old, are visible on the shoulder and waist area.

"Old Paapa says you're awake." The short man approaches the bed. "Come. Everyone is there. We'll listen to him together."

Joel remains silent. He is reluctant, but he is alive, and this man doesn't seem to be here to hurt him. Old Paapa? Who is Old Paapa? The short man helps Joel stand up with harsh toil and grunting. He can barely put his feet flat on the ground. The deep pain weakens him when he forces up. The short man grabs a stick of wood at the bed's feet and places it in Joel's right hand. He holds Joel by his waist and helps him, one step at a time, out of the hut.

There, in the middle of a court, stands the dancing light he was watching, a humble fire illuminating faces encircling a small area. Quiet and attentive faces focus on an old man walking around inside the circle, drawing with his movements what he speaks. He captivates even a baby in its mother's arms.

It is a small group, maybe fifty or more, gazes all following the old man's gestures, silently listening. The short man brings Joel to the circle's edge and helps him sit on the sand. He takes a place by his side and tells him to listen carefully. Joel looks at the people near him, some sitting with legs crossed, others with their bent legs wrapped in their arms. All are looking only at the one standing. Joel turns to the old man.

"And the mighty king kneels. He is weak; he is wounded. He who has never before fallen in front of an enemy sees himself overwhelmed. He, whose power and strength of nature has been feared for centuries, sees himself as hopeless. He never thought his greatest fear would be the one before him. He looks around.

His army is being decimated by the enemy. They are being slaughtered, and there is nothing he can do.

"But he can't give up. He never gives up. It isn't in his custom. Nooo, it isn't what the ancestors taught him. He wouldn't be a mighty king if he gave up. He rises and fights. Only three of his warriors stand by his side. He yells so hard, Nature herself responds. A yell of desolation, a yell of weakness, a yell of despair.

"Greed and his general look at the king. They know anguish got the best of him. The army of Greed seems infinite. They keep coming, despite the tremendous power King Ubuntu shows in his smashes. Despite him destroying many with just one of his blows.

"His second in command has just fallen. The great king is hopeless. He knows this battle is lost, and he can't retreat. The future of the world weighs on his shoulders. He has to protect Odum with his life. The insatiable king and his general advance with their army. They are close to ultimate victory. Whoever controls Odum controls the world, and Greed has sought it since the beginning of time. Now he smiles.

"King Ubuntu calls his two remaining warriors to fall back to Odum. The vast army is advancing on them. They have to act fast. The wounded king kneels before Odum and looks at him.

"'I did what I could to protect you. I can no more. Please use me and my men to protect yourself. Please, Odum, don't change your wisdom for just a few who seek power over others. Please be wise as you have always been and make the best decision for your legacy.'

"The warriors hold hands with the king. Their last gaze upward finds the leaves of Odum before they yell together, 'UBUNTU,' then lay their heads on the bark and transform into roots.

"The infinite army starts to fall, choking to death. Greed and his general, Profit, stare at the legion dropping before them, killed by the unknown. His smile has become quiet rage. They retreat and swear revenge on Nature.

"It is said that Odum walked to a place where he will never be seen again. He changed his size and shape, never to be recognized. Almighty in everything, he controls and regulates our world from his hideout, protecting us from the most terrible disaster: us.

"Everywhere, Mother Nature is abundant beyond our understanding, beyond anything we can hope for. And this is for our need. Not our greed or profit. She is lavish because we are many, because we are different, because we are one. Everyone has the right to abundance, not a few.

"King Ubuntu and his elite warriors gave their lives to protect the tree of life from a few. He wanted everyone to share in the wonders of Odum. He wanted everyone to know how important we are to each other and to others. How important life from Mother Nature is for each and every one of us. So, to him and to ourselves, we say ..."

And everyone says, "UBUNTU."

Hands tap with rhythm, drums resound, and the circle rises up to dance. They emanate happiness, moving in broken harmony with wide smiles and bliss. Joel, still trying to grasp words from what has been told, stares at the quaint tribe, addled by their sudden celebration.

It's a black night with a silhouette of trees all around. The closest huts get a brush of orange paint when the dancing shadows don't interfere. Joel can only see what the fire allows, and it means mostly the crowd before him. How far is he from the road? That's the sole thing bothering him. He has to reach the station, or he has no chance to find his sister. These people saved him; maybe if he asks for guidance, they will help.

The dance of the humble fire and the many feet around it reveal someone walking in Joel's direction. It's an old man with patterned fabric wrapped over his body, exposing his right arm and chest to the orange light. The same man who not long ago was speaking with enthralling gestures. His neck catches Joel's eyes. A prominent cord holding a striped torus of wood lightly dangles on the old man's chest as he walks. One would say it is almost too heavy for someone his age, yet he carries himself straight.

The short man grabs Joel's waist, to his surprise, and helps him stand up with the stick. This old man is coming for him, Joel realizes.

"You can't dance, I know, but don't worry, you'll fully recover in a few days." The old man stops before Joel.

He must be the one who saved me, Joel thinks. Maybe it's inappropriate at this very moment, or downright rude, but he has no luxury of time.

"Sir, I'm grateful for what you did for me, but I have somewhere I need to go. Can you please …"

"I don't want to hear anything," says the old man. "Not before you've fully recovered."

"Sir, my sis—"

"I said, *nothing*. Whatever it is, you can do nothing in your situation. Just recover. Then we will see, okay?"

"Okay, sir." Joel stops talking. Pushing with more words might impede the hospitality he has already been given. Besides, how far could he go if he can't even stay erect for long? The pain is bearable, but he can feel it in the length of his right side.

"Call me Old Paapa," says the old man. "And you have already met my boy, Zonda. He's a djinn. He grew up with the village. He will take care of you."

A djinn. His face, his skin, his height. Zonda does have the same strange traits as the djinn who saved Joel, now that Old Paapa has mentioned this name. But he is shorter and thinner. You can easily mistake him for a less-fortunate ten-year-old. Joel knows he is not young. Nor does he look old. He has an innocent yet somewhat mature cast.

"Come, rest," says Zonda. "We have many things to do at sunrise."

"Many things?" Joel looks at Zonda. "What?"

Zonda smiles. He supports Joel to the hut and helps him sit on the mattress of straw. "Rest." He leans the stick against the table. Joel follows Zonda, taking some of the calabashes out of the hut, and slowly, painfully, lies on the bed. He can still hear the drums, the dancing, people talking. That will probably be a little hard if he wants to rest. Who are these people? It doesn't matter; he has to leave. Maybe not now, but as soon as the pain dies down. Every moment he spends here might weaken his chance to find his sister. But he doesn't even know which direction to take.

The best bet will be going in the opposite direction he ran from these creatures, and that would mean north of the village. But he passed out. Who knows how long they have been dragging him to the village, which turn and contour, which path they followed? This is too random, too risky, and he might easily get lost if he doesn't at least have a direction. Why not ask the villagers tomorrow? He heard a very distinct dialect when they were talking to each other, but Old Paapa, Zonda, and this tall man who saved his life might not be the only ones speaking his language. There could be more. He will have to ask tomorrow.

*

Joel can't sleep tonight. He knows it has been hours since his head touched the pillow, but he can't bring his eyes to shut. Silence reigns outside. It seems he is the only one awake. If there is anyone else, they sure aren't making any noise. Joel sits with a stinging burn. He would have stayed in bed if he weren't sure, but since Zonda forced him out of the hut earlier for the odd story, it should be safe to walk around without causing more damage to his chest. He grabs his stick and leaves the hut. A stool at the entrance is a good spot to watch the sleeping village. He can't go further anyway. This pain is atrocious when he is on his feet for too long. He sits on the stool and takes a look around.

It's calm, peaceful. The chill in the air is delicate. You can pick out the distant cricket chants if you hearken. Joel looks up. The stars have drawn many figures in the blue sky. The slow clouds cover them and reveal a different beauty when they pass.

A tear drops onto Joel's cheek. It is on nights like these that he and Princess play their usual game when he comes home after school. They challenge themselves not to laugh at the other after a series of grimaces. Joel smiles at the sky. He can't understand how someone can be so cute and so ugly at the same time. She is master at these grimaces, simply grotesque. And Joel always ends up cracking up, despite him having the upper hand when the game begins. His smile fades. What has he done? Joel slowly lays his head on the wall of red mud, his eyes fixed on the sparse, drifting clouds. She is out there, alone.

The dark-blue night pales, and stars can now be counted. Someone leaves the neighboring hut with a calabash in hand. Joel slowly opens his eyes. It is Old Paapa. He is rinsing his face. Maybe Joel hears wrong, because it is just a numb stare directed at a shape wrapped in patterned cloth, but it seems like a thank you when the old man looks up to the sky. A thank you with a smile. He watches the old man approaching. Old Paapa stands before Joel and looks down at him. He touches Joel's forehead with his index finger and says, "This ... is your world."

Alertness takes a moment to kick in. There is actually some-one in front of Joel, and he just said something. "What?"

"Do you think worrying will bring her back?"

The haze is brief before Joel realizes Old Paapa is talking about Princess. "No."

"Then why do you do it?"

"She is my sister," responds Joel, still trying to grasp the mean-ing of these strange, almost preposterous questions.

"If she is so important, why don't you take action to get closer to her?"

"What do you mean?" Joel pauses.

"You are your world. Be careful what you think," says Old Paapa.

Joel cannot get more confused than he is right now. Mouth agape, he pauses for a moment. "What I think?"

"Every creature of nature is surrounded by an energy that defines it and affects its surroundings. I felt yours from my hut. Worrying will do nothing but deepen the pit between you and your sister."

"What can I do? You told me not to move because I'm wounded."

"So, you worry." Old Paapa smiles and levels down to Joel's eyes. "You know, the gorilla, when he is hungry, just looks for a tree and eats the fruit. The elephant, when he is hungry, just looks for a tree and eats its leaves. If there are no leaves on that tree, he moves to another tree. The lioness, when she is hungry and sees that her prey is not reachable, looks for different prey and gets it anyway. She doesn't know about *if*. She doesn't know her children won't eat because the prey was surrounded. She doesn't know worry. She just knows and is certain of one thing: she will get food, because this is what she wants."

Joel stares at Old Paapa. Yes, he can. He *can* get more confused than he already was. His brain just froze. Joel is completely lost in these words. He knows Old Paapa is speaking his language, but something is wrong. Why does it seem like he is just mixing words?

"What are you trying to tell me?" asks Joel.

"Start thinking about what you want, not what you don't," says the old man, standing back up.

"I want to get my sister back."

"Then stop wasting time, and let's start."

*

Joel is sitting by his hut, legs stretched, palms joined on his thighs. Old Paapa covers his naked torso with a yellowish cold mud. It will ease the transition, he tells him. Joel glances at the old man and looks back down. Trying to make sense of this discombobulating person might be pointless, Joel thinks. There is no need to ask what he means; there will be another tangled response. Better let him do his thing, recover quickly, and say his good-byes and thank you. Old Paapa makes him eat a mixture of green leaves and grass. Joel's scrunched-up face and slow mashing say plenty about the taste of this quaint, grainy goo. The old man urges him to fully swallow. It is not to be played with in the mouth. The struggle between gulping and vomiting is harsh, but Joel pulls off the feat and shows his greenish tongue to Old Paapa, who wants to verify it. Regret about the choice to agree to all of this is already filling Joel's mind.

After a few moments sitting in the grass, a strange feeling comes over Joel. His concern requires movement, but he can't. He tries to get up, but it seems he only has control over his arms. Panic is about to reach its peak when Old Paapa comes back from his hut and holds him still.

"Don't." Old Paapa repositions him. "Your legs are no longer in charge. You will use their energy to take care of your chest. Now, try to remember how you were before this pain."

These are not mixed words. Joel did understand the sentence, and it genuinely doesn't make a spark of sense. He cannot ignore it. He cannot ignore this old man's words. His whole lower body is irresponsive. What will it be next? His heart stopping?

"Old Paapa, how will I do that?" he asks in a low tone of concern, stating how ridiculous he thinks this sounds.

"I'm sure you'll figure that out if you want to fully recover from this wound," responds the old man, heading for his hut.

*

Morning comes soon enough to the village, already awake, with half-sleeping children going about their chores. Some adults are leaving for the forest, while others prepare and arrange things in the court of sand. Everyone seems preoccupied with something, ignoring Joel by the hut. The few pausing to look at him when they pass and the discomfort of his uncontrolled posture are all he needs now, as if the pain and toil of constantly trying to keep his chest up and spine straight were not enough. Most of them stop briefly, but their long eyeing feels like they have never seen someone behave like this. Children sometimes give Joel a smile and move on. Joel can't smile. The muscles assigned for that have something else to care about.

The pain in his chest is becoming bothersome and seems to intensify. Joel has trouble staying still, and with his hands on the ground, he attempts to stand upright. One wrong move and he might fall on his side. Old Paapa already warned him that it was the last time he straightened him, and if Joel bends or falls, his chest might worsen. So here he is, prisoner of his own legs, trying hard not to tip over. And he is supposed to have his hands free from the ground and joined on his thighs. If he dares shift, there is no doubt his temple will slam into the grass.

"You'll never be able to heal if you keep disturbing yourself."

Joel levels his eyes to Zonda crouching before him.

"What do you want me to do?" The frustration escapes Joel's voice. "Your crazy old man put me in this situation, paralyzing me and feeding me grass. He thinks I'm some rare breed of mutton or something. I never should have agreed to this."

Zonda smiles. "Your thoughts are scattered, and complaining won't help. Whatever you do, you aren't leaving this grass any-time soon. Try to follow what he told you."

"What, remembering how I was before the pain?" Joel looks back at Zonda after stabilizing himself once again. "If this isn't the talk of a crazy man, what else could it be? He should have told me that before making me sit, and I would have found the closest exit from this village. My chest is hurting so bad. If that's not enough, my butt is starting to hurt too."

"He saved your life," says Zonda. "I don't think he would've told you something he doesn't know."

"Then how? How can I do that?"

"Everything is accomplished by one process."

"What?" Joel gives his attention to Zonda. Maybe there is some sense to all of this.

"Silent demand," says Zonda. "Forget about your surround-ings. Focus, and state what you want."

"To whom?" Joel squints.

"To yourself."

A brief silence, then a gasp of pain and disappointment. "You ate way more grass than me, I think. Next time he comes, I won't eat it," says Joel, looking back at his arms to maintain himself.

"Then you're never going to leave this ground."

"Okay, I'll try."

"Don't try, do it," says Zonda, standing up.

He is left on his own yet again, dangling on his waist and occasionally glancing at the villagers passing by. He can't keep doing this. Zonda is right about one thing: Joel is not going anywhere with these loose legs, and no one is to say how long this will last. His only choice is to try to focus, make this "silent demand." As silly as this sounds, there are no other choices to pick from. It's either that or he worsens his condition.

Joel closes his eyes. The pain, the feeling of bending to the left, forces them to instantly open. Nothing seems different. The burn and swarming persist, but he is still straight. Joel closes his eyes once more. He keeps them closed despite the urge to open them. *Forget everything*, Zonda said. He has to try. His flickering eyelids remain shut long enough for this bending feeling of left and right to sink into his preoccupation. He doesn't realize the noises have faded when the need to check on his hands is gone. He can still feel the pain, but it is now part of this dark place with flashing white spots around him. He's forgotten about it.

Old Paapa notices Joel sitting still this morning. The old man approaches and delicately removes Joel's hands from the ground to join them on his thighs. He feeds him the bowl of green mixture, and a constant gulping follows, with no expression indicating taste. Joel is gone, and the old man examines his neck and chest with satisfaction.

The bowl of green comes every morning. Old Paapa cleans Joel and reapplies the yellowish mud before he leaves for other activities. Joel's wound grows less visible as the days pass. He is now a breathing statue, with a relaxed face and a dried tear down his right cheek.

When Old Paapa crouches before Joel to examine him on a sunny afternoon, he smiles and looks at Zonda by his side. The curious have gathered to observe the young man. Children who usually run to Old Paapa when it comes to checking on Joel won't miss today. They constitute most of this small crowd. The excitement on their faces is noticeable yet silent. Zonda bends to verify and smiles.

"This is fast."

"Yes," says Old Paapa.

"How?"

"There is a moment in his life he likes the best. He's living it in a loop."

"What do we do?"

"We wake him up." The old man lays a palm on Joel's back. "Hold here. We have to make sure his body gets a smooth transition."

"Okay," says the djinn, holding Joel's neck.

"Come back, son," says Old Paapa.

The villagers stare at the unresponsive young man.

"Hey, wake up," calls Zonda.

Joel opens his eyes. He first has to find himself, then identify the blurry faces before him: Old Paapa, Zonda, and many others he doesn't recognize. There seems to be a particular interest, especially the children in the front row, smiling at each other and looking at him. Is it his sitting on the grass? They stopped to give him this weird gaze when he was still trying to steady himself, but not that many at once. Speaking of steady, his hands are on his thighs, and he doesn't feel the slightest shake from his waist.

"I can see your trip was rewarding." Old Paapa continues the examination. "You didn't want to come back?"

Joel finds his chest and touches the faded scar. He turns to Old Paapa with wide eyes. So that was it. This strange feeling of nothing—feeling normal. The pinch and strong pain are gone. That's what was so different when he opened his eyes.

"Yes, I've noticed." Old Paapa smiles at Joel. "A very good recovery. I wasn't expecting this so soon."

It wasn't the crazy talk of some old man. Joel can't quite believe it. Apart from a few tingles, the pain in his chest has vanished.

"How long have I been gone?"

"Eight sunrises," responds Zonda.

"We're not there yet," says Old Paapa. "Your body has to solidify."

Eight sunrises. Joel connects the dots. That's long. That's way too long. *Princess.*

"I'm fine, Old Paapa," says Joel, laying his hand on the grass to stand up. The atrocious strike feels like a slashing under him. He loses control of his words and stops for a second before his screams take over the whole village. Joel rolls on the grass in unbearable pain. Villagers are laughing. Children are compelled to hold their bellies, mocking Joel. That's all they were waiting for. "Butttttttt" is the most prominent word in Joel's long shriek.

"Secondary effect of the cure," says Old Paapa. "You'll be fine. And don't worry about your legs. They'll come back."

Joel's ears are plugged by his own screech. It feels like needles piercing his behind. Everyone leaves him moaning on the grass. He needs some alone time to calm down, the children are told, but they can't help themselves at the uncontrolled sounds. The severe cramps make Joel roll for hours before any form of relief occurs.

At night, he can't sit to listen to Old Paapa's teaching. He can barely listen to him. He lies on his belly, his eyes directed at the old man and the quiet circle. The only way to appease these constricted spasms is to lift his waist off the sand at times. When this happens, no villagers will venture in his direction. Old Paapa's teaching is too important to try to contain an inevitable guffaw and miss a word.

Drums resound. It's time for dancing. Some people approach Joel with bright faces. Replying with genuine smiles is impossible in his current situation. He can only fake them.

*

Joel sits with extreme care in the morning. Moving is a luxury. He wants to believe he is okay and this is just temporary, but why does it feel like he just traded one pain for another? He knows there is improvement, otherwise a stool wouldn't cross his mind. He felt like dying the day before when he budged from the grass. He can feel his toes now. Not the big ones.

Bending them is a whole other useless fight. Old Paapa said to be patient. There is no need to force it. He has plenty of time to look around, watch these people go about their daily activities. The children look so happy, helping their parents, playing in the middle of the court. They seem to be doing everything together, sharing, ignorant of anything but their contagious smiles.

Old Paapa massages his legs every morning. Joel also has to stretch many times in the day. He has made friends. They sometimes come and drag him from his stool to the center of the court, sit together, and speak a language strange to him. Why do they sit in a circle and extend their legs for the bottom of their feet to touch? Why do they hold hands for so long? Maybe it's a custom they picked up from their parents. Or it's just the way they play. Joel has no clue. The joy emanating from them, on the other hand, he can grasp. It's hard to follow in their small space if he doesn't fold his legs. He is taller than them. Listening to their laughs and giggles and looking at them makes him momentarily forget his pain.

The stick helps Joel get about. He can't go too far; his lower body fatigues quickly, but he can walk in the village, and no one seems to bother. He has been in a village before, his mother's. From what he has seen so far, the only thing common with what he knows is the name. Calling it a village might not even be the right word. Joel's guess is limited. Whatever he sees here is new to him.

It looks like a thick, curved band of sand and grass bordered by round huts. The huts, with distinct motifs on their walls, are just close enough to be neighbors and tend to form small curves at each side of the band, every five huts or so. The huts, now that he has repeatedly seen them, appear to have been masterfully built, or should he say built at exact dimensions one from the other. He wonders if this is mud. Courts are many and run along the band, separated mostly by the gathering of the villagers. The biggest one is where Old Paapa does his teaching, where everyone gathers at night. Beyond the curved band is the forest, just a few steps past the rows of huts. Joel hasn't managed to reach the limit of the village yet. He will have to walk farther than he usually does if he is to see any end.

The treatment and exercises of Old Paapa are improving his condition rather more quickly than he imagined when he first felt this acute butt pain. Still not fast enough. He is not sure if it's the constant thoughts of recovery Old Paapa asks him to entertain, the massages, the ointments, or the combination of it all, but he won't stop until he is completely healed and has regained full control of his legs. He would have called Old Paapa senile a few days ago, but this thought left his mind when he touched the faded scar on his chest. Many things the old man says and does don't seem to make sense, no matter how he chooses to approach them, but Joel is getting better, and that's what matters now. Every day here is one away from his sister, and who knows at this point if his chances of finding her are down to nil. No, they aren't. They can't be. Whatever may come, he will find her. The only thing keeping him from making any irrational decision is the help Old Paapa proposed if he can walk without a stick.

He starts noticing a scent when the pain begins to lessen. It's a rather thin and delicate, flowery perfume, probably coming from a nearby cultivation or maybe the trees. This enduring scent is only overtaken at midday or night, during cooking time. Whatever waft Joel is smelling every day is always delicious, or rather, soothing.

Joel spends most of his time with Zonda, learning new things about the village when the need arises. He mostly follows him around and assists if the activity doesn't require strain on his body. A walk in the forest pauses at a shy waterfall when Joel asks Zonda the whereabouts of this stable noise that has been following them for quite some time. He can only contemplate the flow of water washing down the big rocks and tree branches extending a bit too far, the lush green following the current, speckled near the source with resilient sunrays. This is where they get the water for the village, Zonda tells him.

Below are a few women dipping their buckets into the stream, speaking their dialect. Zonda warns to be careful. The roots at the edge are slippery. A fall from this height can be fatal. Joel's focus is on what he sees around, this astounding view, this appeasing feeling just looking at the crystal flow, the people underneath, their movements. It looks like each of their steps is carefully taken. It's not caution. The stream is calm and far from deep. They behave as if they were approaching one of their elders. It's all quaint to Joel, captivating in a way. And what is this gesture every time they meet someone? A palm on their chest, with the word *Ubuntu*. He just heard it when a woman with an empty bucket joined the others near the stream. "Let's go." Zonda taps him on the shoulder. They have many things to do today. Gathering fruits, how exciting.

The walk is not long. Zonda always does the climbing, and Joel picks the falling fruits. Zonda has a bag today. He is not thrilled with the impact of the soil on the fruits. Apparently, it softens them. Joel is supposed to catch them in their fall, but most find their way to the ground first, which is not productive, according to the djinn. Only Zonda and his people know the difference. The fruits taste the same to Joel, whether caught in free fall or slammed onto the soft soil. Again, he doesn't know this fruit and has never tasted it before. They call it *naiim*, one of their delicacies. A fruit resembling passionfruit in size, yellowish-green with a velvety feel to the touch. The skin is a little bit thick but edible, as the villagers indulge in it often. The taste does not compare to anything his palate remembers, but it is rather delicious. Joel has free time to spare, and it will be double the boredom to watch someone else get fruits. The only thing he hears from the djinn climbing up is not to go too far.

He couldn't even if he wanted to. His legs perform okay, but he gets tired with the extra effort. And without the stick, the pain on his waist slowly intensifies, until he loses the strength to hold himself straight. So "don't go too far" doesn't apply to him. He advances lazily, looking at the trunks with their rough textures, the tall branches and their leaves lightly dancing around. This constant noise is faint but still present. They are not far from the waterfall. He didn't hear it the day before. This must be a different place for the same fruits. It's all so confusing. As soon as they leave the village, everything looks the same, except when they transition from a dense place to a wider, clearer area.

Joel makes sure not to veer from his straight path, so he will just have to turn around and follow his trail to Zonda when he is ready. How they find their way in a place like this is a mystery to him. He is allowed to wander off from the village, but he never leaves without Zonda—until he is ready to leave for good. Looking up, he sees the naiims. He will have to tell his companion about this tree. That's one of his tasks. Look around with Zonda when they reach an area, and find the trees bearing the most fruit. Only abundant trees should be harvested. A shadow on the trunk. It wasn't here. Or was it? Joel moves his hand. It's not his. How did it appear here? The question quickly sinks into a void when Joel slowly turns to his left. He didn't hear a sound of movement, a noise, nothing. The waterfall is constant, but Joel should have heard something if someone is this close. A man stands before him, his serious gaze pointed down at Joel.

Joel is shocked before he recognizes the tall man. The one who protected him from those creatures after he ran away from the bus. By no means does his fixed stare look friendly, so Joel dares not to speak.

"Is he leaving?" asks the man, looking behind Joel.

"No," says a recognizable voice.

Joel turns to see Zonda with his bag of fruits.

"So what's he doing here?" asks the man.

"He was with me. He doesn't know the limits. Come," says Zonda, walking away with Joel. "I told you not to go too far."

"I wasn't," says Joel.

"Stay within sight range, I meant."

Joel gives a last look behind at the man staring with his intimidating eyes. "He is the one who saved me."

"I know," says Zonda.

"Who is he?"

"Kobile, one of our warriors. They protect the village and its borders."

"From what?"

Zonda throws a quick glance at Joel. "You should know."

"I never see him in the village."

"They rarely come, only to see family." Zonda extends his hand for Joel to take direction. "They make sure we don't offend other tribes and they don't offend us. They also get food for the village."

"I didn't get the chance to thank him," says Joel.

"Your being alive is his reward. Just don't go to the limits. They have orders. We're lucky we met one of our own."

"Were you following me?" asks Joel.

"I was looking for you. It's time."

"For what?"

"Work."

As if whatever Joel has been doing until now doesn't fall into the same category. "What work?"

They make a stop in the village for the bag of fruits and head to an isolated place of deadwood.

*

Now that Joel doesn't need a stick, his tasks have grown heavier. He has quickly learned to appreciate gathering fruits. It's the only moment when he can rest and relax. Delivering logs to the village is what he endures with Zonda, who is clearly used to it. Joel might be the only one who considers it toil. Most of the people his age perform the same task from different logging sources, many without even showing signs of fatigue. The deadwood does feel lighter in these people's hands. It takes him twice the time to deliver them and back. Even Zonda, who is smaller, carries more than Joel could handle. He can understand they have been doing it from an early age, but this ease with which they carry the heavy wood is dazzling to him. Zonda doesn't even bother to glance at Joel's struggle. Only at times does he arrange an unbalanced log in Joel's pile.

Joel finds Zonda by a dead tree on his return from the village. Joel's exhaustion shows on his face.

"Come, sit," says Zonda. "Looks like you need it."

There's no need to say this twice. The leg pain is gone, and he can walk without any hindrance, but this log-lifting is extremely tiring. Joel sits on the grass and sweeps the blanket of sweat from his forehead. He takes a long, deep breath and feels the tension from all this lifting slowly dissipating. Only a few slivers of wood on Zonda's skin will tell you he has been working. He is calm, his forearms rested on his knees, looking at the soil.

"I was meaning to ask you ..." Joel contemplates the lightly slanted terrain of deadwood before him. "Are you the only one here?"

"You mean the only djinn or the only one of my kind?" asks Zonda.

"Both." Joel's tone suggests uncertainty.

"In the village, yes. I'm the only nonhuman here. Elsewhere, like me, I don't know."

Zonda lays his hand on his chest when a young man who came out from the woods salutes him before grabbing some of the logs. Joel seldom sees him here, but this must be his shift.

"I thought Ubuntu was a king."

"Why do you say that?" asks Zonda.

"Everyone says, 'Ubuntu,' with one palm on their chest when they meet others. You never told me it's a salutation."

Zonda smiles. "It's not. It means 'I am because you are.' It signifies deep respect."

The look Joel gives Zonda has become a standard one of puzzlement, so the djinn shakes his head. "I can't explain that one. You have to feel it. If you're keen, you'll understand when the time comes."

It's the second time he's heard "figure it out yourself" from Zonda. The first time was when Joel asked about this "thought of healing." Zonda spoke one incomprehensible sentence after another until he gave up and said the same thing he said today: "If you are keen, you'll feel it." What does that even mean?

Zonda looks down at the soil near Joel's foot and makes a subtle head movement. "You're a lucky man."

Why Zonda will say something like this is beyond Joel, but he decides to check at his feet. He notices nothing but a tiny lime-green plant. He has seen many throughout the day, and this is no different. Maybe Zonda is pointing at something else.

"The plant?"

Zonda nods.

"What about it?"

"It's rare to spot one." The djinn lightly brushes one of the few delicate leaves with the back of his index finger. "Most of us live and die without seeing it. Many don't know they exist. One day they're here. The next day they aren't. They seem like they'll grow into trees, but no. That's about their full size. It's said they represent the very essence of life."

Joel takes a hard, long look at the boring, insignificant plant. Nothing seems special about it. He would have passed it ten times and never paid attention.

"Chop it off," says the djinn.

After all he just said, this is the last thing Joel is expecting. The doubt on his face when he turns to Zonda confirms it.

"Go on," says Zonda.

The plant is quick to give up its fragile upper body to a steady pinch. Attention is at its peak before Joel raises his eyebrows at Zonda when nothing appears different, unless you count the halved plant. Zonda makes the same subtle head movement toward Joel's feet for Joel to look. Joel brings his face closer to the soil, as if it were too far a distance to believe whatever happened during the short time he turned to Zonda. His mind reels between trying to make sense of it and the bewilderment of this sight. He did chop it off and still has proof between his fingers. Only he never touched it. That's what appearance suggests.

Joel does not break his gaze this time when, once again, he chops the plant close to its roots. The moment seems frozen as he witnesses the plant growing in all its majesty before his eyes. The stems slowly push up and bend. The leaves gradually take shape and blossom, green as ever, tiny, beautiful. Joel turns, silent, to his companion. An explanation is required.

"Don't look at me. They've always been like this."

"They don't die?" Joel asks.

"Not this way," responds Zonda.

"The children of Odum." Old Paapa's steady voice comes from near the pile of logs. "To kill them, you have to destroy Mother Nature herself. Their very roots are forest trees. Ancestors say they are all connected to Odum. They are the ones who tell him if Mother Nature is stable. They are the ones who have stopped him for ages from taking action over us." His almost lingering approach stops a few feet from Zonda. "As time drifts, there are fewer and fewer of them. A tiny plant, the unseeing will say. Yet a plant that allows life to exist."

"Old Paapa," says Zonda, casually standing up. Joel follows.

"I thought you had to help the others carry the deadwood."

"Yes. We were taking a small break," responds Zonda.

"How many times did he chop off?"

"Twice," responds Zonda.

"Then you'll have to plant two trees; walk with me." Old Paapa turns away.

Joel taps Zonda's arm and leaves with Old Paapa in the direction of the village.

"Tell me, how did you end up with this precious amulet on your neck?"

He was wondering when Old Paapa would help him with his sister, since he has been walking on his own without fatigue or discomfort for three days now. Joel explains in detail how he got the djinn's amulet. His grandmother, the certain death he escaped from his house, how the djinn who lived in his bedroom since he was a kid saved Joel's life by giving up his; how he met his best friend Roland's guardian, Bredou, the man with two silent djinns who only takes food for compensation. The man who told him to head for Dosoville if Joel were to find any clue about his sister. Only Joel never made it to Dosoville. He tried to warn the people on the bus of the danger ahead of them and had to flee as a result. Joel explains how he ran for his life after the bus and how everything went dark when he met the tall man who protected him, the man he came to know is called Kobile.

"So this djinn who saved your life told you to seek the Djek-oulé stone," says Old Paapa. "This is a forbidden stone. You won't be able to approach it."

"Why does everyone keep saying that?" Frustration slips into Joel's voice.

"Because it's true. Whoever told you that before knows the despair this stone brings."

"What's so important about this stone?" Joel stops. "Why can't I approach it? I don't understand."

"It's not the stone, my son. It's what lies beyond. For centuries, countless powerful warriors have tried to bring what's out there, but none ever came back."

"Old Paapa, my sister is alone somewhere. You told me to be patient, and you taught me many things that I'm grateful for, but I can't … I have to find her. I have been patient enough."

"I know, my son." Old Paapa lays a hand on Joel's shoulder. "There might be a reason this djinn gave his life for you. We will visit the shaman. Come."

"The shaman?" asks Joel.

"The one who knows if you can go or not. You need his approval to begin this journey."

It's the only hut isolated from the curved band of sand and grass forming the village. Joel never made it this far in his convalescent dawdles. And since he first woke up here, he has seen no one use this path. That might be the reason why there are so many eyes following him and Old Paapa when they cross one of the courts for the road of weeds to the shaman's hut. His startling is barely noticeable when a stick of wood ignites by itself in front of the small hut of intricate motifs moments after they arrive.

"Stay here," says Old Paapa, bending at the entrance of cloth.

Joel doesn't wait long, staring at the mysterious fire. The old man shows his head and beckons him inside. Small flames illuminate this eerie dwelling full of bizarre objects. Joel has to step carefully not to kick one of those small sculptures of many shapes with large heads creeping over the hard floor. Sculptures of wood. Though some of them seem to have been painted with bright colors, most have just kept their deep-brown origin.

A dark old man, sitting with legs crossed on a piece of cloth, wears on his neck the same torus Old Paapa drags with him. The carved patterns feel different, but this piece of polished wood is definitely the most prominent object on the shaman's neck, among others. His scrawny hands and bony face indicate someone who has not eaten for days, yet his piercing regard doesn't give any sign of disease or starvation. If anything, he looks healthy. The washed olive-green robe between his crossed legs is a tad too big for him and allows only his heels and feet to be visible.

Old Paapa asks Joel to sit before the bald man. The beaming from his eyes is so long, pressure quickly builds up. Joel has to blink away at times, with the shaman gazing on his face like a statue. He then grabs Joel's hands and examines his palms. He touches his neck and feels his chest. The shaman retracts his hands and looks at Old Paapa.

The quiet is so deep and incommodious, Joel can hear the short sigh from Old Paapa. He is outside an instant later, on the first signal from Old Paapa to follow him after an "Ubuntu" directed at the shaman. Whatever happened inside didn't go well. Joel knows that much. The silence of Old Paapa on their route to the village speaks plenty. It doesn't matter. Joel has already made up his mind. He cannot stay one more day. The nearest bus station first, then Dosoville.

"What did he say?" Joel ventures.

"Your chances are too slim. You'll die if you try, and anyone you approach will undergo the same fate."

"I'm leaving tonight, Old Paapa."

The old man stops and turns to Joel. "You don't know where it is. Where will you go?"

"Dosoville."

"My son." Old Paapa lays a hand on Joel's shoulder. "You will never find the stone on your own. You have no chance at all."

"Then help me ... please."

"Come. Sit, my son. Sit. Listen. If you force your way down this path, you will die."

"I don't care about myself. My sister deserves to live."

"What about you?" asks Old Paapa.

"I made a mistake. If I am to die, so be it. She can't pay for what I have done."

"This is what you think? You think you made a mistake. There are no mistakes, Joel."

"Old Paapa, she's out there." Joel stretches his arm. "I have to go. Help me."

"I can't, my son. What if you fail? What about the people you'll kill in the process? Have you thought of that?"

"I won't approach anyone. If I fail, I'll die alone. Trust me ... please, Old Paapa." Joel's eyes are moist. Maybe it's the uncertainty. Maybe it's the words of Old Paapa. But leaving knowing his chance of finding Princess could be close to none deeply troubles him. Anything he can get before his departure might be decisive in his search.

"Calm down, my son." Old Paapa pauses. "Calm down. I'll tell you a story. There exists a world, a wonderful world where all people of nature dream to go. A world of unimaginable beauty, where flowers have colors still unknown. Where the air is so pure and the water so clear that people have the lives of trees. A world where harmony and respect for nature is the key to life. A world where all is one.

"Some call it Paradise, others, the Pure World.

"It is said that people of this world talk to trees and animals. They have knowledge that has been lost to us since the very first generation with tools, the knowledge to harness the tremendous force of Mother Nature and the Great Void. It is said that they can move mountains and have mastered life itself. Their healing expands far beyond what we know. Their power and strength are far beyond sorcery. Their ken of Mother Nature is unmatched.

"Every creature knows them, honors them, and gifts them.

"It is said that the passage to this place is hermetically sealed, and the knowledge about its location is bestowed on a very few. Only those who possess the language of trees can enter this world.

"One king blessed by Nyame the sky god received the language of the trees. Guided by the torus and the golden monkey, he located the passage to this world and disappeared for three years. When he came back, he was mighty. He had a spirit on his left shoulder, a powerful spirit named Korokou, who made him one of the most feared kings of his time. He reigned over a hundred kingdoms.

"When he realized that he had failed to harness the power of the spirit for the true purpose given to him by Nyame, he decided to let no one near it, because we weren't ready mentally to guide others in peace. He cursed it and hid it somewhere no one would ever be able to come back from. He took his life and his only son's a few days later. Some say the spirit drove him mad. A few thought he became wise before leaving his body. But all remembered how devastating he was.

"What lies after the Djekoulé stone is very old and powerful. All those who have tried to approach it have failed. People so strong you won't be able to breathe if you stand near them.

"I know you want to save your sister, but you'll have to journey in the forest of wisdom, and no one has ever returned from this place. And even if you could, reaching this forest will mean traveling its sole path, heavily patrolled by the warriors. They will kill you without hesitation if they catch you. And there is the bridge. The only link to the forest. The totems of Goumiran will expel your spirit from this space as soon as you set foot on the bridge. It is said they allow only one person to the forest of wisdom every century or so. No one knows exactly when they open their eyes for this to happen, my son."

Old Paapa leaves Joel in the thick grass by the trees and enters the village. His vague staring at the dirt and green blades between his legs long after Old Paapa is gone stops when he recalls that he is in the middle of the road. Joel stands up with a quick brush of his behind and walks away, maybe someplace where calm, with a breeze, might be of support.

The stream at the edge of the village runs even slower far from its source. It reflects the trees on the other side, more beautiful as sunset nears. It seems the best place to spend his last moment here, in this village with the people who saved him. The people who cared for him. He would have shown his gratitude if he could. Given a thank you for all they have done for him. But any word could tip them on the direction he will take tonight. He doesn't want to lose his life before even starting this journey. He has to prepare. When the stars rise, he will be leaving for the forest of wisdom.

*

There is not much to grab on to for defense. The knife Old Paapa sometimes uses for the concoction of Joel's medicine could be useful. Maybe the machete at Old Paapa's hut. But Joel doesn't want to draw any attention and surely not awaken or alert anybody. Whatever he finds in his room will have to do. He wears his old clothes, which have been cleaned since the third day he was in the village, and shoves the knife into an old bag of braided cords.

"You ready? Let's go."

Joel's eyes snap to the entrance, only to see Zonda. His heart almost pops out of his chest.

"Zonda, how did you …? No, I can't. I have to do this on my own."

"Let's go," repeats Zonda.

"Look, I'm putting everyone around me in danger. I can't risk your life. You can't be near me. Try to understand."

"Do you know the place?"

"The forest of wisdom," Joel answers.

"Do you know how to get there?" Zonda asks.

It clicks. Old Paapa said the forest of wisdom, but he never actually showed the direction. Joel's guess would be the path the warriors patrol the most, but to which extent should he follow it? Which turn should he take? He has absolutely no clue. "No."

"Do you want to die before getting there?" Zonda's blank face comes nearly as an insult.

"No."

"Let's go." The djinn turns away.

"Okay." Joel hurries to the door.

"Leave all of this here. Where you're going, a knife won't be of any help. And take off your shoes."

CHAPTER 9

A Dire Path

The direction in Joel's mind, the sole path he knows the warriors patrol the most, is not the one Zonda takes. They should be heading north, but even in this opaque night, Joel can clearly see the djinn has taken another way, an exit via the second court, opposite Joel's assigned hut.

He follows the djinn with the least noise he can produce, between trunks somewhat silhouetted by the moon and the cold blades of thin grass, dirt, and debris under his feet. Zonda's steps are soundless, or Joel's drown them out. Questions rattle Joel about this direction, but speaking here would be risky, especially with his feet already leaving trails of faint but distinct noises. He didn't even realize Kobile was present back at the forest near the waterfall until a shadow on a tree caught his attention. He can't open his mouth, knowing any of these warriors could be in the vicinity.

Joel can't help but notice the crickets' chant growing louder as they sneak through the woods. Zonda doesn't leave the dark of the trees at the sight of the bright field of small lights before them. It becomes clear to Joel. The crickets' asynchronous and overlapped chorus will cover their movement. Though now he questions the accuracy of his assumptions; if those small, bright lights are the creatures making these sounds, they cannot be crickets, and fireflies flash their lights. So they advance by the edge, two rows of trees away from the tall grass bedding the glittering insects. Zonda eschews any light throughout the whole path before they veer again.

Joel sticks as close as he can, about two paces behind his slightly bent companion. Zonda's shoulders are all he really focuses on. The Stygian dimness doesn't allow him to see much other than the field of bright spots on his right, but he can't afford to lose Zonda. The djinn seems to be treading so he can avoid making the slightest noise. Zonda stops at times to give Joel a warning look.

They stop at a tree with an opening in its roots.

"Follow me." Zonda's voice is just loud enough to reach his protégé.

"Wait, where?" whispers Joel.

"Just follow me." Zonda crouches before the opening.

"Where?" presses Joel. "It's a tree, where do you want to go?"

"We're wasting time." The djinn vanishes into the dark of the trunk.

"Zonda?" Joel calls briskly, still trying to whisper. He promptly slides behind the tree, only to see the same rugged trunk. The sudden emptiness of his environs reminds him that he is not safe at all where he is standing right now. Joel takes a quick look around him and gets on all fours to try the opening. Nothing seems to stop him. There's no hitting the inside wall of the trunk. He can still advance. When he gets out, Zonda is standing, waiting for him.

"What took you so long?" says the djinn, turning away. "Follow me."

Joel slowly stands up, agape, as his gaze wanders through his surroundings. Rays illuminate leaves. Birds sing to the clear sky. Trees rise long and large, far taller than where he was a moment ago. Wherever he is, unless he reenters this split, the village is not walking distance from here. That's what the sky suggests.

"I would've never found this place," says Joel in amazement.

"Let's go. We have a long road ahead." Zonda pushes a small branch away.

The djinn's hunched stance has relaxed, Joel notices. It seems the red zone was behind this odd tree he just crawled out of.

He did crawl through a tree, a solid trunk. How is this even possible? Joel can only take it in. There is no making sense of what just happened. Nothing could explain this. Maybe Zonda could, if his explanation were not more puzzle for Joel. But he doesn't look like he is keen to talk about this crazy shift anyway. His priority is to bring Joel to his destination, and Joel can see that, so he follows his companion into this tall forest of widely spaced trees.

Visibility is difficult beyond five steps, with many wild bushes crowding the area. It's mostly one branch sweep after another, but Zonda doesn't only wave them away—he inspects the leaves at times, as if he is reading them for direction.

"How did you know I was going tonight?" asks Joel.

"Old Paapa." Zonda pauses to glance at a leaf and advances.

"I see."

"He can't openly allow you to go. He believes in the trust the djinn had toward you." Zonda bends to cross a taller branch. "Personally, I think you'll die there."

"Geez, don't think. Please." Joel bends for the same branch.

Zonda has been quite bleak since the hut. Maybe it's the circumstances they find themselves in that force Joel to overthink this. Zonda is usually straightforward with his words. Nothing has really changed. But he seems distant. *Perhaps he just needs his focus*, Joel thinks. *Or he doesn't approve of Old Paapa's decision.* He is probably breaking many rules and risking his life and those of the villagers for an outsider, even if Joel has not felt for once treated like one since he woke up in the hut. Or could it be that he believes Joel is throwing his life away?

"Normally it's three sunrises inside the forest of wisdom. I'll be waiting for you at the river."

"How will I know I'm going in the right direction?"

"Ask your way," responds Zonda.

"To whom?" Curiosity pulls Joel closer to the djinn.

"The inhabitants." Zonda examines some bark they paused at and continues on his path. "If nobody wants to help you, you don't deserve to be in the forest, and you'll never find the stone."

"There are people there?" Joel is now walking by Zonda's side.

"No human lives there."

Joel looks at the djinn. "Who?"

"Shh." Zonda halts, with his index finger on his lips. He looks down at nothing, listening.

"What?" whispers Joel.

Zonda gestures with his palm for Joel to remain silent. His head, slightly turned toward his right shoulder, jerks to his left and pauses. Joel stares at his companion, puzzled by this abrupt reaction. Only the slow movements of the higher branches and the far chirping of the birds graze his ears. Yet Zonda is still before him, listening.

"Damn shaman! Ruuun!" The djinn bolts away, leaving Joel a split second to process before the word clicks. Joel breaks in Zonda's direction. The interfering branches crack as he slashes through them, whipping his mouth and his eyes, making him lose control. But he doesn't stop; he doesn't slow down. Joel runs like a crazy man, trying desperately to make up the distance he initially lost with Zonda dashing before him. Ignorant of what's happening and what's behind, he follows the djinn's trail. He can see his back and is slowly catching up, but Zonda is fast, very fast for his height.

Joel throws a look behind when he clears the interminable bushes. It's mostly a daze of green and brown in this rush, but his eyes catch something. Something dark, with red eyes. Two hard shapes with small legs and large torsos disturb their surroundings in their dart toward him. But what flashes is how quickly whatever is behind him is approaching.

"What's that?" Joel screams.

"Fetishes ... guardians of the forest," Zonda throws back.

"What?"

They move with ease between trunks and bushes. This sound pulsing through the forest, this distorted human sound they emit, reaches Joel. He can feel the icy chill running down his spine, his legs already shaking. He doesn't even want to fathom what's on his trail. Joel's ears warn of their proximity.

"Don't let them catch you," Zonda hollers. "They'll chop your head off."

Joel outdistances Zonda.

"Right, right, take the right," yells the djinn.

"They are closing in," shouts Joel.

"We're almost there."

Joel sprints to a bridge he perceives at Zonda's signal. The dark fetish a few paces behind is about to clutch Joel when Joel plunges onto the intertwined lianas. The bridge shakes violently. Joel, on all fours, is forced to make a frantic turn in anticipation. He clearly sees his pursuer, a stiff wooden shape, devoid of the red eyes it flashed a second ago. It stands inert to Joel's panic, tipping to its right and falling from the bridge. Joel follows its fall with his heart pounding and his body trembling before the fetish slams into the roaring river. Joel balances, panting, holding tight to the thick cords.

He can see the wild current flowing under him, his guts wrenching at the distance. He needs a better position, a better grip. The only thing preventing him from meeting the same fate as the fetish is this loose net with large holes he balances on. There is no describing how tight his grip is around the lianas. It feels like one wrong move and the whole bridge could twist, so he keeps on all fours. His feet are unstable. Joel brings his attention to the two pillars of wood planted on the soil before the bridge—the pillars with intricate carvings he passed when diving to keep away from the guardian. Are his eyes playing tricks with the rush of blood in his veins, or did he just witness the carved eyes slowly shut?

"Don't look at them. Go!" barks Zonda.

Joel thinks twice before planting a foot forward. When he turns again in the direction of his companion, Zonda is in freefall, plummeting into the river. His guide, the only person he could rely on, has just vanished into the current. Joel looks up at the land, and his eyes snap to those of the other fetish, glaring at him. Joel exhales and continues his cautious walk.

A sudden disturbance in his grip and under his feet, the hard shake of the lianas, causes him to halt. Joel's right leg drops into one of the large holes, to his fright. He looks back to see the fetish on the bridge, somehow advancing toward him. Joel tussles to pull his leg out of the hole, with the guardian closing in fast, but the shaking sends him back into the trap.

Joel relinquishes the side lianas and forces his stretched arms to the ones far before him. He pulls himself with a grunt out of the hole and rushes to put distance between himself and the fetish, about two feet from him. There is no time for caution.

The hard shape of the guardian remains undisturbed by the trembling bridge. It is relentless. Joel can feel it on his neck, in the tension of the lianas right after he releases them. He can't afford to slip, he can't look back to check, and he can't look down. The other side of the bridge, the tall bushes after the liana ropes, are his only salvation. Solid ground will give him a chance to outrun it.

The disturbing voice pulses by his ears. The fetish is there. It is right there on his back, and Joel is still about three feet from the soil. Maybe it's the whoosh, or the light instantly dimming on his right side, but a quick glance and reflex pulls Joel down with a sharp shriek. The large hand misses Joel by a hair. Joel lurches forward and flattens on the soil, with his arms trying to pull the rest of his body from the bridge. He quickly gets up, drained with exertion and battling to maintain distance.

The guardian doesn't give up. It is chasing the intruder, quickly catching up to him. It swipes Joel off the ground, but upon slamming into the soil, Joel shoots up and runs. He runs as fast as he can, as steady as his body can allow, but it seems pointless. The pulsing is at his back, it's on his head, and Joel's blank mind prevents him from any other thoughts but saving his life. He feels a snapping clutch on his ankle, and before his whole body can react, he is yanked backward. His face slides on the green grass, uprooting a few blades in his mouth. The guardian has caught him. Joel quickly flips and lifts his legs to keep the fetish's face from getting any closer.

It's no use. His shaking legs are slowly bending toward him. The guardian is stretching its hands to Joel's head. Joel, pinned to the ground, fights with all the strength left in his limbs. He holds the palm of the fetish with his shuddering hands and pushes it desperately from reaching his head. He screams and pushes, his eyes shut, his ears vulnerable to the pulsing voice racing through his body, chilling his skin, his senses. Joel screams.

The large palm touches Joel's forehead, the fingers tightening to his temples, pressing his skull. His deafening cry turns dull under the wooden hand. Joel holds the hard wrist, struggling to shake away under the fetish's clench. The scream persists until it stops. There is no movement. The hand on his face is not budging. Joel sharply pulls and jolts his head from the harsh grip. After a frenetic drag on the large shadow over him, Joel stares before him with wide eyes and disturbed, shortened gasps. There lies the fetish of wood, inert, devoid of red eyes, posing with its extended hand like a statue.

His guard remains high, despite the few moments spent staring at it. He has to leave this area. He doesn't know how long it will be before the fetish comes back to life, but his body beseeches him for respite, even if only for a second. He is drained from using his sluggish hands trying to pull himself from the soil. His sharp breathing slowly calms. His slack head meets the grass. It might be true. It might be what briefly crossed his mind on the bridge. But it doesn't make sense. Both fetishes had red eyes, and then no more. But this one is on land, while the other was just after it crossed the bridge. He should leave, before he gets no time to regret his decision to lie on the grass when those red eyes pop back.

The flickering dots on his hands make him pause after he rolls onto his stomach to stand up. Gleaming dust spreads sparsely on his wrists. The green blades next to him present the same properties. Joel slowly rises up. The gleaming particles are not the only things he missed when he was running for his life moments ago. His eyes cannot acclimate to what surrounds him. The curved, twisted trees, the large and strange shape of the plants, the vivid colors of the flowers—this is a forest like he has never seen before. *Is this the forest of wisdom Old Paapa was talking about?*

His gawking ends when he lowers his head to look around him. They are all staring, silent. Are they animals? Some have a resemblance, similarities. A few present the form but don't behave right, afraid and running at the sight of a human. Joel goggles at the masks with long threads suspended in the air, the antelopes, or those resembling antelopes, creatures with limbs he cannot define, animals he fails to recognize or has probably never seen in his life. None of them seems apprehensive. None of them shows any sign of hostility. They just stare, as if it's rare to see something like Joel. A few are leaving their hideout to eye the stranger. *Respect*, Joel remembers.

"Ubuntu." Joel lays his right hand on his chest. "I seek the Djekoulé stone."

No response. No noise. With his arm bare on his chest, Joel keeps eyeing the small group for any sign, anything he could construe as direction, but they don't seem to speak his language. They don't seem to speak at all. They stand quiescent. A white rabbit hops forward, briefly holds his gaze, and then leaves. Joel doesn't need words. It's the only thing that moved in this strange group. His sole chance is to stick to it. But Joel has to go through them, which he hesitantly does as they open up to let him follow the white rabbit. One last glance behind confirms that the guardian is really gone. The small animal didn't wait for Joel. He has to find it.

There, a fluffy ball of white fur hopping and vanishing in a tangled bush. Joel hurries in that direction and reaches the branches. He looks around. There it is, by a curved tree, loping away. Joel follows the rabbit. The white color helps in this deep-brown, green, and yellow forest. He needs to get as close as he can, and running is the only option, but the hanging lianas are an inconvenience, to say the least. One thing he is convinced of: if he loses track of this small creature, he will never leave this place. The rabbit is quick and sneaky, so as soon as Joel perceives it, he rushes after it.

It seems to be pausing before it vanishes again, as if it was waiting for him to catch up. Joel scrambles through the wild leaves and finds himself in a circular space of fresh and decaying short grass, an isolated area bordered by trees. Before him lies a large, polished stone carved with thin and precise symbols on its hard surface. "It's not the stone, it's what lies beyond it," Old Paapa said.

Behind the rock is an entrance to a cave. This must be it. Joel turns to the rabbit and once again places his hand on his chest to give his thanks, then proceeds for the dark hole.

"Don't go inside," a rough voice says.

Joel turns to the fluffy creature after a light jerk. Astonishment and a spark of fear shouldn't be his reaction; dashing away right about now in any given direction is the proper course of action. But with what he has seen, what awaits ahead, he needs to brace himself. How can one prepare for something like this, any of this?

"I have to," he calmly replies before heading into the cave.

Each step is one away from the light behind him. Should he place another foot ahead? He must. There is no other choice if he seeks a chance to save Princess. Joel sees nothing ahead, not a speck. He will need something to rely on for direction; otherwise he will be wandering in a void.

The left wall. The fading rays. The limit between still visible and barely palpable. Joel lays his hand on these ostensibly natural formations. He must keep his arm on it moving forward. Even if he doesn't see, even if he doesn't hear, this rocky sheet will be his guide. So he advances one step at a time, making sure his palm stays in contact with the wall.

The pitch-black, noiseless tunnel presents nothing to Joel when he looks back to check on the far entrance. The round hole of light is gone. Only the smell, his left hand, and his feet propose a sense of earth. Joel continues walking with clearly audible steps.

He doesn't feel it. This immediately seizes his alertness. Joel doesn't feel the wall. It was there a pace before. Joel retreats three more steps when one shows no result. There is nothing. He doesn't feel anything on his left side. The wall just ceased. He was stroking it a second ago. What did he do? He doesn't remember lifting his hand. He can't turn to check. He can't look around. There is nothing to see, nothing to fall back to. If he breaks his angle right now, he will lose his initial direction. Joel keeps his head straight, lowers his left arm, and continues his aimless roaming.

The earthy odor is still present, or is it his brain remembering? No, he is still walking on something. Focus has now shifted to his legs, the only things generating sound as he advances or maybe retreats. He doesn't even know if he is moving. What if he never leaves this area? What if he drifts forever in this dark place? "Clear your mind … calm down." Joel closes his eyes, which makes no difference. "Keep walking," he reassures himself. "Keep walking."

Time seems endless, before a gray dot enters Joel's pupils. Yes, he is seeing something. The dot is growing as he moves his feet. Joel doubles his speed. An entrance, Joel realizes as he draws near. It doesn't take long to reach it. There is no hesitation before he jumps through.

His eyes have to adjust to the gloomy space. The narrow rays forcing their way through the cracks above show a grand room of layered rocks. Humidity has blended with the pronounced dry smell. Faint but constant water drops resonate from the other side, or at least far from him. He perceives sticks stained white on the soil. Squinting quickly allows the picture to clarify. These are bones. He is staring at bones. Limbs are spread all around the room. The confirmation is stark when he jolts sideways in response to the femur at his feet. These are the people who came before him. Something is moving. Something has just lifted from a chair in the middle of the room, which Joel completely overlooked.

"Who dares disturb this place?" A deep voice bounces over the walls.

Waiting for another word would just be silly. Joel's body has already turned for the door before his mind can catch up. His nose faces the wall. It's as if an entrance never existed. He touches the rocky sheet with a sharp gasp. There is no exit. He might actually spray his pants with whatever is ready to leave his body.

"Who dares disturb this place?" the strong voice repeats.

The sweep is instantaneous, and Joel slams into the bed of bones before lifting up from his right leg. Something attached to his ankle drags him upward until his head stops close to the ground.

"It's me, it's me," gasps Joel, hanging in the air. "My name is Kouadio Dominique Joel. I'm sorry, I really didn't want to disturb you."

"Have you come to challenge me?"

"Chal—? No, no, not at all. It didn't even cross my mind." Joel moves his free leg and crosses and uncrosses his arms to prevent the three floating bracelets seeking his extremities from attaching like the first one did. The quartered, skeletal limbs on the soil clearly lay bare what happened to those who came before for a challenge. None of them seems to have succeeded. "I have come to bargain."

"Then die," the voice intones.

"No, wait! Wait!" prompts Joel.

The first slam is against a rocky sheet on his left, then all the way across the room to the opposite wall. The bones' bed comes next, where he crashes into skulls and ribs. When Joel is left hung up in the air once again, the remaining bracelets slide onto his wrists and ankles with no resistance. The mild wooziness and shock have deprived him of any strength to fight. Despite the pain, Joel remains conscious. The bracelets twist on his limbs as they tighten, scraping his skin, squeezing veins and arteries. He feels something more alarming on his chest. His necklace has dug deep into his skin, unable to fall from this position. The gift from the djinn who died for him won't leave his neck with him upside down.

Before he can take another look, Joel is quickly flipped by the bracelets. His head up, his limbs stretched wide, Joel realizes he is about to meet those on the ground.

"Wait! Korokou!" he hollers with wide eyes. "I, I came to offer a deal!"

"I don't make deals with weaklings. You are worthless to me," the cave says.

Joel's limbs are slowly stretching in four directions, and any attempt to bring them closer is pointless. His joints, his skin, his body cry to keep parts together, and only his gritted teeth can be of assistance. "You'll never leave this place if you kill me," Joel finally screams.

The stretching pauses. The water drips. It all becomes quiet again.

"Speak." The voice bounces off the walls.

"Look at all these bones. They're all centuries apart. They've all failed you, and they're probably all stronger than me. You've, you've been waiting for a long time. If you kill me, you'll have to wait another hundred years or more for someone to reach you, if the habitants let him.

"I know that only one should be allowed on the bridge. The guardians chased me to the forest of wisdom. How long will you wait before the totems of Goumiran grant someone else permission to cross again? If they ever do, with the guardians gone? I'm sure you have better knowledge than me about this.

"I'm the only one you have right now. Listen, Korokou, you can kill me and wait. You, you really can … but I just need your help, nothing else. After that, you are free to choose whatever host you will."

"What do you want?"

"My sister is captive of a sorcerer. I'm the only one who can save her, and you're the only one who can help me find her."

"I am a war fetish. I kill. I don't save," the cave says.

"You want out … you can't without a body. I can help. I just need your assistance until I find my sister."

"Only a griot can find your sister."

Joel pauses for a second. Old Paapa didn't speak of this. What's a griot? This is not the time for questions, not while he is about to be dismembered. "Then help me find a griot, and I'll give you your freedom."

"You will die once I leave your body after the bond."

Joel gulps his saliva. "I just want to save my sister."

"So be it," the cave resounds.

"No, ahhh," Joel screeches to the tension of his limbs stretching away from him. "Ko … ahhh, you didn't … get me, that's not—arrhhhhh."

His lids flicker through the excruciating pain. Trying to keep whole is useless at this point. He can control his body no more with the convulsions twenty feet from the ground. He can't keep conscious with his pupils curving into his brain from the tearing sensation.

*

Joel slowly opens his eyes to a roaring sound. The sound does feel very close, maybe right beside him. He lazily blinks, then shoots up when the flash of being pulled apart strikes. Joel frantically turns around, flummoxed, trying to make sense of his surroundings. The river, just three feet away, is as violent as the one he saw from the lianas bridge, with water splashing intermittently on the large, nearly flat stone he sits on. Someone is crouched by the stone's edge with a quiet stare at the spitting flow. Joel recognizes this small stature, this peculiar skin. The djinn glances in Joel's direction, then back to the current.

"Look who's awake," Zonda says neutrally. "You have a strong will."

Zonda, the companion he witnessed diving into a current just like this one, possibly this exact one, since it bears the same intensity. And now that Joel is close, he knows there is no way Zonda could have survived something like this. Not with the visible tips of boulders on the current's surface, splitting the forceful water right after it smashes them.

"Are we …?" Joel hesitates.

"What?" Zonda looks back at Joel.

"Dead?"

The djinn pauses and then turns to him. "You peed yourself."

Joel stares at his torn pants. He can smell the fading stench from where he sits, but he is dry. Did it happen in the cave? It suddenly dawns on him. He is not torn apart. He is out in the open, hearing a din, feeling the flowing air, smelling what could only have been dread in liquid form. Korokou, this invisible thing, this fetish, didn't spread him around in that cave. Where is the cave? Only a towering, crackless cliff with an imperceptible ledge stands behind him. How did he end up here? The burning in his joints and ribs feels very real and forces him to grimace, but his full attention is drawn to the bracelets attached to his wrists and ankles. Strands of white, brown, and black beads of various shapes and forms are woven, somewhat like intertwined hair or thick cords. They are just loose enough to allow for movement.

Joel realizes there are no liquid stains to be seen anywhere near him.

"How long was I out?" He looks at Zonda.

"Three days … You were gone for four."

"*Four days?*" Going through the strange trees of lianas into the dark passage couldn't have taken this long.

"Time has no meaning in this forest," says Zonda.

"And you waited for me," says Joel.

"I had to make sure you were dead before reporting to Old Paapa."

"Thank you."

"Don't thank me. Your sister is still out there." Zonda stands up. "I have to go now."

"What's a griot?" Joel looks up at the djinn.

"A being with the gift to read all lives' paths." Zonda stares at Joel. "Why?"

"Korokou said only a griot can find my sister. He can be of no help."

"He already has. I'll report it to Old Paapa once he is available."

"What do you mean?"

"I was talking to him before you woke up. Something is happening in the village."

"What? Is that because of me?"

"No. People have gathered in the court. Not only our tribe. Warriors from the neighboring villages and some from afar. The last time this happened, there was a sorcerers' war." Zonda looks at Joel.

"Okay, let's go then." Joel contorts to try to push himself up.

"You can't."

"Why?" Joel pauses in surprise. "I got the fetish. They'll let me in."

"They'll kill you on sight." Zonda points to Joel's forearm.

Joel looks at his pale skin. "What's happening to me?" he says with a calm, almost resigned tone.

"The shaman was right. Your body can't sustain the fetish. You're rotting. I can't bring you with me. They'll never risk a villager's safety for you … You broke the rules."

Only a second call forces Joel to look again at his companion. Beside his left eye turning gray, with prominent red veins, Zonda can see, can feel the profound sadness, the dismay permeating Joel. Joel does not keep his gaze for long, but one to two seconds is enough to read him. Joel lowers back his head to his arms, maybe regretting his decision to enter the forest of wisdom, Zonda thinks. Leaving now might seal Joel's fate, but Zonda is compelled to. He was requested by the elders to return to the village. And if they decided to delay the sanctions for what he has done, whatever is happening now is greater than this one's life before him.

"Here." Zonda approaches Joel, pulling a necklace from his head, a long assembly of brown cords with sparse, squarish small beads, woven in thick sewn cloth. The square beads on the string are closely bound next to round and elongated pearls arranged in a repeated pattern. He crouches and lays it flat on Joel's left palm, resting open on his thigh. "Head south. I'll contact you if there is anything for your sister. Try to stick to the wall. You should be okay."

Zonda gets on his feet and walks to the rock's edge. He gives one last look at the young man. "Joel."

Joel raises his head.

"Stay alive," Zonda says before dropping into the river.

"I will," Joel mutters.

Standing up seems like an unreachable feat. A simple movement proves even more burdensome than he thought. His whole body is like another weight he has to drag with him. Joel can observe his strength draining out with his faltering steadiness. He cannot stay here. He cannot die here, Joel reminds himself. This is the impression squeezing his lungs, his stomach, and his back. Their failure to properly operate is a warning. Zonda said to head south, and this is what he will do, even if he has to crawl to get there. Better use whatever little energy he has left to escape this rock before it runs out. Before he is unable to move at all.

Joel winces as he pushes himself up but is constrained to his knees. His breathing is now shallow and stretchy. Joel, on all fours, takes a moment out of exhaustion, out of the intense throbbing meandering his spine and flesh. He stares at his pale hands supporting him, Zonda's necklace clenched in his feeble left fist. He is not dead. He hasn't been quartered. This is a slower, agonizing death. "What are you doing to me, Korokou? This wasn't the deal." Joel struggles to slowly sit once more. With a frail shake of his arms, he manages to languidly bring the necklace to his head and somewhat wear it. He can't die now, not yet. His vision is becoming blurred, his skin drying out. He can barely move without a vein feeling like snapping, a muscle giving up. Joel lugs his heavy body with one hand to the rocky edge and gives himself to the flow.

CHAPTER 10

Watch Me

Try to stick to the wall. Those were the words of his companion, but he can't control this pressure hurling him along the stream. He could be heading straight for a boulder, for all he knows. Between trying to jab his head up for air and the current whirling underneath, Joel's mind reels, his hands flapping desperately for a safer course toward his left, toward the river's edge. Joel is spat out of the waterfall into deep water before he can realize he is no longer in a current.

Joel sinks into the long dive, and there might not be a point of return if he does not act now. The uncertain flailing of his arms and legs is unlike any swimming technique he has been taught during school exercises, but he can see himself moving up. Joel battles to reach the shore with a long, harrowing breath, when he notices his passive right arm drawing along as he crawls, belly flat, on the pebbly mud. It has completely tanned and doesn't show an ounce of life. Joel keeps at it, one pull at a time, until he reaches the closest tree, around fifteen feet from the quiet river. He sits beside it with strenuous effort and slowly lays his head on the trunk. His extended legs slightly apart, hands on the fairly humid soil, he can feel his internal organs struggling, the excruciating pain of blood flowing slowly in his veins.

Eyes half-closed, Joel fights to stay awake. He knows he must not sleep, for sleep itself will be the end of him. His body demands to shut down, but Joel keeps kicking himself where the pain is most piercing. A pain he has no strength to scream about.

Dusk slowly finds Joel lying torpid at the tree trunk, with his chest sparsely paced between breaths. Conserving energy to stay awake is paramount. And now he can only attempt a weak poke in his lower flank to keep the pain vivid and restrain his eyelids from completely closing. What he can see now depends solely on his declining right eye. And he knows that the close waterfall cannot sound this distant.

Was it a deception? Joel should have known. Desperation probably encouraged him to this cave, but he knew somewhat. Old Paapa warned him. Now here he is, pinned to a tree, deprived of anything but his tenuous breathing and tired blinking. He won't be able to go any farther and help his sister. Another poor choice of his. Another after the one that killed his parents and got Princess abducted.

Korokou wants to kill him so he can quickly be free. Of course he doesn't need Joel. Of course he wasn't going to honor their deal. Why would he? Joel is not a warrior. Even a proper challenge, as Korokou requested when Joel entered the cave, was not met. Why would he stay in such a frail body? He doesn't care about Joel at all. He has no interest in whatever they agreed upon. *Maybe there was never an agreement to begin with*, Joel thinks.

There's a blast. Joel weakly jerks his head to look ahead. Another one, a little farther in the same direction. Yes, they are bursts of earth and sand. Branches snapping and slashing away. Voices. People screaming. Roars. Joel can clearly hear them. He can still peer through his one blurry eye. People at war, savagely killing each other behind trees. The explosions continue around at frequent intervals, and not always in his narrow field of view. The night doesn't conceal silhouettes falling on the soil.

Joel notices him, the man standing out of this chaos. The warrior destroying every enemy his powerful fists meet. He wears a golden tissue on his right arm. He is giving orders as he strikes at those who dare charge him with machetes, with swords, with fists. This commandant, this deadly king, suddenly darts in Joel's direction. Wearing a scornful face, spitting a quaint dialect, he walks. No one seems to be able to stop him in his approach. No one can stand before him.

Wavy lights on the battlefield allow Joel to descry a wooden torus strapped to the king's chest, then thin, white ellipses snap his attention to bracelets. But Joel has no time to dwell on the king's wrists for confirmation. He nears, with wide steps, hate emanating from his fierce glare, speaking sounds Joel can only hear. Joel eyes the furious man talking. He slowly raises his left arm to protect his head when the king raises his fist.

"Why did you curse yourself?" Joel understands this sentence before all falls quiet.

Joel lowers his arm. The king has vanished. The night is unchanged.

Someone calls. A voice he can recognize amid anything.

"Mom." The murmur barely escapes Joel's lips. "Mom, where are you?"

It's them. He knows it can only be them, the two silhouettes entering the mist on his left. He can't signal. He can't mouth anything loud enough to reveal his position, to tell his parents he is only a few feet from them. Joel can only watch their backs fade away.

"Mom ... Dad," Joel attempts once more. He leans too far and falls on his shoulder. They are gone. He gazes at the mist, waiting for them to come back, to call again. Someone stands before him. Joel bends his neck. These small feet, this sky-blue gown.

"Princess," Joel breathes out.

"It's okay ... let it go." The little girl crouches next to him.

"No, no ... Prin – ... Princess."

"It's okay." She fades away with a smile.

"No ... no ... no." Joel hauls himself from root to root, peeling underneath, scorching the earth with his powerless fingers. What he seeks is not here. What about the neighboring tree? The one he has to trail for almost five minutes to reach. There is nothing here either. He will look under all of them if he has to, if he still can. They are wild, Old Paapa said, almost pink in color. They scarcely grow under the thickest roots, and even the slightest shade between the myriad pinks means sudden poisoning or slow deterioration of the human bases of life. But when they are used at their exact color, they can help the body heal.

It was fascinating when Old Paapa showed him the sponge-like stem during their wandering for the grass and herbs used for his chest ointment. Stems resembling protuberances under roots in the forest adjoining the village. But Joel didn't really pay attention to the odd, foamy shape. It was mainly what it could do to the body that he was listening to. But he can surely recognize its odd, repulsive form if he sees it.

He is not going to die. No. He is not going to give up just so a fetish can be free. He has something to do, and as long as he can breathe, he will try. Korokou will have to wait until Joel frees his sister. The thick, wet root under the seventh tree seems to hold something. Joel palpates a small protuberance. He can't really see the color with his blurry eye, but the shape approximates what Old Paapa showed him. Joel pulls the stem from the root and swallows it, almost choking with the paucity of saliva in his loose throat. Gulping has never been this painful.

Old Paapa told him to be extremely careful. He told him to walk the other way if Joel ever happened to perceive this kind of shape. The grass of Pougnon, the red grass, the grass that cures the dead. Old Paapa told him to walk the other way, for a single skin contact could be fatal. In all case, things don't look so good right now, so if there is even the slightest chance to recover, he may as well jump on it. Joel slowly rests his left cheek on the dirt, with his numbed lips half open.

The night runs its course, colorless, ready to pass on its moon anytime now, with the root next to Joel's head receding from the dimness it was absorbed in. He can't really sleep. He won't allow himself to. Fear of drifting by when his eye stays shut for too long pinches him to open it. The other cornea, the one beyond his will, flaps its eyelid as it sees fit. The pain did ebb quite a bit since he swallowed the plant, but so did everything else. He might as well be a vegetable left on the dirt. Or is it lack of impetus? He can't even close his mouth. The only thing he still has control over is his right eyelid. This thick root dipping in the soil seven inches before him is the only stimulant he can bargain for every time he commands himself to stay awake. He stares at the root, however dodgy might be these drowses.

The root remains his first sight when he forces his eye open once more. A twitch of his right pinky pushes Joel to pause his daydreaming. He did feel it, the nerve pulling under his wrist bone. It was so blatant, with everything else Joel was experiencing, he completely overlooked it. His entrails seem appeased. Or they are giving up, one after the other. At this point, he doesn't know.

His middle toe just flicked. The toe from his irresponsive leg. Joel blinks, inert, trying to feel if there are changes he didn't pick up on amid these reflexes. Yes, he can tense his right forearm, an unattainable feat moments ago.

Joel lifts his head at dawn to an arm capable of forming a feeble fist. Morning will come soon. He can search for more grass of Pougnon. It's working. Joel can now gulp his saliva without worrying about choking on it. The next abnormal shape he finds twenty trees later has a dry reddish color. He should stay away from it. The rest of the search is to no avail, but it's become much easier to crawl with two arms. Even though he feels some tingling in his right calf, bending the leg is not possible. Twinges are good signs, especially where there were none. Food. He has to find something to eat, with his stomach grinding so harshly. Where can he within this haven of greenery loosely cradling water droplets? "Think, Joel," the young man whispers.

All this time spent with Old Paapa and Zonda clearly wasn't for naught, because he remembers. It might be the situation squeezing his brain out, the dire need for fuel, but Joel remembers. The white sprouts Zonda sometimes plucked from tree bark as they passed along looking for the right fruits to gather. The white sprouts he used as snacks. They were frequent. They stood out, with their color and fibrous shapes. He should seek those. They had a more-than-inconclusive taste when Joel took a bite of one Zonda shared, but it was edible, since the djinn seemed to enjoy it.

There it is. One not far from his reach. He just has to push up with one arm and stretch a little to grasp the sprout. It might be hunger, it probably is, but it does taste good right now, even with the strong sour flavor. And it is quite tender. There's another one on the other side. Joel pushes again to yank it to his mouth. When his hands fail, his teeth aim straight for the bark, kissing it as Joel tries to snap the lime-green-and-white fiber base.

"Think, Joel." Joel is now sitting, back against a trunk, one leg bent toward him. "What else do you know?" There must be more. There is more, when he relives some of the time spent with Zonda and Old Paapa: painkillers. Morsels of tree bark to chew and swallow the juice from. Old Paapa did this frequently. Some of the warriors who came back to the village after duty had those in their mouths. What tree should he use? Old Paapa did not really speak during that time. He was just gathering from what looked like a careful selection and murmuring *thank you* in his dialect, the first word Joel learned in the village. He ought to venture gingerly in this area. He doesn't know which trunk to peel from. The ones with the white sprouts. It clicks. If they offer something to eat, how poisonous can they be?

Joel limps, slanting at times, to the closest tree when he needs a moment of respite. After seeing twice the scornful face of the king who keeps asking the same question, he realizes this must be what his nights have come to: vivid images of a war he knows nothing about. Oddly, the words before the king's question are somewhat starting to make sense. He pauses by a trunk, spits out what he has been chewing for a while, and pulls a replacement from his pocket. It's the last of his peels. His pigment is growing deeper again. He is getting better, so he keeps at it. The other pocket, stuffed with white fibers, has grown light. Only one remains. It wouldn't be a concern if he hadn't left the area they pertain to. He will make it through the day with this one and think about his stomach later.

"You won't die, will you?" A voice whips Joel's head. It takes a second to recognize it, but only because it sounds slightly different from the cave.

"This wasn't the deal. You won't kill me until I save my sister," Joel responds.

"I have no interest in your death," Korokou announces. "Only through you will I be free. This is a normal process, but your body isn't fit for this. You're too weak to bear me."

"Watch me," replies Joel, pulling away from the bark.

"Some of your building blocks are changing. You're showing some resilience."

"I have something to finish."

"I acknowledge your resolve, but it's misplaced. And you're too young for this healing root. How do you know about it?"

"An old man taught me," says Joel.

"You are poisoning yourself."

"Does it matter?" Joel stops. "I have no choice."

"I'm here solely to help you find this griot. After that, you honor your word, or I'll kill you myself."

"You won't have to."

"Joel." Another voice brushes Joel's neck.

"Zonda?" Joel promptly turns to the wide array of trees. "Where are you?"

"In the village," Zonda responds. "You're still alive."

"In the village, how?" Joel pans around, trying to locate the voice. "Is that ..."

"Yes, the necklace I gave you," says Zonda. "Listen carefully. There is a big operation taking place. All the elders and warriors are preparing to strike at someone. I don't know who, but it seems they will attack different places in the country at the same time. Hidden djinns. They need information about a girl who seems extremely important. Go to Yamouego, Blue Bean Cross. One of the operations will take place there tomorrow. Stay out of sight, and do not interfere. When they get what they want, I'll inform you, and you will follow them. Maybe you'll have a chance to reach her location. I won't be able to contact you for a while."

"Why?" asks Joel.

"I have been assigned to coordinate the attacks and make sure the warriors do not lose communication. I'll inform you as soon as I get anything new."

"Okay. Thank you, Zonda."

"Joel, stay out of sight. You're not supposed to be there, and they won't hesitate to treat you as an enemy if they see you. You broke the rules."

"Understood."

"Continue on your left. You are going in the right direction. "

"On my left." Joel turns for a look before reason takes over. "Wait, you can see me?"

"No. I just know where you are."

"You know where I am?"

"No weird questions, Joel, please. Just go," says Zonda.

"Who is that?" asks Korokou.

"A friend," says Joel.

"A djinn is your friend? Times have changed."

"You have been away for thousands of years. Yes, times have changed."

*

At last, a road. A familiar sight after what he knows is weeks spent in the woods, in this village. The heat reflecting off the dried tar is a clear warning, since he walks barefoot. Joel remains on the dirt by the roadside, visible enough for any passerby to stop. Luck seems at play when a vehicle materializes on the horizon moments after he's left the woods. A fancy gray sedan, Joel observes with his hands sticking up. Its approach does not indicate any loss of momentum. The car drives past Joel's frantically waving arms. The following vehicle, after miles of walking, continues on its course. Joel is exhausted. The ache and soreness of his body, the extra weight on his right leg to ease his left one, is afflicting. But he can't stop without the thought of being on time at Yamouego bugging him.

They are scarce, and they do not stop. They don't even bother a glance, as if they don't see him, or they don't want to. In what feels like long hours of unchanged scenery, Joel has waved at only three vehicles, two family cars and one small bus.

He plods down the roadside, half-awake, waiting for another one to come by and to try his chance once again. The afternoon heat is unendurable. He could stay under cover at the tree line, but he will fall out of sight. Joel might have darkened even more with this direct exposure, and the torn clothes don't seem to be of much help. He only hears the clanking engine when a gbacka passes him and stops about sixteen feet ahead. After taking a few seconds to realize that the minibus has parked, Joel limps toward the vehicle.

"Where are you going, boy?" asks the driver, a middle-aged man in a washed-out lemon-yellow shirt. "Never mind, hop in."

"*Vieux père* Moussa, we got clients," reminds the doorman.

"Do we have free seats, Patrick?"

"Yes, *vieux père*, but the clients won't be pleased."

"So what?" retorts the driver. "Should I leave him in the middle of nowhere?"

"Others did. You know what happens on these roads."

"I know, and I'm not the others. Give him a seat. Get in, boy." The driver turns to Joel, still outside with one foot on the first step.

"Thank you, *tonton*," Joel manages in a drained voice. "Thank you."

His last shower was his dive in the river, so he can understand why the passengers in the front row cover their nostrils or look the other way. It is far from a neutral scent, especially with the layers of sweat. But tiredness outbalances his concern for their perception as he occupies one of the only two empty front seats. It's not long before he passes out, after a few bleary glances of unease at the couple across. The driver's "Are you okay, boy?" falls on deaf ears when the vehicle departs again.

"I think he is gone, *vieux père*. Hey!" calls the doorman.

"Leave him be, Patrick. Poor guy," says the driver.

"Chauffeur, what is this?" One of the passengers finally breaks the silence. "How can you grab just anybody on the road like this? We don't even know who this is."

"I don't know you either."

"If something happens, it's on you. And you're making people uncomfortable here," says the passenger. Murmuring fills the bus.

"Settle down, people. The boy is fine, just tired," says the driver.

"That's why I don't like to take gbackas," says another passenger. "They do whatever they want. No respect for clients."

"There are still fancy buses going to Abidje," the driver tosses out. "You can take them if you feel like it."

Night doesn't take long on a flying road. And what is left to contemplate through the kaput windows is a semblance of the same row of trunks running by until the gbacka slows down. It's about to enter a denser area free of paving, one of the shortcuts usually taken to save gas. The sole functioning headlight helps the driver see what he is forcing his tires onto. He advances slowly. A damaged wheel would be the end of the journey. Between the recurrent wobbling of the vehicle and second presses of the gas pedal to quit a few muddier sections, the driver keeps his eyes peeled before him. The sooner he leaves this area and returns to the road, the better. Stacks of broken branches lie thirty feet ahead after a careful right turn.

"*Vieux père*," says the doorman.

"I know." The driver changes gear.

"Whoooa, whoooa, where are you going? Stop the car," they hear when reverse is sharply hit.

"Stop the car or we shoot," says another voice after the driver's disregard for the first one.

"Not good, old man, not good. Are you trying to get away from us?" A man holding a large white bag smiles at the door.

The engine stops. Another man approaches and bangs the door glass with the back of his handgun.

"Open up," he orders.

The passengers are struck with fear at the two men stepping into the vehicle. The others outside position themselves to cover the old minibus. One stands ten feet from the left headlight, while another guards the back. They all mock the driver's reaction after seeing the branches. A spontaneous retreat, they call it.

"That was quick, driver. Damn," says the man with the handgun. "Yeah, that was, huh, that was a good reflex."

"Please take whatever you want. Don't hurt anyone." The driver tries to keep his cool.

"See that? The hero doesn't want anyone to get hurt," says the man with the handgun. The one behind him with the empty rice bag flashes a smirk.

"No, this is good." The man with the handgun turns back to the passengers. "He doesn't want you guys to get hurt. This is good."

They remain mute before the handgun's scraped-black-painted barrel aimed amusedly, randomly.

"You all know the deal, right?" The man with the handgun walks along the narrow path dividing the two sections of seats. "We'll be passing this bag. Put whatever you have in it. *Do not* hide anything, or you'll piss me off, okay? You don't want to piss me off. Give them the bag. We start front right. We have all the time in the world, so make sure you check twice before passing the bag."

"Who is this guy? Hey, get up," says the man, pushing Joel's temple with the muzzle of his semiautomatic.

"He looks like a vagrant." The man with the handgun turns to Joel. "Look at his clothes. Driver, you drag crazies with you? That's not good. No respect for your clients. Don't bother waking him up. Hey fast, fast, fast, put your things in fast."

The bag moves along, one terrified passenger at a time, until it reaches the back seats and rotates across for the left section.

"So are we done? Hey, what are you doing? *What* are you doing?" The man with the handgun approaches the bag. "You want to die?"

"That's all I have, sir. Please have mercy. My baby needs to eat," says a woman frozen in fear, on the brink of tears.

"Do I look like I care? Com'ere." He snatches her hair and pulls it behind him as he walks to the front row. "You'll be a good example."

The child starts crying at the sharp movements. The woman wails, holding tightly to her infant.

"Son, please," pleads the driver.

"*Shut up!*" the man screams.

The passengers start begging on the woman's behalf.

"You all think this is a joke. I said put everything you have in this bag, so why don't you, woman, put everything in, as I said?"

"Please, sir. Please, I have to feed my baby."

"Oh. Okay. So because of your stupid mistake, the child won't have a mom anymore." The man lays the barrel on the woman's forehead.

"No, noo, sir. Ohh, please, please, I am sorry," implores the woman.

"Well, I'm sorry too."

The child is squalling. The people are begging.

"Next time, you'll all know we don't joke."

The din and loud wailing right beside his seat manage to retract Joel's heavy eyelids. The haze is momentary before he spots a gun pointed at a woman's forehead. Joel snaps up, pinning the man's hand to the ceiling so violently that it perforates the metal sheet, breaking bones into pieces. The pistol goes off under the finger's late reflex, then clangs onto the sheet. The man's scream quickly follows after an instant of shock at the sight of his trapped wrist, his hand left bleeding on top of the minibus, with his unresponsive fingers loose on the grip. He screams in agony. In the half second of grasping the situation, the man with the semiautomatic hustles for his finger on the trigger before any aim is achieved. The aim is sharply redirected below by Joel's right hand, with bullets perforating the metal floor and torn fabric. He is hurled through the door, breaking everything, along with himself, on his way out. People have hastened to the closest shield panic can offer, many stooped behind the seats before them. One of the guards outside opens the cabin door and grabs the driver.

"You move, he's dead." He yanks the middle-aged man from his seat to the mud, stretching his yellow collar at the base of his neck. "I said don't ..." A gunshot completes his sentence.

Joel halts to look at the assailant with the pistol trapped in his uncertain clutch. The driver, agape, stares before him. Joel turns with dull interest to the left side of his chest, where the bullet has sunk a few inches into his skin, then looks back at the shooter.

"Boy, boy, get out of here," says the driver to his captor.

"Shut up," says the young man, fixated on the strange person in torn clothes.

"Listen to me. Don't make the same mistake your friends did."

"I said shut up," repeats the confused young man.

"You have a chance to get out of here, boy. If you kill me, you have no leverage. Go, now, before it's too late," says the driver, throwing a look at the man about the age of his captor by the rear of the car. These two remaining assailants must not be more than twenty-five years of age, he realized when he first met their cocky smiles. "Go, now. You still have a chance to get out of here."

"Okay! Okay." The young man lifts his gun off Joel. "We're leaving. We will get out of here."

The dash toward him seems instantaneous before his head is smashed against the side of the vehicle, leaving the driver aghast. He slides and splashes on the mud, lifeless. The last assailant is nowhere to be seen when Joel turns to the rear of the gbacka. He walks dully to the branches blocking the muddy path and removes them with disturbing ease. The passengers are all silent, enthralled at what they witness. Joel pulls away the last branch and returns to the minibus.

"We are good, *tonton*. You can go."

The driver finds his seat with no words and tries the engine, hoping the bullets didn't cause any serious damage to the vehicle.

"Wait."

The driver turns to Joel, walking toward the man with his hand through the ceiling. They had almost forgotten about him after the intense events that just occurred.

"Please," says the man, moaning in pain, weakened by the loss of blood. "Please don't kill me."

Joel widens the hole, freeing his hand from the ceiling, and asks the man to leave the minibus. He walks to his seat and takes the same position as before. The bullet finally drops from his chest. The bleeding is paltry.

"You must be very stupid or really ignorant," says Korokou.

"Why?" murmurs Joel.

"What did you say?" asks the driver, waiting for some response from Joel, whose eyes are shut.

"Do you know what recovery means?" asks Korokou. "You're still adjusting, and you take metal in your flesh."

"I had to help."

"Do not waste me … *Joel*," calls Korokou.

Joel is asleep.

Disconcerted, confused eyes aimed at Joel persist even after the driver pulls away.

CHAPTER 11

I'll Hold Them Off

Reverence demands the Wiseman speak first, but not a word has come out since they all sat before him about ten seconds ago. Instead, everything in his undisturbed gaze suggests a thorough examination of Biafle and Namien's faces. Kobenan follows along, scrupulously imitating every posture and gesture of his highly seasoned partner. There is no space for the slightest distraction as Kobenan warily looks between the old host before him and his still companions to his left. The checking must be ongoing. That's all Kobenan can glean from their behavior, or lack thereof. The one in front of the house where they had to pause before Namien gave them the green light to approach the door is not the sole control point. Kobenan better keep still then, until the situation evolves. Until they are allowed to state the reason for their visit.

"What is happening?" the Wiseman asks.

"A white man is dead," Biafle responds. "A minister. We believe he has been killed by one of us. From what we've gathered, this man was thinking about destroying an entire forest for his personal benefit. We reckon you might already be aware of this, and we could use any help to find out why a non-African died by means of forbidden practices. What were the real reasons for his death? And though we have learned there is a connection, we're still searching for the link between this case and Namien's daughter, the griot. We sought to approach you because we know this death, like any other, is your concern."

"My concern is to make sure everyone lives as Mother Nature intended," says the Wiseman. "It doesn't matter their color, their action, or agenda. I have to make sure, despite all this pollution, destruction, and war, that all receive the bases of life: pure air, pure water. This is my purpose. I am not aware of this incident. I was in the Pure World, negotiating with the trees for air for this part of the world."

"The Pure World?" Kobenan clearly remembers this name from one of his books with a plain black cover. The four descriptive lines were as abstract and confusing as the reading itself. But he did manage to make out the lack of evidence for any suggestion of plausibility. A name given by the elders of ancient ages, which became a story for children. "I thought this was a myth."

"Every myth, true or false, has its source, my son." The Wiseman turns to Kobenan. "It always comes from something true, which has been altered with time."

"They cut all ties millions of years ago," says Namien. "There came a point where they wanted no more of our space. They warned the leaders and kings several times. They said the thought process of man in this world, the way they use what they call technology, the way they behave in front of new discoveries, will lead their world to perdition."

"It is already happening," says the Wiseman. "No matter the ties cut, both worlds are linked, as is everything else. It might be of no importance now, but it will grow. And what flows here will start to affect them. The ancient trees felt a glimpse of corrupted air coming from this world. That is the reason I have been summoned. I knew this would occur, but it is too soon, and this means it is spreading faster than we thought. The chance that the trees were the only ones to sense it is very narrow."

"Millions of years ago?" Kobenan cannot help but linger on words conflicting with his whole knowledge. No books spoke of a grand society existing epochs ago. "I don't think we were advanced then. I don't even think we were standing on two legs."

A faint smile shows on the Wiseman's lips. "You are young, my son, and so are your people. You are just doing more damage than your predecessors."

"Wiseman, do you mean whoever killed this white minister could be from the Pure World?" asks Biafle.

"Or someone well aware of the negative effect of this link between both worlds. Someone powerful enough even to think about changing the fate of this world, regardless of his true motive. Killing a minister will make waves. It is clear he wanted us to know. There is more to just one death."

"He can't sever the connection, so he will change the direction of this world," Namien adds.

"But changing the fate of this world will mean changing the way people think," says Kobenan. "The way high leaders think. It's too late for that. This is centuries … millennia of knowledge wired on profit and control. They can't change that."

"Unless he kills them all and seeds a new way of thinking," says Namien.

"No one on Earth has enough power to do that," says Biafle.

"With a female griot, yes," prompts Namien. "The Wiseman still has my daughter under his protective mantle, so we know whoever killed this minister couldn't access her to do so, but that doesn't exclude her potential use on a wider scale, along with everything else that will be within his reach if he manages to lay a hand on her."

"No one on Earth has the right to eliminate or impose a thought process, on those deemed to deserve it or for any other reason." The Wiseman turns to Biafle. "The underlying principle that the mind is molded to constantly evolve on whatever path it may take is one of the rules that guide us. Mother Nature and the sky usually speak truth of the collective state of mind, but the curve can, on very rare occasions, be misleading. Correction has occurred in the past.

"The other inhabitants of your space are aware and refrain from measures, stay hidden, to avoid conflict. If this is his plan, he knows he is breaking the rules. This means he is prepared to affront everyone. I cannot think of the power he wields if this is the case. We do not know how smart and resourceful he is, but we should not take any risk, and I do not trust Namien with the griot."

"Wiseman," Kobenan calls, "if he's as powerful and resourceful as you may suggest, finding the griot will be a matter of time."

"The choice of the target, the means … He did want us to know about the minister," says Biafle. "If he doesn't know where the griot is and is really looking for her, as the Enkonhi couple implied, what better way to flush her out? He'll anticipate us moving her from her hiding place for more protection. He might only be waiting for us."

"What if he doesn't?" Namien looks at Biafle.

"What do you mean?" asks the head of the S-cell.

"What if he's aware we'll leave the girl where she is because we already planned that he will attack when we move her?" says Kobenan.

"Yes, but we have no confirmation he knows her location," says Biafle.

"He must know the wise circle very well if he is aware that you, Wiseman, are involved with my child. That means he knows how keen you are and how many years you plan before taking an action," says Namien.

"Wait …" interjects Kobenan. "The prime reason he killed the minister was not the forest—it was you, Wiseman. The forest, the method were just means to make us link all of this to him, someone undeniably well-versed in African knowledge. He knew we would approach you if he knew we would approach Namien, for Namien's mind would unquestionably focus on anything that might remotely connect to his daughter. He planned all of this, and he knows you won't let Namien anywhere near the girl, because his erratic behavior when it comes to his daughter can cost us all dearly. He knows you'll never let that happen.

"Our movements … all our movements read as though he seeks for the griot to be in motion, so she'll be detectable, but

... but he knows where she is. He doesn't want her to be disturbed until he extracts her ... Why ... why inform us, then?" Kobenan's enlightened visage meets the Wiseman's attentive eyes.

The old host turns silently to Biafle.

"He might be right, Wiseman. He's a gifted boy," says the head of the S-cell.

"I know he is right. I posted more of my strongest personal guards last year for this eventuality. This is not what bothers me. I am missing something. You have a very smart kid on your hands. So keep close eyes on him. You should go now. I'll give the order to let you approach her. Bring the griot here." The Wiseman stands up. "I have to consult Mother Nature. Your daughter is at the Bengerville Mental Hospital. Go, we are wasting time."

The guests follow the Wiseman with a brief salute of respect before heading for the exit. One last gander over his shoulder when Kobenan is three feet away from the door shows no more than four stools. He should really start adjusting to this, things appearing and disappearing in the blink of an eye, people vanishing with no trace whatsoever, as if they were never there in the first place. His mind has yet to just accept it, but this makes no sense; it does not obey any law or reasoning at all.

"His reaction seemed ... almost spontaneous." Namien shuts the door. "That's never happened before."

"Maybe he found a hole in the griot's protection."

"Euuuh, guys ..." Kobenan interjects, his pupils frozen before him. A sharp chill runs down his spine before he can get a hold of himself.

There they stand, their calm, annoyed expressions locked on the three men.

"We don't have time for a fight now," Biafle says softly.

"The house can help us shift places. Let's go inside," Namien proposes.

There's only flattened grass, shaped by what was present to them before, when they spin for the house.

"Oh my God … it'll take them a while to find us, you said. We are sooo fucked. What do we do now?" asks Kobenan.

"You two go. I'll hold them off," says Namien. "I'm the only one capable of keeping them off your tails for good."

"Namien, you know how powerful these dogs are." Biafle keeps an eye on the creatures. "With your energy level right now, it's suicide."

"Remove these spirit bracelets, brother. We have no choice. If you have to reach my daughter in time, someone has to stay and fight. You two are the best chance she's got."

The brown dogs advance slowly toward their target, one paw after the other, their canines flaring. Biafle removes the spirit bracelets and hands a fetish to the sorcerer.

"No." Namien glances at Biafle's hand. "This is your last one. You'll need it where you're going. You two step behind me and wait for my signal."

The dogs of Kplegba split into strategic position for what resembles a coordinated attack. When they stoop for a leap, Namien grounds himself and charges, aiming for a timely strike. The dogs, which never bark, surge toward their target. The sorcerer swings back his hands and juts them forward, unleashing the upper body of his spirit. The dogs collide and penetrate an unshaped bubble seeming to be in slow motion.

"Now! Fast, they're breaking," Namien calls out, his trembling hands struggling to hold position. "Biafle, please … save my daughter."

Biafle pats the sorcerer's shoulder before they dash for the car. Namien follows the vehicle speeding away, shrinking to a small box, while his body contends to keep the bubble whole. The dogs break through the spirit and with their initial speed lash out at the sorcerer. He rolls back and stops in a crouched position, both elbows on his knees, his gaze fixed on his attackers. The dogs of Kplegba get back up, walk arcs around him, then attack.

*

Kobenan stares through the window, following the moving landscape and occasionally flicking trunks and poles, his mind far away from his surroundings. He hasn't even noticed the low noise sparking from his stressed thumb grinding on his middle finger.

Biafle glances at him and then back to the road. This underage analyst dragged into the field, compelled to do what most would have fallen before long ago. Maybe he is meant for this. Maybe President Dablan's faith was not misplaced. "He was once one of the toughest and deadliest sorcerers on our top list. He'll be fine."

Kobenan turns to Biafle, then looks back at the window, allowing quietness to glide for a moment. "You know, when they taught us about fetishes and sorcerers, they never mentioned what kind of people they were. Just the power they wield. You tend to forget they have a soul … They all look like monsters in the books."

"They *are* monsters," Biafle affirms. "Remember what the Great Chief said. They only think of themselves. Few care about their progeny or anyone else. Don't make the same mistakes."

"What?" asks Kobenan.

"Mixing your sentiments with your work. It's a sharp, double-edged knife. You're getting too attached to this girl. It may cloud your judgment when you need to make the right decision."

"She doesn't deserve any of this. I just want her to be safe."

"We both do," says Biafle.

"The Wiseman said he had posted more guards for her protection."

"It won't be enough. She is the key to the enemy's scheme. I'd throw most of my resources at the mental hospital if I were him. We need the high guardians of Sector 0."

"You mean there will be an army waiting for us?" asks Kobenan.

"There will be an army waiting to take this girl. And right now, we can't expect any backup. We're outlaws."

"We can use it to our advantage and make the S-cell follow us to the hospital," proposes Kobenan.

"S-cell agencies from neighboring countries have had our cell under surveillance since the prison break. I can't rely on anyone inside. It's deemed a national matter for now, and it has to remain so. We can't afford any information leakage, or the other countries will think the prison break was a hoax and we freed Namien on purpose. It will create tension between the associated countries, and we might lose their trust, along with Sector 0."

"What do we do then?"

"We go there and make sure the girl is safe," Biafle responds.

"You mean *you* make sure, because I can't fight."

"I can't protect the girl in combat. I'll need someone trustworthy to watch out for her, and you're the only one I can think of. You'll carry her, update me on her vitals while I'm carving a way out. We've got one shot at this. Let's give everything to bring her back."

"So we fight," says Kobenan with a smile.

"So we fight." Biafle smiles back. "Together."

So we fight. An expression among S-cell agents for situations where violence is the last or sole option to protect or save. It was one Kobenan came across early in his studies about the secret governmental agency. He never thought he'd ever use these words, let alone with one of the most prominent agents in history. He never made the S-cell, but nonetheless, he couldn't ask for better. Now he wonders if this is what he really wanted, after all he has witnessed, after all he has seen and still can't make any sense out of. The thought of permanent brain damage has already crossed his mind twice now. He can still reason and has yet to lose his identity, so that's a good sign.

When Abiba, his mother, agreed to the government men who invited themselves to her house to request her only boy, she never imagined this. She probably still thinks Kobenan is in a safe office at the presidential house, doing paperwork. Kobenan would have still found himself at the presidential house had she said no, but they had to ask. Courtesy demanded it. Being among the top ten most gifted people in the country releases you from any say your parents have in your future. And they are only informed five years after the government has already started training you in the hours between normal school classes. True, Kobenan was aware something was different between his schoolmates and him, but the explanation really occurred on his first day at the presidential house.

*

The dashboard indicates 3:39 p.m. when the vehicle decelerates. Tall, well-groomed shrubs seem to have been planted to purposely shield the property from outward view. Biafle approaches an entrance, a paved road of light-brown bricks bordered by shadowy bushes. It doesn't take long, with the slow driving, to see seasonal plants with bright, colorful petals along the narrow roadside. Moments later, a wide, multistory building emerges a short distance away, with plain white paint and waist-high windows, an establishment spread across a vast terrain with a small recreational garden to its left about halfway between the SUV and the foundation pillars.

"It's quiet." Kobenan peers through the windshield. "Is it the right place?"

"It has already started."

Kobenan turns to Biafle. "Doesn't seem like …"

A window bursts out from the topmost floor, ejecting a broken table onto the lawn.

"They're here," says Biafle.

A growing muffled sound of desperate voices precedes two men hastening to Biafle's closed window. They are in distinct sky-blue uniforms, giving away their staff status. They radiate panic and near incoherence as they repeatedly hit the reinforced glass with their palms, begging for help. Biafle instantly stops and quiets the engine before descending from the vehicle with his partner.

"Our colleagues, our colleagues are trapped in the hospital," gasps one of the men.

"Calm down," says Biafle. "What did you see?"

"Nothing!" presses the other nurse, slightly shorter and leaner than his counterpart. "We don't understand what's happening. There are explosions everywhere, and we can hear loud, strange noises at times, but we see no one. We don't know what it is, but it's, it's not human. The door won't open. We've tried all we could do to free our colleagues, and we don't see any lock."

The agents turn to the entrance. People are squeezed against the main door of square glass, screaming inaudibly for help. There seems to be a fight behind the panicked crowd, Kobenan notices.

"A seal of strength." Biafle steadies his gaze on a slim mesh loosely wrapped around the door handle, probably invisible to the naked eye. "A normal human being won't break it. They're expecting reinforcements. We have to move fast."

"How did you escape?" Kobenan wonders.

"We didn't," says the nurse. "A voice kept speaking in my head to get out of the hospital and go to the park. At first, I didn't want to, thinking I was just tired. Then my head started to hurt, so I decided to listen, and I met this man. The voice stopped when I reached the park."

"I had an urge to leave. I didn't know what was happening until I was here," says the second one.

Kobenan looks at Biafle. "How is that possible?"

"They're protected by their parents or ancestors. It's common among African families. Protection against sorcery and attack since birth."

"Do you know what's happening?" ventures one of the nurses.

"Listen, we don't have much time. I'll have to trust you on this," says Biafle, unbuttoning his shirt. "I'll open the door, but you'll have to lead your colleagues away from these premises. Don't worry, it'll be okay. You're protected. I can't say the same for these people. Send them as far as you can from the hospital. Whatever you've seen or heard until now is only the beginning. It's going to get worse, and you don't want to be anywhere near the building when it happens."

Kobenan gazes as his partner pulls his pants from his heels, leaving him in tight white underwear. "Euuuh, Biafle ... what are you doing?"

Biafle places the pants on the vehicle's hood on top of the shirt, takes off a sock, then glances at his partner, awaiting a solid response, judging by the flat, clouded expression he wears. "The only chance to reach the griot's room is to fight our way through. I'll need my full strength for that. This human form is limited, and the suit will slow me down." He pulls off the second sock.

The nurses stare at each other before looking back at Biafle. One can only wonder what state of mind drives someone to strip before strangers and talk gibberish in a situation like this. Many patients have presented these symptoms before. The dire position of their colleagues pressures them to seek help, but they can't be too cautious about who stands in front of them. They might well have miscalculated this approach.

"Who are you again?" tries the shorter nurse.

Another fireless explosion shatters glass and frames from the last floor, propelling something Biafle and Kobenan follow until it slams the green lawn and rolls for a moment before stopping ten feet from them. Distraught and confused, the creature gains its feet as the head of the S-cell advances toward it, crouches, and lays his fingers on the grass. A small tree forms atop the creature, narrowing his movements to what resembles fingers and split, hard nails. The nurses stand aghast, unblinking eyes plastered on the fidgeting tree, their myringas exposed to the moaning and groaning of whatever may lie underneath. Only his closed mouth and calm demeanor differentiate Kobenan from the nurses.

What could this possibly be? Its face, its rigid limbs, and dark and cracked skin reveal nothing Kobenan can associate with his books. Even under the weight of a tree, it behaves as if it were possessed. Its silhouette superficially identifies as human, a tall human, but it is far from it. This creature tirelessly shaking to break from its shackles easily tops six foot two. And the intent in its small, round eyes shows nothing but rage and some sort of consciousness.

Biafle observes the broken windows on the seventh floor.

"Gold seals ... impossible. We'll have to go through the main door if we want to reach the griot."

"Why?" asks Kobenan.

"Whoever installed these doesn't want any surprises from the outside."

"It might not seem like it, but he's not crazy," Kobenan reassures the addled nurses. "Do what he says if you want to save your colleagues."

"What about our patients? They're still locked in their cells."

"There is nothing we can do for them right now," says Biafle. "There is no time. They'll be safer inside. Better get those who still own their minds and send them away from here. Let's go."

"You aren't taking your normal appearance?" Kobenan walks beside his nearly naked partner.

"Do you want these people to run in the opposite direction?"

"It's strange how some families do anything to protect their own against any threat, for generations, while others move earth and sky to kill theirs."

"What do you want me to say? This is Africa. Stand back."

Despite a second of uncertainty when they see someone approaching a cloth away from nude, those in the forefront who have desperately labored to open the main door recede a step or two at his gesture to move back. Barring his strange accoutrement, the man in front of them doesn't seem to mean any harm. Besides, two staff members they recognize stand sixteen feet behind him. Biafle grabs the door's handles, with his arms slithering to the color of bark. Leaves grow and meander along. Wrinkles shape. The door almost breaks, opening to the sharpness of his pull.

"Here, follow us. Follow us!" call the nurses, herding the panicked crowd out of the building. The doors have opened, and brawling creatures whose priority was to contain the hostages shift their focus to those escaping. The Wiseman's guards clear the ones left to face them and rush after the staff. Creatures drop one after another onto the large tiles before they can harm the few men and women left to quit the building. The last creature, holding a screaming woman under it, with her hair clutched in its tight grip, flattens onto a nearby table after a violent smash to its left temple.

Biafle and Kobenan step into the hospital. The head of the S-cell crouches at the entrance and lays both palms on the floor tile before the door for a moment, then stands up and closes them. A large, curved tree sprouts outside, blocking the sun and the main entrance.

"This will buy us some time."

They hear irregular banging at a metallic door about forty feet from them. As Biafle and Kobenan advance toward the two men approaching, it becomes clear that people are fighting behind this blockade, which is apt to break any time now at these forceful pushes it frequently receives. But it doesn't break; it only bumps inward. There are loud cries of rage and orders. Two men, well above six feet and with defined composure, stop before the agents. There are intricate triangle and diamond patterns blending into the sewing of the cloth around their hips. The men stand large and slightly darker in tone. They are humans, no doubt, yet something about them whispers that they aren't from around here. And Kobenan can't pinpoint what it is that separates them from the humans he knows. But they are unequivocally the Wiseman's guards.

"Mr. Biafle, Ubuntu. We've been advised of your arrival." The one in charge salutes with his right palm on his chest.

"Ubuntu," responds Biafle with the same gesture. "What's the situation?"

"We're outnumbered and losing ground," the Wiseman's guard begins. "This area's the only place in the hospital free of confrontation. Our brothers are fighting to their last breath, but we won't be able to hold out for long. We have orders to protect the griot until you arrive and help you extract her. This metallic door behind me is the only thing allowing us to talk at this moment. We've placed a sorcerer seal on it, though it's getting weak very fast—too fast. The energy spreading here is abnormal. Whoever sent these creatures is powerful beyond what we think possible. Or he's tapping into something completely unknown to us."

"What are they?" Biafle looks down at the dead creature sprawled three steps from him.

"We don't know. From what we've learned, they seemed to be controlled."

"When we parked, you were fighting them." Kobenan looks away from the corpse.

"My squad and I were assigned to protect any sane human in the hospital. During the fight, we managed to isolate them in this area and locked the door. Some creatures were already here. They surprised us, but we neutralized them."

"What are our options?" asks Biafle.

"The surest way to the griot is the stairs, but they're swarming with these creatures. You'll have to go through them to reach her, and that will slow you down."

"I see."

"We did notice something strange," the Wiseman's guard continues. "People here were using a sort of portal to appear on different levels."

"A lift," says Biafle.

"We don't know how to operate it, so we've installed a barrier to avoid the enemy using it to their advantage."

"You don't know how to use a lift?" asks Kobenan.

"They're unfamiliar with this invention." Biafle glances at Kobenan. "Where is it located?"

"At the end of the hall, on your left. I'll advise the team to weaken the barrier and allow you to get in."

"Got it. You and your team install a trap seal at the main entrance, and get ready." Biafle's skin stretches and gives way to roots forming over his body. "More are coming. Stay put and await my orders."

"Understood," responds the Wiseman's guard.

CHAPTER 12

So We Fight

He has read about them and has a good idea of what they are, according to his books. He heard about them during his assignment briefings at the presidential house. He has even studied some to solve specific files. But nothing could prepare Kobenan for the sight of an actual djinn. He had never envisioned one in his lifetime. His life*times*, if rare passages in the somber orange book were to be believed. Here he stands, frozen with awe, gawking at Biafle. A djinn of the forest. A mass of structured and various-sized roots, leaves, and one small carving daubed with sap for an eye, if it is indeed an eye. It's the only carved spot on what is shaped like a neckless, chinless head. His form still is vaguely humanoid, closer than Kobenan imagined. His height has only gained a few inches. The breadth from shoulder to shoulder, on the other hand, makes him look like two Biafles in one, or are Kobenan's eyes failing to adjust? The only reason his feet are still nailed in place is the assurance that he knows the person who was here seconds ago. Kobenan stares at his partner, completing his metamorphosis, leaving the white underwear torn apart on the cracked tiles.

"Listen to me carefully." Biafle's unrecognizable voice strains as if coming through multiple pipes. "It's going to get quickly out of control, so we'll have to move fast. I can't protect you while fighting. Stay close, stay focused, and follow my every movement if you want to survive to the lift. And watch out for your ring."

The harsh realization of the situation and the quandary he finds himself in subdues his thoughts for an instant. His face, his eyebrows, though subtle, scream to back off. His will is dubious to his core. He doesn't know what awaits beyond this metallic frame. He only has to stick to his partner and hope for protection, which the djinn just mentioned won't be forthcoming. Could it be fear, anxiousness? Kobenan isn't shaking, but he takes a long, deep breath before nodding to his partner.

The djinn puts his hand into his chest and pulls out his last fetish, a small black sculpture of wood. He clenches it and releases it. The fetish bounces on the tiles before settling, then grows into a dog of black wood and red eyes. Its almost-rectangular back comes to exceed Kobenan's waist. It is undeniably the same kind of fetish that slowed the brown dogs of Kplegba when they were escaping the prison with Namien. They do look very large when they are still.

"Keep your eyes on him, and help me when you can," the djinn orders the dog.

Kobenan looks at the unstable door and takes another breath. "Here we go."

"Open." Biafle signals to the Wiseman's guards.

Kobenan shifts his weight behind the djinn, his narrow vision split between a mass of roots and half a door. He is on edge, his senses stricken, but his focus lies before him. The tailless dog readies for attack.

The Wiseman's guard unrolls a seal of old braided African hair, with stubborn strands wrapped around the handles, and pulls open the door. Their first sight, the one instantly drawing their attention, is flying toward them, a creature cast away from one of the many confrontations unfolding in the hallway. Biafle nudges Kobenan further behind him before it crashes into the room at the warriors' feet. The one in charge lays his foot on the creature's face.

"Go. We'll take care of this one."

Biafle crosses the metallic door, tailed by his partner. Mayhem encompasses every visible corner of the ward, and Kobenan stays behind the roots. The corridor runs many feet before a larger one attaches perpendicularly on the right side. That's what a split-second reflexive scan between clashing bodies tells him. He sees the Wiseman's guards brawling with creatures double, maybe triple their numbers, destroying everything in their path. The brawl is seemingly controlled, disciplined, and bent on lightning reflexes. A shadow whooshes past Kobenan before his brain recognizes the dog, which just leaped forward. The first foe is seized by its face with large, black jaws. The dog neutralizes it and leaps to the next.

The second foe Kobenan sees charging toward them is belted to the left wall so harshly, its head indents into the bricks. Biafle jolts his arm from the impact, sending debris flying in his vicinity. He swiftly avoids the third foe before thrusting it to the next ally, who smashes it with a powerful shinbone. The fourth's impetus toward the agents is abruptly redirected when the wooden dog swipes it away. It all cascades around and above Kobenan, barely aiming to keep pace, with his right arm constantly protecting his head. He follows, he stumbles, he hurries on all fours and sticks to the djinn of the forest.

The fifth foe is brutally pinned to the ground by its neck with arms of roots, shattering tiles on impact. Biafle catches an ally reeling toward him, following a hard blow to the temple, and pushes him back onto his opponent, which is bashed into the next. He propels the seventh foe against the far wall with a powerful back-foot kick.

Kobenan collapses onto a corpse with ill-balanced legs, rushes up, and quickly falters over to Biafle, advancing inexorably down the corridor as he carves his way to the lift maybe thirteen feet past the wider perpendicular hall. He watches him step with the tremendous strength and heft of a tree. Kobenan attempts to remain in his shadow, clutching onto Biafle's foot at times while being dragged about. The intense interaction between his partner and these creatures leaves him trying to catch up with his mind and limbs.

The next foe is thrown to an ally, who finishes it off. The twelfth is a warrior overwhelmed by multiple hits. Biafle fiercely strikes one of the attackers, sending it rolling up to a wall next to the stairs and halting its course. The guard clears the rest with the assistance of the wooden dog. The lift is within reach. Biafle blocks a hit, repels it, and taps the button to call the lift.

The enemy spots the agents settling before a small, glowing blue ring encircling the metallic painted button, a light-emitting shape signaling activation of the machine. The assault from all possible angles restricts options and movements. *Defense at all cost* is Biafle's new strategy, smashing, hurling seemingly infinite creatures with their accretion and recurring onslaught. Guards blitz to aid the djinn under multiple hits, and the wooden dog, prominent in this chaos with every jump, eliminates as many as it can to assist its master. A *ding* sounds, and the doors slide open.

"Get in!" shouts Biafle.

Kobenan lunges for the lift, but the repulsion when he is about to reach the door is so sharp, he feels rocketed to the opposite side. He collides midair with the wooden fetish, which leaped, directing its flank to cushion the impact between the white wall and his back. Kobenan has trouble finding his feet, even with the absorbed shock. The dog hastily leaves Kobenan slumped on the cracked bricks and charges its next target.

"Lower the barrieeer!" hollers Biafle, smashing creatures left and right.

"*Damou kie yeyiiii leeeee!*" A warrior relays the order.

The closest ally rolls and touches the wall before the lift. A creature rushes to Kobenan, still on the ground, when Biafle kicks it away. The djinn clutches his partner by his damaged blazer and throws him into the lift. Biafle strikes a creature, smashes another, and crosses the entrance, repeatedly hitting the button for the seventh floor, then presses the lock button. A continuous beep with the doors slowly but gradually sliding inward indicates they will not reopen for any interruption. The guards have formed a human shield in front of the lift. Most sustain ferocious attacks and severe damage, but under no circumstances if not death will they lower their arms or stop pushing back. Creatures scream and rage with their extended arms to try and force their way in. The wooden dog hops next to his master before the doors lock, and the lift is ascending, soft music trickling from the roof.

Kobenan is still recovering from the shock. He repeatedly blinks, his mouth lightly agape and his hands shaking from the trauma. He crouches in the corner with one leg straight, breathing heavily but sparsely. He lowers his head to his ring, which has turned dark green. This is bad. This is really bad. It took a heavy toll. When Biafle gave him the ring, it was clear gold. Now it is somber and worn out. His body must have suffered many hits. Hits he probably didn't notice because of the ring. He doesn't feel pain at the moment, but the slight dizziness from the repulsion persists. He'd better keep an eye on the straying color. It might be the only thing allowing him to keep on.

"Are you okay?" asks the djinn of the forest.

Kobenan looks at Biafle's misconstructed face, trying to find any angle to give sense to this question. How could someone with working synapses ask something like this?

"No! No, I'm not okay!"

He surely isn't the only one who sustained damage, if he reads well the djinn's back, permeated with a mixture of blood and sap. Biafle turns to the square display, indicating six. "Get up. We're almost there."

Kobenan glides up as quickly as his body permits and slides to the other corner as the djinn retreats one step, waiting for the lift to settle. The dog readies for attack.

"Stay close," says Biafle.

The lift has stopped, the doors are opening, and Kobenan whisks behind his partner at the sounds and arms protruding from outside. Biafle raises his foot and thrusts the first creature grinding in as the wooden dog lashes out at the next. It is fast, solid, and shifts like no vertebrate ever could.

The Wiseman's guards, as they did below, protect the lift at this floor. Many have fallen, and more are following. The two agents seek their way through the bedlam to the griot, two rooms ahead, Kobenan mainly giving in to his body's reflexes to dodge and hide behind or beside his partner. More creatures swarm here, and everyone is battling for her. The enemy's overwhelming numbers seem to claim the floor, and the only advantage is corridors restricting their formation, almost nullifying the weight of their numerical advantage. The remaining warriors struggle to hold position and protect the griot.

Biafle is now at arm's length from the room. He glances inside for a quick confirmation of the objective, but his focus immediately veers outside to his left, toward a cluster of warriors thirteen feet past the door. These are a defined group, if he is not mistaken by the purple bands above their elbows, maybe the finest, and they are all aiming to contain a relentless eight-foot beast blasting away everything it strikes. How this large thing got onto the floor is not a question for right now.

Kobenan cannot peel his eyes from the battle inside once he falls into the room, warriors clashing with creatures, bashing each other, destroying everything around them, but under no circumstances do both sides so much as brush the griot lying on the white bed. She is paramount.

"Kobenan, secure the griot," orders Biafle, bashing creatures in front of the room. "I have to neutralize this beast, or we have no chance of leaving with her."

Kobenan remains before the door, unconsciously sizing up the situation, watching allies and enemies fighting savagely around the griot. He looks at her. He has never seen such a beautiful face. He has never seen such a fragile being. Her skinny body wears a white robe. Her silky black skin wears thin symbols. Her curly red hair touches the floor. She is lying on her back, her head turned toward the door, with no expression, calm, a tear on her cheek. Kobenan meets her obsidian pupils, and everything else suddenly seems unimportant. The quaint and loud barking of the wooden dog is muffled as it attacks the rare foes daring to approach. No more sound occurs around him. No more fear or apprehension inhabit him. It is as though he and she are connected, isolated, far from all this confrontation.

He feels a glimpse of the pain she has endured since birth, a glimpse traveling from his small toe to his left eye, stretching and contracting tissues as it meanders. Flesh, emotion, mental, but something else pertains. Something he cannot relate to. Something he doesn't know but understands. Something just beyond. No words could describe it. No thought could capture it. Nothing compares to it. A tear runs down his cheek. He understands this tremendous amount of energy pulling her life away. She can't speak or walk. She is simply a vessel, a body fed and consumed by what flows through her veins. He cannot imagine what kind of agony she is going through. He only has his watery eyes to watch.

"You should have never come here ... Kobenan," a female voice echoes in his head.

Kobenan has no time to grasp these words before the circumstances of his position suck him right back. A chinbone to his sternum hurls him toward a wall facing the griot's room. Kobenan slams into the bricks and falls flat on his face. The noises have stopped long ago. Pain is still nowhere to be found, but Kobenan wheezes as he slowly lifts his head for a blurry look in the room before him. He makes out only two shapes standing beside the bed. They look different. They feel different. One of them is taking the girl. Nothing around challenges them. They are all dead in the room. The wooden dog, appearing from nowhere, leaps with all the speed and ferocity at its disposal. One of the newcomers strikes it with the back of his fist, propelling the fetish to the third following room, ravaging everything on its way. It is no more. The two shapes jump through the window and disappear with the griot.

Kobenan accounts for less of his body. He feels his lower lip and the saliva-turned-blood stretching thin from it. His limbs are numb, but now more than ever he senses the ring wrapped around his finger. He slowly turns toward it, only to see a dark circle. It has reached its limit. It can sustain no more wounds or the pain his body has suffered. Kobenan knows he would be long dead with no support. Can he move? He ought to at least try, for he can hear no more, and his sight doesn't seem to readjust. Biafle—he has to find his partner and inform him of the situation. The main reason for all this violence is gone.

Kobenan sluggishly pulls the arm bearing the ring before him. He slowly drags his knee to his hips and pushes up. He pushes again and manages to get up on all fours, then both legs, unable to rise further. His whole body cries to respond, but he is desperately trying. Focus seems to be scattered among corridors and rooms all at once, or is it nowhere at all? His thoughts are drifting, but nonetheless, they do help him single out the creature charging in his direction. The enemy set to shatter the ring's limits. He slowly blinks, awaiting the fist to his temple, when it brutally changes course toward a broken wall behind him. Someone, who just terminated the attacker, approaches Kobenan and helps him straighten up.

"They got the griot," says Kobenan, barely keeping on his feet, looking straight ahead at nothing. "You can still … save her … the window … they fled by the window … Don't veer."

"I'm on it." Kobenan hears a young man's voice. "Can you hold yourself up?"

"I'll be … fine … go."

The young stranger hastens to the room, halts for a brief second by the bed, and then continues through the window.

"The griot is gone! I repeat, the griot is gone!" A dialect rings in Kobenan's ears. One of the warriors is hollering to alarm the others. She has been gone for more than a minute. The whole company, including Biafle, not noticing it means something here concealed her energy. Something these two strangers left in the room before quitting the area. It's too late. They are unreachable.

"Dammit!" Biafle spits out, glaring at the beast's deadly arms. "It's too powerful. We can't let it position itself ag—don't let it take this side! You, move here, fast. We have to encircle it."

Kobenan's sore legs, partly held up by the ring, make him stagger. Everyone battles around him, and no one seems to care for his small form, stranded between the griot's room and the wall behind him. He is probably a dead man standing, with his body ready to part ways once the ring gives in. There is no use for him in this battle; there has never been, and the enemy seems aware of this. They have a more pressing concern to eliminate: the Wiseman's guards.

*

The unbent, undying beast, despite all the blows it has received, confirms to the djinn of the forest that they will all be dead before it gives up. It is weakening, true, but at too slow a rate to be able to eliminate it and the rest of the creatures shrieking around before they can search for the griot. He can feel the number of allies dropping considerably. At this point, staying alive and escaping this ward is the priority.

"Biafle, can you hear me?" A voice echoes in the djinn's head.

"Wiseman."

"We made a terrible mistake. The griot was never the prime target."

"*What?*" Biafle avoids a heavy strike from the beast that cracks bricks and glass.

"Protect Kobenan at all costs. He is a channel," the Wiseman commands.

"A cha ..." It takes Biafle a split second to comprehend before he spins to search for his partner. "Make a ring around Kobenan!" he screams. "Protect Kobenan!"

The order is not even complete before a creature brutally snatches Kobenan and dashes away, breaking walls in his path and vanishing. Biafle falls to his knees, laying his hand on the floor to locate the creature's steps. He cannot avoid the blast this time. A heavy strike from the beast bounces him off the wall, shattering it. It takes him a moment to move his head. More are coming through the stairs. They finally broke through the main entrance. The warriors on the ground floor are surely all dead. Those who remain on this floor will not contain the coming wave. The situation is out of control.

Biafle lies on the scattered tiles, compelled to witness everyone fading under the engulfing enemy that keeps flooding from the stairs. He hears the beast's deathly cry as it hurls his allies. There is no choice. No more thinking. No more strategizing. Biafle pulls a small ball the size of a pearl from his chest, clenches it, and releases it. The ball rolls a few inches, then stops. Biafle lays both hands on the floor, and they grow, deepening into the broken floor tiles, penetrating them. A few grains detach from the ball's perfectly round shape. The beast is about to end the djinn of the forest when he hollers, "Kuyuleleeeeeee."

"Kuyuleleeeee," repeats one of the warriors.

They all brace themselves, protecting their faces. Some clasp the nearest immovable object. But nothing and no one can withstand the powerful blast of compressed air. The first shock is sharp, harsh, and disastrous, blowing everything away in an instant, forcing the djinn of the forest to immediately lose his right fingers. The following explosions are condensed and continuous, whirling, hurling all away. Many smash pillars and door frames before hurtling through windows, pushing through weakened and broken walls. The bomb clears corridors and all rooms, making structures vulnerable with holes and cracks. The bomb clears all but a slashed, beaten, and bleeding djinn. Biafle's three remaining left fingers of roots deep in the floor still maintain him before he falls flat, chest-first on the tiles, when all sucking and swirling sounds stop. He can barely move from the severe disorientation, his fingers of root slowly receding from the now-crumbly white cement and detached tiles as he attempts to get on all fours.

Though the wounds stretch deep, the pain is bearable, forgettable in light of what just happened. It takes him twenty seconds to stand up; then he trudges toward the hole where his partner was taken away. He knows full well the answer to his query, but he has to verify it. He has to take a look at the blank path of scrambled bricks used by whoever abducted his partner. A long look in the direction shows three holes in a row, three rooms before stalling. How could he miss this? How did they all fail to foresee through Kobenan: the Great Chief, the Third Great Chief, the Wiseman? It can't be. A channel. This can't be happening. Today's failure is crushing his head. The only thing left to him is to track down Kobenan. A forlorn quest with the elapsed time. He has the soil and the trees for a start, even with improbable odds. Reaching the ground floor is next.

Noise emanates from the stairs below. Biafle listens, following them until they show themselves. More, many more creatures. It seems never-ending. They are on the seventh floor, coming toward him. He takes a stance, for he is about to drag as many as he can with him. He swings his fist at the first foe when something drops from above, smashing the crowd and the floor, breaking everything and forcing all to recede one story to the floor caving in, crumbling upon the massive impact. Biafle, caught off guard, is standing up. His shoulder withstood the fall. He knows only one being capable of such a din with his entrance. He glances at the djinn of the mountains before whacking the first creature in proximity.

They are now on the sixth floor, fighting creatures, synchronizing, coordinating their attacks at times to eliminate each and every one of them. Biafle pins the last one to a wall. It coughs a sharp shriek and then gives its last breath. Biafle sits on the floor, succumbing to depletion, subsiding to the calm.

"The boy's gone."

"What happened?" asks the djinn of the mountains.

"We completely missed it. He's a channel."

"A channel?" His broad, low voice tone settles. "I thought those kind of people were extinct."

"Apparently not." Biafle looks at the djinn of the mountains. "They have the griot too."

"We can't worry about that now." The djinn treads toward Biafle with heavy steps. "I saw an army on my way here. This structure is weak. If we get caught in a fight, the roof won't hold."

"Why are you here?" Biafle is standing up, with assistance from the djinn of the mountains.

"The Wiseman. He contacted all of us and gave your location. The Great Chief released me. The prison is under attack."

Biafle pauses for a brief moment with an intent stare and then gets back to straightening up. "He's smart. Attacking Sector 0 head-on. A bold move. Keeping the great chiefs occupied while he takes the hospital. That's an important message."

"Who is this *he*? Do we know?" asks the djinn of the mountains.

"No," Biafle responds.

"He has resources, I give him that. Willing to sacrifice an entire army to slow down the great chiefs. He didn't want them or any of the high prison guards interfering."

"They're here," says Biafle.

"I know. Let's get out of this building."

The ground ripples from a blast outside. It seems to have originated from the hospital's main entrance. The top story is collapsing, freeing mainly its large blocks. The djinn of the mountains grabs his old friend and jumps through the closest window. Biafle's position under the djinn's arm grants him a narrow view to follow his large, overlaid feet of well-connected rocks as they descend through the air until they land with a boom from his whole weight, deepening a few inches in the soil and flattening grass under them. Biafle relies on his right knee's contact with the ground to recover his balance. He then stands up with assistance and gets back on his feet.

"You okay?"

"I'll manage," responds the djinn of the forest, observing a wide crater with stacked corpses lying where once was a curved tree.

This signature is unequivocal, and sure enough, the Great Chief is here, standing by the large hole. His dusty, half-clenched fist confirms that he engendered this blast. They are all present: the Third Great Chief, the pygmies, and some of Sector 0's highest guardians. The S-cell agents and a few Biafle does not recognize roam with seemingly distinct tasks on site. Some are closing the area and setting perimeters.

"The djinn of the forest in all his grandeur." Djengdjeng, the pygmy with short braids, faintly smirks at the djinns' approach. "Must be liberating to be out of that human shell. You don't look so good."

"Why would you drag the boy into battle?" asks Nianbou, the pygmy with long braids.

"And where would I leave him?" Biafle retorts calmly. "There is no place on this Earth you can hide from Sector 0 once you're a target. I had no intel on what has been decided for both of us by the S-cell or Sector 0. Kobenan would have not fared thirty minutes on his own if we were already condemned."

"He would have been among us … safe," says Djengdjeng, his demeanor more serious.

"I didn't know what he was," says Biafle.

"Still, he'd have had a better chance if you'd left him out of this building," Nianbou adds.

"We freed one of the deadliest sorcerers from Sector 0. No, I wouldn't know his chances of survival if I left him on his own."

"We're long past all of this," the Great Chief interjects. "Biafle had no time to hide the boy. We weren't going to kill him." He turns to Biafle. "You, on the other hand … So, they have a channel and a griot. Whatever they're preparing will be catastrophic."

"Why a channel?" Djengdjeng turns to the Great Chief. "Why does he need a channel when he has a female griot?"

"The very medium for the universe to express itself. Reckon the past, shape the future. Connect with every being and influence their unfolding. Provide energy to each individual and create life. The channel is the ultimate ally and the ultimate foe. Energy at its most whole self before it is branched out to Mother Nature. Whoever harnesses a channel harnesses the full power of the universe."

"Wiseman." The Great Chief places his hand on his chest to greet an old man approaching. Everyone in the circle follows suit.

The Wiseman lays his hand on his own chest in response. "Contrary to the talented sculptor, the incomprehensibly skilled builder, the one who understands all languages or constellations … or the gifted analyst whose sole bond is inherently limited to a grain of information in the universe specific to him and his ancestors, from whence he unconsciously draws inspiration and knowledge of his craft, Kobenan has access to them all. He is the beacon of energy and information from which all proceed. And so long as he lives, all will proceed through him until it is returned to the universe upon his last breath … and passed on to another soul in this space or another." The Wiseman turns to Biafle. "What Kobenan unveiled about the assassination of this minister when you visited me was not an analysis or a deduction. It was a revelation. Up until now, his life was a series of revelations based on whatever his mind focused on. Even heavily blocked, residuals of the stream were being fed to him whenever he required it."

"No one can harness this raw energy," the Great Chief proceeds. "It's foolish to even think of nearing it, let alone use it."

The Third Great Chief steps in. "Maybe foolish, but not impossible if you have a tool powerful enough to control it."

"Eyra is right," says the Wiseman. "Not if you have a catalyst to control the tremendous stream of energy and information channeling through this boy."

"A female griot," says Biafle.

"So, using Namien's daughter, he can now draw what he needs from the channel," infers Nianbou, the pygmy with long braids.

"And this is how powerful our enemy is," the Wiseman continues. "If we don't find this channel, I can't imagine what will befall us."

"How come we know only now my partner is a channel?" Biafle turns to the Wiseman, his tone calm and balanced. His frustration, though in check, threatens to spill out with every word. "How come, in all these years, nobody was aware beside our enemy?"

"Because he wasn't a channel until now," says the little girl. "He wasn't meant to be activated. Whatever they did to him, long before his conception, to contain the channel couldn't challenge the griot's energy and his will to protect her. I felt him when it happened."

"His ancestors were contacted about the coming of a boy in the fifth generation who might be a medium of the universe," the Wiseman begins. "Knowing that death will only bridge the path to a distant soul, they decided to embrace the arrival for better control over it. They sealed and concealed his energy for when the time was to come and passed down the information to their children.

"Since then, the grandparents prepared the parents to conceive a child deprived of power so he wouldn't be able to channel energy. They sent the parents—at their infant stage—to live in town, where cosmic thought is at its lowest, to avoid any suspicion. Whatever information the universe channeled through him wasn't leaving his body. He was meant since birth to block any transmission he received. There was no way for us to know a channel was alive."

"It was said the universe wouldn't allow for their existence. Why is he here?" asks the djinn of the mountains.

"Channels vanished millions of years ago, and nobody really knows the reasons," the Wiseman explains. "The ancients say the universe created them to regulate Mother Nature, but something happened, and it gave this energy to every being to express themselves through it, making them master of their path. The reason why a channel is living, I do not know."

"My name is Alla Rodolphe, new head of the Spectrum Cell. Permission to talk among such eminent people of our motherland," requests a lean, tall man in a marine-blue suit.

The little girl nods.

"If our enemy knew this information from the beginning, it'll mean he somehow tapped into the Wiseman's information sources, which would be highly unlikely, and more so improbable, to localize the channel, or he acquired it at the time of the ancestors and lived through five generations to get to this moment. It's not possible. That's at least five hundred years."

"He could have passed down the information as Kobenan's ancestors did," a high guardian suggests.

"He could have, but beside the fact that you have to be of Dogo blood to even fathom the intricacy of this mechanism, no one would be able to weave these Dogo seals on the windows if he wasn't at least five hundred years old or more. This is not only about knowledge. Someone far older and more experienced is pulling the strings," says Biafle.

"My point exactly," Alla Rodolphe agrees. "No human can live for this long. We have no record of it, except from the Dogo people and the Triniguiri, who have far surpassed the 460-year mark and are both extinct. Yet we have Dogo seals all over this hospital."

"The Dogo were wiped out from all spaces. It's not them," affirms the Wiseman.

"Then who?" asks the Great Chief.

"His proceedings, the energy he uses to control these creatures. They all read as human," says the Third Great Chief.

"I have never seen a human with such degree of patience and control. That's too many souls to bear," says the djinn of the mountains.

"A misleading?" proposes Alla Rodolphe.

"If he is able to fake an energy signature, we might be against something entirely different," says the Wiseman. "In all circumstances, he possesses more than a thousand years of knowledge, and this makes him one of the most dangerous enemies we are facing. Biafle, were you able to follow your partner?"

"The trees lost him at the entrance of Ghana."

"We have to find them before it is too late, and gathering information is our best chance. Do the other countries know what we are up against?" The Wiseman turns to the Great Chief.

"Yes, they're sending reinforcements. The president gives us full control over the situation. We're in S code."

The circle lapses into silence as someone limps toward the Wiseman. Biafle examines the wasted individual covered in severe cuts and bruises. Her tall, rectangular stature and flat shoulders, her accoutrement, her perfectly patterned and symmetrical tresses tightly braided to the base of her neck—one survivor of the wind blast has managed her way back to the hospital. The warrior arrives and whispers in the Wiseman's right ear.

"Someone is in pursuit of the griot," relays the Wiseman

"Who?" asks Biafle.

The warrior looks at the Wiseman for permission to talk and is granted with a barely perceptible nod.

"We don't know. He was very different from all the people we've seen. He's not from the Pure World, not a djinn or a sorcerer. He spoke to the channel before launching his pursuit."

"You mean he's a common man." Nianbou shows reservation.

"Could this be possible? How did he survive the pressure on the seventh floor?" asks Djengdjeng.

"It's the troubled energy I felt when we arrived here," says the little girl. "The guard is right, he is neither of the former. Certainly a human, but it seems like he's followed by something ... a spirit I knew ages ago."

"What spirit?" asks the Great Chief.

"I'm not sure. It looks like a very old fetish."

"Very old, you say? I know of only one ancient fetish still existing on this space. It was imprisoned a long time ago. No, no one leaves that place alive."

"There's no one in the registries matching this description," says one of the men in suits standing beside the circle, typing on what appears to be a field laptop.

"His acquisition of the fetish must have been very recent then," says Alla Rodolphe.

"It is, otherwise the information would already have circulated." The Great Chief turns to the crater. "We know nothing about our enemy, but this ... this is an awful mass of trapped souls. He must have performed vast sacrifices throughout centuries to amass an army this size. The S-cell should have spotted this."

"We would have, unless the frequency were very sparse. And I'm talking decades of intervals," says Alla Rodolphe. "But if it's the same suspect, he must have accelerated his activities recently. When was the last one, Marcel?"

"Today, sir, an attempt," says the agent, typing on his laptop.

"An attempt?" The head of the S-cell looks at his agent.

"Yes, sir," confirms Marcel. "A sorcerers' report says someone walked in front of a bus, forcing it to stop. Two djinns have been killed by the authorities in a place near Blue Bean Intersection, one of whom was often sighted at grave accident sites. Analysis suggests they've been weakened by a confrontation with two individuals, including the one who stopped the bus."

"The authorities killed a djinn, how?" asks Djengdjeng, the pygmy with short braids.

"Two djinns ... and weakened," corrects Nianbou.

"Five BMPs fired at them," says Marcel.

"Tanks. White people's gear," says Alla Rodolphe.

"Do we know who these two men are?" asks Biafle.

"No," responds Marcel. "The agents on site reported that one was significantly taller than the other. The safety distance between them and the confrontation wouldn't allow for clear identification, but the shorter man appeared significantly younger. Maybe early twenties. The agents reported that he was fighting as though he was not in control of his limbs."

"Two men fighting djinns ... that's very unusual, unless ..." says the djinn of the mountain.

"Unless they're not common men or have some serious protection," completes Biafle.

"A fetish." The djinn of the mountains looks at his friend. "A few of the ancient builds used to share body control with the wielder. The younger one seems to fit the description."

"He could be same person who was here," says Biafle.

"Someone forcing a bus to stop. Probably to avoid collision, to save lives. Can't be his first time. Look for similar events in these past months." Alla Rodolphe turns to his agent.

"Five weeks ago, sir," says Marcel, "there was a terrible bus accident on Agbaville Road. Only three out of the forty-two passengers survived. The report says all three confirmed a boy warned them of the accident. Marina Ake, the only woman survivor, said he was sitting right next to her."

"A boy, did she say his name?" asks the Third Great Chief.

"No, but she recognized his face from a newspaper. A murder case in Novalim City, she said."

"Kouadio Dominique Joel," an agent next to Marcel speaks up, typing on his keyboard. "Seventeen years old, student. First son of Kouadio Philipe and Koukoume Alida. Lives in Novalim City, Abidje. Wanted by the national authorities for first-degree murder. Official report says he killed his parents and ran away.

"Sorcerers' report says there had been a confrontation between unknown creatures and a djinn. Kouadio Joel and his sister were the only ones missing from the crime scene. Both parents were killed. They found the djinn's body six miles away at the edge of the highway to Ebile. Analysis suggests Komanko."

"Komanko, suicide to take a life … What kind of djinn does that … for humans?" a high guardian says.

"What's the name of the sister?" asks the Wiseman.

"Kouadio Melanie Princess," responds the agent.

"Someone came for the boy and his family. Why?" asks the Great Chief.

"Reckoning?" proposes Nianbou.

"Djinns don't interfere with reckoning. Whoever he is, he gave his life protecting the family or someone in the family," says Biafle.

"I do not think so." The Wiseman's calm voice seeps through the conversation.

The circle turns to the old man as though awaiting concrete elaboration.

"There was a similar event in Dodoma. The little sister went missing, and the brother, who was a clairvoyant, was assassinated by a djinn. We found out later that the girl was a vessel. There are many vessels around the world …"

"But the ones who can support a channel's energy …" says the Third Great Chief.

"Yes," the Wiseman nods. "One of a kind."

"So Kouadio Joel's sister is a vessel?" asks the Great Chief.

"She might be," says the third Great Chief. "She is the remaining piece that completes the functioning of the channel and the female griot."

"Why would a djinn who is supposed to eliminate the clairvoyant brother give his life to save him?" asks Biafle.

"That's a question we need answered," says the Wiseman.

"Get a search warrant here and in all neighboring countries based on what we've gathered on Kouadio Joel," orders Alla Rodolphe.

"Understood," responds Marcel.

"Wiseman!" A voice echoes in the old man's head.

"Yes."

"At last I can reach you."

"What is it, Zonda?" asks the Wiseman.

"I lost him."

"Who?"

"I've been trying to contact you, but you and Old Paapa were out."

"Tell me, Zonda, who did you lose?"

"Joel."

"Kouadio Joel?" asks the Wiseman.

"Yes, yes."

"Give me the details."

CHAPTER 13

A Brief Meeting

A minibus gently pulls by a station entrance, turning, driving slowly toward similar vehicles, gbackas, arranged in a line yards from the entrance. Though they are notorious for their defective shape, their working engines grant them a green light despite several other ignored criteria for a proper minibus to run. This specific gbacka stands out, with its torn door and perforated ceiling. It attracts attention as it approaches an open spot with its clunky, deceivingly faltering sound.

The driver finally kills the engine after a few tricky maneuvers to properly park. "Terminus," he hollers. "Patrick, check the door for the passengers."

"You got it." The doorman descends from the vehicle and warily pushes back the protruding torn metal segments to make sure no one is hurt on their way out.

They are in Abidje, 2:30 p.m. The bright, hot rays have followed the gbacka through the ceiling's hole until its last stop. They are persistent inside the minibus while the passengers fetch their bags and belongings before alighting. They all descend with an apprehensive side-eye at Joel, still asleep in his seat. The unknown and what they vividly remember from the night before hasten their steps when they reach his section before exiting.

"*Vieux père* Moussa," calls the doorman. The driver turns to his employee to see his gesture toward Joel, the last one in the minibus. He quits his driving seat, approaches Joel, and takes a good look at the young man, or maybe questions the safety of the action he is about to take. Joel is sitting bent on the front seat. His feet on the ground, head and folded arms in his lap, he emits a faint snore.

As gently as he can, the driver touches Joel's shoulder blade. "Kid … we have arrived."

"Hm?" Joel lifts his head, with saliva half-dried by the left side of his mouth. "*Tonton.*"

It's the same word the boy used when he got on the minibus the day before, and when he cleared with frightening ease the branches blocking the vehicle's path. *Tonton* is very much like an unrelated uncle, like *vieux père.* It somewhat reassures the driver that there is no threat, even if deep down he knows. "We have arrived," he repeats. "Where do you want to go?"

Joel collects himself and wipes his saliva with the back of his hand. "Yamouego, *tonton.* I'm going to Yamouego, Blue Bean Cross."

"We're in Dabanville right now. You'll have to take another gbacka to reach there. It's about forty minutes from here."

"Okay. Thank you very much, *tonton.*"

"No, thank *you,*" says the driver, laying his hand on Joel's shoulder.

At this emphasis in the driver's words, this momentary yet direct eye contact, Joel is taken aback, but only his short silence can express it. He grimaces to a needle pain in his left chest when he readies to stand up. He lowers his head to take a look and notices his right arm, then the other one. The chest pain is present but declining. His arms are regaining color. His skin's elasticity shows improvement. Grayish blotches persist, but not as prominently as yesterday. They have shrunk to disproportionate small patches all over.

"Are you okay?" asks the driver, staring at Joel examining his skin.

"Yes," Joel snaps out of his contemplation. "Yes, *tonton.*"

"Here," says the driver, handing him coins. "It's not much, but it'll get you to Yamouego."

"Thank you, *tonton*."

When his feet touch the aging pavement, Joel follows the doorman's chin gesture in someone's direction by the gbacka's flank, near the row of uneven windows. The face is unfamiliar. Joel watches, not really knowing what to make of her eyes watering as she carefully, respectfully approaches him with a baby lovingly wrapped in her arms. Now tears are running down her cheeks. Joel gazes with bewilderment.

"Thank you," she manages under her trembling breath, then looks down at her baby, blissfully asleep. "Thank you ... for my son's safety."

His chest instantly contracts at her tears, but he is unable to place an event on her face. Joel tries to recall looking at the baby in her protective arms, his eyes filling up. His mind is blank. It's been blank since he looked on her exhausted, lean visage. What happened? What did he do? Is there any connection with this wound in his chest? The only thing he remembers is a void after he sat on the bus's seat.

Joel hesitantly nods to her before turning away. He meets the doorman yet again. Patrick, if Joel's feeble recollection when he got on the minibus yesterday holds. He meets Patrick's eyes, which were following this queer interaction all along, just watching, silent, as if they know what this woman is talking about. They do, the driver as well, considering what he said earlier. Joel must be the only one oblivious to what occurred.

"Go to the far-end buses." Patrick points behind him. "They leave for Yamouego in a few minutes."

Joel navigates the mobile obstacles before halting to try to locate once more the direction he was given. Though it is straight ahead, peering clearly through the line of buses southmost of the station requires neck-stretching, with all the bustle. People roam about, many seeking clients for their goods, most aiming for their respective rides. The noise, the frequent calling out to remind future passengers of the departure time, and the controlled chaos all around can easily intimidate a newcomer. Luckily, Joel has already received direction.

"Shit!" Joel sharply retreats to find himself hiding behind a gbacka tire.

Joel gingerly sticks his forehead out from behind the wheel. Two people by a cashier stand are conversing with a woman. Their clothing stands out from their surroundings. He does recognize these suits: the S-cell. He acutely remembers them from Roland's panic in the taxi when they were going back to his apartment following the visit to his guardian, Bredou. They must not see him; that's all he knows. Now they are looking about. The station is crowded but filled with too many pockets for him to blend in. He might be seen if he doesn't think this through. He estimates at least a minute's walk. If only it weren't so far.

Why are they here in this station, at this moment? This is no coincidence.

"Korokou, what happened yesterday?" whispers Joel, with one eye on the two men speaking to random people passing their way. "Korokou?"

"You wasted me."

"What? What did I do?" The needle pain spikes with a jerky movement of Joel's shoulder, forcing him to look down. "How come I have a hole in my chest?"

"You really don't remember. Your subconscious is more reckless than I thought."

"What are you talking about? Are you going to tell me what happened?"

"Kid?" Joel starts to a voice behind him.

"Shewww ... *tonton!*"

"What are you doing?" asks the driver.

Joel carefully points to the men in suits.

"Yes ... these guys. They must be here for the rumors about my gbacka. We don't like people asking too many questions around here. Don't worry, nobody will rat you out. We mustn't be seen together. They will be looking for me. Wait here."

A moment later, Patrick appears. "Let's go."

Joel remains by Patrick's left side, using his thin profile as a screen from the agents' field of view. Patrick knows the station like the back of his hand and takes a few paths farther from the S-cell agents. Every prominent gbackaman they cross and Patrick salutes seems to know who Joel is, judging by their prolonged eyeing.

"Information spreads fast here," says Patrick. "Don't bother."

"What happened?" asks Joel.

The doorman looks at Joel. "You don't remember?"

"No."

"Wait, any of it?"

"No." Joel shakes his head.

"Damn … you're messed up. You saved us. That woman would have been dead if not for you." Patrick fist-bumps another man his age and asks for a name, Bamogo.

"*Vieux père* Bamogo, Patrick's here," calls the doorman.

Joel observes as people enter the white-striped yellow gbacka to claim their seat. A short man with an uneven gray beard descends and approaches Patrick. His prominent belly pushes his shirt in front of him, drawing attention first before his face.

"Patrick, how's it going?"

"I'm good, *vieux père*. *Vieux père* Moussa sends me," says Patrick with a nod toward Joel.

"Hm. Oh, they're here for him?"

Patrick nods.

"I suspected that. Get in, boy."

"Thank you, *tonton*," says Joel, boarding the minibus.

"Grab the middle back seat," hollers Bamogo.

The minibus fills up to two empty seats. The driver starts the engine. The doorman warns imminent departure for those who haven't got in yet. When nobody shows up, Bamogo reverses gear for the exit. The white-striped yellow gbacka is leaving the station.

Forty-five minutes feels like two hours when you are wide awake and counting every second because you know you are indisposing the people next to you. Though they do avoid eye contact with Joel, the small facial hints and involuntary subtle nose coverings say it all. He is called out by someone next to him after fifteen minutes on the road. The man reminds him in a whispery voice that he should clean up more often. Joel does apologize for the inconvenience and comes to know the passenger as Fabrice, a medical student who is visiting his mom in the Red Roofs and inquisitive about where Joel has been, why this particular state. It's a difficult reply for Joel, who has no conventional name for the place he is coming from. "Forest of Wisdom" will only stamp the peculiar mental illness dossier. The passenger wishes Joel good luck and leaves the gbacka two stops later. When it's time, Joel is one of the first to quit the vehicle, with a thank-you to the driver.

Yamouego, the City of Joy, as they colloquially call it, gets its fame from Queen Avenue, with its line of well-known bars and nightclubs. Anybody who has ever stayed in Abidje for more than a month has heard of Queen Avenue. This place here must be far from it, a busy street with restaurants, small shops, and multiple-story buildings sprinkled around. There, about thirty feet away, is a crossroads surrounded by people waiting for the green light to reach the opposite side, probably going about their activities after the midday break. Kids are heading back to school, some with their hands held by grownups. When Joel inquires of one of the pedestrians, he obtains confirmation of Blue Bean Cross.

"Zonda?"

"Yes, I'm here," responds the djinn.

"I can see the crossroads."

"Good. Lay low and wait for my signal."

"Okay." Joel walks to a corner near a pharmacy, where he can sit and rest without making a disturbance. All this food on display around reminds him of the last time he swallowed a proper meal.

"Stop." A voice freezes Joel, already well on his way to bending his knees.

"What?"

"This place is wrong," says Korokou.

"Did you sense something?"

"It should be in a forest. What's it doing here?"

"Who?"

"There is another one. Leave," commands Korokou.

"What? No. Zonda warned me about a warrior from the village. He told me about the djinn they want to capture."

"Joel, your body is still in recovery. Leave this place now."

"Wait, something is moving." Joel peers through passing vehicles to the other side of the road. "It's the djinn. Zonda, he's getting up."

"Wait for my signal, Joel."

"All right," says Joel, gawking at an elongated creature straightening up. Its brown-black tone matches the average human skin color, but its size and hands long past its knees are bizarre. It advances a few inches along the road, very mindful of the pedestrians, and looks left, as if waiting for something. Joel follows its gaze and spots a bus from afar turning in its direction after a few sedans.

"Zonda, if your guy has to act, it's now. This thing's here for the bus."

"Just follow the plan, Joel."

"Yes, but …"

"Don't move," interjects Zonda.

"They're going to die, Zonda," insists Joel.

Korokou weighs in. "Joel, you have no idea what will happen here. Leave now."

The bus is approaching. The creature has its eyes fixed on the long vehicle. "Zonda, I don't see the warrior. Where's the warrior?" demands Joel.

"Listen to me, I warned you. Do not jeopardize this operation. This djinn is very important. Let the bus drive," says Zonda emphatically.

"No, I can't." Joel is leaving the pharmacy's façade. "They're all going to die."

"What are you doing, Joel?" Zonda calls. "The country depends on this operation. Stop. *Stop!* Breach, I repeat, breach."

"What are you doing? I told you to leave," says Korokou.

Joel walks the lane between vehicles, careless, drawing all gazes. A fool seeking death. He draws the attention of the brown djinn, redirecting its globular eyes to Joel's path toward the bus. Drivers brake to look at him in the middle of the road. Honking surrounds him. Pedestrians stare. No one approaches. No one will dare to, when many suspect there may be a curse afflicting this individual. The bus stops seven feet before Joel.

"Hey! You're on the road. What are you doing?" yells the bus driver.

"Disembark," orders Joel.

"What? Someone drag this fool out of the road."

Joel goes to the bus's side. He will pull each one of them out if he has to. No accident will happen today while he is here. And if pulling doesn't work, if there is resistance, he will lie down before the front tires. Joel clutches the locked doors, aiming with a forceful attempt to pry them open, and with an effortless yank snatches them so hard, they stick in his hands. Faces widen in the bus, even Joel's, but he can't dwell on it. He has a point to make. Joel releases the doors on the road, walks back to the front of the bus, and looks intently at the driver. "Disembark ... now," he says firmly.

The tense yet composed driver quickly ushers his passengers out of the vehicle while keeping panic at bay, but it all spirals into turmoil, with everyone screaming, running for their lives, when the young fool suddenly flies toward a building, as if struck by something. Joel smashes into a fourth-floor window, rolling, trashing everything on his course into the living room before being stopped by a TV stand next to a wall.

"Miserable human," screams the djinn. Its distorted voice resonates all over the area. "Do you have any idea what you have done?"

"Korokou," calls Joel, disoriented. It hurts to stand up, with his feet failing on the first two attempts.

"You didn't listen," says Korokou.

"We have a d—"

The creature snatches Joel by the neck, lifts him up, and lobs him into the next room. Obstacles can only stop Joel's impetus in the next apartment, where families are rushing out, seeking safety outside the building. Joel leans on the bed frame to try to stand up. The only urge lingering at this moment is to take hold of his dysfunctional body so he can escape. The bent creature, filling every room it steps into, approaches Joel.

"Korokou? Ahhhh, Korokou. Are you in this boy?" asks the djinn. "A fossil in a weak piece of meat. So, you are the one the sorcerers are talking about. You've been a lot of trouble these dayyyyzzz. Hahahaaaaa, Zooeeelllll. I'm going to bring your head and those bracelets to him. It'll be a gooood compenzazionnn."

Joel has trouble relying on his right leg to stand up. The distortion tells him his head, his eyes have yet to adjust to the shock he received. The brown djinn raises its long right arm and flings it at Joel, who dodges with a wrench of his upper body and emits a shrill cry from the immediate back pain.

"You had to move. This strike would have killed you," says Korokou.

The long left arm is slashing through the air toward Joel, when the creature is walloped by a stout man thrusting it into the living room. The man seizes Joel with one hand, walks toward a blasted window, and tosses him out of the building with no particular attention. Joel flinches, but he is already in free fall, watching himself cross each story and slamming into the tiled bedrock. He is flattened, sprawled, eyes opened. Seconds are frozen until he blinks once, then sits and with both hands holds his head, his countenance crumpled with pain. He felt the rock under his shoulder blades, his tailbone, his heels, the back of his skull. He felt his entrails crushing his spine, demanding room to spread, yet he is still breathing. They ache like hell, but they have not shattered, they have not burst. How is this possible?

This hard face, this thick black beard from ear to ear, this tall and burly stature, Joel remembers the man who released him like garbage. They have never talked, and frankly Joel never approached him, nor did he want to, for he was far from welcoming back in the village. Or should he say indifferent? So was Kobile, his little brother, the man who saved him and brought him to Old Paapa.

Joel slowly stands up, confirming with pressure applied that nothing is actually broken. He looks around. He is in the building's backyard. The exit is through the left corridor. Once he reaches the road, he locks eyes on the agents staring at him from afar. The seriousness in their eyes, their serenity. Every inch of his body warns him to keep his distance. The momentary exchange lasts until a short explosion presses Joel to instinctively jerk and cover his head. Skyward, he perceives the djinn spat out from the building, followed by dust of destroyed furniture, then Kobile's brother, who shows himself by the edge. He lands, uses his hand to retain his balance, and strides toward the dazed djinn arising farther by the crossroad. The warrior skirts a mis-aimed strike and smites the creature to the asphalt.

People have deserted Blue Bean Cross and the vicinity. The S-cell agents Joel saw at Dabanville observe the scene, one of them preparing something on the ground next to the crossroad. The warrior is on the djinn, delivering a series of powerful blows. The raging brown creature grips him with a sharp, stretched groan and hurls him by the side of the road. The warrior digs himself out of the debris of ruined buildings and reflexively bends his head at a strike deepening in the rubble. He uproots his opponent and splats it before him, then lifts both fists to aim for its head, when something bashes him away. The warrior slowly lifts his heavy build from the asphalt, rests on a knee, and surveys straight ahead. The brown djinn is approaching with another one by its side, red, slightly taller, more human-shaped but fuller, with indescribable facial features.

"Another djinn! Korokou," calls Joel.

"He doesn't stand a chance," says the fetish.

The S-cell agent, with a knee on the driveway, is now mounting a device.

"We have to help him," declares Joel.

"He's already dead."

Joel breaks toward the djinns. "You're going to help me, or you won't leave this body."

"What are you doing?" Korokou asks calmly.

"He's the only lead to the griot right now." Joel is nearing the agents.

"Jump."

Joel leaps before dark strings jet out of the ground, only to miss and brush his left heel nearly five feet above their heads. The S-cell agents fixate on Joel as he bunglingly falls on the battlefield.

"Don't touch the red djinn," advises Korokou.

"Got it. Be careful with my body. I'm too young for a broken spine," says Joel, avoiding a blow meant for the warrior.

The stout man is fighting both djinns, powerful and brutal, dodging, withstanding blows. He fights with decreasing vigor and a skin clearly suffused with rot. The moment is now, or what is about to happen might end it all, so Joel dashes to the brown djinn, with a kick in its right flank as it is winding up for what would be a conclusive strike.

The blow forces the startled djinn to instinctively retreat near its partner and assess the new threat. There's not much to consider besides the surprisingly audacious action of this weakling. It probably felt a sting because of Korokou. It should keep an eye on Joel.

"I'll help you with this one. I have a fetish."

"I know." The warrior gets back up, waving away Joel's helping hand. "Avoid its arms. Its strength comes from them. And don't get close to me."

The fight restarts, wasting everything in proximity. Joel engages cautiously, landing blows when the frequent opportunities present themselves, eluding or flat-out leaving the brawl when the red djinn shifts aim, when the brown djinn shifts aim. He is aggravating, and his kicks are nothing less than painful. The warrior locks the djinn's neck at times or restrains its short legs, landing consistent blows on its back, flank, or neck until it refocuses on its old target.

There's rage in the brown djinn's sharp screams. The annoyance of this boy is immeasurable. Joel knows it only requires one blunder for the brown djinn to tear him into small pieces. Korokou does not only warn him to split when it becomes too hot; his limbs disobey when he fights. They even disobey when he's running from the djinns, causing a stumble or a trip to miss a strike on his back. His movements deviate from conventional coordination. He battles as though his body struggles under two managements.

*

It quickly gets crowded at the edge of Blue Bean Cross. The army is on site. Tanks are in strategic position after a trail of wrecked vehicles lines up on their periphery. Choppers surround the area.

"What's the situation?" A high-ranking officer stops next to an S-cell agent.

"We're almost ready," responds the agent. "The S-cell has been briefed. There are several confrontations like this going on in the whole territory."

"We're aware. The national army is getting mobilized."

"I'm afraid you won't be of much help, Colonel."

"We're all you have right now," affirms the colonel. "Try to get something out of it. The whole country is on alert one, and I received report of S-cell heads en route to Bengerville."

"Make the choppers leave the area," says the S-cell agent.

"Why?"

"There are frequency variations on these battlefields. Trust me, you don't want your choppers to fall into the bad ones."

The colonel thumbs a button on his walkie-talkie. "Chopper one and two, move two miles away from Blue Bean."

"Two miles. Roger," responds a pilot.

One of the officers approaches the colonel. "Sir, our electronic equipment isn't responding properly."

"What about the tanks?"

"We have control over the cannons, for now."

"Get your tanks ready," the S-cell agent advises.

"How many?" asks the colonel.

"All of them."

"This area is pretty small for five tanks."

"Colonel …" The S-cell agent looks at the high-ranking officer. "Apart from those cannons, none of this will do any serious damage to these creatures."

The colonel locks gazes with the agent, as if giving it thought, and then turns to his officer. "Have the people been evacuated?"

"Almost, sir. We weren't prepared for this."

"Do it fast."

"Yes, sir."

"This place will be a mess after those tanks," says the man, eyeing Joel fighting the void.

"As soon as you see them, fire your cannons," says the S-cell agent.

"How many am I looking at?" asks the colonel.

"With the teenager, four. A djinn of the east, one of the north, and a warrior from the forest of Agbaville. The only one we don't know is this young man. Judging by his movements, he has one or more fetishes in his body. He's a threat."

"What about the warrior?"

"He's already dead. The djinn of the north's skin is cursed."

"So, we fire on the whole?" asks the colonel.

"Yes … target the young man. The radius will have them all."

"Colonel, the population has been evacuated," the officer returns.

"This is Colonel Tizie. Target the boy."

A blast heightens everyone's senses. The sudden gust shakes many to the flank of their military vehicles and flips others' hats.

"What was that?" exclaims the colonel.

"A wind blast," responds the S-cell agent. "The warrior. He got rid of the djinns."

"He got rid of them?"

"Not for long."

"Boy, get to cover," commands the stout man, sighting the far-away crowd peering at them, at Joel, probably the sole being in their spectrum. It only requires one of their tools to incapacitate him permanently.

Joel looks behind him and then to Kobile's brother. "What about you?"

"I'm done." Joel knows what he means, or at least he thinks he knows what the word *done* means, yet the spoken word and the demeanor of Kobile's brother diverge so stiffly, he might just be conveying that he can fight no more. "Zonda what's the situation?" the warrior asks.

"Nobody is responding. We lost all the battlefields. They knew we were coming," a voice echoes in the man's head.

"All the battlefields …" he repeats in disbelief.

"All of them," confirms Zonda. "The last communication was Kobile's. They've been ambushed by djinns they didn't sense when they reached the area."

"I didn't sense this one either."

"We should have been able to detect something. Even you missed the djinn of the north. It doesn't make sense."

"Somebody is helping them," says the warrior. "These djinns don't leave their dwellings. Do you have something for me?"

"There has been a lot of communications since we deployed. I managed to extract a few based on the information Kobile and Tigam sent. I don't understand, Dangbe. These sounds are very old."

"How old?"

"It looks like … Triniguiri," says Zonda.

"Triniguiri? You need to inform Old Paapa and the Wiseman."

"I can't reach them."

"Then make this your priority," orders the warrior.

"Understood. From what I've gathered, it seems there is a lot of activity at Bengerville, a mental hospital. Right now, it's the only place. And, Dangbe … Sector 0 is under attack."

"By who?" Joel can only follow the warrior's words, but even he knows the stout man barely believes whatever has just been told to him, judging by his shocked expression.

"We don't know," responds Zonda. "They're still fighting. Whoever it is, he's powerful."

"I don't think 'powerful' is enough to hold the whole Sector 0 guardians. We're missing something. Can you confirm the presence of the griot at Bengerville? They're coming back. Fast."

"I can't, but every piece of information leads me there," replies Zonda.

"Okay, boy." Dangbe turns to Joel. "It seems you can defend yourself. Hold this. You'll get better vibrations. Go to Bengerville, and get the griot to a safe place. Zonda will guide you. I'll take care of those djinns."

Joel accepts a rough piece of broken stone dropped into his palm with doubt flooding his face. The djinns are imminent, and processing a thought in this situation is just not possible. Kobile's brother is disturbingly composed. His stark countenance betrays no weakness, but his deterioration is more apparent by the minute. You would think only a benign skin disease affects him if you were solely relying on his facial expression. However, he's now made of two colors, and black is losing ground.

The warrior was surely talking to Zonda with the words he mouthed moments ago, and now Joel is tasked with the safety of something they all consider extremely important. Has this responsibility just been entrusted to him?

*

"It's ready," informs the S-cell agent, kneeling on the blacktop, activating the device he was manipulating.

The sound of a charge loads, and a pulse flashes, rushing toward Joel. The djinns stop to look at themselves. The warrior glances at his chest, then the army, and with one smooth maneuver positions himself before Joel.

"F-i-i-ire!" yells Colonel Tizie.

The bombardments are deafening, exploding at short, consistent intervals, wildly disorienting. They are continuous, while the agents and the colonel observe from a bearable position an ever-growing foam of smoke, swallowing whole the targeted area and firing debris and concrete morsels out of its shapeless sphere. The foam does not decrease in volume and size until Colonel Tizie orders a stop. Silence dominates the scene as the army watches the black-and-gray screen growing thin. They hear it. They can all hear it: a faint moaning traveling across Blue Bean Cross. A barely audible wretched chant capable of inciting any bowel to contract, any skin to crisp, and any limb to fail if the mind is not prepared to face the unfaceable.

Soldiers retain their focus despite the unsettling sound, their barrels aimed at the vanishing smoke, ready to unload on whatever might be coming their way. When the dust clears, they perceive only a calcified body, but this vile moaning suggests something alive, something in a great deal of pain. Something only visible to the S-cell agents. It is torn in half. Its upper body lacks an entire arm, and its skin is dark and crusty. The brown djinn is somewhat alive. Not really an event for the agents.

"It's still alive," murmurs Colonel Tizie, trying to wrap his head around the idea of anything surviving this much firepower. "One of them is still alive."

The agent who handled the pulsing machine flicks his hand in a beckoning motion to the officer next to Colonel Tizie, as if requesting something. The officer looks at his superior, and when Colonel Tizie agrees, he passes his walkie-talkie to the agent.

"We were lucky those tanks were working. We would have been their primary target," says the agent, quitting his strategic position for the field of smoke.

"It's okay, Colonel," says the second agent, pulling a small bottle from the inner pocket of his suit. "We'll take it from here."

They approach an area of blood and flesh painted on the road and standing foundations, charred, reeking of burnt meat. The gray smoke barely clinging to the points of impact leaves fumes unlikely to dissipate anytime soon. The first agent advances toward the dying brown djinn. He crouches and studies it as it helplessly looks back with a weak squirm, a plea emanating from its mutilated protruding pharynx. The agent pops open the small bottle and leans in for a scrape. The second agent walks farther, to the calcified body visible to all, and he too observes.

"The teenager ..." He turns to his colleague. "He's still out there."

"Colonel?" The walkie-talkie sounds.

"Yes." Colonel Tizie freezes an officer coming toward him with an outward palm.

"We'll need a chopper," continues the agent. "One of them survived."

"Sir," the officer insists.

Colonel Tizie turns to him. "We've located him."

"Who?"

"The young man. He's on his way to Yamouego's exit," responds the officer.

"Then stop the vehicle! Where are the police?"

"He's running, sir," says the officer.

"There's only one exit, we ... What do you mean he's running?"

"He's running ... sir."

Colonel Tizie lets the words sink in for a moment. It can't have been more than five minutes since the cannons. Nothing should be close to Yamouego's main exit road on foot. "What are these people?" his tone spikes. "Where are the choppers?"

*

"Which way, Zonda?"

"Left, left."

Joel manages an angular veer past a house, almost losing his balance and quickly reclaiming it with a palm to the ground, his momentum broadly conserved, a large portion of his body smeared with ash and brick dust. He navigates through a neighborhood baffled at the sight of him and the fleetness of his movements.

"What's happening?"

"What?"

"Why is everything blurred?" Joel eases on his feet.

"Stop!" Zonda calls. "This is too soon ... Your body has to adjust. You're stressing your senses."

"Not good, I can't see anything, Zonda."

"Give it time. It'll come back."

"Okay." Joel pants, on his knees, spent but not out of breath or stamina. Blotches of color are all he seems to be able to process. There are no people where he paused, or else they are incredibly still and quiet.

"We'll have to use the main road for a while. That's the fastest way," declares the djinn.

"They have choppers, Zonda. I'll be too exposed."

"Our choices are few. We just have to reach the Bienga Reserve, but it's through the main exit road. The other way will be between neighborhoods. It doubles our time."

"We'll take the road, then," asserts Joel.

"Let's weigh our options. Your body is clearly straining."

"We have to. There's no time."

"How are your eyes?" asks Zonda.

"They're getting better."

"They're all looking for you, Joel, and they won't stop until you're dead or can't move a muscle. Don't slow down, even if your sight recedes."

"I won't. Let's go."

"Walk," commands Zonda. "Give time to your mind. Once we get out there, that's it. You're not far from the main road."

It's hard to walk unnoticed with the powder of dust and ash defining Joel's face. The few people he passes watch but maintain their distance. Maybe they have figured out he is the reason for all this din of sirens and rotors and choose not to approach, or they are just dumbfounded by the extravagant makeup. What is certain is he should not linger wherever he passes. There it is, Zonda confirms, a long, narrow alley opening to brightness.

Is there time to gather his nerve? There is no time at all. The griot, that's all that matters. The only person, according to Korokou, who can help him get his sister back. He must think five times before he gets out of this alley. People who fire explosive projectiles mean to eliminate him, whatever the circumstances. So better not to think altogether of what awaits ahead. Caution will only slow him down.

"All right … all right, let's go." Joel accelerates on the narrow path between rows of houses and springs out in the open about thirty feet before the barrage of police vehicles.

Choppers surveilling the area now have a lock. Joel races right for the overpass. Police cars skid into pursuit. Motorbikes have already launched. One of the choppers follows, lowering altitude, the dot becoming a fast-moving individual capable of challenging a sedan's speed in urban settings. It will soon be within sniper range. They are on a highway, and the police vehicles are closing fast. He is in the open, but his nimbleness is a slight advantage over tires.

"Stop, or we will open fire," warns the S-cell agent, looking down at Joel, a megaphone in his hand.

"Find something, Zonda." Joel flicks his head up to the chopper on his left.

"I am, I am. Give me a moment."

"We don't have a moment," stresses Joel.

"The road becomes a bridge a few miles farther down. We'll exit as soon as we can."

"Holy shit! They're shooting!"

"Don't, *don't!*"

Joel smacks the asphalt headfirst, rolls along the white lines, and then stops. He immediately half-rolls, nearing a motorcycle's tires inches from his skull. The second vehicle is about to ram him. Joel jumps up and barely dodges the police car, scratching the doors. A biker at the tail of the vehicle, aiming his machine pistol, causes Joel to make an abrupt movement to remove himself as a target before he slugs the pursuer off his motorbike. These bikers are not policemen, he realizes, now that he has crossed one. Beside their unique uniforms, dirt bikes and this type of gun are not used by the police he is accustomed to. Disorientation has yet to settle away, but his priority lies somewhere on the road. When Joel finds the small piece of stone that escaped his hand during the fall, he lunges for it, clenches it, and shoots forward.

"You cannot look behind at this speed, Joel," yells Zonda. "You'll lose balance."

"*Yes*, I figured that out." Joel jerks at a bullet's swoosh piercing his hearing. "There are civilians on the road."

"You represent a national threat. The S-cell will lose civilians to stop you. Don't run straight."

"Shit, shit, I have to leave the highway, or someone will die."

"We're almost at the bridge," assures Zonda.

"Behind," says Korokou.

The word is calm and the tone unbefitting the situation, but Joel has learned the value of Korokou's shallow warnings by now and does not lose a fraction of a second to veer aside. He hears a loud shot bursting in the spot he just vacated. This sound is different, singular, and it hitting the road means it came from above. The chopper is the only vehicle that has been constant, whatever evasion Joel has performed. Flying bitumen debris hits his heels. He should really get out of sight before another shot is fired.

"Can you get him?" the S-cell agent asks a man with a patchy beard. He wears a marine blue military outfit tucked into black boots and a bulletproof vest.

"He's too fast, sir," responds the sniper.

"As soon as you have a clear shot, take him." The S-cell agent peers through the windshield. "The bridge ... of course. All units, do not let him reach the bridge. I repeat, do not let him reach the bridge."

Bullets zip by Joel's head. Civilian vehicles in the way are mere obstacles to the flying projectiles. Joel cannot grimace enough to convey the burning ripping his back, when two bullets sink into his skin. The urge to halt at the unbearable pain taunts him, but he might as well agree to die if he doesn't reach this bridge.

"What are you doing?" the S-cell agent asks impatiently. "He's slowed down."

"The tanker truck, sir," responds the sniper.

The agent locks eyes with the sniper. "He is heading to Bengerville. Have you ever in your whole life seen someone moving this fast? Do I need to remind you what's at stake here?"

The sniper takes a second to consider. "I cannot, sir." He confirms his decision. "There are too many civilians on the road."

The agent glares at the sniper, unused to someone refusing to execute an order, a direct S-cell order. "Move." He shoves the man from his position and snatches the rifle, which the sniper does not oppose. Disobeying these people is already career-ending, if not jailable. He is unsure what thwarting them will lead to. The S-cell agent locks himself in for safety and takes aim at Joel.

An explosion ahead, a tire succumbing to one of the multiple bullets chasing Joel, does not stir his attention from the bridge. A low, heavy skidding noise, however, demands a glance. It's a tanker truck, slowly going out of control as the driver attempts to maintain a straight course. He won't, from the angular direction the tank is deviating to.

"Where are you going?" asks Zonda.

"The driver," says Joel, distancing himself from the bridge side.

"Joel, the explosion won't spare you if you get caught in it."

Joel rushes to the vehicle and with a slight jump clings to the driver's door. "Let me in!" he hollers at a fat man whose grip on the wheel and desperation for control deprive him of any other focus but the road ahead. Joel pulls the door open and instantly feels a metal sheet next to him pierced when he hears the now familiar single shot. He does not wait for another and pushes the driver, while getting in the truck and holding the steering wheel.

The S-cell agent strikes a seat with his fist and looks once more at the sniper. The tank topples, dragging the truck along, scrapes the asphalt, and is set afire. Police vehicles brake, causing collisions among themselves, civilians, and motorbikes. Those who can manage to the best of their ability try to retreat from the flipped tank. The blast on the bridge sweeps away any vehicles in its vicinity, prompting the pilot to maneuver away from the intense explosion. The S-cell agent and the pilot stare at the explosion, and so does the sniper.

"No sign of the target," the pilot finally says.

"He's already gone," says the agent, grabbing a phone from his inner pocket.

*

Joel writhes, scratching at the metal shell deep in his back until he can get a hold of it with his fingers and pull it out of his skin. Then comes the second bullet. His fingertips daubed with blood, he manages to remove the second bullet and lets it fall onto rich, uneven soil. The instant relief is indescribable. He gets to his knees, his forearm still on a long trunk he used for support, and exhales. Joel made sure the driver was still breathing when he ditched him on a slanted, grass-carpeted hill leading to the reserve entrance. The blast they barely escaped left him unconscious in Joel's hands. A heavy load to carry on his back.

The chopper is still disturbingly prominent at a distance. Staying in this area would be ill-advised, especially this close to the entrance, with those long, spaced trees giving way to a noticeably sunny sky. Joel pulls himself up and dives into the Bienga Reserve. Now that no one is on his tail and the burdensome sound of rotors drowns in the background, he finds room for an attempt to grasp what's happening to him, to his body. He doesn't really think so much as explores the question, discovering. He cannot really understand; he doesn't try to. It is just boggling his mind. Bullets failing to penetrate him. The pain is horrendous, but nonetheless, he felt pain. No matter how atrocious it was, he felt it, he didn't collapse, and they were certainly not rubber bullets.

What about his legs? He meanders through the Bienga with a certain swiftness he knows he has never dreamt of until it was possible moments ago. He is just *fast*. That's what he perceives, grazing through whipping branches and leaves. He is fast, at least unreasonably faster than the average person. And it all unfolds before him. Unbelievable, hard to conceive, yet shockingly factual in his firsthand experience.

"They're fighting," informs Zonda. "Turn left here."

"Who's fighting?" Joel takes the recommended path.

"Everyone in the mental hospital."

"Did they get to her?" Joel asks apprehensively.

"I don't know. We have to move fast," says the djinn.

"I'm following you."

"Here."

Joel halts in the midst of the forest. "Where?" He looks around.

"Wait ... I'm not sure which one of them," says Zonda.

"Which one what?"

"The two trees in front of you. One of them leads to the mental hospital."

"Okay." Joel pauses. These trees are large but very distinct from the ones he and Zonda passed through when the djinn helped him leave the village for the forest of wisdom. They have no openings at their roots, just long, straight trunks.

"You're not sure which tree we should use?" Joel reiterates.

"No." Zonda pauses. "Their patterns are pretty similar, but their connections are very different."

"Then let's pick one."

"*Don't* do that, Joel. One of them brings us close to the mental hospital. The other will send you to the central forest of Ghana. Even if you're the fastest person in the world, you won't be able to get to Côte d'Esperance in time. Believe me, you're far from fast. And you're wounded. Just be patient. Let me analyze the patterns and make sure we take the right connection."

"How long?" ventures Joel.

"About ten minutes."

"We don't even know what's happening out there! We can't wait ten minutes."

"It's the surest way to get there," says Zonda.

"Korokou, what do you think?"

"I don't care."

"Pff, why do I even ask?" Joel throws his arms up in despair and covers his face.

He cannot stand quietly. His hands either crossed by his neck or resting on his waist, he paces by the designated trees. Head down at the soil, head up at nothing, his concern grows. They're wasting valuable time right now.

"Zonda?"

"Calling my name every five seconds won't increase my reading ability, Joel."

"Please hurry."

"What do you think I'm doing? The patterns on the left tree are starting to shape like ..."

"We go for it," says Joel.

"No! ... Wait ... Let me confirm. It's only been a minute. It's too premature."

"We have to go, Zonda."

"Do you ever listen? Just listen for a moment." Impatience seeps into Zonda's tone. "If I am wrong, I fail at my assignment, and you lose your sister forever. Do you understand that? Give me a few minutes to confirm the patterns."

"Our chances grow thin every second."

"Wait, *wait!*"

A garden. That's what Joel sees when he exits the fuzzy path. An enclosed, well-managed yard of circular, square, and personalized flower blocks, plants of diverse origins arranged in specific fashion so as to evoke beauty or religious care. An even, masterfully trimmed green hedge high enough to conceal all surrounds it. When Joel turns, he perceives the tree he just passed, a very dissimilar species from the one he entered by. A kind he can at least recognize among many, with its popular fruits, as they grow in most home courts: a mango tree.

Noises beyond the garden draw Joel's attention. He then notices a large building through an opening serving as entry to the garden.

"Zonda?"

"Yes, it's here."

Joel cautiously approaches the opening and takes cover behind a vaguely square corner of green leaves, reconnoitering about. They have swarmed the area. Humanoid creatures concentrated at the building's main door try to bypass in bulk an extensive curved tree, which they only manage to push through a pinch at a time. Though their exceedingly large number gravitates toward the entrance, very few are sprinkled about on the wide terrain. Joel needs to be extremely careful if he wants to avoid attention. It only requires one to alert all.

"What you're looking for is up there," Korokou says indifferently.

Joel looks up. He cannot quite distinguish the noise of the fight, but even from here he catches grunting and screeching from the floor above.

"Zonda, the griot is still here." He relays the information.

"I'm reading that."

"The main entrance is not an option."

"What do you see?" asks Zonda.

"There is an army of creatures trying to break in."

"Those inside don't have much time," declares the djinn.

Joel observes the enemy's relentless struggle. The proximity of this curved tree against the main entrance has no purpose whatsoever from a construction standpoint, but it keeps them occupied. "What do we do?"

He describes the top windows at Zonda's request. The djinn is adamant about specifics of meshes enveloping the yet-to-be-destroyed metal frames. They look like worn-out ropes of goldish color, with fibers straying all over their main knots and whorled bodies. They are not attached securely enough to keep anything from getting in, rather loosely hanging over the frames with a few lazy knots. Most of the windows, the ones still intact, present the same characteristics. Zonda does not embrace the description at first, demanding confirmation of the color.

These seals don't exist, he says. They shouldn't. Yet there they are, protecting the enemy from a surprise attack through the windows. They are Dogo seals, Zonda explains, genius, from one of the most powerful civilizations in African legend. They should be lost in time, buried in the woven history of forgotten songs, but they aren't. Someone managed to replicate the Dogo knowledge here, in this hospital. The only people who could weave a Dogo seal were the Dogo, and they went extinct epochs ago. For the first time, Joel can feel that Zonda is genuinely trying to understand something he says doesn't make any sense.

"We can't penetrate those windows," he finally announces. "If you touch them, you'll die instantly, however strong you are. It's a very ancient seal, and I don't know how to break it."

"Korokou says he does," says Joel.

"Korokou?" Zonda falls silent momentarily. "Yes, King Condo, his first host in this space, acquired him from the Pure World, and the Dogo were believed to have permeated numerous spaces during their ascension."

Spaces, more than one. Whatever they are has no correlation with Joel's current understanding, but there are more pressing concerns at this very moment, and one of them is finding a way inside the hospital.

"So, what now?"

"First, you have to be out of sight. The back side of the building might do. You won't stand a chance if these creatures spot you deactivating one of the seals."

Joel squeezes into the hedge's corner through a hole he uncovers by pulling tangled branches out. He surely is visible, though if he is heedful of their position, it might help him get to the rear without raising any attention. There is not much between the garden and the building other than elegant concrete flowerpots and sparse benches.

The sounds of violent interactions emanating from the building are muffled but clearer at the rear in the oddly quiet surroundings. This side does expose more Dogo seals than the façade, with all its windows intact. His position shows another building connecting to the one of interest in an L shape. Another ward bearing the same deadly mechanisms. He finds his grip and begins planting one foot above the other, very mindful of any proximity to the seals. Supporting his weight on his fingertips and toes takes a toll on his stamina. The only respite is air conditioners spaced all over the wall.

Joel reaches one of the windows, the fifth past the left corner, positions himself so as to secure a semblance of stability with one of the radiators, and stretches his arm to approach the golden mesh.

"Count the straight fibers from left to right. Don't touch them," Korokou says suddenly.

"What straight fibers? There are zillions here," says Joel.

"Look carefully. There are straighter ones."

Joel studies the mesh between his right arm, tiring from his firm grip and the feeling of his toes on the verge of slipping off. Korokou is correct. After a slow glide, his gaze stops at the bottom half of the frame. The strands in this section look definitely straighter than any other ones around. These lightly bent fibers appear like nothing but a natural result of a frayed rope. One needs a very close examination to notice the different forms of curls and bends running over the rope.

"Where should I stop?"

"Rikiery," responds Korokou.

Joel starts counting, patiently, as one should in this situation. A single erroneous slide, and he falls from this building. The dripping sweat on his forehead and under his armpit seem to be the result of his apprehensive body over his precarious resolve. *Rikiery* swiftly translated to 213 in his head, and he is now at 105.

"Okay, 213," says Joel after a silent moment, his eyes peeled on the strand so as not to lose it among a sea of near-identical shapes.

"Touch it slightly."

"Are you sure?"

"Touch it and nothing else."

It requires an enormous effort to compose himself over the piercing shriek below. One of the creatures has spotted him and is alarming the others. It's climbing up, Joel senses. He touches the fibers and follows Korokou's instructions, though his main concern lies underneath, with the vicious grunt, until it suddenly stops. Joel gingerly peers down, only to see the inert creature flattening on the soil.

They have responded to the call, and more are converging. Joel tries to concentrate on the seal, to complete the discombobulating deactivation pattern. The movements and frequent shrieks indicate they are closing in. Joel glances down to observe many of them falling while others strive up. Their behavior shows an awareness of the seals' effect, although the rashness of some provokes contact with the strands. Joel maintains focus on the mesh. Korokou has yet to hint at any concluding steps. He will be helpless if one of those creatures reaches him in this boxed-in position. There are not many options for evasion besides entering this window.

"Touch twice the twelfth curved fiber," Korokou commands.

"The ... twelfth ..." Joel carefully begins the count.

"They're not far. Take your time," Korokou says passively.

"It's my life on the line here!" replies Joel.

However one defines Korokou's brash behavior or insulting lack of interest, each of his uncommon words proves verified, and sure enough, Joel can effortlessly isolate the prominent cry above all else growing underneath him. It won't be long, he can feel, before this creature pulls him off the wall.

The calm is starting to break, and Joel can see his finger's mild quivering. All he can do where he stands is to count and touch fibers, with no sign whatsoever of an ending or even progress. He is to reach for the left side, identify semicurved strands, count until the seventh, and touch three of them at once. He cannot really take time or focus, with the grunting probably at his feet now. He counts, convinced he has skipped one in this bustle, dismayed, yet he continues. Joel stretches his gripping arm, so he will be at a proper range for his fingers to touch all three simultaneously, when he is violently yanked down, loses his toes' grip, and scrapes his knee on the bricks but manages to hold on to the air conditioner. An involuntary squawk puffs out of him, followed by a series of short, uncontrolled groans. He will not let go, despite the creature pulling with all its strength and weight on his ankle.

Joel consolidates his position with his free hand, reaching for the air conditioner, the unstable object only inclining further, cracking cement as though it's going to detach under the weight. It only takes a fraction of a second for Joel to reflexively let go. They drop like flies as the seal grazes them in its fall. Joel manages to touch all three strands without even realizing it. Now he has to get rid of this clingy creature without dragging them both down. He needs a better support; this unit won't hold for long.

He pulls himself above the radiator and reaches for the open window. When both hands have found stability, he uses his left foot to repeatedly stomp the creature until it gives in. Joel climbs, slumps into an office, and remains on his belly for a moment to recover something, anything, from all that was drained outside. The clashes are violent here, as the reality of his location barges in. He jerks up to a thump on the wall, then another one near the broken doorframe. Joel stands up. Walls bulge to heavy blows, tiles explode into many pieces, unsettling screams and roars emanate beyond the door, and sounds of violent impacts reverberate nearby. He takes a deep breath. "Zonda, I'm h—" An arm grabs his neck, hauling him to the window.

The abruptness takes him off guard, but he manages to unhook himself and thrusts the creature off the frame. More are coming up. Joel locks the window and drags a bookshelf by it, then a table.

"Zonda, I'm in."

"Good. Let's find the griot. The mass of energy has expanded, but it's still here."

"Okay." Joel steps out of the office.

Chaos cannot describe what he witnesses. Creatures are violently propelled to the corridor's edges, soaring black men dropping in batches. Inhaling instantly grows laborious, although bearable, with his chest visibly pumping air. His stupefied gaze has yet to take in the area as he briskly steps back to avoid a creature slammed against the doorframe. Joel does not wait and keeps it there with a swift kick to its face. To his left is a struggling group of a few, trying to restrain an unspeakable beast filling the area's height and width. Another creature, a humanoid made of roots, seems to be the leader of this group, shouting orders and repositioning itself.

"Him." Korokou refocuses Joel.

He looks right and perceives a man in a damaged suit, lying on his bleeding face, trying slowly and desperately to stand up. He reckons it is a girl he seeks, but there is no time to argue. Joel, while maintaining complete awareness of his extremely hostile surroundings, is making his way to him when he spots one of the creatures running toward the man in the suit. He rushes over and whacks the creature to the wall behind the man, then lunges to terminate it with a stomp on its face at its attempt to get back up. Joel approaches the man in the suit, crouches before him, and helps him straighten up. The young individual, about Joel's age or maybe few years older, is looking straight ahead, as though he has lost sight, his face expressionless. It looks like he might collapse on the floor if Joel doesn't support him.

"They got the griot." His efforts to speak appear strenuous and his voice frail. "You can still … save her … the window … they fled by the window … Don't veer."

"I'm on it," prompts Joel. "Can you hold yourself up?"

"I'll be … fine … go."

"You're leaving him. Why?" asks Korokou.

"What? You heard him." Joel hastens for the room.

"You're in the area, Joel," informs Zonda. "The girl should be close by."

"There's no girl."

"Search, Joel. Search the rooms."

"There is no girl, Zonda. Someone just told me they got to her."

"Then what is this energy?"

Joel halts in a room facing the young individual, where corpses lie about at all angles. "What should I do?" The shrieks at the door directed at him when he spins clearly define his next move. Joel lurches for the window without a second thought.

He lands, and in seeking immediate balance, sprawls on the grass cheek-first. He jumps up without delay, in anticipation of any pending attacks from above or sideways. No one is there. The green yard is actually empty. "Oh, shit." Joel stares at the main entrance.

"What?" asks Zonda.

"They've broken in."

"There is nothing we can do, Joel. What did that someone tell you, exactly?"

"He said they got the griot and that I could still save her. He told me to use the window and not to veer."

"Not to veer. Go straight," prompts the djinn.

"We're going back in the garden, Zonda."

"Go, go!"

Joel runs for the high hedge and halts at the crossing of the entrance.

"Do you see anything unusual?" asks Zonda.

Unusual—a preposterous use of the word. "Nothing, it's the same garden."

"The tree," says Korokou.

Joel approaches the mango tree. "What about … Zonda, there's a blue ball by the root."

"A blue ball?"

"Yes." Joel crouches for a closer look. "Sand, it's like a ball of sand, blue."

"Blue sand. How is it … Joel, jump in the tree," orders Zonda.

"What?"

"Jump in the tree before the ball fissures."

Joel follows the command.

CHAPTER 14

Otiose Sacrifice

They walk at a steady pace, unconcerned and silent. The smaller one, about six-foot-three, wears a white-painted mask of wood strapped to his shaved head, a folklore piece carved at the eye sockets and smooth, as though polished by expert hands. His sturdy, naked torso ends in a belt of brown, neatly separated, with thick strands, and short pants of odd, somber material. His bare feet step on the strange soil of shiny black pebbles, sharp gray rocks, and strong roots. His right hand, wearing a ring only a shade deeper than his skin, maintains the griot bent in half over his shoulder while his left hand, free, wears a wooden ring of the same shape and color. The griot's red hair caresses his heel at each step.

The second one, far past seven feet and almost double the thickness of the first, walks by his side, dark, with a face one would doubtfully consider human, bearing tiny round balls for eyes encased toward the center of its features. It appears naked, with dangling genitals.

The noiseless forest carries the minimal sounds of the soil displaced under their weight. They pause for a moment. The masked man looks at the large creature by his side and gestures with his head, as though giving an order. The dark creature presents a sign of respect and then leaves in the opposite direction.

*

"Where am I, Zonda … Zonda?"

"He can't hear you," says Korokou.

"Why?"

"You're in transition."

"Transition … where to?" Joel stares at a cliff about fifteen feet from where he stands, giving way to a large landscape of lush vegetation on uneven terrain stretching to the horizon.

"Let's get the griot."

"Yes, but I don't know which direction."

"To your right."

This dirt almost resembles what he has already seen, if not for the shiny pebbles scattered about. Gray rocks of various sizes, maybe granite, also scatter the area in less abundance. Geography was a boring subject, he reckons, but even he knows those rocks should pertain to an environment distinct from here. Joel pulls the small piece of stone from his pocket and turns away in Korokou's suggested direction.

Joel freezes five steps onward to a vibration traversing his skull. He has to assure himself of its veracity, confirm it's not just a product of his saturated mind. He did hear something. He does not need to wait long, since the sound whips once again by his left, by his right; it is overhead. Joel snaps in each direction of this heavy breathing. It hovers everywhere at once. Joel spins around, listening but blind.

"Korokou?"

"Quiet," prompts the fetish.

Only branches, trunks, and leaves present to him. Something is here. The breathing sweeps behind him, and in following it with a wild turn, he barely evades a blow, deforming the bark on impact.

Joel bends to a resounding swoosh, recedes to another burst of bark, stumbles, and gets bashed toward a trunk nine feet away, where he splats against it. He does not linger waiting for the next blow, which ravages the trunk his head just banged into. He keeps his eyes open and his mind clear. Joel retreats until he falls, keeping his eyes on the entity whose contours he has yet to fully grasp. Its breadth blocks the sky, and each miss is a firm blow on impact. Joel keeps moving frantically backward, avoiding the hammering. An attempt to turn for an escape will surely be the end of him. One of these blows would suffice to crush him into this deep-toned soil.

His blank mind has given up to dread and sharp senses. The creature lifts both hands to constrict any angle of evasion and in doing so, aims for Joel's head. Joel dives at the sole window available to him, the creature's stomach. He'll be at its mercy, to be snatched and torn apart, for there is no escape where Joel just lunged. The dark creature grabs his head underneath it with a ferocious swing and pulls him into sight while Joel struggles to prevent the dislocation of his neck by holding tight to the thick forearm. His right hand extends a series of blind punches toward the creature's face until one pokes its eye. The creature reactively relinquishes and almost instantaneously pins Joel by his neck. He lies on the dirt, a portion of his head protruding from the cliff, his pharynx pressed so hard, it provokes a violent grimace. The creature leans further, about to crush Joel's face.

With both hands holding the dark, pillar-like arm squeezing his neck like a sponge, Joel manages to stick his feet under the creature's stomach, and with a strength of an origin he ignores, he unbalances it, tipping it off the cliff by rolling himself backward. Joel catches a root extending into the void and reflexively bends his legs upward to prevent the creature from grabbing them in his arm fling. Its intense stare does not wither as it falls, haunting even in death. Joel pulls himself up and remains for a moment on all fours. He then stands up unsteadily and lays a hand on a trunk for stability. The double vision is aligning.

"Oh ..." Joel softly breathes to a localized pain after a few steps. He leans on a tree with the back of his forearm for support and slowly puts his head on his arm.

"Joel," Korokou calls.

"Hm ..." He shakily wipes the blood he tastes dripping from his nostrils. "I'm okay."

"Let's get the griot."

"Right." Joel takes an instant to answer. He gulps his saliva and slowly pushes himself off the trunk before realizing a hollowness in his hand, the absence of the rock fragment. He looks below in his circling vicinity, with dizziness guiding his faint movements. There is no doubt how it quit his grip. He can still run faster than the average. He is not hopeless. He won't stay here searching for something probably unrecoverable, so he launches into pursuit, limping at first but pressing through the pain to continue. He lost time, a lot of time. Maybe that was the goal all along. A crucial delay, yet paling in comparison with death itself. He is still alive. There is a chance to make it if he keeps pushing. He would never have made it past the first strike if not for Korokou. Of that he is certain.

Joel advances into the wild, forcing himself to ignore the twinge running down his ribcage or the numbness enveloping his right arm. The very arm that almost took the full brunt when he smashed against the tree. His head throbs, but he cannot allow himself to slow down and take a break. His body demands respite, and once he has recovered the griot, he will capitulate. There, perhaps a thousand feet or so away, stands a clearing, followed by another batch of trees. Joel accelerates. A human silhouette who has just installed something on a pile of rock is approaching a girl lying behind him. Joel observes the masked man lifting her, as he strives with every cell of his body to reach him.

"No, no, no, no, no, no." It can't be now. His senses cannot stress at this moment.

"Slow down, Joel," voices Korokou.

"He's getting away!" Joel leaps, abandoning himself to his momentum for guidance toward what was a masked man turning after having picked up a girl on his shoulder, now blurred patches.

Pain is not what Joel experiences. More a metallic, rigid surface against his cheekbone. He doesn't feel himself smacking the dirt. All he knows is someone, something, clobbered him, along with the ripples of the recoil when his other cheek hits the soil before sinking. A hopeless feeling quickly rises when he realizes this divergence is permanent. His will to see, to comprehend the situation, won't change the current state of his eyes. As if this doesn't already cause enough anguish, receiving no responses to his commands is piercing. No limbs, no torso, not even his lids nudge at his signals. He is trapped in layers and layers of unmovable tissue. He might suffocate if he doesn't calm down, if he doesn't descend from the rising panic.

"I c – ... I can't m've, Korokou."

"You've reached your limit."

Joel maintains a shuddering, controlled breathing. "C-can't ... let him ... scape with'v griot." He lies torpid in the dirt, sensing his lungs poorly functioning. He is a mass awaiting the final blow.

"Impressive." The masked man removes a piece of flesh from his knuckle with a nonchalant wipe. "How did you get rid of my warrior?"

"D'somthin ... please," begs Joel.

"Who are you talking to?" The masked man about three feet from Joel inspects him, noticing the wrist bracelets. "Are you ... you are Joel." he says with a concluding tone. "So, it's true. A boy hosts Korokou. How does the fetish of one of history's greatest warriors fall so low?"

"If you want me to help, I'll have to take control over your body," says Korokou.

"D'it," prompts Joel.

"I'm sure it never occurred in King Condo's vision that his valuable fetish would bind to such a frail and immature body after all the sacrifices he's made."

"I don't know pain, Joel. That's why you failed to gauge your body's warnings. You could die if I take control."

"We'v deal ... Kr'kou, d'it," repeats Joel.

"You do realize what you've done, Korokou. Don't you?" The masked man lays the griot on the soil a few feet away from what seems like an intricately arranged pile of rocks. "By lending yourself to this boy, you've broken all vows toward your king, your former host. You've allowed yourself to grow weak, limited, and at the mercy of anyone. Maybe you're outdated. It was ages ago when the world thought whoever possessed you controlled history and men's evolutionary path. A lot has been rediscovered since. A lot has been understood since. Nonetheless ..." The man stands up and turns to Joel. "You remain a very valuable asset. I'll bring him those bracelets. I'm sure he'll be pleased. You'll be serving under a worthy and powerful leader."

The masked man observes Joel, who has gone silent. "How interesting," he calmly whispers, scrutinizing a few details on Joel's body. The sparse and light fidgeting of the fingers, the barely visible bend of the toes, and most noticeable of all, the right iris settling to the eye's outer corner. He knows better than to stop or even approach such a mesmerizing process: the bind of a man's spirit and flesh with his fetish, or in this case, at this very moment, a bound fetish taking full control of flesh and bones. "Korokou?" he ventures.

The young man is silent. The fidgeting has stopped. The masked man observes, patient, cautious to a certain extent. This has never happened before.

"Why do you need the griot?" A broken voice emanates from Joel's throat. He then rises as though unconstrained by the rules of his osseous frame.

"This is quite intriguing, I must confess. A fetish controlling a body. You've proved my point. This boy was never meant for a binding. You wanted to escape your cage."

"Why do you need the griot?"

"You know why. You were present the last time this happened."

"Condo hid me to make sure this day never arrives."

"Yet here you are," says the masked man. "King Condo hid you to make sure no one like him finds you. His will is dead, Korokou. You saw to that. You should choose your side wisely."

"There's no side," says the body, head lightly bent down and eyes directed nowhere. "There is only SEKI. Condo sacrificed himself for it."

"What, enlightenment?" Even through his inscrutable mask, the air of mockery is almost palpable. "Ohhh, Korokou, you're aware of the stages required for SEKI, aren't you? Of course you are. You come from a space that had reached some of these stages. Even with a body this desperate, I'm sure you've felt it from the very moment your host's feet touched the soil. Does the collective mind state reflect any approach to the first step? Don't be a fool. King Condo wasn't. He failed, but he had foreseen it. They've long deviated."

"Only time dictates that," says the fetish.

"Time dictates when the mind is collective. It'll never be. Not in this space."

"No one is ready for a griot."

"*He* is." The masked man pulls off his two crafted wooden rings and lets them fall on the ground. The rings grow into black fetishes of wood, two solid humanoid silhouettes, one or two inches taller, standing on each side of their summoner.

"Who is he?" asks Korokou.

"I present to you Goure and Fiatre, my guards. Everything has evolved, Korokou. You were the fetish of one of the greatest warriors of Africa. It's pitiful to see you like this."

"Who is he?" repeats Korokou.

The masked man makes a head gesture to his fetishes, and they converge on the young man. Korokou briskly moves past his opponents as though disregarding their existence. He halts by the pile of mounted rocks and kicks it, sending its components flying about. He then turns to the masked man and charges. The interception is brutal as one of the fetishes throws him to the next one, which bashes him into a tree.

The masked man looks at the destroyed portal, then at Korokou stumbling off the trunk he slammed into. He taps one of his fetishes' shoulders and with vehemence strides toward the enemy. Korokou stands, eyes aimless, awaiting the first strike. He senses them approaching, he sees them, and the delay in his movement seems voluntary. The masked man starts jogging. One, two side-to-side jerks, before lunging to his opponent with a fist, then, at the critical moment of contact, with incredible control of his body, deviating from his path. Korokou does not see the fetish's sole burying Joel's head into the same tree. He drops on one knee and almost instantaneously rolls sideways to avoid a fist jolting the soil. The masked man does not wait for any settling. His next blow, drawn like an extension of the first, finds Joel's temple in devastating ways, instantly followed by a fetish's knee to his sternum. A subsequent third strike from the second fetish, mere milliseconds after the previous one, is sharply blocked. Korokou seizes the fetish's head and smashes it into the trunk he is leaning on.

The near-perfect coordination of his opponents is a spectacle to behold. Their strikes are rarely void, yet they do move cautiously, for Korokou's retaliation goes beyond the flesh that encases him. He is intense, with a deceiving speed, brutal with powerful fists, and makes use of his environment like no other. Broken branches and heavy rocks fitting in Joel's palms belong in his arsenal.

Despite severe injuries, Joel's body does hold, and Korokou makes full use of its capabilities and size. From a feint, he pins one of the fetishes to a trunk and bursts its wooden head with his fist, shattering two fingers in the process. He is about to end the second fetish with a rock when a large branch bashes him away. The partial thud against bark provokes a violent partial spin, ending in a drag on the dirt. Korokou hoists himself up on straining limbs.

The large creature releases the branch and tramps decisively toward Korokou. The long fall earlier at the cliff didn't end the being. Korokou rolls from the exploding ground under the being's fierce stroke, and as he leaps for its head, the creature snatches him by Joel's ankle and throws him to the wooden fetish, which whacks him to the soil. Joel's mouth is bathed in blood. Korokou tries to get up, but the masked man kicks Joel's chin.

"*Pointless!*" His tone is exasperated. "You, fighting us, for what? Feeble and controlled minds? What? You can't get up? I know you don't feel pain, but he does. And once he's gone, you'll follow. I must admit, I'm surprised he's still alive. He's resilient."

The large creature lifts a rock worthy of its size and walks toward Joel with clear intent for his head. An incoherent, abrupt whisk of Joel's body avoids the dropping boulder by an inch. Korokou sweeps the creature's leg and whirls, bashing the wood fetish out of sight, then cracks the large being's skull against any obstacles within range. It does not rise when Korokou releases it.

At this instant, this frozen second, the slight body Korokou inhabits vanishes. It is Joel the masked man observes declining, yet it is Korokou, unhampered, vicious. King Condo's fetish stands before him. He radiates through this small and fragile frame like darkness swallowing light. The tales and ancient writings did not paint fantastical praise; they described what this fetish was. The songs were not in vain. What could have been the extent of his reach with a body like King Condo's? The man was chosen for his extraordinary physique and singular thought process.

The masked man, brisk and agile, moves around his formidable opponent, the one who planted fear and reverence in the heart of the multitudes at the peak of his host's era. The very same who was cast away and sealed, for he was perilous to the human mind. The very same is here, unconstrained with a merely functional system. Awe and rage traverse the masked man before logic regains control. Joel stands, his eyes undirected, his broken jaw leaving his mouth open, dribbling blood. Korokou awaits the next attack.

He violently turns and slugs the wooden fetish, which was coming from behind. The masked man sees an opportunity: the boy's heart. Korokou sharply switches to his main enemy, and in all but a complex strategy, they start smashing each other with their powerful fists. Neither is avoiding the other. Strokes to the chest, neck, cheekbone, throat. The mask splits when Korokou is still pounding his opponent. The wooden fetish charging against Korokou suddenly stretches on the soil, lifeless. The masked man is no more. Korokou remains atop his opponent for a moment before standing. He walks to the griot gazing at him, silent.

"Joel ..." he calls.

Korokou scoops the girl up to his shoulder and dashes through the forest. He passes the tree Joel came in from and drops into the midst of a market, causing panic and frenzy. Dread spreads contagiously, while screams extend further, and Korokou, with the griot on his shoulder, watches the populace running for their lives in all directions. It quickly gets quiet in the empty market. The most daring of them, maybe two at the most, the ones whose sight and brain did not suffer at the appearance of a bloody entity from above and who for some reason won't follow the whim of the masses, observe, ready to dash away at any moment. They shakily watch it descend from a stable and notice a corpse attached to it, trailing long red hair. Their bravery snaps at this point. The chill in their spines makes them sharply realize they are gambling with their lives, so they clear off, one after the other.

A woman is looking at a bloodied and deformed visage, unafraid, tranquil. Korokou turns to her and exchanges an eerie silence with her for a moment. Her face is worn from time and toil. She has not stopped cleaning the article in hand, but she has considerably slowed down, with her attention on the fetish before her. She is the only one who has not budged an inch.

"Oma ... healer," Korokou tries with the tools still at his disposal.

"There is no one here," the old lady responds. "But there is a hospital not far away."

"Where?"

"Go straight in this direction," she says, pointing down a path. "You can't miss its size."

Korokou nods to the woman and vanishes in the direction indicated.

*

The fetish crashes into a large hall, busting the aluminum-framed glass doors open and startling everyone around him. People gasp at the sight of him, with their wide eyes trying to process whether they should start a panic, but blue uniforms they are familiar with stand behind the frightening individual, so they wait, frozen. It is the largest edifice Korokou has noticed since the market, and the hall itself exhibits its grandeur, with its rows upon rows of seats, where people who were sitting before his arrival are stark on their feet, many protecting their little ones. About thirty feet ahead stand a few alarmed people wearing blush uniforms, probably the ones caring for others. The road to the building, approximately three miles from the market, was not without commotion, and Korokou has stirred multiple police vehicles onto his tail.

"Do not move!" shouts a stern voice nine feet from his back.

Korokou, with Joel's dead eyes and his face directed at one of the nurses, lifts the griot off his shoulder.

"*Do not move!*" threatens the voice.

Korokou gently lays the little girl down on a polished tile floor and flattens abruptly next to her. The police officers on the verge of firing release their fingers and gingerly approach with their barrels pointed at him, puzzled by the sudden change in the situation. The nurse does not wait for the firearms to be holstered or any safety signal. She rushes to the two individuals on the floor, followed by a colleague, despite multiple warnings from the police. "How much harm can they do?" she argues, examining the silent girl.

"Look at your door. You've not seen what we've seen, madam," says the police officer.

"Oh my God, we're losing him," says the other nurse, checking the unconscious young man with a bloody, sandy, floating jaw. "He has internal bleeding; his heart might give in at any minute. We have to bring him to the emergency room." She looks impatiently at the officer in charge.

The officer nods and holsters his firearm. The five others follow. Two stretchers finally arrive, and a nurse who helped carry one of them crouches by Joel. "Okay, on three. One, two

…" And they lift Joel onto the stretcher. The little girl seems stable, the nurse gathers, after inquiring about her status from his colleague. They hasten for the lift, the nurse who examined Joel trying to pump oxygen into his lungs with a device connected to a pocket mask covering his nose and held-in-place jaw.

"What have you got, Nadine?" says a man in a white coat, hurriedly approaching Joel's stretcher.

"Male, eighteen or younger. Concussion; possible skull fracture; internal bleeding; multiple bullet wounds; several sprains; dislocated sternum; broken jaw, forearm, fingers, and ribcage; punctured lungs; potential perforated liver; and that's what we've diagnosed so far. I don't know how this boy is still alive, Doctor Asumu."

"What happened to him?"

"We don't know," responds Nadine. "He came bursting in with a girl on his shoulder."

"Bursting?"

"The main entrance is destroyed."

"He was conscious?" asks Doctor Asumu.

"He was, and then he wasn't," says the nurse.

"To the operating room."

"You got it."

*

"Can you hear me, cutie?" attempts the nurse. "What's your name? All right, let's go." She and three others proceed to install the little girl on the second stretcher and push her out of the hall into a large corridor of aligned lifts.

The nurse smoothly sets the little girl on a bed and starts prepping the equipment. "Don't worry, cutie. You're safe now," she says with a faint smile at the impassive visage.

"Anything, Murielle?" Another slender man in a white coat enters the patient's room.

"No. She hasn't said a word."

"Give her some time to rest. We'll try again tomorrow."

"Okay," she concurs. "What the hell happened to those two?"

The man sighs. "I've never seen a body in such a state. I don't even understand how this boy is breathing. Doctor Asumu is trying to keep him alive. It'll be a miracle if he survives."

"Doctor Asumu is the best this boy could hope for."

"You're right. I've called Doctor Pembe. He's on his way."

The nurse turns to the little girl. "Those eyes …" She slightly shakes her head.

"They're beautiful," the man agrees.

"Doctor Onyumbe," calls Murielle, turning the girl's arm, revealing a prominent, patchy bruise.

The man lightly bends and rearranges his spectacles. He glances at the nurse and looks back at the arm. "Severe … molestation?"

"I don't know. I haven't done a full checkup yet."

"Well, let her go under, and do a full examination," says the man, reaching for the door.

"Understood. Doctor?"

"Yes." He turns the lever.

"I think she might be … Oh-h, Lord!" cries the nurse, staggering backward and finding stability on a table, where Doctor Onyumbe instinctively lunges to gets a solid grasp of her.

"What is it?" he hastily inquires.

The nurse points her quivering index finger at the ground by the bed. Doctor Onyumbe approaches a syringe on the floor and then looks at the little girl. He grabs another syringe on a reflective metal plate and brings it near the thin arm. The needle curves as it approaches the sleek ebony skin.

"We need … we need to inform the authorities," utters the rattled man.

"It's okay, we'll take it from here." A group of five men barges into the room.

"Doctor Pembe?" Doctor Onyumbe recognizes one of the men, the shortest of them, plump in a brown suit.

"Did you do anything?" asks one of the taller men by his side in a dark-gray suit.

"The … the needle," stutters Murielle, her troubled countenance unaltered. She can hardly align her thoughts, but she certainly doesn't recognize these faces from earlier. These are not the policemen who chased the young man into the hospital.

"Where's the other one?" the man in a gray suit demands.

"In the operating room with Doctor Asumu," responds Doctor Onyumbe.

The man in a gray suit looks at one of the police officers, who instantly leaves the room. "Okay, you can leave us now, please." He turns back to the perturbed doctor and his nurse.

"What's happening, Doctor? Who … what is she?" Doctor Onyumbe turns to his colleague.

"Please do as they say," Doctor Pembe softly replies.

"Can you please leave us, Doctor?" The man in a gray suit firmly reiterates his request.

The two police officers walk both doctors and the nurse out of the room.

*

"Stop everything!" The police officer forces his way into the operating room, startling the people around the surgeon. "Move away from him!"

"What are you … you are not allowed in here," yells Doctor Asumu.

"Don't touch him," repeats the police officer.

"He's in a critical state. If we don't do anything, he'll die."

"I said, don't touch him." The police officer does not hesitate to push them away from Joel.

"I don't care what he did," Doctor Asumu snaps. "You won't stop me from helping this boy. You'll have to shoot me. Go on."

"How many syringes broke on his skin?" prompts the police officer.

An assistant looks at Doctor Asumu, then at a plate of bent and broken needles.

"But he's going to die if we don't do something," another assistant says in near despair.

"Move this scalpel away, Doctor Asumu. They're coming for them."

"Who?" His incredulous face flares. The General Hospital of St. Benedict has the best equipment in the country. Unless a technology he is not aware of is coming from the Western world.

"Those who can help him," responds the police officer.

"Who?" Doctor Asumu insists.

"That's all I know."

There may be hope for this boy, Doctor Asumu thinks, *if the incoming technology can manage to penetrate his skin without breaking or inflicting more damage.* Though he ought to try all he possibly can, the tools in this operating room present illogical limits on this skin. The boy is fighting, clinging to life despite these dreary odds, and Doctor Asumu does not need a machine beeping at very distinct intervals to know that time is running out.

*

Two old men step above the debris of fragmented glass and bent aluminum frames to enter the hospital. Their stature, and that of a barefoot girl following them in a white gown, with short, braided hair, does not stir much attention from the people chattering about the troubling event from earlier. Some begin to take notice when two men in dark-gray suits, the ones who enflamed the conversation, as they are believed to be secret services, approach them. A boy about seven years of age, sitting by the end of the second bench, holds tight to his mother's palm. A long, disproportionate, dark creature and this short being he observes behind the old men and this girl just spotted him yet ignore him.

"Where are they?" asks the Third Great Chief.

"Fourth floor," responds one of the men in gray suits. "The girl isn't speaking. We tried to make her sleep, but nothing worked."

"She doesn't sleep. She doesn't speak," asserts the little girl. "I said, nobody touch her. Who touched her?"

"A nurse and a doctor when they first came in," says the agent. "We weren't on site."

"You're protected. They aren't. Where are they?"

"Second floor."

"My guard will follow you. We have to make sure they haven't been harmed." The Third Great Chief makes a sign to the long creature, and it follows one of the agents.

"How is Joel?" asks Old Paapa.

"The boy, his state is critical, sir," answers the second agent. "We made sure nobody touches him."

"Guide me to him, please."

"Did you inform your government of our arrival?"

"They know, Wiseman," replies the agent. "We sent them a full report of the situation."

"Then clear the fourth floor," orders the Wiseman. "We don't want anyone hurt. She's unstable."

"Understood."

*

Doctor Asumu eyes an individual in a dark-gray suit entering the operating room, followed by an old man. With an air of disbelief and inescapable inference, he stares intently at the old man approaching.

Old Paapa lays his hand on his chest and walks by the top side of the bed. Though the doctors do not recognize the gesture, it does appear to be a salutation of some sort. Old Paapa puts down his small bag of well-knit, broad cords and takes a long look at Joel.

"Wait, what's this?" Doctor Asumu finally voices. "This is the one who's going to perform the operation?"

"What operation?" asks Old Paapa.

Doctor Asumu looks at the police officer. "You aren't serious. This must be a joke. There is a life on the line here! What are you doing?"

"Can you please leave the room?" Old Paapa demands calmly.

"You heard him," says the police officer.

"Zonda, prepare the concoction."

"What was that?" asks Doctor Asumu.

"Oh, sorry. I wasn't talking to you."

"Goodness! You put the life of this boy in the hands of a senile. You won't be getting away with this. Believe me."

"Do not force our hand, Doctor. There is no need for it. Leave," the agent says sternly.

The police officer locks the door behind Old Paapa.

*

"Is she harmed?" asks the Wiseman.

"No, but she's unbalanced." The Third Great Chief pulls her hands back from the griot's forehead. "I have to stabilize her energy."

"There is no time, Eyra," says the Wiseman. "We need to know where the vessels are hidden before something happens."

"Wiseman, it's risky to contact her in this state." She turns to the old man. "We aren't in Côte d'Esperance."

"You are the Third Great Chief. Figure something out. We cannot miss these vessels. You have seen what our enemy can do."

"I'll try," says the little girl.

A man in a pecan-brown suit enters the room, followed by someone wearing a skirt of wheat straws and cowrie shells. The grooming and strong posture of the man in the suit dwarf any other traits that might seem prominent about him, namely the wholly white hair. The visage of the man in straw seems well seasoned, yet one would fail to accurately guess at his age, despite his bearing white in his eyebrows.

"My men are in position," says the old man in the suit. "We've been looking everywhere. It's impossible to find them. We need these locations, or at least to narrow the search area."

"We are trying to get them, Dadie," says the Wiseman. "She has been under a lot of pressure."

"I understand."

"Did you move your great-granddaughter to safety?"

"She's under protection." Dadie scratches his eyebrows. "Don't worry."

"I'll need the room," the Third Great Chief announces.

They follow each other without a word and stand by the glass window, exposing the room.

"Who brought her?" asks the man in straw.

"Korokou."

"*Korokou?*" Dadie looks at the Wiseman.

"Who's the host?" asks the man in straw.

"A young man named Kouadio Joel," answers the Wiseman.

Dadie turns to his companion.

"You know him?" The Wiseman picks up on the subtlety of their reaction.

"He's the one who saved Dadie's great-granddaughter," the man in straw explains.

"How did he manage to host Korokou?"

"We do not know yet," says the Wiseman. "Old Paapa is healing him. He might not survive."

"The days ahead are dark, Wiseman," declares Dadie. "We have to prepare for what's coming."

The lack of decisive or concrete information among the three of them is a monumental concern. It is the first time in existence that the Wiseman cannot link anything from all that has occurred up to this moment. The enemy communicates in Triniguiri, has the knowledge of the Dogo seal, and travels with blue sand. Each of these billions of years apart from the next, as Dadie lays out. Each of these inhering from a definite and extremely powerful civilization that was not, in any form, time, or space, connected to the other. Their leader, whoever he might be, is a well-prepared and outrageously resourceful individual, if it is indeed one being who orchestrated all these events.

"Blue sand," says the man in straw.

"Yes, blue sand," repeats the Wiseman. Only the four of them, he states, are old enough to know what lies beyond.

How, where did the enemy acquire a material as preternatural as blue sand? The last grains were sighted in the Pure World fifty-eight million years ago and were believed since then to have vanished from the surfaces of Mother Earth. Old Paapa and the Wiseman, he mentions, have been searching in the archive for any traces of blue grains. None was found, and no records or tales spoke of this unique compound. The enemy is prepared. He has been for a very long time and was simply waiting for the opportune moment. He has an army, no doubt, the Wiseman elaborates, when Dadie requires an exploration of his train of thought, but they do not know how powerful he is or who has sided with him. Yet the need for more allies is plain in many of his actions. The enemy, the Wiseman continues, does aim to defeat them not only with overwhelming numbers but also allegiance and belief, and what better time than now to make anyone join your cause?

"The evolution of science and the destruction of Mother," the man in straw extends the train of thought. The subject has long been a concern of the wise circle.

"It is not science," the Wiseman elucidates.

The evolution of man and striving for a better life pertains to the affairs of SEKI. It is the consciousness behind searching for any means of profit and control, willing to break the curve every time it attempts to expand, to bloom their minds. A substantial incentive for any creature of nature to join the enemy's cause, the man in straw expresses, and factually so, as he caught wind that many who have learned the supposed intentions of the enemy, judging by his actions, intend to align themselves with him. The enemy has already assassinated a prominent figure who proved to be a threat to nature, thus sending word among all: the ones who deliberately make decisions to scorch the earth and the ones who depend on her. He has attacked Sector 0, one of the most powerful prisons on Mother Earth, and though the guardians repelled the attack, it clearly demonstrates the potential and extent of his army.

Then comes the language: Triniguiri. A series of exceedingly intricate vibrations ranging over a vast spectrum, a communication canal of a civilization believed to be the most advanced that has ever inhabited Mother Earth. A civilization before known consciousness. One so ancient, none of the old inhabitants possess an epistemic understanding of its existence, and for the very few who do, it has been forgotten from memory for as long as they could remember. Yet the language resurfaced. One believed to be the most difficult language to understand. If those under his control can utter the sounds, it entails according to Dadie that the enemy had more than enough time to create his own method of communication that could have been undetectable, or at the very least unintelligible. So the reason for his exact choice remains a mystery, unless he needs Triniguiri for something or someone.

Someone. Nothing since the restart of time has ever suggested a presence, but the tenet that a few of the Triniguiri age live on Mother Earth has always circulated among ancients. The understanding, the Wiseman conveys, is that they shall never align with this cause; they cannot. It is not ingrained in their being to take these kinds of actions, for their brainwaves, their train of thought, very much like the Dogo yet very opposite, are a wide deviation. The Triniguiri lived by respect of nature and balance of life. The natural evolution of a species must occur, even if their failure to mold their thoughts should bring their extinction.

"Then how come he speaks Triniguiri?" Dadie asks calmly. "Unless he is himself a Triniguiri, he could learn this language only from one of them. No amount of scrolls or artifacts, if he even had managed to find one, can teach this language. We've lost balance for a very long time, Wiseman. Why else would he speak the language of the most powerful civilization that ever walked Mother Earth? We have to face it—everything is changing, and balance, balance is among all, not only with one group of inhabitants."

The fact that the Triniguiri have doors on Mother Earth only their language can unlock could be one of the reasons for this choice, but the man in straw is reluctant to pursue this conjecture, because no one knows their locations, not even the enemy, or the four of them would have known one way or the other. Unless the channel is the means of finding them.

The Dogo seal. A marvel of engineering from the Dogo age, yet bland in comparison with the Dogos' other creations. Though many of their handprints persist to this day as natural formations and inexplicable phenomena, their technology has been lost for billions of years, unattainable. For a tool like a Dogo seal to exist in this age means a spark of fathoming their technology has been attained. One demanding a mind that has traveled several spaces. Only a Dogo can weave a Dogo seal, for the required brain patterns are specific to Dogos, and one cannot align with these patterns and speak Triniguiri.

"He's toying with us," the man in straw says confidently. "The Dogo civilization is no more. Their own experiment destroyed them."

The consensus on the course of action is to recruit. Assemble as many allies as they can in a close time span. Steal them before the enemy does. An enterprise that might prove challenging, even for them. How do you convince a creature of nature when the supposed enemy is fighting to protect the very place that allows all to be? They have to concede, Dadie points out, that nothing is on their side in this undertaking, and much of the world, bound to follow either by choice, if not the imposition of misconceived power, will be of no help. They might actually force the hands of those still in doubt to join the enemy. The fact that they are not aware and can surely not understand or perceive what's happening, says the Wiseman, might be the most help they will lend. The firm belief of their technology leading everyone bends their perception of this world.

"Their secret societies suspect something," adds the man in straw.

"Nothing of concern," confirms Dadie.

"We need intel. I'll deploy my men on Mother," announces the man in straw.

The Wiseman watches the Third Great Chief leave the side of the bed and hasten for the door.

"Ethiopia, the hidden forest! Gabon, the forbidden forest!" she hurries after half-opening the door, her hand holding the metal lever.

"Let's go," says the man in straw.

"I'll head for the forbidden forest," says Dadie. "Wiseman, please contact the respective authorities."

"I will take care of it. Is the griot okay?" The Wiseman turns to the Third Great Chief.

"She'll be fine. She wanted to help. You have to act fast. He'll be moving them shortly."

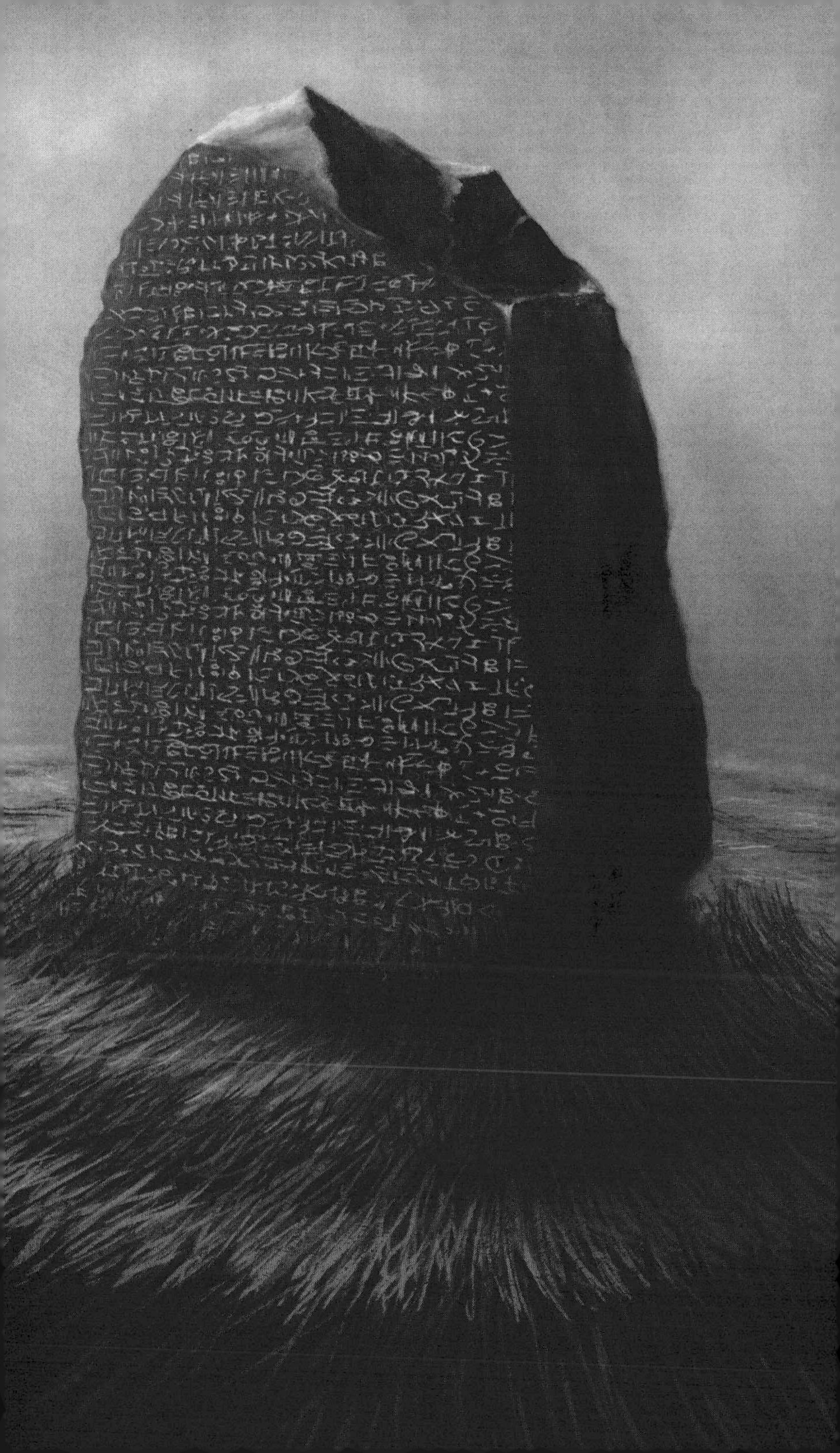

CHAPTER 15

Pain of Joy

The slight chill shrouding him is hard to locate. It does slant a little stronger through his sides, but which sides? He sees nothing but pitch black, omnipresent wherever he aims to look, if he is actually seeking for sight. There is no sight. There hasn't been any for a long time now, or did it just occur? He does smell something. A quite delicate redolence he is not fond of. It reminds him of something painful, stinging. In fact, as far as his recollection stretches, even since his childhood, he has never liked it; he wailed loudly to his mother when he knew he was going to dwell in it for hours. It is an aseptic smell. Maybe he knows where he is. But why is everything dark? Joel hears a clank and then a barely audible squeak before what seems like a door closing. He patiently opens his eyes, which draw blur and brighten at first but don't take long to readjust.

"Old Paapa says you're awake," says a familiar voice.

"Zonda." Joel gives a clumsy smile. "How are you?"

"I should be asking you this question." The djinn goes to the right side of the bed, by the unplugged machines meant to monitor or sustain Joel's health.

Joel weakly moves his tongue. "I taste blood." He gently readjusts his position on the bed with a slight grimace. "And I'm in a lot of pain. But apart from that … yeah … I'm okay."

"You'll be fine. And you won't have to visualize your recovery." Zonda fails to conceal an air of mockery.

"I'm not doing that." Joel's countenance does not follow the joke, if Zonda is poorly attempting at one. "Got ass cramp for two days. Remember?"

"You'll be fine," says Zonda. "There's a recovery pot under your bed. You'll walk before you know it."

Joel utters a sound of assent while delicately rearranging himself on the bed once more. The pain pervades everywhere, and lying for too long on a spot worsens it somehow.

"Hey," Zonda calls. "She's safe. We got her."

Joel looks at the djinn, trying to process the words with this momentary silence, yet bringing himself to believe what he just heard. Could it be what he desperately wishes Zonda is saying? "Princess?" he ventures carefully. Zonda nods with a smile.

His face agape and nearly vacant, he stares into the djinn's eyes, wanting to believe, bringing himself to the thought that his little sister might be—no, *is*—by some miracle, alive and safe. Joel's eyes turn red and fill up before Zonda. His lips tremble. Thick tears roll down his cheeks, while he remains motionless in the bed, fixated on the djinn. Joel breaks into soft sobbing. He whimpers with the delayed and frail shuddering of his body.

"She's okay," Zonda repeats, understanding the disbelief, the surge of emotion enveloping Joel.

"How's my boy feeling? Ohh, what did you do, Zonda?" Old Paapa enters the room.

The excitement has killed the pain, or subdued it so deeply Joel can barely contain himself. "Is it true?" Joel is sitting up.

"Don't! Don't move." Zonda hurries to hold Joel in the bed. "You're far from healed, my friend." He smiles after laying him carefully back down.

"Apparently Zonda couldn't hold his tongue," Old Paapa says passively. "I told you to wait until he's better."

"He's all right. He's a tough young man," Zonda declares.

"He is." Old Paapa smiles. "It was very courageous what you did, giving your body to a fetish. Ignorant, foolish ... but courageous. Nobody before you has done that."

"Because they were not as weak as he is." The Wiseman steps

in the room. "Nobody in their right mind would. But you have a strong will. That is all that matters in this life."

"Where is she?" Joel asks impatiently.

"In the village," answers Old Paapa. "You'll see her once you can walk. She's a wonderful little girl."

"Yes. That's my sister. That's how she is." Joel cannot stop his tears.

"You have had quite a journey for her. The inherent beauty and ineluctable fate of connection," says the Wiseman. "You have uncovered things on your route that nobody before you achieved. How did you convince Korokou to join you?"

"Hmm ..." Joel slowly wipes his face with a ponderous wrist. The languor and uneasiness of his body, he feels, is rather flagrant and tiring at any exertion. "I made a deal with him."

"Korokou does not make deals," asserts the Wiseman. "He saw something we have yet to see."

"You'll have to train your body if you want to be able to control his movements," says Old Paapa.

"I don't know. Now that she's safe, the terms are met. I should be gone by now."

"You should listen to your elders," says Korokou.

"You should." The Wiseman gives a faint smile. "He will be with you. Will you be able to bear him? Only you can answer this question."

"Wait, you can hear him?" asks Joel. The relaxed look on this strange man's face speaks volumes. Awaiting an answer might seem pointless.

"And yes. You are going to visualize your recovery," says Old Paapa.

"No, I'm not."

"Yes, you are."

"Zonda, you said ... Don't do this, Old Paapa. Please."

"You have to fully recover, my son."

"No, no. I don't need to. Seriously."

"We informed the authorities of your innocence," says the Wiseman. "And your friend Roland is doing well."

"Thank you, sir. Thank you for everything."

The Wiseman nods and leaves the room. Old Paapa smiles at Joel and then follows the Wiseman into the corridor.

"They got to his grandmother before she could warn her daughter," says the Wiseman.

"Joel's grandmother?" asks Old Paapa.

"Yes."

"So, who is this person who visited his parents?"

"We are still looking into it, but if his parents were deceived by the appearance ..." responds the Wiseman.

"A complete transformation ... it can't be." Old Paapa looks at the Wiseman. "There are only two or three of them left in this world, and they vowed to protect humans."

"Many rules have already been broken. I informed the leaders of each tribe. There will be a tree of counsel," says the Wiseman.

"There will be opposition this time," says Old Paapa.

"We have to try, or we will have to deal with a lot more enemies."

"Some leaders have started to speak for him."

"I know," says the Wiseman. "They have to hear the truth. We cannot allow him to have them on his side."

"He's off to a good start." Old Paapa flaps the hanging portion of his African fabric over his shoulder and tightens the overall fit.

"I will need your help, Old Paapa," says the Wiseman. "War appears inevitable with these circumstances. Whatever form it takes, when the time comes, we will have to protect as many as we can. Those who do not know are part of it."

"This will upset many," Old Paapa says. "Most think they're the reason we're in this situation."

"Everyone is at fault. Those who do harm as much as those who are silent. Mother Earth is round, Old Paapa. Until the sphere of each of their selves expands, we are compelled to protect them."

"I understand, but will it expand? It seems they're adamant on containing it."

"The occasional fluctuation when a prominent event occurs is sizable, and it is a good sign. Only time will tell us, Old Paapa."

"Then they should remain in the dark, or they will be a thorn."

The Wiseman nods. "Let's observe the evolution of this situation."

"I'll prepare my warriors and those of the neighboring villages. We start recruiting."

The Wiseman looks through the glass into the patient room. "I am concerned about him."

"Korokou?"

"He took control once. He can do it again. We still do not know why he accepted this boy as a host. He has no guidance."

"The boy is strong," says Old Paapa. "I'll take care of him. He has much to learn. And the village will restrain Korokou."

"His sister?"

"He doesn't know."

"Then when the time comes ..." The Wiseman looks at Old Paapa.

Old Paapa nods. "What about the griot?"

"I will take care of her."

"The enemy will find other ways to control the channel," says Old Paapa.

"This is what troubles me," confides the Wiseman. "We could not figure out his plan. We cannot read his action. It was too easy to get back the vessels. Let us focus right now. The tree of counsel is our priority."

"Wiseman!" The old men turn in the Third Great Chief's direction.

"The channel, she can't feel him anymore."

"He has already started. I have to consult. Eyra, send her to the Pure World. Explain the situation, and plead for their acceptance. Cameroon authorities allow three more days before we are no longer welcome in this hospital. They want to still be able to keep a blanket on all of this and control the damage. I will see you very soon." The Wiseman fades away.

*

"You did it." Zonda sits by the beige wall near Joel's bed. "I'm sure your parents would be proud."

"I was lucky," says Joel.

"Luck came because you wanted it."

Joel goes out of his way to look at Zonda. "Please don't talk like Old Paapa. He's too much on his own."

They both crack up a bit before Joel abruptly stops, with a muffled moaning. He was not meant to open his mouth this wide, and his skull felt it. "Get out, Zonda. You're killing me."

"I'll let you rest." Zonda stands up and heads for the door.

"I want to see her."

"Soon, my friend, soon."

"Hey," Joel calls when Zonda turns the lever. "Is the griot okay?"

"She is, thanks to you." Zonda closes the door behind him.

"Thank you, Korokou."

"You're weak."

The surprise demands a brief silence. "Okay."

"Get stronger. War is coming."

"War? Which war?"

"Get stronger."

"I don't understand. I thought you were seeking a stronger host."

"I don't need one."

"Thank you for believing in me."

"I don't believe in you."

"Well … thank you anyway."

"Don't thank me."

"It's called being polite, old fetish."

CHAPTER 16

Though dim overall, the room receives a fair amount of bright spots from the stairlike, staggered row of screens, illuminating the faces sitting before these displays, typing silently on their keyboards. A projection on the wall before them fills its side of the room. They all seem absorbed, seeking or uncovering something on the large map before them. A man in a suit, unbuttoned at the vest, enters the room. He is approximately six-foot-three and walks with confident steps. He approaches one of the displays and stands behind the operator.

"What is it?"

"SAR-2 took this image thirty minutes ago."

"Where is this?"

"Côte d'Esperance, town of Yamouego."

The man stares, hands in pockets, at the wide display on the wall. "What are they shooting at?"

"This." The operator types some commands and zooms in on a specified spot.

The man in a suit squints. "What the hell is that?"

"There's more, sir." The operator continues his functions on the keyboards. "That's ten minutes after the tanks."

"It's a man," says the man in a suit.

"They're chasing him."

"Yes ... but this is ..."

"That's a lot of forces for one individual," says the operator.

"No." The man pulls his hands from his pockets and bends to the operator's display. "He's on foot." He touches the display. "Get me the CIA and DARPA."

THE WALL

BOOK I: KNOWLEDGE

"FOR WHAT DEFINES YOU WILL
HELP YOU FIND WHAT YOU SEEK"

Acknowledgements

Book 1 would not be what it is if not for the expert hands of some great editors. Allister Thompson, Lara Kennedy, and Joel Pierson, thank you for your invaluable corrections. I am grateful to have met you in this interesting journey.

Allister, your remarks, questions, and advice paved the way for a better book. I am grateful.

Stephanie Cohen, your insight as a beta reader, your inputs and suggestions for better words were incredibly helpful. Thank you.

Of course, book 1 would not be whole if not for the amazing illustrations of some fine artists. Cristiana Leone, Charlie Utting, and David Leahy, thank you for your special touch and signature in this book. I was fortunate to find artists who would bring such life and precision in my book.

Euan Monaghan, your work just shines between pages. Thank you for this interior design.

To my beautiful family, I pay tribute to you for your unwavering support, your voices, your silence, your smiles, your joys, your love.

To my friends who read the very first collage of ideas and inspirations of a book, Juba, Temidayo "TD," Divya, and who were even thrilled back then, thank you very much for your incredible support and encouragement. I am grateful to have met you.

To all Africans whose extraordinary sculptures and patterns inspired this book—Thank you. Thank you. Thank you.

Mom and Dad, I wouldn't be the man I am if not for you. You are the first molders before I could shape myself in this world. You are my very first pillars. I cannot thank you enough.

About the Author

Yessoh G. D. is the author of *TA LẸ Book 1: Knowledge*. He grew up in a small city of warmth and joy in Côte D'Ivoire. When he was not going to school, he was lost in his thoughts on various subjects. He still is, but now on specific subjects, from his own personal experiences to the knowledge he acquired since birth on his African heritage. He believes that books have the power to change people for the betterment of the whole. When he is not daydreaming about stories and the world, he is a visual effects artist, or a gamer. He currently lives in Vancouver, Canada. You can find him online at www.thetaleseries.com.

I hope this book brings you joy, calm, wonder, excitement, and food for thought. Because ultimately it is you who incites and allows one to share his story, even though the process is, at its core, one with oneself. UBUNTU.

If you enjoyed TA LẸ Book 1: Knowledge, please leave a word in the review section. This will help me share the story with more people. Thank you.

I believe word-of-mouth to be an amazing force for spreading the word, especially when that word brings happiness. Please tell your friends and family about this book, if you think they would enjoy it. Publishing a post on social media to recommend this book as a must-read will also be greatly appreciated. Thank you.

Thank you for buying this book.

For bonus content, info on new
releases and other great reads, sign up for
our newsletters or visit us online at
www.thetaleseries.com

Made in the USA
Middletown, DE
19 January 2023

22554064R00194